The Death & Times of Mark Ferris

Alex McIntosh

Published in 2012 by FeedARead.com Publishing – Arts Council funded

Copyright © Alex McIntosh.

First Edition

The author has asserted their moral right under the Copyright, Designs and Patents Act, 1988, to be identified as the author of this work.

All Rights reserved. No part of this publication may be reproduced, copied, stored in a retrieval system, or transmitted, in any form or by any means, without the prior written consent of the copyright holder, nor be otherwise circulated in any form of binding or cover other than that in which it is published and without a similar condition being imposed on the subsequent purchaser.

A CIP catalogue record for this title is available from the British Library.

To George
I finally finished it.

FRESHLY DEAD

My demise was sudden enough. There was no pain. No lingering disease. No burning, drowning, or starving. I didn't get assassinated, set upon by wild animals, go down with the ship, or get lost in the mountains. My last living transaction was a quick fall through the hatch whilst visiting the attic. My gravestone reads:-

Mark Ferris,
slipped and fell.
Is he in Heaven,
or is he in Hell?

That's Elaine's sense of humour for you.

My life hadn't exactly been dangerous. A standard upbringing accompanied by a normal schooling, had, in turn, been followed by an unexceptional puberty all topped off with an undistinguished career pushing letters through letter boxes. I never smoked, only drank when there was reason to do so, and my gambling career consisted of putting a pin in the newspaper whenever the Grand National came around. My extra-marital dalliances amounted to occasional flirting with a work colleague, Grace, who was a good twenty years older than me, only had a small percentage of her own teeth, and liked to quote passages from the Bible.

I'd gathered no kids, no pets, a semidetached mortgage, and a twenty year marriage to the aforementioned Elaine; caught on the rebound from a rock-drummer, who'd dumped her to go on tour with his band, *The Doctors of Destruction*. I couldn't believe my luck. A month after I'd met her, well before she could recover her senses, I whisked her off to the local registry office and married her.

It was the most reckless thing I'd ever done, but believe two factors played their part in my rashness. Firstly, I'd received limited female attention up to that point in my life. Secondly, Elaine was a stunner. Loving my wife was the one thing I ever did to excess, but how she put up with my colourless life was a mystery to everyone who knew her, and an even bigger one to everyone who knew me. Some people, Mother in particular, reckoned Elaine didn't treat me right. But I never complained. Did I mention she was a stunner?

Then, a week after my fortieth birthday, my uneventful life came to an end. I fell out of the attic, broke my neck, and found myself sitting in a wooden chair staring wide-eyed at the committee.

The committee. In the chair, Mr Theostopholes, or Mr T. for short. No, he's not black with medallions weighing him down, and, as far as I know, he doesn't drive around in a tank advertising confectionery. Actually, by the look of his hat, I think he's Greek Orthodox. To his right and left sit two heavily bearded, turbaned, undernourished paper-shufflers, who I simply refer to as the sidekicks. The three of them sort of run this place. Whatever this place is.

On that first wide-eyed meeting, during which Mr T. rummaged through swathes of paperwork, he explained that I had not met the criteria to be sent straight to the *Sanctum*. His manner suggested I should know exactly what he was talking about, but on seeing my mouth opening and closing, but no words actually forming, Mr T. pointed to somewhere behind me. I turned to find a large wooden door, maybe only twenty feet away, which I somehow must have missed when I'd first arrived. The door had the word *SANCTUM* in bold letters decoratively carved around its top, and reminded me of the heavy oak door that led into the church I attended as a child. Below the word, hung off a large nail, was a small, well detailed painting. The painting looked like it had been completed by a child, albeit with some idea of colour and depth. It consisted of a flowerless green meadow full of brown rabbits, a huge orange sun filling one corner of a cloudless blue sky, and 2 rainbows arching from the top of the frame down to the meadow. Here, however, is where the artist's grasp of colours let them down. Both rainbows were solid black.

Mr T. smiled proudly at the door for some time before turning his attention back to the paperwork in front of him. He then started off on some lecture about how much trouble sudden deaths like mine caused them. At some point he also gave me a number: 7359. I must admit, most of the episode went by me in a bit of a fog. After all, you don't die every day, do you?

The discourse ended with Mr T. announcing the committee's decision was always final. Their final decision at that first meeting was to send me away to a holding area until they'd apparently completed some paperwork and reached a final decision. Mr T. once again pointed behind me. The Sanctum door had disappeared and in its place stood a much less impressive structure with the word *DENTIST* crudely cut into its wood.

"You can wait in there," Mr T. said, waving towards the door. "Don't look so worried, Seven-Three-Five-Nine," he added, obviously noticing that I was frantically looking around for whatever was making doors appear and disappear at will. "It's all standard practice. We'll send for you when we're ready. Off you go."

I found myself at the threshold of the door. I had no idea how I'd gotten there from the wooden chair - after all, I'd been hanging onto it for dear life - and turned back to Mr T. and the sidekicks for enlightenment. They were heads down in paperwork. Mr T. looked up and frowned.

"You still here, Seven-Three-Five-Nine?" he said. "Off you go." He waved his hand to send me on my way, then immediately went back to a document he was studying. A force beyond my knowledge pushed me through the door.

The small, airless room I found myself in wasn't just *like* my dentist's waiting room, it *was* my dentist's waiting room, and I appeared to be the only patient. The high-pitched screams of dental drilling tools resounded from a place I couldn't see, and I started shaking involuntarily. I'm sure I heard the odd scream of pain, and my whole body felt cold, which struck me odd as I'd undoubtedly found myself in Hell.

I'd often been known to pass out whilst waiting for the dentist. Not a complete state of unconsciousness, just a sort of self-ignited sleep. A defence mechanism against the look of terror on the bloated faces of patients who'd had their injections and were awaiting further torture. Elaine would insist on coming with me on my appointments, waking me up when my name was called by tickling me under the chin and saying, *'So who's a ickle baby?'* in that voice kept for addressing children under 2.

Evidently, in Hell, the mechanism didn't work. I tried with all my might to send myself to sleep, but the best I could manage was to close my eyes, stick my fingers in my ears, and hum as loudly as I could muster. Despite pushing my fingers into my ears as far as they would go without causing brain damage, the sounds still resonated, and how long I sat there, shaking and humming tunelessly, I don't know. It felt like a lifetime.

I was eventually forced to open my eyes when one of the sidekicks tapped me on the shoulder. He silently helped me to my feet, and ushered me out of the room back to the wooden chair.

"Ah, hello again, Seven-Three-Five-Nine," Mr T. said, his head stuck in a file. "After due deliberation, we've unanimously decided to appoint you as one of our designated watchers." He pushed a dossier across the desk in front of him. "I suggest you read this thoroughly. It'll give you all the information you need about your first assignee."

I tried to speak, but only managed to emit some dolphin-like noises; odd clicks and clacks that, as far as I could remember, I'd never managed to emit before.

"Just calm down," Mr T. said. "Try taking some deep breaths." He demonstrated how to take deep breaths. "Scores of people have been through this process before you, and they've all survived perfectly well. Now, we've done our best to find you someone... interesting." He tapped the dossier. "Although, I must admit, Seven-Three-Five-Nine, we never let you loose on anybody high up the social ladder when you're freshly dead. It's all standard practice." He went back to his mound of files and papers.

Without any conscious instruction to do so, my shivering body decided to enter Mark Ferris security mode and began curling into a ball on the chair. I believe I was one step away from putting my thumb in my mouth and calling for Mother, when my brain found a morsel of coherence and instructed my mouth to ask the first words I'd managed since my arrival. "Am I in Hell?" I asked. The words had definitely formed from my mouth, but it appeared I'd been given a new voice. My voice had always been that of a standard postman, not a mouse. Although, Elaine had often referred to me as one.

Mr T. let out a solitary laugh. "Do I look like the Devil?" he said.

It was slightly comforting to note that Mr T. looked about as far away as possible from how I'd been taught the Devil might appear. No horns. No pointy tail. I was also still shivering, and surely the one undeniable thing about Hell was that it was meant to be hot, wasn't it?

I coughed hard to try and clear the mouse out of my throat, but he seemed determined to stay. My body was too frozen and too confused to form any logical thought processes, however, with the aid of the mouse, I did manage to ask, "So where am I?"

Mr T. put down the file he'd been studying, smiled, opened his arms wide, and looked around. I followed his eyes, but could see nothing. It was like looking out of the window of an aeroplane at 30,000 feet. But without the window. Or the aeroplane.

"Why, you're here with us, Seven-Three-Five-Nine," he said. "About as dead as dead can be and not a fiery pit in sight." He put his arms back down and immediately went back to concentrating on the file in front of him. "Now, as you can see, we do have quite a lot of work to get through, so any further questions will have to wait. Here's what I suggest."

In a voice that smacked of a headmaster talking to a pupil of limited capabilities, Mr T. advised they would send for me when they had completed all the paperwork and appointed me a messenger.

"In the meantime," he said, before either the mouse or I could think about asking what he meant, "we'll send you off to have a nice little chat with Old Eric. He's sort of the elder statesman around these parts. We send most of our freshly dead to Old Eric for a chat before sending them on their way. It's all standard practice. I'm sure he'll be delighted to see you. He tells the most wonderful stories."

One of the sidekicks leaned over and whispered something in Mr T's ear. Mr T. nodded, a small frown creasing his brow. "Excuse us for a moment, Seven-Three-Five-Nine," he said. The three of them turned their chairs around and had a brief conversation in whispers before turning back.

Mr T. narrowed his eyes and tapped his chin with his index finger. "My colleagues have reminded me that Old Eric is currently assigned to watch Elaine," he said. "Be warned, Seven-Three-Five-Nine, there is a strong possibility he may be eager to… now, how can I put this?... fill you in about her activities."

I had no idea what Mr T. was talking about, but the sound of my wife's name squeezed my chest. If I was about as dead as dead can be, why was I struggling for air? As was normal for me in times of high anxiety, I could feel my bottom lip quivering. I'd always found crying such an easy thing to do, much to Elaine's dismay. Sad films, funerals, weddings, dead hedgehogs in the road, news reports about starving Africans, pain, the list of things that would get me going was long, and I could hear Elaine telling me to, *'Act like a man, Mark, for God's sake you're embarrassing me again.'*

I whispered back that I was doing the best I could under the circumstances.

I tried to keep the tears at bay by persuading myself that any moment now I would wake up and realise my being about as dead as dead can be was just another one of my big bad dreams, or as Mother used to refer to them - BBD's. In an effort to break the BBD, I closed my eyes and willed myself awake, allowing a few seconds to pass before slowly reopening one eye. I repeated the process several times. Each time, Mr T. and the sidekicks were still there, sifting through files.

"This isn't a dream, Seven-Three-Five-Nine," Mr T. said, rifling through yet more papers in front of him. "It says here your neck snapped as easily as a rotting twig when you nose-dived out of that attic. Instantaneous it says. Not the way we like it I must admit, but there you are. Now, we'll send your messenger to you when we're good and ready. It's all standard practice. Off you go."

Mr T. once again pointed behind me. This time a door had materialised with the word *IKEA* carved on it. Before I could get any words beyond the mouse, I found myself standing in front of it, dossier in hand. "You'll find Old Eric in the little office at the end of aisle forty-two," Mr T. said to my back. "Now, off you go."

Beyond the door wasn't something that just looked *like* the inside of an Ikea superstore, it *was* the inside of an Ikea superstore, and I appeared to be the only customer. Elaine loved Ikea; I hated it, and would navigate my way round by holding onto Elaine's hand for dear life. The very second contact was broken was the second I'd be swept away to be undoubtedly destined for a lifetime of arrows sending me round and round in circles. If this was no BBD, and I really was about as dead as dead can be, then I now knew I had definitely been sent to Hell. I turned with the intention of leaving, but the door through which I'd entered had gone. When I turned back, I found myself on the foot of an escalator, which, moments later, duly deposited me at the start of the Ikea trail. After subconsciously collecting a pocket full of pencils, I took a deep breath, closed my eyes, crossed myself, and entered the sheer bewilderment of Swedish superstore lay-out policy.

I eventually found aisle forty-two. It had taken me three hours. I'd meandered through the kitchen department at least eight times, gone round and round the bedroom section until I'd felt physically sick with dizziness, got stuck in the marketplace somewhere around lighting, and actually fallen into a huge wooden crate containing cuddly dinosaurs.

At the end of the aisle was a door, on which the letters O.E. had been ornately engraved onto a brass plaque. I knocked twice before being invited in by an authoritative voice from within. I tentatively opened the door and allowed my head to enter.

Mr T. had not lied when he'd said the office was small. It contained an ancient wooden desk, behind which, on an equally ancient arse, sat who I assumed was Old Eric. The desk was bereft of any items except for a small, framed print of *The Last Supper.* The white-washed walls were also bare. Old Eric looked up slowly from a crossword that didn't appear to have any of the grid completed, removed his half-moon spectacles, revealing sparkling eyes, and greeted me with a smile. He was, quite possibly, older than trees, and yet wore a purple robe over a white linen shirt and trouser combo, giving the impression he'd once belonged to a late-sixties rock group. His long grey hair and lined face put me in mind of someone.

"Hi," I said, letting the rest of my body follow my head and closing the door behind me. "My name's Mark." I placed the dossier on the desk, offered out a hand, and returned Old Eric's smile. "Nobody told me I'd died and come to Hogwarts."

Old Eric frowned, although his smile remained in place. "I'm sorry?" he said, taking the offered handshake. "Hogwhere?"

As was usual, my attempt at humour had backfired. Elaine would cringe whenever I decided to tell a story in public. I would get punch lines wrong, stumble over names and plotlines, repeat myself, and generally dig myself into caverns from which there was little chance of recovery. To avoid embarrassment, and any possible hindrance to her career, Elaine therefore rarely invited me along to any of the swanky parties her law firm threw, citing I would only be bored at all the legal talk.

"No, I'm the one who should be sorry," I said, shaking my head to indicate Old Eric should ignore my flippancy. "I've never been good meeting new people. Elaine reckons I suffer with foot and mouth disease. Every time I open my mouth, I put my foot in it."

Old Eric continued to smile and motioned for me to sit opposite him. I looked around but could see no other chair, so remained standing. I'd never seen a face as furrowed as Old Eric's; it was certainly well lived in. He looked a bit like that guitarist from The Rolling Stones, but more alert. He put his elbows on the desk and rested his chin in his hands. "So, Mark, what can I do for you?" he said.

I had no idea whether Old Eric could do anything for me or not. I didn't know where to start. At least the length of time taken to get through Ikea had helped de-ice my brain a little, and there were a million questions I now wished I'd asked the committee. "Well, for starters, I don't really know where I am," I said.

Old Eric stretched out his arms. "Why, you're in MY office, son," he said. The purple robe had multicoloured strips of material hanging from the sleeves, creating wings even the most colourful of parrots would have been proud of. They reminded me of similar things that, instead of doors, used to hang inside the doorways of our house when I was a child. Mother was nineteen by the end of the sixties, and for most of her life had embraced the vibrant style, if not the lifestyle, of the era. Father used to say Mother was one of the few people who could remember everything about the sixties; no surprise when considering her hatred of anything alcohol orientated, drug related, or, much to Father's disappointment, sexually liberated.

Eric's smile was trying to catch up with his outstretched arms. I don't think I'd ever seen anyone beam so much. Not even Elaine when she'd been made partner three months prior to my launch from the attic had offered as much excitement as Old Eric announcing that this was indeed HIS office. "I'm the only person here to have an office," he said. "How cool is that?"

I couldn't quite find the same enthusiasm as Old Eric. After all, the office wasn't much bigger than a broom cupboard. "Yeah, very cool," I said. "But honestly, I don't know where I am. One minute I'm in my attic, the next I'm sitting on a wooden chair in front of someone calling himself Mr T. It's like a BBD."

Old Eric dropped his arms. "What the hell is a BBD?"

"Oh, sorry. It's something Mother used to say. It means big bad dream."

Old Eric reapplied his glasses and went back to his crossword. "It's no stupid BBD, son," he said. My indifference about his office had obviously disappointed him. "You're dead."

I hoped I hadn't upset Old Eric too much, although, upsetting people did seem like something of a forte of mine. Given enough time, most people I met got bored or angry with my ordinariness eventually. How Elaine had found enough patience to stick around for twenty years was a wonder of the modern world.

No matter what point in my life you cared to choose, my back-story contained very little of interest, and, as I watched Old Eric ponder over his crossword, I wondered what must have happened for my normally reliable imagination to come up with something so cryptic as this BBD. I made a mental note to boast to my wife about how off-the-wall my mind had suddenly become as soon as I woke up. Even if it meant phoning her at work; something which she expressly forbade.

I attempted the will myself awake exercise again, this time opening the other eye, but Old Eric was still sitting in front of me, concentrating on the empty crossword. I therefore decided, for the purposes of reaching the end of my BBD as quickly as possible, that just for the time being, I would have to play along with this being about as dead as dead can be thing.

"So are there any other dead people about?" I asked. "I've been wandering around for hours trying to find you and didn't see a soul. Ikea is normally very busy."

Old Eric stood up, stretched himself, and rolled his head from side to side, giving out a satisfied grunt at the click of a bone. "Trust me, son," he said, sitting back down. "There's plenty milling around."

"So where are they all?"

Eric laughed and removed his glasses. "Oh, I do love you freshly dead," he said. "Always so clueless." He made a steeple of his fingers. "Think about it logically, son."

I made a face I hoped at least looked like I was trying to think about it logically, but when it became obvious no amount of thinking logically on my part was going to help, Old Eric took it upon himself to move the conversation along.

"Imagine how you'd feel if you suddenly bumped into your arch-enemy?" he said. "That old bully from school say? Or maybe the boss who wouldn't give you a raise? Perhaps the next door neighbour who played music until three every morning? What about the drunk-driver who mowed down your family like they were nothing more than a row of skittles? Worse still, imagine turning a corner and finding yourself face-to-face with a grudge-carrying ex-girlfriend? The one who found you in bed with her sister. Or brother. Or, perish the thought, her mother! Get my drift, son? There's no way the committee can risk it. There'd be mayhem."

"So I don't get to see any other dead people at all?"

Old Eric tutted and shook his head. "Now I didn't say that, did I?" he said. "I said the committee can't risk you randomly bumping into someone you may have issues with. Don't worry, if the committee think it worthwhile, you'll find other dead people along the way. How do you think you're in MY office talking to me, son?"

In its confusion, my mind hadn't even considered the supposed fact that Old Eric was a kindred spirit.

"I see," I said, not really seeing at all. "So do you think it could be arranged for me to see Father?" A sharp intake of breath stung my lungs as certain possibilities started to form. "Or?" I launched into my best Elvis pose; head glancing down to one side, one arm up in the air, a single finger pointing to the heavens. I put on the Southern drawl and curled the corner of my upper lip. "The King?" I remained in Elvis situ for a while before glancing at Old Eric. He had his head cocked to one side, studying me as if trying to solve some puzzle.

"I'm talking about Elvis Presley of course," I said, resuming a normal standing posture. "I've always dreamed of meeting Elvis. I know all there is to know about him. Although, Elaine reckons my repertoire of Elvis stories is another reason she doesn't invite me to her work parties. She says my Elvis trivia would bore a convention of chartered accountants, let alone some of the best legal minds in the country."

"Doesn't matter what she says, son," Eric said. "You've got no chance of meeting Elvis." He shook his head slowly and went back to his crossword. "He isn't dead."

I sat down on the edge of the desk before I fell down. I tried to speak, but the mouse had returned to his lodgings in my throat and wouldn't allow anything out.

"Anyway," Eric continued, ignoring my trauma. "I reckon the only way you can live the death you always dreamed of, son, is to get yourself packed off to the Sanctum. How you do that I haven't worked out myself yet. My advice would be to keep your head down and do as you're told. The committee can't stay pissed at you forever."

I vaguely registered Mr T. having said something about me not meeting the criteria to be sent to the Sanctum, but my head was too full of the revelation of Elvis being alive to give it much thought. I felt a certain naughty power surge through me. The sort of naughty power you get from holding knowledge that other people couldn't possibly know; like when I'd been the only person to know what had happened to Granddad's teeth. But then I remembered this was all just a BBD, and as soon as I awoke, Elvis would be dead again. The naughty power bubble burst as quickly as it had filled. As Grace would say, *'What the Lord giveth, the Lord taketh away.'*

Deflated by the real knowledge I would never meet Elvis, I latched on to Old Eric's terminology, and asked, "But why would the committee be pissed with me? I'm only a postman."

"Because you died quickly," Eric replied. "They really don't like that. Causes them all sorts of problems. Gives them a real headache with all the paperwork amongst other things." Old Eric slowly placed his glasses and crossword away in a drawer. He crossed his arms and studied me with those super-bright eyes of his. "Don't know about you, son?" His smile filled the room. "But I'm getting a bit bored."

Familiar ground, I thought. In fact, I was surprised it had taken this long for Old Eric to become weary of me.

"So, tell you what we'll do to cheer ourselves up." Eric unfolded his arms and clapped his hands together. "We'll talk about Elaine. After all, it's what you've been dying to do since you set foot in this office."

The sound of my wife's name once again put a payload on my chest. I gripped the edge of Eric's desk with as much force as I could manage, whitening my knuckles. Through intermittent darkness and light, I could see the whole of Old Eric's face sparkling. Even his teeth were glistening. I felt like I'd been caught in some sort of trap and sensed an increasing anxiety creeping up my back ready to smack me in the back of the head. Hadn't Mr T. given me some kind of warning about Old Eric talking about my wife?

I performed the will myself awake exercise as hard as I could, even resorting to poking my fingers into my eyes in a desperate attempt to break the BBD before Old Eric could start talking.

Eric waited patiently for me to stop the exercise, then leaned back in his chair and put his hands behind his head. He closed his eyes; a look of total satisfaction washed over him. "Ah, Elaine, Elaine,

Elaine," he said. "She sure is one sexy hunk of woman, son. Okay, so she's pushing forty and I usually like them a bit younger, but when you've got a body like Elaine's, age is superfluous, don't you think?"

I waved my arms about in front of Old Eric's face, and my voice did that dolphin thing again.

Eric slowly opened his eyes. "What?"

It had perhaps been true I'd been curious to know where, or how, Elaine fitted into my BBD. After all, I couldn't really expect her to appreciate how fantabulous my imagination had suddenly become without involving her in some way, but I didn't feel particularly comfortable receiving the information off some ancient, robe-wearing hippy. Especially one who referred to her as, *'one sexy hunk of woman.'*

"Eric, enough," I said, fighting with the throat-mouse and the dolphin. "That's my wife you're talking about."

Eric shook his head slowly. "I'm sorry to have to be the bearer of hard facts, son, but technically she's now your widow."

I could feel the bottom lip going again. Despite having only just met him, something told me if I'd started crying like I wanted to, I'd get as much sympathy from Old Eric as I'd ever received from Elaine. *It's just a BBD* I reminded myself, biting the quivering lip and looking at the ceiling.

Eric stood up, made his way to me, and put his arm around my shoulders. He moved with the ease of a twenty year old and smelled clean, like a freshly polished cabinet. The brightness from his eyes put me in danger of snow-blindness and I had to turn my head slightly. He put his mouth to my ear and whispered, "You do know that when we watch our assignees, we get to see *everything*, don't you?" He nudged me with his hip, winked, and almost skipped back to his seat. "The committee assigned me to Elaine about six months ago." Eric made it sound like we were talking about nothing more serious than the weather. "It was the day after she started shagging that lawyer…"

…At last! The BBD was breaking. My eyes flickered, and I could hear someone calling my name in a voice that was only vaguely familiar. I sensed an all encompassing brightness bearing down on me, and, in slow motion, my mind replayed my fall from the attic. Was I waking up in hospital? - Or? - Were all those stories Grace spouted about the path to Heaven true after all? The soft calling of my name;

the bright light. I forced my eyes open expecting either a host of relieved medical staff or the faces of cherubic angels to be looking down on me, only to be confronted with Old Eric's shining, smiling face. He held out his hand to help me up. I'd no recollection of falling off his desk.

Eric helped me around his desk like a boy-scout taking an old-age-pensioner across the road. He deposited me safely in his chair, then leaned against one of the sidewalls. "My, you are a touchy one, aren't you?" he said, folding his arms. "Now listen, son, I like you, so I'll be as gentle as I can. But you're going to have to face a few facts around here. The biggest of which is, you're dead. Doesn't matter how much you cry or faint or shout or moan. You're dead. Period."

I once again recollected my fall from the attic, and began, slowly but surely, to believe Old Eric may have a point. But if I was dead, why had the mention of Elaine's infidelity hurt so much? It wasn't like it should have come as a shock. I looked at Old Eric and wondered if he'd cried over someone or fainted at the mention of their name. Actually, I wondered if he'd ever cried over anything. From the radiant way he was smiling at me, it was difficult to imagine.

"Were you *'watching'* Elaine when I fell out of my attic?" I asked, doing that annoying quotation thing with my fingers around the word watching. The words floated in the air between us, like I could have reached out and touched them. I wasn't even certain I'd spoken them. Perhaps it was the mouse.

Eric winked at me. "Sure was, son."

The last thought I remembered having just before I'd allegedly hurtled to my death had been to consider what Elaine might have been doing at that precise moment. "Where was she?" I asked. I knew the answer. It lurked somewhere within my soul, but I guess my ears felt left out and needed to know as well. I felt my lungs constrict at the question, let alone the probable answer.

"Sure you want to know, son?" Eric looked at me like a loving grandfather. I felt like I should be sitting on his knee.

I nodded my head slowly, catching hold of the sides of the chair and bracing myself. Even so, I hadn't bargained on Eric's reply being quite so brutal.

"Going at it like hammer and tongs on his kitchen table, son," he said, belying the look of gentleness.

Waves of nausea crashed over me like I'd angered the Gods of wavy nausea crashing; every last one of them. As I started dry-retching, Eric moved from the wall, produced a brown paper bag from one of the desk drawers, and held it over my mouth. "Breathe," he said. "That's it. In - and out. In - and out." Eric continued talking as the bag inflated and deflated. "Tell you what, son, if I'd been in your shoes, I'd have fought a bit harder to keep her from his clutches. That body of hers is to die for. How could you just sit back and watch it slip away?" If this was Eric's way of easing the pain of my wife's indiscretion, it wasn't working. The bag moved in and out quicker. "As we all know, son, every wife expects a good seeing to now and again. Your job, as a loving husband, is to make sure you're the one satisfying those expectations, not some crazy son-of-a-bitch lawyer with an oversized libido."

Eric removed the bag from my face to check my progress. I felt like both lungs had collapsed and I started making strange gurgling noises. The dolphin was actually drowning.

"I don't know why you're so upset," Eric said, replacing the bag over my mouth. "You made the choice to sit there and listen to all those excuses. Working late, weekend business trips, sudden interests in hobbies taking her away from the house for hours, sometimes days. Christ, you even rolled over when she went shopping to Asda at midnight, coming back two hours later with nothing more than a loaf of bread and a limp. You knew exactly what was going on. I was there, remember? That's it. In - and out. In - and out." The darkness surrounding me took away the power of sight, yet I could still hear Eric's voice chirping away like we were talking over the garden fence. "They met at court. The poor bugger's daughter had killed herself a few weeks before. Elaine helped him get over the death by getting over him, if you know what I mean? Like I said, the committee put me on the case the day after. They know I like a bit of action." Eric removed the bag from my face and looked at the ceiling. "Do you know that after the shock of finding you without a pulse had worn off, the first thing she did was go and buy herself a puppy? Nasty little thing it is too."

The information didn't really surprise me. Elaine loved dogs; I hated them. Twenty-three years as a postman had served to embed a natural hatred of man's best friend in me. I reached to try and take the bag from Eric's hand, but he took a step away.

"Of course," he said, "the second thing she did was go and get herself liberally rogered by that lawyer."

I clutched at the air, trying to scoop handfuls of it into my mouth.

"The bag," I croaked. "Need the bag."

Eric placed the bag back over my mouth. "At least she waited until after the funeral," he said. "You see, son, you actually died a fortnight ago. The committee put a fourteen day turn-around period in place quite some time ago. Just after they'd had an unfortunate incident where some poor sod ended up attending his own cremation. Now that was one busy day, son, I can tell you."

It seemed having palpitating, freshly dead postmen in his office wasn't something that Old Eric was particularly fazed about, and he continued his ramblings with occasional requests for me to, "Breathe. That's it. In - and out. In - and out…"

Despite the bag's best efforts, it took some time before my breathing reached a level Old Eric deemed safe. He put the bag away in a drawer and stood behind me, massaging my shoulders.

"Guess I'll have to be a bit more careful what I say when you're about, eh, son?" he said. "Wouldn't do to have you passing out on me all the time. What fun would that be?" He stopped massaging and made his way to the front of the desk. "Hey, tell you what, why don't you read this?" He picked up the dossier Mr T. had handed me and waved it in the air. "Might help take your mind off things and keep you conscious for five minutes."

In all the panic I'd completely forgotten about the dossier. I took it off Eric, gladly accepting an opportunity to occupy my mind with something other than mental images of Elaine and that lawyer doing things on his kitchen table. I shakily opened the dossier, and, despite my head playing host to an internal jazz-band, and my eyes finding it difficult to focus properly, I was still surprised to discover it only contained one piece of lined notepaper.

"Come on," Eric said, clapping his hands. "I love this bit. Who've you got?"

I persuaded my eyes to concentrate and my hands to still, and read down the list on the handwritten, bullet-pointed note aloud.

"David Williams: Unmarried: Thirty-two years old: Ill-educated: Welsh: Part-time debt-collector: A man of very few words, when they run out, it's time to leave: Known locally as *Dai the Murderer* on account of him having once strangled his pet budgie in a fit of rage: No children: Lives alone in a small council house with a new swing in the backyard and a rusty Metro in the front garden: Has quite a lot of pictures of his dear old Mum scattered around the house." I turned the note over, but there was nothing else. I picked up the dossier and shook it. "Is that it?" I said. "I thought Mr T. said I'd have all the information I needed."

"Ah, I remember my first," Eric said, gazing at the ceiling. "Lots of souls been through my fingers since then, but you never forget your first."

"Who was it?" I asked, still checking the dossier for extra instruction.

"A real lowlife," Eric said. He watched as I turned the dossier over and over. "Killed his brother in a fit of jealousy, then ran away somewhere never to be seen again. Good riddance to the jealous murdering bugger I say."

Eric took the dossier off me as gently as if he were taking a book off the chest of a sleeping child. "There is no more, son," he said, placing the dossier back on the desk. "Actually, for them, that's more than normal. Now, if you're feeling better, is there any chance I can have my chair back?"

I tried standing up, but my legs were unable to support my limited weight - just under 60 kilos when I'd last weighed - and I had to use the edge of Old Eric's desk to pull myself out of his chair.

"So what exactly am I supposed to do?" I asked, crab-walking my way round to the front of the desk and sitting down. "You know, when I'm watching this... this, David Williams? Am I some sort of guardian angel?"

Eric laughed and opened his mouth to reply, but was interrupted by a knock on the door.

"Who's that?" I said, jumping off the edge of the desk and instantly crumpling to the floor.

Eric leaned over the desk and looked down at me. "I'm afraid I haven't yet developed the ability to see through doors," he said, raising his eyebrows. "Come in."

The redheaded girl who entered was, at a guess, in her late teens or early twenties. She was wearing tight fitting jeans tucked into boots, and a t-shirt with *Doctors of Destruction* written on the front. She seemed flustered and out of breath. "Seven-Three-Five-Nine," she said, taking a rest between each word. "I'm your messenger. The committee have completed all the paperwork and it's time to go." She looked at the arms of Mickey Mouse on her watch. "Actually, it's well past time to go. So can you please get up off the floor and come with me?"

"But I can't go!" I said, panic rising from somewhere near my shoes and engulfing my body like a fast-acting snakebite. "It's not my time. I'm not ready. What about Elaine? Oh dear God, Elaine! I never said goodbye to Elaine."

"I'm afraid it's a bit late for that, son," Old Eric said.

"But I don't think Mr T. has put everything into my dossier." I used the desk for leverage to get to my knees and looked from the messenger to Eric, then back to the messenger, and finally back to Eric again. "I have no idea what I'm supposed to do." The bottom lip started quivering its merry dance.

Eric and the young girl exchanged knowing smiles. "Perhaps you'd best take this with you, son," Eric said, holding out the paper bag.

I struggled to my feet, and, thanks to my trembling hands, took an inordinate amount of time to get the bag into my trouser pocket. The length of time spent staring down at my trousers brought a startling revelation regarding my attire; one that had obviously escaped my attention until now.

I was in my postman's uniform.

I looked myself up and down several times, and once again replayed my visit to the attic. I knew I hadn't been wearing it when I'd climbed in there. I distinctly recalled having on my favourite clothes; the cream sweater and brown cords Mother had given me last Christmas. I looked to Eric and tried to speak.

"Elaine thought it's what you'd like to be buried in," Eric said, giving me that grandfatherly look again. "Still, it's not as tasteless as her insistence on using *Return to Sender* as your filing out song, eh? She really has got a wicked sense of humour, don't you think?"

The young messenger coughed for attention. I turned to find her tapping her foot and her watch simultaneously.

Believing if I engaged her in small-talk it may delay whatever was coming next, I pointed at the name on her t-shirt, my hand bouncing as if I had some imaginary basketball, and asked, "Do you like them?"

She pulled the bottom of the t-shirt out and looked down at the name. "God, no," she said. "They're like ancient. No, I borrowed this off my Mum on the day I died. I was running late and couldn't find anything clean. This was the best she could do. Told me she had a thing for the drummer or something." She looked at her watch again and grimaced. "Come on," she reached over and grasped my oscillating hand, "let's get you gone before the committee find out how late I really am."

As she led me towards the door, I noticed the back of the t-shirt listed all the dates for the *Doctors* 1992 Scandinavian tour.

"Oh, I nearly forgot," the girl said, slapping her forehead. She turned and looked over my shoulder at Old Eric. "Mr Eric, the committee have suggested you may want to return to your assignee. Something about a table?"

"Ah, that would be that lawyer's kitchen table again." Eric winked and disappeared.

I stared at the empty chair. I turned to the girl and opened my mouth, but not one syllable got past the mouse.

"He's Old Eric," she said, as if I was about to ask the most stupid question in the world. "Now come on, hurry up."

MY FIRST

I never believed people like David existed. He was the stuff of novels and films. The archetypal muscle brought in to help when negotiations weren't going your way. Six-five in his bare feet, bald and flat-nosed, he looked like he'd been constructed from two men. He certainly drank enough for several more.

Dead or alive, I was five-eight on a good day and had spent the majority of my adulthood delivering bills, greeting cards, and pizza delivery adverts. The giant David delivered mayhem.

It had been five months since the young messenger had walked me out of Old Eric's office and straight into David's living room. She'd disappeared moments later with a quick look at her watch and a gasp, leaving me staring mutely at the snoring hulk of David sleeping soundly on his sofa. It had been five months in which I'd never felt so alive.

I couldn't believe I was accompanying a heavy. Me? Mark Ferris? Mother would have had a fit if she'd known. All my childhood playmates had been handpicked by Mother and had names like Timothy or Christopher. They always lived in the same street and were deemed to be *nice*. Toy weapons and violence were frowned upon in the Ferris household. My parents were more peace and love than push and shove, and didn't believe in beating their only child, although, to be honest, apart from the episode with Granddad's teeth, I couldn't recall having ever done anything that would have warranted a beating.

I could imagine Mother's torment if I'd ever brought someone like David home.

"Mum, this is David."

"Oh, hello, David. My, aren't you big?"

"He's known as Dai the Murderer, Mum."

"He's what?"

"Is it all right if we go and beat the living daylights out of somebody because they owe somebody else money? Is it? Please say yes."

"I don't think so, Mark, do you? Why don't you go and ask that nice Timothy from down the street if he'll come and play with you instead? Now, let's stop all this silly talk about beatings, and I'll get Father to take David home."

I was getting such a buzz from David's work it was unreal. Okay, so there were some areas of the operation I had to turn away from. The sight of blood or the snapping sound of a bone in a much needed limb were things that would leave me a bit woozy, but the anticipation David generated in the preamble more than made up for my timidity.

Hey, Elaine, why don't you put that lawyer down and come and see how exciting your dead husband has become? Perhaps I'll even introduce you to my new friend, Dai the Murderer. Yes, that's what I said - Dai the Murderer.

David had a generic name for his prey: Mr Unlucky.

His preparations to visit the Mr Unluckys of this world were of military precision.

First - bath, shave, and brush teeth - then, whilst still nude and singing along loudly to Bon Jovi's greatest hits, David would proceed to iron his best white shirt and smart black trousers. After liberally spraying cheap deodorant in places only mothers and wives should know about, David would progress to the dressing stage: Black boxers and black socks would be followed by the freshly ironed shirt and black trousers. The shirt would then be patriotically adorned with gold-plated cufflinks decorated with the *three feathers*, and a bright red tie with the word *Cymru* written on it just below the knot. The ensemble would get finished off with polished black lace-up shoes and a black suit jacket. Into the right-hand pocket of the jacket would be placed the details of the job - name, address, and any other relevant information - and into the left-hand pocket would go a set of gold-coloured knuckle-dusters. Finally, before leaving, David would double-check all windows and doors were locked. After all, there were some shady characters living around David's way.

Watching David go about his business of demanding money by snapping limbs, breaking jaws, hitting people with garden implements, and using menaces I never knew existed, wasn't something I thought would ever be factored into my life-plan; and it certainly bore no resemblance to the path my school's careers officer had wanted me to follow. She'd tried to persuade me to go into chartered accountancy; a dream shattered when she realised I was useless at maths. Mother, as most Mothers do, wanted me to be a doctor, but stated she would settle for me doing anything, *'as long as I was happy.'* Secretly, I knew she was devastated at me becoming a postman, but I guess if it had been a choice between that or becoming a non-registered debt collector's dead assistant, perhaps she would have tempered her disappointment.

Despite David doing his best to take my mind off things, the last five months had brought two major problems. Firstly, I'd neither seen a single dead person since my arrival into David's world nor heard a word from the committee. The meeting with Mr T and the sidekicks, along with my time with Old Eric, all seemed such a distant memory, and thoughts I had been forgotten about often had me reaching for the paper bag. Had my details got lost in all the paperwork perhaps?

Secondly, no matter how hard I'd tried, I hadn't yet found any way of communicating with David, or, for that matter, any of the other living souls we'd come across. For the first few weeks after Crimson had left me in David's living room, I'd screamed a lot. I'd screamed at David. I'd screamed at anyone who wasn't David. I'd screamed at inanimate objects. Basically, I'd just screamed. Oh, and cried. Actually, I'd probably cried more than I'd screamed.

The screaming, over time, had eventually reduced itself to shouting, then to talking, and finally to rarely speaking at all. The crying, however, hadn't really subsided at all. It appeared as though my existence, if that's what it could be called, was unnoticeable to the masses; and it seemed as though the dead, or at least this dead, had no way of making himself known.

David's office was a corner table in his local Wetherspoons, *The Three Buckets*. He took each case on its own merit, but rarely refused his services. No paperwork was involved, and the fee for David's assistance was 10% of amounts owed. Up-front. Cash only. It wasn't a hugely lucrative operation, but the job satisfaction David took from his profession more than compensated for the lack of prosperity.

One night, a wiry man by the name of Tim, who looked vaguely familiar, walked into the Buckets seeking out David's help. As with a lot of David's clients, Tim walked by several times before plucking up the courage to approach.

"Are you Dai the Murderer?" he eventually asked.

David took a long draught of his pint of Guinness. "Who wants to know?"

"Of course, where are my manners? The name's Tim," he said, offering his hand.

"And what if I were this, Dai the Murderer?" David said, finishing his drink and ignoring the handshake.

Tim removed an official looking document from his pocket and grabbed a chair. "Well it's like this," he said, sitting opposite us. I couldn't work out if the document was shaking because he was nervous or excited. "About a month ago," he seemed to count something off in his head. "Yes, it must have been a month, because Julie, that's my daughter, had just returned from spending the summer with her Aunt in Dundee…"

David closed his eyes and started mock snoring. "Keep your life story for someone who gives a bollocks," he said. "All I need from you, Tim, is three facts." David held up three fingers. Unfortunately, he used his right hand, where he'd previously managed to lose half an index finger. "One, who fucked you over?" David lowered one finger. "Two, where will I find them?" He looked at his fingers and lowered his hand. "And three, how much am I politely asking them for?" David picked up his empty glass and waved it in Tim's direction. "Now, all this negotiating is making me thirsty. So why don't you put that worthless piece of paper away?" David nodded to the document Tim was still holding, "and go get us a drink."

The facts were this. Tim had bought a timeshare that didn't exist from a local conman known as *Tony the Pony*. Why someone who seemed as nice as Tim was dealing with local conmen never got discussed, but as soon as Tony the Pony's name was mentioned, David's eyes somersaulted.

"Did I just hear you right?" David said, spitting out a mouthful of Guinness. "Did you just say the twat who sold you this non-existent suntrap is Tony the Pony?"

"That's right," Tim replied. "I suppose he's got something to do with horses with a name like that. Do you know him?"

"Oh, I know him all right," David said. "And I can assure you he's got fuck-all to do with horses. Now, why don't you go and get us another drink? Then we'll talk finance."

Tim had paid Tony a £6000 deposit for exclusive rights to a fortnight every August in a luxury apartment on the Costa Del Bravo. The apartment never existed, and, for £600, David agreed to help Tim recover his outlay. The look on David's face as Tim handed over the crisp £20 notes suggested he may enjoy this job a little more than usual.

Later that night, David's good mood flourished in his performance of naked gymnastics with Shaz from behind the bar. The old Metro complained on rusty springs.

"By Christ, Dai," Shaz pleaded. "You're gonna snap me in two. Why don't you get yourself a bigger car?"

David tried to manoeuvre Shaz into a more accessible position. Shaz was shorter and lighter than me, but with the three of us in the car it was still a bit tight. I had to be careful to avoid body parts I never thought I'd need to avoid.

"Sorry, Shaz," David said. "I'm just in the groove tonight. I had some good news earlier."

"Well you just watch what groove you're pointing that thing at," Shaz said. "Good news or not, I'm strictly a front door girl, all right? And don't do what you did last time either. Twenty quid this hair-do cost me."

Thanks to Shaz, in the five months I'd been with David, I'd gained more knowledge about the noble art of love-making than I ever thought existed. Mother and Elaine would have been mortified and delighted respectively.

The levels of abandon Shaz and David displayed were things I could only have dreamed of producing in Elaine, and, amidst the creaks and groans of David and Shaz's enjoyment, thoughts of my own regular sexlife with my wife came to mind.

Every second Thursday, without fail. Unless it was the wrong time of month, Elaine had a headache, she was tired, or simply didn't feel like it. On high days and holidays, Elaine would occasionally suggest something other than the missionary, but as not many holidays fall on a Thursday, variety was at a premium. Still, I never complained. Did I mention she was a stunner? The odd session was good enough for me, although, as it turned out, it appeared it wasn't good enough for her.

Despite my inability to keep Elaine away from that lawyer, I couldn't help but believe Eric must have been wrong when he'd said she'd been *doing it* on his kitchen table. Elaine always insisted on being comfortable before penetration could take place, often stating, *'Why pay good money for a bed if you're not going to use it?'* So it would have been impossible for her to entertain the thought of getting on a table. Wouldn't it?

David and Shaz finally finished grunting an hour later. David only stopped then because Shaz started complaining she thought she'd cracked a rib.

"What the hell am I supposed to tell my husband?" Shaz said, trying to straighten clothing. "I can hardly bloody walk." She moved the interior mirror to look at herself and let out a small scream. "You bastard! What did I tell you about getting any in my hair?"

David was attempting to retrieve a shoe from under the driver's seat. "If he gives you any grief just tell him to come and have a word with me," he said. "I'm sure I can put his mind to rest."

Shaz thanked him for the offer but politely refused. "The fat useless twat is probably asleep by now anyway," she said. "Will we be seeing you in the Buckets tomorrow?"

David had finally found all his bits of clothing and was readjusting the seats. "Is the Pope Catholic, sweetheart? I have a little job to take care of first. But I'll be in for a celebratory drink after. Tell you what, wear something easy to get off."

Given his exertions, David slept with a well-earned smile on his face that night. I sat on the chair in the bedroom and watched him in his contentment as I tried to block out the noises of the slumbering house. Night-noises had always put the fear of God into me, much to Elaine's amusement, and David's house had the habit of complaining bitterly during the dark hours. No matter how hard I'd tried over the last five months, it seemed the dead, or at least this dead, didn't sleep.

As I'd done almost every night since I'd been with David, I checked under the bed for monsters before entering into conversation with his mum to help me through the darkness. "Well, as you can see, Mrs Williams," I said to the picture he kept of her on his bedside cabinet. "I've managed to get your son home all in one piece, which is more than can be said for poor old Shaz."

David's mum smiled back at me from underneath a huge sombrero whilst sitting astride a stuffed blue donkey, and asked after her son's welfare.

"What's that, Mrs Williams?... Yes, I'm looking after him... No, he's not drinking too much. I'm sure ten pints a night is normal for a man his size... Yes, I'm sure he'll meet some nice young girl and settle down soon... Of course I'll make sure he doesn't get into any trouble... No, I know he..."

"Who are you talking to?" The voice came from behind me. I screamed and leaped out of the chair like a gymnast. I turned, fully expecting to find an axe-wielding creature of the night ready to flay me alive.

Standing in the doorway, looking at her watch, was my messenger.

"Jesus Christ," I said, clutching my chest. "You scared me half to death. What are you trying to do, give me a heart-attack?"

"Sorry," she said. "But it's not like I can phone and say I'm coming. Anyway, come on, the committee want to see you." She reached over and took hold of my hand. "I've got to get you to them like," she checked her watch and groaned, "before now."

"Listen," I said, standing my ground. "Here we are holding hands and I don't even know your name." I was quite surprised, and, even though the mouse had returned to make my voice barely audible, I was also a tad proud at my bravado. Could it be that some of David's forthright manner had begun to rub off on me? I sincerely hoped so. It hadn't been unknown for me to palpitate to the point of collapse whenever I'd had physical contact with girls. And yet here I was, a young female clutching my hand, and I hadn't fainted yet. In fact, I'd asked her for her name. Not like me at all. The first time Elaine and I had held hands, I'd squeezed too hard and almost dislocated her little finger. At the time she'd said it was painful, but cute. The first time we'd kissed, I near knocked her teeth out. She'd said that was painful, but cute, too. When she took my virginity, she'd said that was just cute.

The young girl looked around as if to check there was nobody listening. "I shouldn't really," she said. "The committee go mental if us messengers get too familiar."

"But the committee aren't here," I said, duelling with the mouse. "It'll be our little secret. I'm Mark by the way."

The messenger continued to check the corners of the room for intruders into our conversation. "Okay," she said, "but if I get caught, I am so blaming you."

Her real name was Scarlet, on account of her mother being obsessed with Gone with the Wind, but all her friends called her Crimson, which she thought way better.

"In that case, Crimson it is," I said. "So tell me, Crimson. Why do the committee want to see me? Am I in some sort of trouble? Have I done something wrong?"

"I wouldn't know," Crimson said, looking at her watch again. "But I'll be in trouble if we don't get a move on. Come on, let's go."

Mr T. didn't look up from the file he was reading. "We were just wondering how you're doing, Seven-Three-Five-Nine?" he said. "Are you all right? Is there anything we can do?"

I turned in the wooden chair and scanned the area behind me, seeing nothing but empty space. I quickly checked to my right. Nothing. And then to my left. Still nothing. Apart from checking up Mr T's sleeves, I was sure there were no strange doors around me.

"Thanks for your concern," I said, sitting on my hands to stop them shaking. "Under the circumstances, I think I'm doing okay." I decided to leave out the fact I was still bursting into tears quite regularly. "I hadn't heard from you for so long I thought you may have forgotten about me."

"Don't be so silly," Mr T. said, still not looking up. "There's no need to worry if you don't hear from us for a while, Seven-Three-Five-Nine. As you can see, we are very busy." Mr T. scanned his hand over the mounds of paperwork in front of him. "We can't keep in touch every minute of every day. You're just going to have to learn to fend for yourself. You're not the only one on our books you know."

I bowed my head and was about to offer my apologies for my ignorance, when the new, David inspired, forthright Mark Ferris took control of my voice and decided to speak for me. "There is one little thing that's been bothering me," he said. I noticed not even the new forthright Mark Ferris could get rid of the mouse.

Mr T. continued to read over some documents. "And what's that, Seven-Three-Five-Nine?"

I removed my hands from under me and placed them in my lap. If the new forthright Mark Ferris was going to fight my battles for me, I assumed he'd need my hands. "What am I supposed to be doing?"

Before Mr T. could answer, one of the sidekicks passed him a note. He read it quickly before screwing it into a ball and throwing it over his shoulder. "Looks like you're going to have to hang around, Seven-Three-Five-Nine," he said, forcing a smile. "Your messenger is… temporarily otherwise engaged." Mr T. went back to the paperwork in front of him. "Don't worry. We'll get you back to your assignee as soon as we can. It's all standard practice."

"That's okay," I said. "I imagine David's exhausted after the night he's just had. Probably won't surface until at least noon. I've got plenty of time."

"Unfortunately, we haven't," Mr T. said, without taking his head out of the file one of the sidekicks had just given him. "So, as much as I'd love to sit here and carry on with this idle chit-chat, here's what I suggest."

Mr T's suggestion was I spend whatever time I needed to kill in the company of Old Eric. "I'm sure he'll be delighted to see you again. Off you go, Seven-Three-Five-Nine." Mr T. nodded to somewhere behind me.

Before the new forthright Mark Ferris or I could ask, *'Where the hell did that door come from?'* we found ourselves standing in front of it, staring at the words *EXCELSIOR STREET*. I turned back to Mr T. and pointed at the door. "But… how?"

Mr T. waved his hand. "We'll send your messenger for you when we're ready. Off you go, Seven-Three-Five-Nine. It's all standard practice."

Excelsior Street was the worst street on my round. Only fourteen houses long, it contained, in order, a vicious Alsatian, a merciless Bulldog, a ruthless Poodle forged from the fires of Mordor, and finally, a homicidal mongrel that believed itself to be Cerberus. Of course, through the door wasn't something that just looked *like* Excelsior Street, it *was* Excelsior Street, and I was wearing a postman's uniform. I could see Old Eric's office door offering sanctuary at the end of the street, the brass plaque glinting at me like a light-house.

I took a deep breath, closed my eyes, crossed myself, and ran the gauntlet of Hell itself.

I burst through Eric's door and landed on the edge of his desk with a thump. I was breathless, covered in sweat, had poodle teeth-marks on my shoes, and one of my trouser legs had been ripped.

Eric looked up slowly from his still empty crossword and studied me over his glasses. "Don't we believe in knocking any more?" he said.

I put my hand out to indicate he'd have to give me a minute to find enough air to speak. "I'm sorry," I eventually managed. "But what are they trying to do to me? First they make me wait in my dentist's waiting room, then they send me through Ikea, and now they make me run Excelsior Street. If they carry on like this they'll kill me."

Eric smiled, then giggled, and eventually burst into laughter. For once, the laughter didn't seem to be out of pity, or spite, or embarrassment. It was genuine laughter. I'd actually told a little ditty and made someone laugh.

What do you think of that, Elaine? The new forthright Mark Ferris was a hoot, was he not?

When Old Eric finally finished laughing, he removed his glasses and put away the crossword. "Okay, so the dentist and Ikea I can understand," he said, "but what's wrong with Excelsior Street?"

I displayed my gnarled shoes and ripped trousers. "What's wrong with Excelsior Street? I'll tell you what's wrong with Excelsior Street, Eric. It's full of insane dogs whose favourite meal is leg of postman. That's what's wrong with Excelsior Street."

Eric's smile competed with the white-washed walls for dazzle. "So what brings you back to MY office, son?" he asked.

I replayed the conversation with Mr T. in my head. "I'm not really sure. I think the committee just wanted to check I was okay."

"And are you?"

After five months liberal usage of Eric's paper bag, the panic attacks had now subsided to only a few a week. Also, thanks to David's mum, not every bump in the night now sent me into spasms of despair. Watching David go about his business often had me forgetting I was dead, so, all things considered, I guessed I was okay. Sort of. Except for the crying.

"I still don't know what I'm meant to be doing," I said. "I can't communicate with a living soul. Is that normal, or am I doing something wrong?"

Eric shook his head and re-applied his glasses. "No, you're not doing anything wrong, son. That's just the way things are."

"But that doesn't make sense," I said, playing with the print of the Last Supper. "If I can't talk to anyone, what's the point of me being there?"

Eric let out a deep breath and rubbed his face with his hands, pushing his glasses to the top of his head. "Well what did you expect to be doing, son?" he said. "Changing the world? At the expense of repeating myself, you're dead. D.E.A.D. Dead. And, in case it's escaped your attention, son, dead postmen are not the most influential of creatures."

The new forthright Mark Ferris struggled to find the quick witty comeback he was looking for, so as an alternative, he scrunched up his face and poked his tongue out at Old Eric.

"You look like you've had a stroke," Eric said, replacing his glasses and retrieving his crossword. "For God's sake put it away."

My tongue disappeared and my face returned to normal. "But really, what's the point of it all?" I said, placing the print back on the desk. "If I've no influence on David's life, what possible reason is there for me to be there?"

Eric threw his arms upwards. The wings on his robe created a wave of air which ruffled my hair. "Aha!" he said with some triumph.

From Eric's reaction I thought I'd at last asked the question to end all questions. That I'd broken some secret code; that I was about to be enlightened with the very meaning of life and death itself. My whole body began shaking and I found myself sitting on my hands to keep them still. "What? What is it Eric?"

"Melancholy," Eric said, grabbing the crossword and waving it in the air. "Seven down. Deep and long lasting sadness. Ten letters." He sighed heavily and put the crossword away in a drawer, staring at its disappearance. "Taken me ages to work that one out."

I tried to hide the bursting of my excitement bubble. "Oh, right. Yeah. Of course. Deep and long lasting sadness. Melancholy. Well done." I released my hands from under me and pointed to the region of where the crossword had disappeared. "Uh, Eric, aren't you going to fill it in?"

Eric hadn't taken his focus from the drawer, and shook his head slowly. I'm sure some of the glint disappeared from his eyes. "That's something else you've obviously let escape you, son," he said. "The dead don't write. Sure as hell makes doing that crossword harder."

I tried to shake the confusion out of my head. Suddenly remembering I still had a pocket-full of Ikea pencils, I eagerly tipped them out onto the desk. Old Eric and I both looked at them forlornly for some time before the realisation set in that I had absolutely no idea of how to use them.

"Think about it logically, son," Eric said, putting the pencils away in a drawer. This time he didn't wait for me to even try. "The committee can't risk having dead people leaving notes all over the place. Can you imagine? There'd be mayhem."

"But what about all the paperwork surrounding Mr T. and the sidekicks?" I said. "Where does all that come from? And what about the hand written note inside David's dossier?"

As far as Eric was aware, the sidekick sitting to Mr T's right was responsible for keeping all written information up to date. He was apparently the only dead person ever granted the ability to write. "Been that way for as long as anyone can remember, son," Eric explained. "That's why sitting to the right of the chairperson is such a coveted role. It's high honour indeed if you ever get offered to sit there."

"So I really have no way of making David aware of my existence?" I said. "I just have to bumble about behind him like a mute dummy?"

Eric stood up and made his way to me. "Listen," he said, putting his arm around my shoulders, "there's no use beating yourself up about not being able to communicate with the living, son. Forty years you trudged your sorry living arse around, right? Now in all that time did you ever once base any decisions on some voice in your head? Fairies at the bottom of the garden? A native American spirit sitting on the edge of your bed? A gremlin on your shoulder? Luke Skywalker's father telling you to, *'Feel the force, Mark, feel the force,'* mm?" Eric didn't wait for a reply. "Of course you didn't." He squeezed my shoulders. "That's because the living can only hear the living, son.

Think about it logically. If they could hear us dead folk, there'd be mayhem, yes?"

"But there's loads of people reckon they can communicate with the other side, Eric."

Old Eric looked at the ceiling and crossed himself theatrically. "Yes, but thank the Lord they're all strictly monitored and not allowed to use anything sharper than a crayon." He smiled and made his way back to his chair.

"So that's it then, is it?" I said. "I'm destined to follow David about forever and do nothing but watch?"

Eric stretched his back and rolled his head from side to side. There was a click and a sigh of relief. "Ah, that's better," he said, rolling his shoulders. "I'm afraid these bones aren't what they used to be, son." He looked at one of the walls as if staring out at some wonderful vista, a rueful smile creasing his lips. I followed his glistening eyes, but saw nothing other than bare wall.

Eric's daydreaming brought back memories of the early stages of Father's Alzheimer's. He'd sit there for hours staring at nothing, then tell you something of little importance, only to tell you the same thing again moments later. At first, Mother and I took fun of his seemingly poor recall, putting it down to old-age. Mother even used to quip it was a burden women had to carry if they would go around marrying men who were considerably older than themselves. But when the diagnosis came in, it stopped being funny.

Somehow, I couldn't quite believe Old Eric was suffering with Alzheimer's, and allowed him a few moments before waving my hands in the path of his stare.

"Sorry," he said, shaking his head quickly to disperse whatever thoughts were pleasing him. "Where were we?"

"We were talking about David."

"Oh, that's right," Eric said, slapping his thigh. Despite Eric's dramatics, I didn't think for one minute that he'd actually forgotten. "Well now think about it logically, son," he continued. "You won't be following David around forever, will you?" He rolled his eyes as if I should have known this all along. "After all, he's bound to die one day."

David's mortality, or the lack of it, had never crossed my mind. I guessed his lifestyle didn't really lend itself to a long and healthy run, but he was still only in his early thirties. The possibility was he could still have many fruitful years ahead of him.

"But that could be years away," I said. "What if he lives to be seventy? Eighty? Ninety? That would make me…" I looked at the ceiling and closed one eye in concentration, struggling to do the maths.

"Forty!" Eric said, interrupting my calculations. "How many times do I have to keep trying to get it through that thick skull of yours, son? You're dead. Dead, dead, dead. Doesn't matter if David lives another week or a thousand years. You denied yourself any more birthdays by free-falling from that attic. Understand?"

What I did understand was Old Eric seemed to take great pleasure in reminding me I was dead. How many times *had* he mentioned it? Perhaps he was suffering with Alzheimer's after all.

"Okay, okay, I understand," I said, not fully understanding anything.

Regardless of the amount of times it had happened, I'd always hated it when people got to raising their voices at me, and I could feel the bottom lip starting to quiver. I closed my eyes and willed the new forthright Mark Ferris to make the lip stay still. "So what does happen if David dies?" I eventually asked, opening my eyes.

Eric leaned back in his chair and put his arms behind his head. "Well, fourteen days after that inevitable day comes, he'll find himself in front of the committee waiting to be told whether he's going into the Sanctum or not, then…"

The new forthright Mark Ferris crept up on my blindside. "I meant to me, Eric!" he said. "Not David. What in God's name will happen to me?" I could see this new forthright Mark Ferris was going to cause me a few problems.

Mother would have been dismayed at the way I'd spoken.

"You're bothering with the wrong crowd, Mark. You seem to have found a new forthright manner which doesn't become you. I think it's best you stay clear of that David the Murderer. He's obviously a bad influence on you. I also think it's about time you found yourself a nice girl. What about Timothy's sister?"

"But she's got buck teeth and spots all over her."

"Yes, but she's very nice."

Old Eric retrieved his crossword, opening and closing the drawer with slightly more force than normal. I heard him mutter something about respect, and started to feel awful. Eric must have been at least twice my age, although even three times wouldn't be out of the question, and I'd shown no regard for my elder. I made a silent apology to Mother before making an audible one to Old Eric.

"Eric, I'm sorry," I said, my voice as soft as a doctor about to tell parents their child hadn't made it through the operation. "But, you see, I've got this new forthright thing going on, and I think it's getting frustrated at not getting any answers around here."

"Death isn't meant to give you answers, son," Old Eric said, without looking up from his crossword. "You're supposed to find all the answers you want when you're alive. Death is a mystery. Always has been, always will be. If you only thought about it logically, you'd realise the committee can't risk having it any other way. If people knew exactly what death entailed, there'd be mayhem."

There was a tiny bit of me wished I had David with me to do my bidding. When David asked questions, he got answers. Not that he asked many questions. If I could have just found a way to leave David alone with Old Eric for five minutes, I'm sure I'd get all the answers I needed, and more.

However, given *that* scenario wasn't possible, I would take Mother's advice, and put David's impressions on me away. I would be the Mark Ferris she knew and loved. The one who made allowances for people's age. Eric wasn't an imbecile, far from it, but obviously certain tolerances would have to be applied to take into account his advanced years, not to mention the possible onset of Alzheimer's. I made a mental note to adopt a more forgiving policy.

"Would you like me to help you with that?" I said, nodding at the crossword. It was a token gesture as I was useless with words. Now jigsaws, that was a different matter. I loved jigsaws; Elaine hated them. She couldn't understand why anybody would want to spend all that time putting something together, just to tear it all apart and put it back in the box never to be seen again. She had a point I suppose. The last time I'd been in the attic, I'd noticed a neatly stacked pile of them in the corner.

"No thank you," Eric said. "I'm perfectly all right." He still didn't look up from the crossword.

I wondered if I could retrieve the situation with a little tale about a debt-collector, a rusty Metro, and a barmaid? Something told me if I could tell it correctly, Old Eric would enjoy it.

"You'll never guess what David got up to tonight?" I said.

Eric looked up gradually. "Let me try," he said. The brightness from his face gave me the sinking feeling I'd fallen into another trap. "Did he practice bondage on his lover? Then, when she was all tied up, did he smother her in whipped cream and slowly lick it off until she begged him to take her roughly?" Alarm bells were ringing and my chest started collapsing. Eric slapped his forehead. "No, wait! Me and my memory, eh? That wasn't your night was it, son? It was mine."

If there had been a window in the room, Old Eric and I would have undoubtedly witnessed the new forthright Mark Ferris flying right out of it. Subconsciously, I retrieved the paper bag from my pocket and found myself breathing into it. I closed my eyes to avoid looking at the darkness advancing towards me, and wished I could have closed my ears as well, but Eric's voice was loud and clear.

"You wouldn't believe the things Elaine and that lawyer get up to, son. I'm sure most of what they do would be considered illegal in most civilised countries. Let me tell you about last Tuesday…"

I heard Eric say something about a restaurant, followed by the details of Elaine dropping her napkin whilst they waited for dessert. I then heard something about oral stimulation. On my way to the floor, I wondered how the lawyer had managed to get her to do it on a Tuesday. It hadn't even been a holiday…

…When I came round, I was sitting in Eric's chair. He was up against the wall, arms customarily folded. He nodded to the doorway.

Crimson stood there, shaking her head and tapping her watch. "About time," she said. "If the committee roast me on this, I am so feeding you to the vultures." She moved to me and caught hold of my hand.

As Crimson marched me towards the door, Eric winked and gave a little wave of his fingers.

I decided my forgiveness policy may need re-evaluating.

THE HEARING

I was wrong. David's eagerness to pay Tony the Pony a visit had him up and about well before noon, and I joined him in a noisy rendition of *Living on a Prayer* as he finished his nude ironing. An hour later, ready for action, and with all windows and doors checked, we skipped out the door. There followed a moment of anxiety when the old Metro wouldn't immediately start, but after David had thumped the steering wheel a few times and uttered some magic words, it finally sparked into life and we were on our way.

I never felt safe in the car with David. He insisted on only driving at whatever top speed he could get out of the Metro; a speed that was effectively unknown thanks to the speedometer being broken. Apparently, the gear-box was also on its way out, and, as I bounced around on the back seat, David used much of his considerable strength and limited vocabulary to get the car's gears to change.

My knowledge of vehicles was worth diddly-squat, and my failure to have ever passed my driving test had been a constant source of embarrassment to Elaine; who'd passed first time at eighteen. Whenever we were in company, if asked what car I drove, I was under strict instruction to say I had been banned from driving for speeding and had sold my Toyota coupe. Apart from finding this less embarrassing than having to admit I'd never passed my test, Elaine also reckoned it gave me an air of dangerousness people really wouldn't be expecting.

Elaine loved anything on wheels, often reminding me that rock-drummer used to drive the band's equipment about in a van, which she thought sexy. She'd even hinted they'd once made love in the back of it, although, given her insistence on being comfortable, I doubted if that were true. My understanding was that lawyer drove a Mercedes sports-car of some description. Presumably she found that sexy too.

Thankfully, we reached the street mentioned on the piece of paper Tim had given us alive, and David stopped the car at a corner shop on the pretence of buying some bread. A few minutes flirting with the shop assistant told him Tony drove a second-hand BMW and lived at number 42 with his girlfriend, who was referred to as, *'The Trollop.'*

David parked the Metro a few houses away and waited. We sang *Wanted, Dead or Alive,* and other Jovi classics as loudly as we could until a dapper looking man eventually popped his second-hand BMW onto the drive of number 42 and made his way inside.

"There's our man," David said. "I'll give him fifteen minutes to get comfortable and then I'll truly go and spoil his day." I loved it when David spoke to himself before a job. I could pretend he was speaking to me. Boy, did it add to the tension.

Exactly fifteen minutes later, David gave the door of number 42 his special aggressive knock. If possible, David preferred to enter the houses of his Mr Unluckys with the minimum of fuss, however, he was prepared to bide his time if necessary, and continued hammering on the door until it finally got opened by *The Trollop*.

She was seemingly wearing nothing but a bathrobe, high-heeled shoes, and one false eyelash. She brushed the hair extensions from her eyes and smiled; her whitened teeth showing extra bright against her fake orange face.

"Sorry I didn't answer straight away," she said. "I was in the bath." If this was true, it had obviously been a bath with no water in. Apart from a trickle of sweat disappearing into her ample cleavage, I could see no trace of wetness.

David said nothing, which was odd, but simply stood there smiling, the sun on his back casting an enormous shadow over *The Trollop*.

David's incessant knocking had brought at least two neighbours to their curtains, and his silent stillness was troubling. Past experience told me the longer we spent in full view, the more likelihood someone was to get a case of nosinessitis and come and see what all the bother was about. It wouldn't even be beyond the realms of possibility that one of the curtain-twitchers would call the police.

Mother would never forgive me if I got brought home by the

authorities.

"Hello, Mrs Ferris, is this your son?"

"Oh, hello officer, yes it is. And please, call me Margaret."

"We found him loitering with intent on a doorstep, Margaret. If you ask me, I'd say he was up to no good."

"Thank you for your diligence, officer. He's been such a naughty boy since he started bothering with that David the Murderer. You just leave him with me. I'll get Father to sort him out. Would you like to stay for tea? I've got Timothy's sister coming over anyway, so one more would be no bother."

It was *The Trollop* who finally broke the silence. "Still see you're kicking about in that old rust bucket, Dai," she said, nodding towards where the Metro was parked. She allowed the bathrobe to loosen slightly, revealing a faded tattoo of a heart just above her left breast. Inside the heart was the name, *Dai,* although, the *i* had faded so much it looked more like *Da*; the Russian for yes.

"You didn't complain about it at the time, Liz," David said.

"Yeah well, I was young and naive then. Didn't know any better, did I?"

David still didn't move. "Young I'll grant you," he said. "As for naive, I'll beg to differ. Now, as much as I'd love to stand here and shoot the breeze about old times, Liz, I've got some business with Tony I'd like to discuss. So, do you mind if I come in?"

"He's not here. Haven't seen him in days."

Oh, how David and I laughed. David put his massive hands on Liz's shoulders and gently moved her to one side. It wasn't how David normally gained entry, but I was comforted we were at last getting out of sight.

"Oh, Tony," David sang, entering the house. "Where are you? Time to come out and play." He turned to Liz. "Sorry, sweetheart," he said. "But you know how these things work, so don't get any funny ideas about phoning the police, there's a good girl. We wouldn't want to make matters worse, would we?"

To my relief, Liz nodded her agreement. "Please, Dai," she said, following David as he started searching rooms, "do me a favour for old times' sake?"

"What's that, sweetheart?"

"Try not to break his dick. Break anything else, just not that, okay?"

We eventually found Tony cowering naked in the bottom of a bedroom wardrobe. "There you are," David said, dragging him out by his hair. I couldn't help but notice Tony fully deserved his *Pony* tag.

Elaine had always told me not to worry about size, stating, *'It isn't the whip, it's the way you crack it that counts,'* but I'd always thought it would be handy to at least have a decent whip to crack in the first place, and felt a pang of male jealousy at Tony's inches. I'd also once overheard a conversation Elaine was having with one of her friends on the telephone, in which she'd said, with some rapture, *'Oh my God, Janet, I tell you, it was so big it was tickling my belly button. From the inside!'* I hadn't picked up the extension quick enough to catch the beginning of the conversation, so had no idea who she was talking about, but persuaded myself it was some ex-lover she'd had before we met; maybe even that rock-drummer. Although, she had just returned, slightly worse for wear, from a golfing weekend away.

"Now, here's the deal," David said, dumping Tony at his feet. "I need six thousand pounds in the next five minutes. If, for some reason, I can't get six thousand pounds, my client has given me permission to forget to be nice."

There was no six thousand pounds: David forgot to be nice.

I sat on the edge of the bed and listened as Tony begged for mercy, promising to find the money if David would only give him a few more days. It wasn't an option David was prepared to discuss, and I was forced to turn my head as he removed the dusters from his pocket.

The first sickening crunch to Tony's head brought a loud scream from Tony, strangely accompanied by a female shriek from somewhere on the bed behind me.

"Is that you sneaking up on me again, Crimson?" I said, turning to find the girl sitting there, hiding her face behind her hands, obviously wasn't Crimson.

I leaped off the bed as if the girl was diseased, and had to use the bedroom wall to keep myself upright.

"Please sit back down," the girl said, without taking her hands from her face. "I was using you to hide behind." She peeked at me from between her fingers. "Please tell me he's not a real murderer. I can't lose another assignee. The committee will go ape."

I scanned the room trying to find the new forthright Mark Ferris, but he was nowhere to be found. Without him, my legs took it upon themselves to be unsupportive, and I slid down the wall until I was sitting on the floor. The angle at which I'd landed meant I now couldn't see the girl, and I convinced myself she'd been nothing more than a figment of my imagination; an illusion brought about by the strain of being dead, possibly coupled with having not slept for the last five months. I forced myself to crawl across the floor until I reached the foot of the bed, and slowly peered over the top with more reluctance than a WW1 soldier in a trench. The girl was still there, face behind hands. I yelped and ducked back down.

"It's okay," the girl said. "You can come out. I don't bite. Well, not much."

My breathing quickened to dangerous levels and I reached into my pocket for Eric's paper bag. My panic increased to worrying proportions when I realised it wasn't there. Eric must have kept it on my last visit to his office.

"Are you okay down there?" I heard the girl ask.

Without daring to look over the edge of the bed, my mind digested the mention of words such as *committee* and *assignee*. I put two and two together - even my appalling maths could manage that - and, despite the throat-mouse narrowing my airwaves, managed to ask, "Are you... dead?"

"Ten out of ten for observation," the girl replied. "Now will you please get back on this bed?"

I pulled myself up, slowly crawled up the bed, and sat as close to the girl as I had the nerve to do. I could hear Father warning me to, *'Never believe anything you hear, and only half of what you see, Mark,'* and still half-thought the girl may just be a trick on the eyes. Despite her face being hidden by her hands, I could tell she was young; same sort of age as Crimson I guessed. Her blonde hair was tinted with strands of black, and she wore a short denim skirt topped with a t-shirt emblazoned with, *Boys are stupid, throw rocks at them.* She was slim, but not pitifully so like me, and I noticed the nails on her little fingers carried black varnish. The girl parted her hands slightly, revealing matching black lipstick.

"The name's Mary," she said, some form of piercing glinting from inside her mouth. "Please tell me your murderer isn't going to kill my Tony."

I turned to look at the scene. Tony was lying pulped face up, unconscious, but still breathing as far as I could tell. David was wiping the dusters on a discarded sock.

"No, he won't kill him," I said, not entirely convinced. "He's just here to try and get some money Tony owes someone. Anyway, what makes you think he's a murderer?"

From behind her hands Mary told me Tony and Liz had been enjoying each other's company when David's knocking had disturbed them. At first, they'd ignored the intrusion and went about their business, but when it was obvious whoever was at the door wasn't going away, Liz climbed off Tony, looked out the window, and announced in some panic that *Dai the Murderer* was at the door.

"That's when Tony hid in the wardrobe and I climbed under the bed," Mary said. "I mean, I assume he's not called *Murderer* for nothing?"

"He strangled a budgie."

"Well that makes me feel a lot more comfortable." Mary shuffled herself closer to me. I gasped as I caught a waft of her perfume. It was the same as Elaine's.

"I can't believe this," I said, sniffing the air with delight. "Do you know you're the first dead person I've spoken to since I died? Well, excluding Old Eric and Crimson. Oh, and the committee of course. This is so exciting. I'm Mark by the way."

I felt like a high-spirited kitten, and, despite being forty years old, I couldn't help myself from bouncing on my knees.

"How long have you been dead?" I asked. "You look so young. So you're assigned to Tony then? What's he like?" I couldn't seem to stop my lips from moving. I was talking faster than David; and he was Welsh. "Honestly, I really can't believe this, Mary. I mean, look at you. I can see you, I can hear you," I reached out a shaky hand and lightly touched Mary's elbow with my finger. "Wow! I can even feel you."

Some song by *The Who* flitted across my mind. I hated the band; Elaine loved them, often reminding me, *'Put it this way, Mark, whether you like their music or not, I'd never crawl over the singer to get to you.'* If I remembered rightly, the singer in question was number

20 on what Elaine referred to as her S*hag-list*. At least none of the other members of the band had made it onto the list, unlike every member of some new group I'd never heard of called *One Direction*, who were collectively in at number 16.

"Please tell me all about yourself," I asked Mary, shaking Elaine's fantasies out of my head.
"Only if you stop bouncing," Mary replied. "You're making me feel sick."
"Sorry."
"And stop saying sorry."
"Sorry."
The twenty year old Mary had been dead just about a year. She'd thrown herself off Waterloo Bridge, and not just to give the tourists in the *Eye* something to talk about.
"I was having a hard time at home," she said. "My father was continuously on my back about sociology not being a *proper* degree. He had these grand ideas about me following his footsteps and doing law. God, he was such a bore. Do you know, he took me to a theme-park for my last birthday. A bloody theme-park! Who the hell takes their twenty year old daughter to a theme-park? My mother was no help. All she was interested in was nagging me about my boyfriend - *Star*. He's too old for you. He plays drums in a rock band so he's bound to be on drugs. His hair's too long. He's scruffy. Etcetera, etcetera, etcetera, blah, blah, blah. The pair of them drove me mental."
Whilst fully sympathising with Mary's plight, I couldn't help but think If I'd had a sister, Mother may also have had difficulty if she'd brought someone home called Star.

"Mum, this is my new boyfriend, Star. He's a rock-drummer."
"Oh, hello, Star. My, aren't you old, scruffy, and in need of a haircut? So what's the difference between a rock-drummer and a proper drummer then?"

"His real name was Darren," Mary explained. "He was a big fan of The Beatles, and, being a drummer himself, Starr seemed the obvious choice for a stage-name. He had to drop the extra 'r' for legal reasons.

Anyway, my parents were doing my head in so much, that one afternoon I packed up a few belongings and decided to go and surprise Star by moving in with him at his Elephant and Castle bed-sit. Turned out the surprise was all mine."

"Another woman?"

"Worse. There I am hammering on his door when the landlord appears. He tells me Darren has pissed off and would I like to pay the rent he owes?"

"That's terrible. Any ideas where he went?"

"God knows. The last the landlord seen of him he was disappearing into an old Transit van which apparently carried some faded artwork suggesting the van belonged to some *Doctors* or something."

"Doctors?"

"Or something. Anyway, I was so upset I went to the nearest pub and got myself liberally rat-arsed. I even got a bit naughty with a guy in an alley before I threw myself off that bridge. And all before teatime. I don't think I really meant to kill myself. It was only when I was halfway down I remembered I couldn't swim."

"Well Darren's loss is my gain," I said. "I can't believe I've found someone to talk to. You really wouldn't believe how excited I am, Mary."

"Well, actually, I might," Mary replied, a slight smile curling her lips. "Because do you always rest your hand on a young girl's knee when you're excited?"

I looked down. Oh my dear God! I removed my hand as if I'd touched a hot grill-pan. The new forthright Mark Ferris had obviously taken control of my hand when I wasn't looking and decided to do inappropriate things with it. He was a dangerous thing, this new forthright Mark Ferris. I would need to be vigilant. How long had my hand been there? What type of man was I to go touching up young girls? Mother would go mental if she ever found out. She didn't believe in sexual contact before marriage. According to Father, she didn't believe in much of it after marriage either. Hence the lack of siblings I assumed.

"Please, please, forgive me," I said, not sure if I was speaking to Mary or Mother. "I'm really not that good around new people. I always seem to say or do the wrong thing." The mouse had taken complete control of my vocal chords and my breathing was reaching hyper-speed.

"It's okay," Mary said, taking hold of my renegade hand. She stroked it gently before placing it back on her knee. "I really don't mind. It's actually quite nice to feel a man's hands on me again. It's what I miss the most, I think. You know? The physical stuff. Star had wonderful hands. He used to do things with them that no other man I know could do…"

"Uh, shall we check on Tony," I said, the mouse playing hopscotch in my throat. I left out, *'Before I faint. Right here, right now.'*

"You look," Mary said, putting her hands back over her face. "I can't."

I turned and dangled my legs over the edge of the bed. Tony was prostrate at my feet. A dark pool of blood was slowly spreading across the carpet from his head, courtesy of a severed ear. He was still unconscious, but at least his chest was rising and falling. "Um… I think he'll be okay."

Mary came up behind me, put her hands on my shoulders, and peeked around my head. "Oh… My… God," she said.

I could understand how Mary might be a bit taken aback by the carnage David had meted out. However, I was a five-month seasoned pro, and used the new forthright Mark Ferris to nonchalantly say, "I don't suppose you're used to seeing men like this, are you?"

"No, I'm not," Mary replied. "The size of it always takes me by surprise."

Liz appeared in the doorway, a tumbler of something dark in hand. By the look of her she'd managed a few tumblers of something dark whilst David had been going about his business. "Finished, Dai?" she said, the bathrobe hanging on by a thread.

"Just give me five minutes to gather up some saleable bits and pieces," David replied, straightening his jacket and adjusting his tie in a mirror. "Then I'll be on my way. Best call an ambulance before Tony here bleeds to death. Tell them he fell down the stairs or something."

Liz tottered into the room unsteadily in her heels. She put the drink on a bedside cabinet and helped David with his tie, her tongue lapping around her smudged pink lipstick. "Why don't you stay a bit longer?" she said. "I'm sure Tony won't mind. By the way, how can I say he fell down the stairs when he's in an upstairs room, Dai?"

David smiled and ran his hand slowly up Liz's thigh until it disappeared underneath the bathrobe. Liz flung her head back and gasped. I can't be sure, but I think I also heard Mary moan.

"Well then tell them whatever the fuck you like," David said, removing his hand and pushing Liz to one side. "Now, where's the keys for the BMW?"

Liz tightened the robe around her and retrieved her drink. She tapped the glass on David's chest. "You really don't know what you're missing," she said.

David took the drink off Liz and swallowed it in one. "Oh yes I do," he said, handing the glass back. "The keys, Liz? Before I forget my manners."

The keys were kept on a hook by the front door. David thanked Liz for the information and left the room.

I was prepared to do my duty and follow David when Mary reached out from behind me and put her arms firmly around my chest. I could feel her young, firm breasts pressing into my back and found myself dangerously short of air. I think I let out a small squeal. Or was it the mouse?

Mother was livid.

"Mark! Put that girl down immediately and stop behaving like a heathen. Public displays of affection are so embarrassing. In fact, they should be forbidden by law if you ask me. Now put her down I say, before I call Father."

And what could be more embarrassing than one particular public display of affection that Mary's actions had started to grow inside my postman's trousers? I covered the offending area with my hands and begged the new forthright Mark Ferris to stop me from fainting.

"It's a shame you have to go," Mary said. "I was hoping we could get to know each other a bit better. Perhaps you could call round again? We could call it a date if you like." She pressed her lips to my ear. "But be warned. I normally allow a bit more than knee touching on a proper date."

I don't know, but I think I screamed as I leaped from Mary's embrace. What I do know is I lost the top two buttons off my postman's shirt in the process. I was out of the front door before David.

That night, David was indeed in celebratory mode. He downed a dray-load of Guinness and couldn't wait for closing time to find out if Shaz had taken his advice and worn something easy to get off. He took her outside during her break, bent her over some conveniently placed beer crates, and rutted as if his life depended on it. After ten minutes of furious pumping, David gave out a groan.

"There, finished," he said, rubbing his hands together. "How about you, sweetheart? Did you make it?"

Shaz removed a vanity mirror from her leopard-skin clutch-bag and looked at herself. "For Christ's sake, Dai, look at the state of me," she said, attempting to put her hair back in order. "But if you must know, yes I did. Twice. You pig."

I would have paid more attention to David's face if I had known then that a dead, black-haired woman by the name of Jody was going to make sure this was the last time David would smile. She appeared in the corner of my eye. Smart, tall, businesslike; white blouse, black pencil skirt.

Despite the click of her heels on the concrete, David and Shaz seemed oblivious to the woman's imminent arrival and went about their business as normal. David was bent over, drunkenly attempting to pull his trousers up, and Shaz was searching through the beer crates looking for her underwear. I jumped in front of David and spread my arms, somehow believing I could hide his modesty from view.

"Hi," the approaching woman said, giving a wave of her fingers. "I'm Jody."

I looked from David to Shaz, but neither of them seemed to have heard anything and continued fumbling with their respective bits of clothing. The woman stopped a few feet from me and nodded in my direction. "You can see me I assume?" She flashed a worried smile.

It was the dossier she was carrying under her arm that finally helped me register I was in the company of another dead person. I nodded slowly and tried to cough up the mouse.

"Good," Jody said, turning to where Shaz was leaning over the crates, her bare behind sticking in the air. "Now, tell me, does this arse belong to," she opened the dossier, "Sharon Brittany Paris McDermott, twenty-nine year old married barmaid?"

I'd gone well past the idea that this whole being about as dead as dead can be thing was a BBD, but I still pinched myself and slapped myself across the face nonetheless. I'd waited five months before seeing any dead people at all, now, like animals drawn towards the

Ark, two had come along in no time. I looked around for the new forthright Mark Ferris, but he must have been busy and my legs customarily gave way.

"Well?" Jody said, without turning around.

"I guess so," I said from the floor, the mouse just about allowing the words to pass. "I only know her as Shaz."

Jody turned to me and immediately froze like she'd been hit by a spell. The dossier fell from her hands and a solitary lined piece of notepaper fluttered to the floor. Aside from the fact she was dead, Jody really didn't look very well. She was staring at something behind me. I followed her eyes to find David had finally managed to get his trousers in order and had brought himself to his full height.

"Oh, don't worry about him," I said, turning back to Jody. "He's mine. He's known as Dai the Murderer." I hoped the mention of me being assigned to someone with such a nickname would help detract from the fact I'd collapsed at Jody's arrival. As it was, I think I could have been dancing naked through rings of fire and Jody wouldn't have noticed.

"Jody, are you all right?" I said, struggling to my feet. "You look like you've seen a ghost."

Jody staggered to me and collapsed into my chest, knocking us both back to the ground. I landed on my rump, and, without any invitation whatsoever, Jody put her head in my lap. We silently remained that way for a few moments.

Jody's shoulders started heaving, and I was aware my lap was moistening. "Oh sweet Jesus," I whispered, looking at the stars. I sincerely hoped the dampening was a result of Jody's tears, and not anything to do with my inability to keep control whenever contact with a woman was established. I prayed I could remain calm enough to stop yet another public display of affection from stabbing Jody in the ear, but it was no good. What with the movement of Jody's head, coupled with the moistness, the public display of affection was inevitable. It was so inevitable, the loss of blood to my head almost made me pass out.

Jody obviously felt something stir.

"Urgh!" she said, snapping her head up from my lap. "For God's sake! Bloody men! You're are all the same."

"Jody, I'm really, really, really, really sorry," I said, trying to push the swelling down. "But you have to understand. I'm not that good around new people."

"You need special help," Jody said, standing up. "Bloody pervert." She smoothed herself down. "I didn't even know dead people could get… those." She pointed in the general direction of my lap.

"Nor did I until earlier this evening," I replied. I realised this probably wasn't what Jody wanted to hear. "No, what I mean is… you see… it was all this young girl's fault…"

Jody raised a hand to stop me. "If I was you, I'd shut up now," she said.

"Yes, okay, probably a good idea."

Jody turned to survey the scene. I followed her eyes to find David and Shaz had reassembled themselves to somewhere near passable and had slowly started making their way back to the pub. "Dai, you did use protection just then, didn't you?" Shaz asked, sounding slightly worried. "Because I'm right in the middle of my cycle. Somehow, I can't imagine you being the fatherly type."

"David Williams!" Jody shouted after them. "You are nothing but an evil bastard. I hope you rot in Hell!"

David stopped like he'd walked into a closed shop door. "Of course I did, sweetheart," he said. "Listen, you go on in, Shaz. I think I need a bit more air." Shaz rolled her eyes and made her way inside the pub.

Jody retrieved her dossier and single piece of notepaper, lifted her head high, threw back her shoulders, and followed her.

David then did something odd. He sat on a beer crate, put his head in his hands, and cried. I'd never seen David cry before. It went against all forces of nature. I'd always believed men over six feet tall and built like elephants got their tear ducts removed at birth.

I slowly crawled towards him, lifted myself onto the beer crate beside his, and cried too. Like I said, crying had always come easy for me.

But what was David's excuse?

BITTER PILLS

I'd never been a great lover or imbiber of alcohol, much to Elaine's bewilderment. I'd therefore never experienced its full effects and could only assume that several pints of Guinness helped you cry. Ten minutes after Jody and Shaz had disappeared back into the pub, David was still sitting on the beer crate blubbering like a baby. I'd never seen David so distressed and wondered what could have got to him so badly. I replayed the scenario with Jody, and if I hadn't known any better, would have said David had somehow been effected by her screaming at him. But then that was impossible. Wasn't it? The new forthright Mark Ferris decided to try and find out.

"I'll just be inside if you need me, David," I said, standing up and making my way into the pub. "I'm just going to have a quick word with that Jody woman, okay?"

"Listen," Jody said, after I'd put it to her that I thought David may have heard her scream at him, "I don't care whether he heard me or not. Just keep the big bastard away from me, okay?"

I wondered how I was supposed to keep someone who couldn't hear me from doing whatever they liked. Of course, it was also possible that even if David could hear me, he wouldn't take an iota's worth of notice; not even if I got the new forthright Mark Ferris to speak to him. Also, with Jody being assigned to Shaz, keeping David away was a request I felt beyond reasonable.

I begged Jody to come back outside and scream at David again, just to prove or disprove my theory. She told me to, *'Piss off,'* and marched away to the ladies' toilets.

Despite being invisible to the living, I still couldn't find it within myself to enter that particular sanctuary. Mother would still be reeling from my recent displays of affection; she'd have an apoplexy if I started visiting ladies' toilets as well. I waited for several minutes before concluding Jody wasn't going to reappear any time soon, and decided I would wait for a better opportunity to find out what David had done that she found so repulsive. Even to my untrained eye it was obvious Jody was upset. I would leave her to calm down.

I made my way back outside to where I'd left David sobbing. There was no sign of him.

After a few frantic minutes of searching, I eventually found David in the car-park. He was struggling to find the right key to open Tony's BMW.

"Don't you dare drive home," I shouted, running towards him. "You're not safe to drive at the best of times, never mind when you've had a drink. What if you lose your licence? What'll you do then, eh? How will you get to work? If you want to kill yourself, David, that's fine, but think of the innocent people you might take with you. Think about me! Come on now, have a bit of sense. Let's just walk home. It's not far."

David fired up the BMW and drove home.

Mrs Williams looked at me from under her sombrero. She looked less happy than normal; reproachful even.

"I'm really, really sorry, Mrs Williams," I said, as David collapsed into bed. "I couldn't stop him... Yes, but you know what he's like?... Well luckily the roads were quiet... Yes, I know he's a naughty boy... Yes, I'll try harder next time, honest... Of course I won't let any harm come to him... Don't suppose you know anything about someone called Jody do you?... No?... Oh well, goodnight then."

Despite the Guinness dulling his senses, David struggled to sleep. He woke several times through the night in baths of sweat screaming the name *Claire.* I looked to Mrs Williams for help, but it seemed she had as much knowledge of anyone called Claire as she had of Jody.

The following day, David remained at home. He spent all day on the sofa watching daytime TV, and didn't even dress. By half-seven in the evening, I started worrying we weren't going to make it to the Buckets. David was normally on his fourth pint by eight, and yet showed no signs of getting ready to go out. In all the time I'd been with David, I'd not once known him to spend the night at home.

Something didn't feel right. At half-eight, David rummaged through a kitchen cupboard and found a bottle of cheap Brandy he'd been keeping for best.

By half-nine the bottle was empty.

The following afternoon, David did go out. He went to the corner shop in slippers, ripped jeans, and a scruffy t-shirt for more Brandy. Twice.

Within a fortnight, David was up to three bottles a day. He continuously failed to make it to bed, using the sofa as his constant refuge. Personal hygiene became something belonging to a bygone age, as did any inclination to leave the house - unless it was to purchase more Brandy.

Since the night Jody had turned up at the Buckets, I'd tried screaming at him from every angle I could think of. Up close, far away, from behind, from the front, upstairs, downstairs, mid-stairs. Nothing.

Over the next two months, the nightmares about Claire got progressively worse, as did David's ability to function properly. In an effort to exorcise whatever demons were haunting him, David took to devouring ever larger quantities of Brandy. Gone were the heady days of nude ironing, Bon Jovi, crazy car rides, hitting people over heads with shovels, and pleasuring barmaids. The last time we'd set foot in the Buckets had been the night Jody had turned up. No visits to the Buckets equalled no jobs, no Shaz, and endless days stuck in David's living room. I started believing that the committee had definitely forgotten about me this time.

Mrs Williams and I were very worried.

"I just don't know what to do with him, Mrs Williams," I said to the picture on the living room table; the one where she was standing outside Blackpool Tower, arm in arm with a coloured gentleman. "I've tried to speak to him, but I just can't get through. I mean, just look at the state of him." I pointed in the direction of where David was comatose on the sofa. "It's half-eleven in the morning and he's already drunk enough Brandy to pickle twelve dead sailors. What are we going to do, Mrs Williams? I'm starting to believe I'm not cut out for this sort of thing. Did I ever tell you I'm only a postman?" Mrs Williams continued to smile at her affro-haired friend. "And who the hell is this Claire he keeps shouting for?" I flopped down in the living room chair.

"Ah, well, I suppose we're in for another long afternoon, Mrs Williams. Still, at least he can't get into any trouble if he never goes out, can he?"

I closed my eyes and wished with all my might that David would come out of whatever fog was surrounding him and go back to the way he was. My mighty wishing scrunched my face up like somebody had put their fingers up my neck and squeezed.

"Are you all right? You look like you're in pain." The voice came from behind me.

I screamed and leaped out of the chair. I opened my eyes to find Crimson standing in the doorway leading to the kitchen.

"I wish you wouldn't do that," I said, putting my hands on my knees and doubling over.

"What?"

"Just suddenly appear like that. You're going to be the death of me if you carry on."

Crimson made her way into the room and sat in the chair I had just vacated, crossing her legs.

The best pair of legs I knew belonged to Elaine, but Crimson certainly run her a close second. Not that I was an expert on women's legs, but like most men I knew what I liked, and I very much liked Crimson's legs filling her jeans the way they did. I suddenly realised I was staring. Oh God! Was that also the early indication of another public display of affection I could feel?

Crimson stared back at me with a grin across her face. She slowly uncrossed her legs, and then crossed them again the other way. I tried, unsuccessfully, to stifle a little moan. Crimson looked at her watch.

"Bloody hell!" she leaped out the chair quicker than I had. "Come on, the committee wanted to see you like ages ago." She reached over and took hold of my hand; the one that wasn't attempting to cover the display.

I sat in the wooden chair and waited whilst Mr T. and the sidekicks passed files back and forth. "We'll be with you in a moment, Seven-Three-Five-Nine," Mr T. said.

They could take all the time in the world as far as I was concerned. Firstly, if David was following the pattern of the last few months, it would be around teatime before he woke up reaching for his next fix of Brandy. Secondly, it was going to take me ages to finish apologising to Mother for my decline into sexual depravity.

"Right, I think we've got everything in order," Mr T. looked from one sidekick to the other. They both nodded their agreement. "You know, I can't wait until we go computerised," Mr T. announced. "Can you imagine how much easier it'll be just to press a few buttons and have all the information you need right there at your fingertips? I really wish that Gates fellow would hurry up and die." The sidekicks made assenting grumbles. "Anyway, that aside, the reason we've brought you here, Seven-Three-Five-Nine, is to let you know that if anything… now, how can I put this?... untoward should happen to your assignee, then not to worry. We're on the case and are happy to advise that we would be in a position to move you to a new assignee in double-quick time. That's how efficient we are here, Seven-Three-Five-Nine."

I clutched the side of the wooden chair. "Sorry? I don't understand. What do you mean untoward?"

"I'm afraid we haven't got time for all this idle chit-chat, Seven-Three-Five-Nine." Mr T. nodded at all the paperwork in front of him like a chicken pecking at corn. "Suffice to say you can't expect to stay with the same assignee for ever."

I recalled Old Eric telling me the only way I would stop watching David was if he died. Was Mr T. trying to inform me David was going to die? The idea made the bottom shelf of my stomach collapse. Mr T. and the sidekicks started swimming from side to side in front of me, and my chest felt like someone had lit a campfire inside it. I searched desperately for the new forthright Mark Ferris to help stop the advancing darkness, but I must have left him in David's living room. Without him, it wasn't long before the darkness took control…

…When I came to, I was still in the wooden chair. The sidekicks were standing over me fanning my face with files. Once they were satisfied I was fully revived, they made their way back to their seats and went about their business.

"Ah, welcome back, Seven-Three-Five-Nine," Mr T. said, passing a document to one of the sidekicks. "Old Eric mentioned you had a tendency to pass out every now and again. I really don't see what the problem is. It's all standard practice. Now, when you were away with the fairies, we received information that your messenger is… temporarily otherwise engaged, so you're going to have to stay here for a while. Here's what I suggest."

Mr T's suggestion was I spend some time with my good friend, Old Eric.

"I'm sure he'll be delighted to see you again. Off you go." Mr T. pointed behind me. "We'll send for you when we're ready."

Almost as soon as the words were out of Mr T's mouth, I found myself standing in front of a large wooden door staring at some sort of timetable. I turned back to Mr T. and the sidekicks. They were all busy passing files around. Via the mouse, I managed to ask, "Is this a bus timetable?"

Mr T. looked up and frowned. "Why I do believe it is, Seven-Three-Five-Nine," he said. "Now off you go. You haven't got all day."

I scanned my eyes down the myriad of names and numbers in front of me until I found something marked, *Old Eric's Office*. It was followed by a jumble of numbers and letters in boxes: the secret code of bus timetable compilers.

Through the door wasn't something that just looked *like* my hometown bus depot, it *was* my hometown bus depot, complete with a host of identical looking buses all docked in numbered bays. Even the graffiti was the same. There was, *Sandra loves cock,* and, *Beware of the dyslexic with a Gnu,* and, *Gaz takes it up the arse,* and, my personal favourite, *The genetically identical circus is in town - send in the clones.*

Time had also been taken to ensure the depot smelled like an open urinal, just like normal. What wasn't normal was the fact I was the only person to be seen. At least this meant the tramps and alcoholics who usually used the depot as their base were absent.

I could never get my head around buses. I'd used this depot to get to and fro the sorting office a thousand times and more. Even then, I'd still occasionally found myself on the wrong bus. The secret society of bus timetable compilers obviously had no consideration for those of us who had never worked on *Enigma*, and I hated this place with a passion. I could hear Elaine reminding me, *'Well, if you were a real man and passed your driving test, you wouldn't have to use it, would you?'*

I took a deep breath, closed my eyes, crossed myself, and entered the mystifying labyrinth of the depot.

I'd taken twelve buses, each journey lasting twenty minutes through emptiness, only to find myself back at the depot each time. The thirteenth, number 42, finally dropped me outside Old Eric's office door. This time I knocked.

"Ah, young Mark," Eric enthused. "Come in. Take a seat."

"Eric, you know full well you haven't got a seat," I said, sitting on the edge of his desk.

"Oh dear, is someone having a bad day?" Eric said, removing his glasses.

"You could say that," I replied. "If there's one thing I can't work out in this world, it's buses. Taken me over four hours to get here. Four hours! There were no drivers, no passengers, nothing. Just me and a pile of identical buses. How the hell was I supposed to know which one to jump on?"

"Didn't they give you a timetable?"

"Oh, please. What use is something so mathematically complex to me? You might as well ask me to work out the Duckworth Lewis system, or the off-side rule."

Eric laughed until he started complaining his sides were hurting. "Well, I've never known them to use buses to kill time before," he said. "Virgin trains, yes, but buses, no."

I waited patiently for Eric to stop laughing, rather pleased I'd once again told a ditty that had produced such merriment. When Eric had recomposed himself, I told him about my conversation with the committee.

"You told me the only reason I'd stop following David about is if he died," I said. "So what's going on, Eric?"

Eric brought his crossword out of the drawer and reapplied his glasses. "Must be getting close to David's time, son," he said. "Sorry."

I could feel the mouse scratching around in the bottom of my throat. "But he can't die, Eric," I said. "I promised his mother I'd look after him."

Eric looked up quickly from the crossword. "His mother?"

"Yes. He keeps photographs of her everywhere." I picked up the print of the Last Supper and studied it. "She sort of helps me through the night. What am I supposed to tell her when I get back?"

I envisaged her smiling at me from underneath her sombrero and from aside her coloured companion. I really didn't want to be the one to wipe those smiles off her face.

Mother would be so disappointed if I'd made promises I had no powers of keeping.

"You made the promises, Mark, it's you that's going to have to keep them. It's no use looking to me or Father for help. This is your problem."
"But I don't have any means to keep the promises, Mum."
"Well you should have thought of that before you told the poor woman you'd keep her son safe, shouldn't you? Nobody likes a big fat lie teller, Mark, nobody. Honestly, what am I rearing, a politician? It's that David the Murderer I blame. You would never have gone round making wild presumptions before you started bothering with him. Now, you best get round there straight away and put things right, Mark. Otherwise you and I are going to fall out. And be back by teatime. Timothy's sister is coming over again. Oh, she's such a nice young girl, don't you think?"

Eric looked at me over the top of his glasses. "So, you've taken to talking to photographs to help you through the night, eh?" he said, his smile widening.

I thought about telling Old Eric all about Mary and Jody to detract him from poking fun at my problems with night-noises, but something held me back. Somehow, I didn't think I could give an accurate account of the meetings without making myself sound slightly less than normal.

"David can't die, Eric," I said, the bottom lip starting again. "It's just not fair."

Eric put the crossword away and made his way to me. He took the print off me and gently placed it back on the desk. He put his arm around my shoulders. "Death isn't meant to be fair, son," he said. "It's one of life's levellers. It makes no allowances for age, colour, creed, or station. A bit like diarrhoea. Like I told you before, son, David's days were bound to come to an end sooner or later."

"So why can't it be later?" I said, the bottom lip now quivering like it had been electrocuted.

Eric tightened his arm around me. "Tell you what, let me take your mind off things with a little story about one of my old assignees," he said, the room brightening with his smile. "A famous airman he was, name of Pontius I think…"

I let Eric talk, but took no notice of what he was saying. During the four hours I'd spent on those buses, the new forthright Mark Ferris had come up with a whole bunch of questions he was determined to ask Old Eric, but it now seemed those questions had been relegated to a point in my brain which couldn't recall a single thing. Bugger! Did I have Alzheimer's as well? They say it's hereditary.

Eric took his arm from around me and made his way back to his chair. "Now that was one busy day, son, I can tell you," he said, oblivious to the fact I'd not been listening. He went back to concentrating on his crossword.

We sat in silence for a while, then a brief moment of clarity worked its way through my mind, and I managed to ask, "Eric, how do the committee *know* David is going to die?"

Eric replied without looking up from his crossword. "Well, let's see," he said. "What's your assignee been doing for the last few months?"

If Mother had been in the room, she would have reminded Eric, in no uncertain terms, that answering a question with a question was frowned upon in proper social circles. But then I supposed a confused postman talking to an ancient, purple robe wearing voyeur, both of whom were dead, couldn't really be considered a proper social circle.

"He's gradually been drinking himself to death."

Eric looked at me slowly and waited for the irony of what I'd said to seep through my brain. "So there's your answer, son," he said. "The committee have no actual idea when any of us will die. If they did, there'd be mayhem, don't you think? But as long as we give them fair warning, they can at least make some educated guesses and start preparing the paperwork. That's why they get pissed when it's quick. Give them long, lingering diseases, and they're as happy as sin. Even soldiers going off to war they can sort of prepare for. But give them a healthy twenty-something who suddenly keels over with a heart attack, or someone who plunges out of an attic, and they go mental. After all, they only get fourteen days to put everything in order."

"So how did you die, Eric?" I asked, my brain struggling to digest the information it was being given.

"Ah, a sufferer of the end syndrome," Eric said. For a moment I thought perhaps he was reading out another clue. "You're one of those people who have no intention of enjoying the journey in getting to the destination, aren't you, son? I bet you always look at the last page of a book before even starting it, don't you? You neither have any idea how I lived my life, nor what I did with it. You're not interested in my high-points, low-points, or any points in between. You don't care about my achievements, and you couldn't be damned to hear about my losses. You just want to skip it all and get straight to the end. How did you die, Eric?" He looked at the ceiling. "God save us from sufferers of the end syndrome."

How did this always happen? I'd asked what I thought was a perfectly logical question, yet somehow managed to upset the person I'd asked. Elaine had obviously been right about the foot and mouth thing.

"Sorry, Eric," I said. "Actually, I'd be more than interested to hear your life story. I have no doubt it will carry more eventfulness than mine." From the way Eric's eyes and teeth had started glistening, I expected there to be a toothpaste commercial involved along the way at the very least.

"Well, if you insist," Eric said, putting the crossword away. "But I don't know if I can remember it all."

Another sign of Alzheimer's, I thought.

"Now, where shall I begin?" Eric rubbed his hands together. Unfortunately, Old Eric had no chance to begin anywhere before we were disturbed by a knock on the door. "Oh bugger! I was just getting to the good bit," he said. "Come in."

Crimson entered the office clutching at her side and gulping for air. "Mark, the committee has asked me to take you back to your assignee immediately," she said, looking at her watch. "In fact, it should have been quite some time before immediately."

I turned to Eric to bid him farewell to find his smile had reached epic proportions. He looked from me, then to Crimson, and then back to me again. "First name terms, eh?" he said, winking at me. "What have you two been up to then?"

I looked nervously at Crimson before walking round the desk to Eric. I leaned down and whispered in his ear, "Eric, we're not all perverts you know. She's old enough to be my daughter."

"Ah, but she's not," Eric said, not lowering his voice at all. He punched me playfully on the shoulder. "Which makes it a-okay."

"Come on, let's go," Crimson said, reaching over and grabbing my hand.

"It's a shame you have to leave so soon," Eric shouted at my departing back. "I haven't had time to tell you about the nurse's outfit that lawyer bought for Elaine."

David was waking from his afternoon's unconsciousness when I returned. He got up off the sofa and stretched himself, holding onto his jeans with one hand to stop them from falling down. Since the night Jody had shouted at him, David had stuck rigidly to a liquid only diet and all his clothes were now several sizes too big for him. David sat back down and poured himself a large glass. At least he hadn't yet degenerated to drinking it straight from the bottle, I thought. He took a hefty swig and was about to make himself comfortable when we were both surprised by a knock on the door. As far as I could remember, David hadn't had any visitors to his door since the very first day Crimson had delivered me to his living room, although, my recall would of course now need questioning thanks to the possibility of my hereditary Alzheimer's. David got up and made his way to the front door, keeping a thumb through one of the belt-loops of his jeans as he went.

David opened the door to find Shaz standing there in all her brilliant garishness. She'd had a new hair-do and was decked from head to toe in all things pink.

Standing behind Shaz, but with her back turned to us, was Jody.

"Oh thank God!" I screamed, looking at the heavens. I felt months of tension, and dare I say, boredom, release from me like water from a tap. "Are you pair a sight for sore eyes or what? Please, please, come in."

Neither Shaz nor Jody took any notice of my invitation. Jody remained staring towards the road, and Shaz looked David up and down, frowning.

"Bloody hell, Dai, you look like shit," she said. "Where have you been? Everyone at the Buckets is asking after you. I keep telling them I'm not your bloody keeper, but you know what people are like?"

David shrugged his shoulders. "Been busy, sweetheart."

"Is that so. Well listen, it's my night off, and I was wondering whether you'd like to do something?" Shaz paused, but David offered nothing. "Perhaps we could go for a ride?" Shaz nodded at Tony's much abandoned BMW in the garden. "See you finally took my advice and got something bigger."

I started jumping up and down. "Yes, yes, a ride," I said. "Ooh, Jody, you wouldn't believe what happens when these two get in a car." My enthusiasm waned slightly when I remembered Jody already believed me to be some sort of depraved sexual deviant. God knows what she'd think if we both had to sit in a car and watch our assignees getting it on. Knowing my luck, David and Shaz's antics wouldn't fail to produce a certain recent excitable part of me from rising to the occasion.

"Go away, Shaz," David said. "Go back to your husband, sweetheart. Our time is done."

My enthusiasm dimmed further and I stopped jumping.

"Wow, let me down gently why don't you?" Shaz said, her voice cracking. "Okay, well can I just come in and talk for a few minutes? There's something I need to tell you."

David looked back over his shoulder. "Uh, it's really not a good time, Shaz," he said. "You see, I've got company."

I turned to David. "Ooh, you big fat lie teller," I said. "Mother was right. I do get it from you." I turned back to Shaz. "He's lying, Shaz. Don't take any notice of him. He's not got anybody in there." I peered around Shaz. "Jody, please tell Shaz there's no one here."

Jody still wouldn't turn around. "Tell her yourself," she said. "She doesn't take any notice of me."

Shaz coughed lightly and produced a tissue from her pink clutch-bag. "I'll go then, shall I?" She dabbed the tissue at her eyes.

"Good idea, sweetheart," David said. "Thanks for calling round."

Shaz put the tissue away. "You know, I'm thinking of leaving my husband," she said. "Does that makes any difference?"

David said nothing and looked straight over Shaz's head, pretending he found the guy tinkering with his caravan across the road more interesting. Shaz followed his eyes. She nodded slowly, then turned and walked away. Jody dutifully followed her.

Before I could think about what to do, I found myself running after Shaz. More particularly, I found myself running after Jody.

"Jody, please don't go," I shouted. "Jody, please, I just need to talk to you. Five minutes. It's all I'm asking."

Jody turned quickly. She was about to say something when she caught sight of David standing in the doorway. "Jesus Christ," she gasped. "What in God's name have you done to him?"

I turned and realised David looked even worse in daylight than he did in the confines of the house.

"I meant it when I said I hope you rot in Hell!" Jody screamed in his direction.

I studied David hard, hoping for some reaction to Jody's shouting, but he simply stood in the doorway and waited until Shaz was well out of sight before making his way back into the house. Bugger! I thought. I'm locked out.

"Okay, you've got your five minutes," Jody said. "Then I have to go. Sharon has got an appointment at the clinic in half an hour."

I had no idea what Jody was talking about, but put it to the back of my mind. There were a few people milling about the street, and I would have preferred to find somewhere more private to discuss things, but decided to cut straight to the chase.

"Jody, since that night you shouted at him behind the pub, David hasn't been the same person. I really don't know what to do. I'm floundering like a goldfish on a carpet, Jody. I mean, you just saw the state of him. He spends all his time cooped up in the house drinking Brandy like it's milk. I've lost count of the number of bottles a day he's up to. To top it all off, the committee have as much as said he'll die if he doesn't pull himself together. They've even got my next assignee all lined up ready. Please, Jody, I need help." I looked at my teeth-pocked shoes in a show of humility. "Besides which, I don't know how I could ever face his mother again if something happened to him."

"His mother?" Jody gave out a snort. "What the hell are you talking about? His mother came out of prison in a body-bag just after I'd met him. She was serving time for aggravated burglary. Got diagnosed with lung cancer during the trial. Doctors gave her a year, the judge gave her eight."

I snapped my head up. "You're kidding?" I said. "She looks like such a nice, happy-go-lucky person." Proves Father was right all along, I thought, *'You can't judge a book by its cover, Mark. Unless it's by that Archer chap, in which case you can safely assume it'll be shit.'*

"Right, time up." Jody turned to leave.

I grabbed hold of her arm. "Jody, listen, I'm sure he heard you that night."

Jody looked down at my hand on her arm. "And that interests me, because?"

I removed my hand. "Jody, he really needs someone to talk to. I've tried all ways to get through to him. In any event, I'm thinking twenty three years as a postman isn't the proper training to talk to a lonely, depressed, drunken debt-collector. I don't want him to die like this, Jody. I know him and I'm sure he doesn't want to die like this either."

Jody's face reddened and her hands squeezed to fists. "Oh, you know him, do you?" she said. I looked around nervously, wishing she'd keep her voice down. "Let me tell you all about your wonderful David Williams."

The story took us well over the five minutes Jody had allocated, but once she'd started, it didn't look like she had any intention of going anywhere until she'd finished.

Jody explained how she'd first met David whilst working as a receptionist in a second-hand car dealership that employed David's services to repossess cars from clients whose loans had gone sour. Apparently, he wasn't anywhere near her type, but he'd eventually worn her down and persuaded her to go for a drink, and, ultimately, to his bed.

"We stayed together for seven months before I ended it all," Jody said. "I think seven months was probably a record for David."

"So you dumped him?" I said. "That's brave."

"Shut up and listen will you?"

I shut up and listened.

Jody fell pregnant a month into the relationship. According to David, the condom must have split, but Jody didn't think he was telling the truth.

"He was far too excited for it to be an accident," she said. "He even picked out names. Claire for a girl, Troy for a boy. He also went out and bought a swing for the backyard. Stupid bugger."

By her second month of pregnancy, David had moved Jody into his house, much to the worry and anguish of Jody's parents, who didn't think David was the right stock.

"They much preferred my previous boyfriend, Tony," Jody said. "A real dapper fellow who I met when he came to the dealership looking for a second-hand BMW. It looked very similar to the one you've got parked in the garden there." Jody waited to see if I had anything to offer. "In fact, I'd go as far as to say it was identical."

The cogs in my brain suddenly aligned. "Bloody hell, Jody!" I said, grasping at a garden wall to keep me upright. "You used to go out with Tony the Pony?"

"Indeed I did," Jody said. "Wasn't easy when David and I reached that part of a relationship when you talk about ex-lovers. I mean, the basis of a good relationship is truth, don't you think? So I didn't really want to lie when David asked me why Tony was called *the Pony*, although, I must admit, I did take an inch or two off."

"I'm not surprised," I said. "I've actually seen it." I thought about qualifying this statement given Jody's belief in my perversions, but decided to let it lie.

"David reassured me he was okay with it all, but deep down I could sense his insecurity," Jody said. "After all, you're a man yourself, sort of. Imagine how you'd feel if you knew your partner's previous boyfriend had an enormous weapon?" Jody gave me a moment to do my imagining. "Now imagine what a proper man like David would think about it?"

I opened my mouth to protest at the belittling of my manliness, but Jody put a finger to my lips and reminded me I was shutting up and listening.

"Those insecurities really came to town when David was in drink," Jody continued. "One night, after a particularly heavy session at the Buckets, David came home and started with the questions. He wanted to know what it had really been like with Tony. How many times did Tony make me come in a session? What positions did we do it in? Had we ever done it in the car? The bath? Outdoors? In the George at Asda changing rooms? Was Tony better than him? Was it really that big? Etcetera, et-bloody-cetera. I was six months pregnant, fed up, and feeling very much below par, so I told him straight. Yes, it had been amazing with Tony. Yes, I'd orgasm so many times in each session they were uncountable. Yes, we'd done it in every position conceivable. Yes, we'd done it in the car, the bath, and up a mountain. And yes, yes, twenty times yes, the bloody thing was huge!"

"Oh, oh," I said. "I bet that didn't go down too well."

"You could say that," Jody replied. "David went mental. He told me there'd been rumours circulating at the Buckets that I'd been seeing Tony behind his back. Apparently, I'd even been spotted with Tony that afternoon in the supermarket, supposedly looking all loved up and buying wine and chocolates."

"All lies of course?"

"Well, sort of. I told David it was true I'd been to the supermarket. I also told him it was true I'd bumped into Tony. He'd been buying wine, I'd been buying chocolates. But it was a chance encounter, nothing more. My pleadings made no difference. David even said he wouldn't be surprised if the child I was carrying wasn't his. After a while, David ran out of things to say. We all know what happens when David runs out of things to say, don't we?"

I was apprehensive to hear what came next. But come it did.

According to Jody it wasn't the first time David had hit her, but it was certainly the hardest. She'd tried to run and lock herself in the bathroom, but her six-month bump slowed her down. She'd only made it halfway up the stairs before David caught up with her.

The doctors apparently believed her when Jody told them she'd fallen down the stairs accidentally. Whether they believed her or not made no difference to the baby girl they'd been forced to prise out of her. Claire was dead.

Jody's story was taking its toll. At the mention of her dead child, the bravado she'd been displaying so far collapsed, and she fell into my chest, wrapping her arms around my waist.

"He begged forgiveness," Jody mumbled through her tears. "Told me he couldn't live without me. Cheeky bastard even said we could have more kids."

"But you left him anyway," I said, my arms outstretched to avoid any inappropriate touching. "Under the circumstances, I'd say that was perfectly understandable."

Jody lifted her head and used my shirtsleeve to dry some of her tears. "Can you imagine trying to leave David and living to tell the tale?" she said. Despite being distraught, Jody still managed a wink and a smile.

"Yeah, it must have been difficult," I said. "He strikes me as someone who wouldn't take lightly to being dumped."

"I'll say again," Jody said. "Can you imagine leaving David and *living* to tell the tale?"

Those cogs in my brain clunked and grated again. Just like the rusty Metro, they took a while to find a gear. "Jesus Christ, Jody! Are you trying to tell me David killed you?"

"No, you imbecile." Jody put her head back in my chest and cried hard. "I killed myself."

My bottom lip started vibrating in sympathy. I looked up and down the street, but couldn't find the new forthright Mark Ferris anywhere. Within seconds, I was crying equally as hard as Jody.

"I took a shit-load of pills," Jody said. "I thought if I killed myself and left a note telling him it was all his fault it would be something he'd have to carry for the rest of his life. Something to remind him of what he'd done to me and my child. More fool me, eh? I bet he forgot about me even before my body was cold in the ground."

Jody had a point. Up until that night behind the Buckets, David looked like a man with very few cares in the world. But then I guessed men like David very rarely wore their hearts on their sleeves. "I think it's a man thing," I said, balling like a baby. "We don't like to let our feelings out."

It took a while for Jody and I to compose ourselves. We used a sleeve each to dry our tears.

"Well he was certainly letting everything hang out the night I stumbled on the scene, wasn't he?" Jody said. "If I remember rightly, he had a smile on his face from ear to ear."

"Maybe," I said. "But things have definitely changed, Jody. He's been a completely different man since then. Do you know he even cried after you went back in the pub?"

"So what?" Jody turned and started moving away. "I couldn't care less."

I ran the few steps to catch up with her. "Jody, please don't go. Come back inside with me. I'm positive he heard you that night." I went to put my hands on Jody's shoulders, but then decided against it and kept them firmly at my sides. "If you could just tell him everything is going to be all right. Perhaps even tell him you forgive him. Do you think you could do that, Jody? If not for David, then do it for me. Please?"

I couldn't remember if Mr T. or Old Eric had ever said anything to me about the relationship between being dead and feeling pain, but I can vouch that the slap across the cheek I received from Jody stung like I'd been attacked by a horde of angry bees. It brought fresh tears to my eyes. I couldn't recall ever being slapped by a woman before, but then maybe my Alzheimer's was playing up. Once again, I'd obviously misjudged the situation and said the wrong thing. Bloody foot and mouth.

"You bastard!" Jody screamed. "I pour my heart out to you about what that animal did to me, and you want me to just waltz in there and tell him everything is all right? Fucking men!" She took another swipe across the other cheek. It was hard enough for me to see stars.

I used a nearby garden gate to stop me from falling over and watched as Jody marched away. She'd only gone a few paces when she suddenly spun back around.

"Oh, and if by some miracle you do ever get the big bastard to hear you, then you can tell him from me that the day Tony and I were spotted in the supermarket I'd just given Tony a blowjob in the back of *that* BMW." She pointed to the abandoned car. "And one other thing.

Sharon is just over two months pregnant. You do the maths."

I thought about pointing out I was useless at maths, but under the circumstances decided it might not be appropriate.

BAD MEDICINE

I'd been sitting on the bonnet of the BMW for about half an hour before David emerged from the house. In the light of day, it was noticeable he'd taken on a very unhealthy pallor. He looked like something from one of those cheaply made Zombie movies Elaine liked to watch. I jumped off the bonnet and followed him as he shuffled his way the few hundred yards to the corner shop. Compared to the days just a few months previous when he would have left the house dressed as if he were collecting a medal from the Queen, he could now easily be mistaken for one of those homeless guys Mother always told me to avoid. He didn't even bother to shut the front door behind him.

As was normal now, David walked with his head down, and I often had to apologise to any passers-by who got bumped or nudged during his progress; the ones who hadn't already crossed the road before he got to them that is.

The shop door chimed as David entered. He made his way straight to the front of the small queue, and once again it was me who was forced to apologise for David's drunken unwillingness to follow British etiquette.

I thanked God that Mother wasn't anywhere to be seen.

"Uh... excuse me young homeless man, there's a queue here and I suggest you wait in it like normal people. We're not in Germany. I also suggest you have a darn good wash and put on some clean clothes. I mean, you haven't even bothered to put shoes on. Honestly, I don't know what this country is coming to."

"Mum, please, keep your voice down. David's not homeless. He's *just not coping very well at the moment."*

Fortunately, the three people in the queue were not of Mothers ilk, and, apart from a few mutterings, turned a blind eye to David's presence.

Over the last few months, David must have increased the profits of *Patel's mini-mart* by a healthy margin. It was this profit that had obviously helped Sundip Patel himself to conveniently forget about certain laws regarding serving alcohol to customers who were plainly already drunk.

"Usual, David?" Sundip asked, showing a mouth that could easily have matched Old Eric's for the whiteness of its teeth. Without waiting for an answer, Sundip reached to the display behind him and brought down a bottle of Brandy. "One or two?"

David held up two fingers, or at least would have if the one had not been the index finger on his right hand. Sundip placed the two bottles of Brandy into a self-branded carrier, using as little eye contact with David as he could possibly get away with without seeming rude.

"That will be thirty one pounds and ninety eight pence please, David." Sundip held out a hand which I couldn't help but notice was trembling slightly.

"I'll pay you tomorrow," David said, reaching to grab the carrier.

Sundip tugged the carrier back towards himself. "No, no, no," Sundip said, pointing to a sign that reminded customers the shop didn't do credit. "Like I told you before, without money I am sorry to say I cannot sell goods. Please, I do not want trouble, David, so I am asking you nicely to leave now and come back when you have money." Sundip showed as many of his teeth as he could. A collective intake of breath from the queue sucked the air from around us.

Sundip had indeed told David he couldn't have his Brandy on credit once before. That time, David had stormed out of the shop pushing and kicking displays over as he went. This time, David forgot to be quite so nice.

Despite having been out of practice for a few months, David reached over and caught hold of Sundip by the lapels of his shirt in the blink of an eye. He dragged the hapless, screaming shopkeeper head first over the counter and dumped him at his feet.

Without saying a word, David landed a kick to Sundip's head that sprayed a few of his lovely white teeth across the floor; no doubt keeping Sundip's dentist happy for the foreseeable future.

The three queue members disappeared quicker than Olympic sprinters, some of them strapping mobile phones to their ears as they left. David calmly picked up the carrier bag and limped out of the shop, leaving poor Sundip fighting to remain conscious.

In the absence of the new forthright Mark Ferris, my bottom lip had given way as soon as David had grabbed Sundip by the collar, and I cried like a fool as I followed David home.

"David, you can't just take things," I said. "It's not right. Just take back the Brandy and apologise. Tell Sundip you're not well. I'm sure he'll understand. They're a very understanding people you know?"

David took no notice and almost took the front door off its hinges when he slammed it shut behind us.

"You do know the police will be here any minute, don't you?" I said. "Did you not see those people on their phones?"

Mrs Williams caught my eye from in front of Blackpool Tower. She looked sad, and very worried. "Mrs Williams, I'm so, so sorry," I said. "But you know what he's like when he's in a mood?"

And boy, was David in a mood. He finished off half of one of the Brandy bottles in one go, straight from the bottle. He then made his way upstairs, stripped off all his clothes, and started running a bath.

Part of me was delighted. David had recently started to take on the same aroma as my hometown bus depot, and it had become increasingly difficult to stay close to him for any length of time.

"Excellent idea, David," I said, watching the water flow. "At least when the police get here you'll be nice and clean. But, David, you haven't put the plug in and you're only running cold water."

David ignored me and went back downstairs, where he promptly finished off the rest of the first bottle in two gulps. He wiped his mouth clumsily with the back of his hand, let out a satisfied grunt, and staggered to the CD player. It took several attempts before he finally succeeded in getting *Bon Jovi's Greatest Hits* into the machine. David turned the volume to full. *You give Love a Bad Name* filled the house.

I noticed David's foot had swollen to twice its normal size. I guessed it might even be broken. However, the Brandy had obviously deadened the pain, because David danced around the living room like someone being poked with an electric cattle prod. After a few minutes of tripping the light fandango, David collapsed exhausted into a chair. He reached for the second bottle of Brandy and took a hefty swig before picking up the picture of his mum outside Blackpool tower. He gave the picture a quick kiss, then made his way to the kitchen where he extracted a large, rusty scissors from a drawer. He left the kitchen and began making his way back upstairs.

"Now that's not going to help, is it?" I said, following him as he climbed the stairs on all fours. "If the police turn up and you've got a half-drunk bottle of Brandy in one hand, and a scissors in the other, my guess is you could add a few years on to whatever you're facing already. And what the hell do you need a scissors for anyway?"

Despite the problems I'd undoubtedly encounter in trying to explain to Mother why I was on my way to prison, the thought of David doing some time was appealing. At least he wouldn't be able to drink in prison, and maybe, with a sober head, he could somehow re-establish communications with Shaz and find out he was going to be a father again. I was sure he'd be over the moon. Also, secretly, I was getting quite excited at the thought of doing my time. My stretch. My bird. My porridge.

Hey, Elaine, guess what? I'm off to prison for attacking a shopkeeper who dared to upset me. Well, actually, it wasn't me. But I was there. How dangerous is the new forthright Mark Ferris then, eh? Answer me that.

I looked at the wall clock on the landing and wondered how much longer David and I had left as free men. Surely the police were only moments away.

"David, I'm not sure you've got time for this bath," I said. "Maybe just give yourself a good wash, eh?"

David took another slug of Brandy as he crawled into the bathroom. With some effort, he eventually climbed into the bath, his head at the tap end.

"Now that's the wrong way round, isn't it?" I said. "You'll never get comfortable that way."

David didn't seem to care and sang tunelessly along to Bon Jovi wafting up to us from downstairs. He also didn't seem to care that the plug still wasn't in and only cold water was running down his back.

"Ah, what the hell?" I said, sitting on the toilet and joining in the singing.

As Mr Jovi launched into the second verse of *Bad Medicine*, David finished off the Brandy and allowed the bottle to fall to the bottom of the bath with a clunk. He then rested his head on the taps, and, with one deft movement, used the scissors to slice open a six inch gash up his left wrist. He immediately repeated the process with his right wrist, before resting the scissors on his chest. I stopped singing.

I tried screaming, but just as in nightmares, nothing would come out. I jumped off the toilet and started running around slapping my head. I ran into David's bedroom and picked up Mrs Williams on her stuffed blue donkey. I tried asking her what to do, but I couldn't get any words out. I put her back down and ran downstairs in the vain hope that Mr Jovi himself was actually in the living room and would offer some assistance. I ran all over the house looking for help. There was none. I eventually forced myself to re-enter the bathroom.

David's eyes were wide and unblinking, his body shivering. Rich Welsh blood fountained from either wrist, getting carried away by the water into the dark recesses of David's plumbing system. I immediately collapsed to the floor. I could feel the darkness creeping up my spine; any moment now it would take me completely.

"Is that you, Jody?" I heard David say, his voice barely a whisper. "I'm so sorry. I didn't mean to do it. Tell Claire she can play on the swing any time she likes."

I crawled to the bath and used my last dregs of energy to lift myself to my knees.

"Don't do this to me, David," I said, trying to cradle his enormous head in my hands. "I'm only a postman." I allowed my tears to fall freely onto David's chest.

A gentle cough from behind me turned my head. Crimson's image materialised in front of me, blurred by the stinging in my eyes.

"Mark, we really do have to be going," she said, looking at her watch and holding out her hand.

I turned back to the bath. David's eyes were still wide, but the shivering had stopped. The blood coming from his wrists had slowed to a gentle ooze.

"But the police will be here any minute," I said. "They'll call for an ambulance and then everything will be all right. I bet the hospital will even fix his foot. Just you wait and see. A minute or two. That's all. I promised his mother I'd look after him. He needs to know Shaz is pregnant. A minute or two, Crimson. That's all."

Over the strains of Mr Jovi, I heard the sound of pounding on the front door.

"Come on, Mark," Crimson said, taking hold of my wrist. "There's nothing you can do for him now."

MY NEXT

Mr T. and the sidekicks were busy passing files around.

"We can see you're upset, Seven-Three-Five-Nine," Mr T. said, concentrating on some papers. "And that's perfectly understandable. But death must go on. I'm pleased to say that thanks to our preparations we've almost completed the paperwork and will be in a position to send you off to your new assignee within the hour." Mr T. waved a dossier at me as if it were some sort of prize. He pushed it across the desk. "In the meantime, I imagine Old Eric will be more than delighted to see you again. Off you go." He pointed behind me. "It's all standard practice."

The thought of spending time with Old Eric didn't particularly fill me with desire, and I adopted all the Mark Ferris defence mechanisms I could think of. I didn't care that Elaine was screaming at me to stop embarrassing her. I curled myself into a ball, closed my eyes, put my fingers in my ears, and hummed loudly. Just like I had when the committee had made me wait in the dentist's. Just like I used to when Mother tried feeding me cabbage.

I felt a sensation of moving; the sort you get when dreaming of falling. I opened my eyes to find myself standing directly in front of Old Eric's office door, the brass plaque shining proudly, new dossier tucked safely under my arm. I looked behind me to find Mr T and the sidekicks still passing files to one another.

"Under the circumstances we thought we'd send you straight there," Mr T. said, without looking up. "Off you go. We'll send for you when we're ready."

I told Old Eric all about my time with David. I told him everything

I could remember, which given the possibility of Alzheimer's turned out to be quite a lot. I told him about nude ironing and Bon Jovi. About Shaz and the pregnancy. I told him about Tony the Pony, and about meeting Mary and Jody on the same day. I decided to leave out how I'd managed to lose the top two buttons off my shirt and the public displays of affection, but did mention how I was sure David had heard Jody scream at him. I told him about Claire, and about Sundip's jaw. I described the large, rusty scissors that ended David's existence. Finally, I told him how, right at the end, I believed David had felt my presence.

"I know it's hard, son," Eric said, getting out of his chair. "Losing your first is never easy." He made his way to me and put his arm around my shoulders. "But people on the brink of their last breath say and do all kinds of weird stuff. Trust me, he wouldn't have known you were there."

"But what about that night at the Buckets?" I said. "That night Jody screamed at him. You should have seen him, Eric. I swear he heard her."

Eric cocked his head to one side and adopted his grandfatherly face. "If what you've just told me is true, son, wasn't your man full of Guinness at the time?"

"Well yes, but…"

"But nothing, son. Drunk people say and do even more kinds of weird stuff than dying ones. You just have to accept the fact David had reached the end of his willingness to live. There's nothing you could have said or done to change that."

"But he had so much to live for," I said, using one of the multicoloured ribbons on Eric's robe to wipe the tears that had started to roll out of my eyes. "If only I could have told him Shaz was expecting his child. I'm sure things would have been different."

Eric released his arm from around me and made his way back to his chair. "Listen, it's no use beating yourself up about things you have no control over, son," he said. "You might as well blame yourself for the Holocaust instead of Hitler. The sinking of the Titanic instead of Captain Smith. Or Jedward instead of Louis Walsh. You just have to accept what's happened and move on. It's the only way."

Eric took his still completely blank crossword out of the drawer. "I worked out three across the other day," he said, tapping his finger to his temple. "But do you think I can bloody remember what it is?"

That's what Alzheimer's does to you, I thought.

I digested what Eric had said, but it took none of the feelings of helplessness away. The vision of David's life literally disappearing down the plughole brought fresh tears running down my cheeks.

I looked at the dossier sitting on Eric's desk. "And in what industry can a man watch someone die and then be expected to be back at work an hour later?" I said, pointing at the dossier.

I'd meant it as a rhetorical question, but Eric looked at the ceiling and concentrated for a moment. "The military comes to mind," he said. "What about nurses? Priests? Mountaineers? Lifeguards? Firemen? Paramedics? Ooh, and serial killers?"

"Okay, point taken," I said, holding up my hands to stop him. "But it doesn't matter if you reel off a hundred professions, Eric, because I'm none of them. Putting bits of paper through people's doors has given me no training for watching naked people die in their baths. I never even did basic first-aid."

"Think about it logically, son," Eric said. "Sending you back into the firing line straight away is probably the best thing to do. It'll stop you from brooding over David for too long. You know, kind of take your mind off things. Give you something else to concentrate on other than the horrible picture of someone bleeding to death. Someone that you've come to like, dare I even say love. Someone who's been a huge part of your death so far. Someone who showed you excitement and adventure beyond your wildest dreams and introduced you to a world far removed from your own boring existence. Someone who…"

"Eric!" I forgot all my promises about being more tolerant and forgiving. "Please give it a rest will you?" I couldn't work out whether the new forthright Mark Ferris had entered the room, or if my shouting had come from the real me. Either way, I immediately apologised to Mother for raising my voice.

It took a long time for the conversation to get going again.

"Illusory," Eric eventually said.

"Pardon?"

"Three across. Perceived to be real, but not actually so. Eight letters." Eric put the crossword away. "I finally remembered."

"Eric, I'm sorry for shouting at you," I said. "But I can't just push David's death to one side and carry on as if nothing has happened. Doesn't matter what you or the committee say. I'm in pain here."

"But that's my point, son," Eric said. "You won't be hurting for long will you? You've got someone new to get worked up about now haven't you?" He pointed at my dossier.

"I don't care who's in there," I said, refusing to pick it up. I felt like if I'd shown any interest in the dossier, it would have been the first step to accepting David's death. I started playing with the print of the Last Supper.

"If you don't read it, I will," Eric said, leaning over and taking the print off me. He started tapping the dossier. "Come on, don't keep me hanging. Who's next in line for the Mark Ferris treatment?"

"What treatment, Eric?" I said. "A fat lot of good it did David to have me following him about."

Eric continued tapping the dossier. "Come on," he said. He looked at me like a puppy abandoned on boxing day. "You know it makes sense."

I sighed heavily and picked up the dossier. Once again, it only contained a single piece of lined notepaper. I went through the ritual of checking the dossier was empty before reading the note aloud.

"Sarah Lloyd: Thirty-one years old: Single parent: Eleven year old daughter by the name of Emma-Lou: Works from home as an aromatherapist: Doesn't smoke or drink: No current love-interest."

Eric feigned a yawn and rested his head against the palm of his hand. "Sounds a bit boring," he said.

"I haven't quite finished yet. Had another daughter when only sixteen: Child was given up for adoption straight after birth: Hasn't been seen since." I turned the note over but there was no more.

"Ah, now that's more like it," Eric said, rubbing his hands together. "I love it when there's a skeleton in the cupboard. They're always likely to jump out and say boo!"

"Is that right?" I placed the note back in the dossier.

"Too bloody true it is, son. Let me tell you a little story about an old assignee of mine whose skeleton jumped out and truly ruined his day."

I sat and listened as Old Eric told me all about an Asian gentleman by the name of Kapel Omar who owned a cash-and-carry business called *Kapel Omar's Koral.*

"As is quite often the case, Kapel was from a big family unit who all lived within a few doors of one another," Eric said. "Now, in theory, that may be fine. But in practice, my experience tells me the best thing between families is distance. I always find the more people there are in any mix, the more likely it is things will go a bit pear-shaped."

"You reckon?"

"Too right. Anyway, there I am doing my thing," Eric continued, "when Kapel starts to take an unhealthy interest in his youngest brother's new, and highly nubile, young bride. Said young bride quite likes the attention, and before you know it, she and Kapel are regularly playing at being the two-backed monster. Now, far be it for me to pass judgement, but let's face it, they're breaking the same rule your sexy wife decided to break, namely, rule seven, the one about adultery. But they've gone one further and broken rule ten as well, the one about coveting your neighbour's bits and pieces. Now, over time, the situation starts to play on our young bride's sense of family fairness, especially when she finds herself carrying a child she's not sure which one of the Omar brothers has fathered."

"Eric, what's this got to do with anything?" I said, playing with the Last Supper.

"Patience, son," Eric replied. "We're just getting to the good bit. One foggy night, in a complete moment of madness, our young, pregnant bride confesses to her husband that Kapel has been keeping her regularly orgasmic. Now, as you of all people will understand, the husband is not a happy bunny. So, armed with a pistol he's been keeping for special occasions, he marches off in the direction of the *Koral*, where he knows Kapel is working late. Our young bride's sense of fairness then takes another twist. She telephones Kapel and warns him of the impending visit of his very annoyed, and very tooled-up brother. However, what she doesn't know is that like most careful Asian cash-and-carry business owners, Kapel keeps a loaded firearm under the counter. Just in case of undesirables."

Eric paused.

"So what happened?" I said.

Eric smiled and his eyes sparkled like royal brooches. "Just checking you were listening," he said. "A full-scale war is what happened, son. By the time anyone in authority arrived on the scene, Kapel, his young brother, and a few co-workers, were all fourteen days away from their first visit to the committee. Guess what the press called it?" Eric started laughing.

"I have no idea."

Eric's laughter exploded, echoing around the small room. "Gunfight at K.O's Koral," he said. "Now that was one busy day, son, I can tell you." He was slapping his thigh so hard it must have hurt. "Don't you just love the press and their way with words?"

I had to raise my voice to get over Eric's laughter. "And the point of telling me this is?"

Eric eventually got himself under control. "Oh, stop being so melodramatic, son," he said. "Not everything in death has to have some deep and philosophical meaning. Occasionally things can just be fun you know."

"I doubt whether Kapel, his brother, or any members of their family thought it was fun."

"Ah, I give up," Eric said, taking his crossword back out of the drawer. "If you want to mope around like Mr Grumpy Grump the Grumpy, be my guest. But don't expect me to join in."

I stood up and paced back and forth in front of Eric's desk. "Have you got a thing about brothers killing each other?" I said.

"Not really," Eric replied, without looking up from his crossword. "But when you've had as many assignees as I have, the same circumstances are bound to crop up from time to time. After all, when all you've got is those ten miserly rules to go on, you're certain to get a bit of duplication every now and then."

I sat back down and started playing with the Last Supper again. I wondered how Eric stopped himself from dying of boredom whenever he was in this room by himself. The only thing he seemed to have by way of amusement was a crossword he had no means of filling in. "What you could do with is a jigsaw," I said, not realising I was talking out loud. "Thousand piece minimum."

The light from Eric's face could have easily lit up a small town. "Now don't you go worrying yourself about how I find my kicks," he said, putting the crossword away. "I've got two pieces of information I'd like to share with you, son. Firstly, that wife of yours sold on that vicious bloody dog she bought. Secondly, she's suffering with cystitis."

I gripped the edge of the desk.

Eric opened a drawer and pulled out the paper bag. He stood up and reached over to place it over my mouth, but I swatted his hand away. I stood up and turned my back on him with the intention of making the few paces to the door and marching straight out of the office. Unfortunately, as I tried to put one foot in front of the other, my legs acted as if they were being controlled by Pinocchio's father, and I had to use the desk to stop myself from falling to the floor.

"By the way, that dog really didn't like you," Eric said, ignoring my despair. "You see, for some reason best known to herself, Elaine keeps a picture of you on her bedside cabinet, and by God did he used to growl at it every time he saw it. Of course, whenever Elaine and that lawyer decide to get naughty in the bedroom, she turns the picture to the wall. I must admit, you spend a lot of time looking at the wall, son."

I tried to sit back on the desk, but missed the edge and ended up on my knees.

"Now, seeing as we're on the subject of coupling," Eric said to the back of my head. "How are you and your messenger getting on?"

A series of noises came from my mouth which should have translated as, *"What the hell are you talking about?"* but came out as something like, "Wharayatalaboo?"

"Oh come on," Eric said, making his way to me. He lifted me up by my elbows and sat me on his desk. "Are you trying to tell me you've not even thought about what she might look like naked? Or what she sounds like when she orgasms? What she's like in the sack? Is she dirty? Is she demure? Does she like to be tied up?" Eric made his way back to his chair.

Before I could find enough air to formulate anything resembling a reasonable answer there was a knock on the door.

"Come in," Eric said.

Crimson entered with her legs all wrapped up in those jeans and I immediately wondered what she looked like naked. Or what she sounded like when she orgasmed. What *was* she like in bed. Was she dirty? Was she demure? And, God forbid, did she like to be tied up? I think I even licked my lips and let out a small grunt.

Mother was going ballistic.

"Women's bodies are not to be ogled over, Mark. They're built the way they are for perfectly good biological reasons. None of which include being tied naked to the bedposts. I can't blame that David the Murderer any more can I? He's dead. So this must be all you're doing, Mark. Wait until I tell Father."

I looked down at the floor and immediately had to use my hands to cover the display of affection that had started to appear thanks to my improper thoughts. I suddenly felt extremely cold and began shivering. With my hands where they were, and my body shaking as it was, I can perhaps understand how things may have looked.

Mother referred to it as, *'Godless self-gratification,'* whereas Father preferred, *'Introducing John Thomas to Mrs Hand and her five lovely daughters.'*

"When you've quite finished," Crimson said, tapping her watch and nodding to my groin area. "It's time to get you gone." From the thickness in her voice, I could tell she was on the verge of laughter.

I slowly lifted my head. "Crimson... I... you... Eric... he mentioned... and... it's not what you think."

Crimson and Eric simultaneously launched into fits of delight.

I called upon the new forthright Mark Ferris to be displeased at their merriment and held out my wrist for Crimson. "Don't we have to go?" I said, collecting the dossier off the desk. "I assume we're late?" My moment of sudden indignation was ruined by my legs. They buckled as soon as I stood up and I sank back to my knees.

Crimson did her best to be professional. "Of course, Mark. I'm sorry." She looked over to Eric who was still quietly chuckling away. "Mr Eric," she said, "the committee has asked me to inform you that your assignee and her partner are currently involved in an indecent act behind the recycling bins of Asda. Apparently, they are causing quite a stir in the staff room, where they are being watched on CCTV."

I didn't bother to look; from the way the light in the room had dimmed, I knew Eric had disappeared.

Crimson looked down at me. "Come along, Mark," she said, still stifling laughter. She took hold of my hand. "You were right. We're late."

THE SKELETON

Sarah Lloyd may not have had any men in her life, but she did have a dog. He came in the shape of an ebony-black cross between a wolf, a bear, and a hippo. At four-feet tall and weighing in at somewhere around 7 squillion tons, Toby put me as much at ease as someone with a rucksack on a tube. He possessed the wildest, piercing green eyes I'd ever seen, and trust me, as a postman, I'd seen a lot of wild and piercing eyes.

"Oh, don't worry about him," Sarah would say whenever any of her clients showed discomfort at his sudden appearance. "His bark is worse than his bite."

Bloody well doubt it, I thought.

"I can't believe the woman who sold him to me didn't want him any more. He's so cute. He's taught himself to open all the doors in the house. Isn't that clever?"

To my mind it wasn't clever at all. There's damned good reasons why all things mental are kept behind locked doors. Imagine a prison officer glibly dropping into conversation that the axe-wielding, murdering paedophile he's been looking after has taught himself to open doors. I don't think he'd be ending that conversation with, *'Isn't that clever?'* Anyway, why Toby bothered with doors when he could simply knock down walls was beyond me. If my dealings with beasts of Toby's nature were anything to go by, I pitied Sarah's postman with all my dead heart.

Of course, Sarah also had her daughter, Emma-Lou, to keep her busy. Elaine had never wanted kids; said they'd ruin her career. I never argued, although deep down I would have liked to have been a dad. I think it would have been nice to have had someone who loved me unconditionally for at least the first thirteen years of their life. I guessed now I was dead, having kids was out of the question. But if by some miracle I ever did find myself creating a daughter, I wouldn't go far wrong to model her on Emma-Lou. Despite my limited knowledge with the ways of children, I believed Sarah's daughter was quite possibly the loveliest creature I'd ever met.

She was always polite and sweet; a real credit to her parent. Even at the tender age of eleven, it was obvious she would be breaking the hearts of lovesick males, or females, before many more sunsets. Graced with beautiful pools of blue for eyes, a blemish-free round face, curly blonde hair reaching halfway down her back, tall and thin, she was the epitome of girl. She was forever receiving the plaudits of her teachers and brought home the most glowing reports. There was no subject at which she didn't excel.

Sarah earned enough to keep herself and Emma-Lou in reasonable comfort. The modern three-bedroomed semi was clean and tidy with a normal collection of mid-income commodities. There was a large television in the living room that the furniture pointed at, and a smaller one in Emma-Lou's bedroom, only ever used if Emma-Lou was ill in bed. The fitted kitchen contained an American style fridge, a dishwasher, a washing machine you needed a degree in physics to work out, a tumble dryer, and a 6-ring cooker. Sarah slept in the front bedroom in a king-sized double bed, whilst Emma-Lou made do with a single in the middle bedroom, which she kept in good order herself. The small third bedroom contained a horde of things kept *just in case*.

Toby slept wherever he wanted.

Sarah's existence was quiet and comfortable. She liked routine, and kept herself in shape by finding an hour in every day for an aerobics work-out at home. She made sure Emma-Lou ate healthily, and promoted a typical middle-class interest in the natural world by making sure she recycled.

A normal day for Sarah and I consisted of getting Emma-Lou off to school, then dealing with Sarah's morning clients. After a light, fruity lunch, we'd deal with her afternoon clients, then pick Emma-Lou back up from school. Over a healthy, dietary controlled tea, we'd all chat about the day's goings-on before sending Emma-Lou off to do her homework. In the evening, we'd all settle down in front of the TV, unless of course Emma-Lou needed to practice her flute, in which case complete silence was called for. After we'd tucked Emma-Lou up in bed, Sarah and I would watch some more TV before turning in for the night ourselves. Very occasionally, Sarah would indulge in some quiet

Godless self-gratification under the covers; which seemed to be enough satisfaction for her as far as that type of thing was concerned.

In some circles, I could see how Sarah's life may be considered a little boring. She didn't even do jigsaws. In the three months I'd been watching her, the most excited I'd seen Sarah get was when her and Emma-Lou's favourite TV programme came on.

Billy's Belters was one of those programmes where viewers sent in tapes of cats going round in tumble dryers, or people getting their heads stuck in railings and the like. Emma-Lou loved it, and would roll around laughing from start to finish, whilst Sarah would watch starry-eyed and groan quietly whenever Billy himself filled the screen. She told Emma-Lou he reminded her of a young George Clooney, (number 5 on Elaine's shag-list) and Sarah's *Godless self-gratification* always seemed more intense on the nights she'd been watching *Billy's Belters*.

I tried my best to get Sarah to do something, anything, that would break the tedium. Naturally, none of my helpful protestations were heeded. She ignored the advice to get a man, or a woman. Similarly, she never got drunk, found some friends to go out with, or attempted a hobby. I wondered if this was what it had been like to live with me. Poor Elaine. No wonder she did what she did. Imagine twenty years of this.

The only source to stop me from going completely stir-crazy was Toby. He had sensed my presence from the very second Crimson had landed me in Sarah's living room. Whenever I got get anywhere near him, a low growl would start somewhere in his abdomen, slowly building until he was howling and snarling like he'd contracted rabies. The next time you think your favourite family member is barking at nothing but the wind, think again. I was supposed to be the spirit around here, but he was the one who made people jump. Toby, very much like Crimson, was highly adept at silently appearing behind me. It didn't matter what time of day or night it was, what I was doing, or where I was doing it, there he'd appear, growling and shouting with real menace. He wouldn't stop until I'd retreated into some dark corner of the house out of sight. I'd never been so bullied in all my life. Not even the daily harassment meted out by Bryan Bryant and his cronies when I was at school instilled as much fear in me as Toby.

I took some consolation from the belief that Mother would undoubtedly be happier there were no more beatings, no more Mr Unluckys, and no more randy barmaids to occupy my day. For the last three months I hadn't once needed to offer her any apologies, and knew that if I'd taken someone like Sarah home, she would have probably been delighted.

Accepting she didn't find out about the single mum part of course.

"Mum, this is Sarah."
"Oh, hello, Sarah, my aren't you a lovely little thing?"
"She's an aromatherapist, mum."
"She's a what?"
"She uses aromatic oils obtained from plants to heal people and promote their wellbeing, mum."
"Oh, so she's a doctor is she? Well, I must say I'm impressed, Mark. Do you think you could ask the nice doctor Sarah to cure Fathers Alzheimer's?"

In order to get me through a standard day, I replayed certain events over and over. I wondered how Jody was getting on. Shaz would be well into her pregnancy by now, and I hoped Jody had enough character to handle the fact her assignee was carrying a child that by rights should have been hers. What if Shaz had a girl and called it Claire? Boy, would that be cruel. I also wondered what might have happened if I'd stayed on that bed with Mary much longer. In the clear light of day, I persuaded myself that if I should find myself in a position where a young girl, or any girl for that matter, made such blatant advances again, I would make sure the new forthright Mark Ferris took full advantage of the situation, even if it did mean facing Mother's wrath. After all, how many opportunities to fill one's boots did dead postmen get?

Then all reminiscing got put to one side. The skeleton arrived.

It was a Sunday evening and we were all nice and comfortable in the living room. Sarah and Emma-Lou were wrapped in a blanket, fused together on the sofa. Toby was stretched out on the floor like an oil slick. I was in my corner conjuring up images of how the new forthright Mark Ferris was skilfully persuading a large percentage of the female population to disrobe for his benefit. We were part way through the *Wizard of Oz* when Toby's head jerked up and his ears pricked. Seconds later we were disturbed by the doorbell.

"Who could possibly be calling on a Sunday evening?" Sarah muttered, disentangling herself from her daughter and making her way to the front door.

Toby and I both followed. One out of duty, one out of curiosity. I thought it odd that Toby hadn't gone mental like he normally did whenever the doorbell went.

Standing in the doorway was a beautiful young girl. Graced with beautiful pools of blue for eyes, a blemish-free round face, curly blonde hair reaching halfway down her back, tall and thin, she was the epitome of trouble.

"Hello, mum," the girl said.

Toby gave one excited bark. He bounded out of the door and started circling the young girl, his tail thumping against his haunches. Sarah on the other hand had obviously decided the visitor was a Gorgon and had turned to stone.

I put my fist to my mouth to try and stifle the outpouring of air that was leaving my chest. I felt as excited as Toby looked. I started hopping from foot to foot, before breaking out into a little *Things might be getting interesting* dance. As it turned out, interesting didn't really do the situation justice.

Toby allowed the new family member to ruffle his head as he chased around her feet. Something which no other person on the planet had done and lived to tell the tale, not even Sarah.

Emma-Lou's voice drifted in to us from the living room. "Hurry up, mummy," she said. "Dorothy is about to do something momentous."

Sarah was incapable of replying. She was far too busy dealing with her own momentous occasion. She remained as rooted, and as silent, as an ancient graveyard Oak.

"I love your dog. He's so…" the stranger looked to the sky, "…powerful," she finally settled on.

Sarah started sliding down the hallway wall just as strains of *Ding, Dong, the wicked witch is dead* reached us from the living room. As Sarah reached the floor, Emma-Lou repeated, "Mummy, hurry up will you?"

Emma-Lou must have eventually got curious at the lack of her mother's response to Dorothy's adventures, and poked her head into the hallway. She immediately got scared at the sight of her mother sitting on the floor, gasping for air, and rushed to her side. "Mummy, what's wrong?" she said, grasping Sarah's hand. "Why are you so white?"

"If I was you I'd go and get her a paper bag," I said.

"Your mum has just had a bit of a shock, that's all," said the stranger at the door. "You must be Emma-Lou, right?"

Emma-Lou narrowed her eyes and cocked her head to one side as she stared hard at the smiling mirror-image looking back at her. She eventually turned back to her mother for support. "How does she know my name, mummy?" she asked, stroking Sarah's hand. "Mummy, why can't you talk?"

"Tell you what I'll do," the stranger said. "I'll leave you two alone to have a nice little chat and come back tomorrow. Does that sound fair? Perhaps we can all sit down and introduce ourselves properly, eh? That would be nice, wouldn't it?"

Neither Sarah nor Emma-Lou found the means to answer.

"Excellent," the girl continued. "Then that's settled. Shall we say around six?"

There was still no response.

"I'll take that as a yes then, shall I? All righty, I'll see you both tomorrow. Bye for now."

The girl turned and started walking away, but was forced to come back when Toby insisted on following her.

"No, no, no," the stranger said, leading Toby back to the door by his collar. "You have to stay here, Toby. But don't worry, I'll be back to see you tomorrow as well." She pushed the dog through the door and handed him to Emma-Lou.

Emma-Lou got up and closed the door on the departing stranger. "Who was that, mummy?" she asked, sitting back down by Sarah's side. "Do we know her? How did she know my name? How did she know Toby's name?... Mummy?"

"I think I'm going to be sick," Sarah said. And then she was.

A few hours later, with the aid of a long bath and several cups of free-trade decaffeinated coffee, Sarah finally composed herself enough to sit Emma-Lou on the sofa and give her the story I suspected she never wanted to tell.

"I need you to listen carefully to what I'm going to tell you, Emma-Lou," Sarah said. "Please don't ask too many questions, and please don't be angry with me."

"Why would I be angry with you, mummy?" Emma-Lou looked at her shoes and started playing with her fingers. "What have you done wrong?"

Sarah took a deep breath.

She'd given birth to the child just after her sixteenth birthday. Sarah's mother, on finding out her daughter was pregnant, swore Sarah to secrecy and sent her away to stay with an Aunt in Dundee until the child was born. Not even Sarah's father was to know, let alone the child's father. Whilst Sarah was gestating in Dundee, her mother arranged all the procedures for the child to be adopted, telling anyone who asked that Sarah was simply enjoying an extended summer holiday in Scotland. Almost as soon as the child said hello to the world, it was whisked away and never seen by Sarah again.

Until now.

Emma-Lou played with the edge of her dress and listened carefully as she'd been instructed to do. "But why would your mummy do that?" she asked. "Didn't she want a granddaughter? I'd love to be a grandmother, although not until I'm really old. I need to go to university first. It's a good job your mummy was dead before I was born, isn't it? If she'd still been alive, I might have been born in Scotland as well."

Sarah got up without replying and made her way to the kitchen where she started unloading the dishwasher. If it was to give herself some respite, it didn't work. Emma-Lou instinctively followed to help.

"I expect she was worried about what people would say," Sarah said, handing Emma-Lou some plates to put away. I noticed Sarah's hands were shaking badly. "You have to remember, sweetheart, I was only sixteen, and your grandmother was a prominent member of the church. In her own way I think she was just looking out for me."

Sounds like she was looking out for herself, I thought.

Sarah and Emma-Lou made their way back to the living room and sat back in their respective seats on the sofa.

"Let's watch some TV before we go to bed?" Sarah said, picking up the remote control.

Emma-Lou frowned and twisted her mouth in concentration, closing one eye. She tapped a finger to her temple. "Mm, not yet," she said. "Were my daddy and her daddy the same person?"

Sarah replaced the remote on the coffee table, hands still shaking. In a voice that played host to several octaves she told Emma-Lou that they most definitely did not share the same father. "Absolutely not," she said. "I've told you before, your father was a musician."

"A drummer!" Emma-Lou announced, as if Sarah may have forgotten what instrument he played. She leaned forward and banged out a rhythm on the coffee table with her hands. "But he had to go away on tour."

Sarah sucked her teeth as if she was in pain. "That's right," she said, forcing a smile. "I'm sure it was purely coincidental the tour started the day after I told him I was pregnant with you. And then I expect he just got so busy he simply forgot to keep in touch."

Emma-Lou stopped drumming and cocked her head to one side. "Are you being sarcastic, mummy?" she said. "Because Mr Wilkins, that's my Geography teacher, says that sarcasm is the lowest form of wit. That was after Brian Fletcher asked him if all the starving people lived in Hungary."

Sarah apologised, and agreed she may have been a little sarcastic, but pointed out that, in her opinion, she and Emma-Lou had done perfectly well without Emma-Lou's father about anyway. "Who needs smelly men around?" she said, picking up the remote and clicking on the TV.

Emma-Lou gently took the remote control off Sarah and clicked the TV back off. "So who was my sister's daddy?" she asked, placing the remote behind a cushion out of Sarah's reach.

Sarah looked confused at Emma-Lou's insubordination. "Let's just say he wasn't a very nice person," she said, closing her eyes and rubbing her temples. "Can we watch some TV now?"

Emma-Lou ignored the request. "But why did you have a baby with him if he wasn't very nice, mummy?"

"Oh for God's sake!" Sarah said. "What's with the interrogation? I thought I told you not to ask too many questions."

In the three months I'd been here, this was the first time I'd heard Sarah raise her voice to her daughter. Obviously, Emma-Lou didn't appreciate being shouted at and started sniffling. I knew how she felt. She'd asked a perfectly reasonable question and been answered with anger.

"I'm sorry," Sarah said, quickly gathering her daughter in her arms. "But you have to understand, Emma-Lou, I was very, very young. I didn't really know what I was doing."

"You mean you didn't know how babies were made?"

I couldn't help but feel slightly sorry for Sarah. Emma-Lou wasn't making things easy. But then I guessed eleven year old daughters were not designed to give their mothers an easy time. If I was to have kids, I would hope for boys. At least I'd once been one, so would hopefully have half an idea of what they were thinking.

"Of course I knew," Sarah replied. "What I mean is, I was naïve. I sort of got caught up in the moment and forgot to be careful, that's all."

Emma-Lou extracted herself from Sarah's embrace. "Careful about what, mummy?"

If Mother had been in the room, she would have unceremoniously reminded Emma-Lou that children were meant to be seen and not heard, and actually, wherever feasible, they shouldn't be seen that much either. She had a point. I was glad it wasn't me under Emma-Lou's spotlight.

Sarah struggled to keep her parenting skills in check. "Please don't pretend you don't know what I'm talking about, Emma-Lou," she said. "I signed the consent form for you to learn all about this sort of stuff in school."

Sarah stood up and made her way to the kitchen, where she began sorting out some clothes in the washing basket. Once again, Emma-Lou dutifully followed and started helping.

"I wish I'd had the same opportunity when I was in school," Sarah said, putting all the darks together. "But your grandmother wouldn't allow it. I honestly didn't think you could get pregnant the first time you, well, you know?... did the thing."

Emma-Lou tutted and raised her eyebrows. "Silly mummy," she said, sorting out the colours. "Of course you can. Although, Grace says that in order to go to Heaven, you have to fall in love with someone first, then get married, then do the thing, then have babies."

Sarah had no idea who Grace was.

"She's the new crossing patrol lady outside our school," Emma-Lou said. "She's like really, really old. She's retired from the post office or something. She started talking to me because she said she used to go to church with your mummy. Anyway, Grace says that if girls don't have babies in that order, then they end up in Hell as Satan's whores. She also said that if your mummy was alive today she'd turn in her grave, although, I don't think I was supposed to hear that bit."

Sarah's fingers clenched around the t-shirt she was holding. "Tell Grace to mind her own sodding business," she said, throwing the t-shirt in the wrong pile. "Now, can we please go and watch some TV?"

Five minutes later, Sarah and Emma-Lou were cuddled up on the sofa watching some programme about penguins.

"What do you think she's been doing all this time, mummy?"

Emma-Lou asked.

"Who, darling?"

"My sister of course. What do you think she's been doing since she was born?"

Sarah gently pushed Emma-Lou from her embrace and ran her fingers through her daughter's hair. "Well I suppose we'll find out tomorrow, won't we?" she said. "Listen sweetheart, mummy can feel a headache coming on, so why don't we have a nice early night? Just so we're not all tired out when she arrives."

"I can't wait," Emma-Lou said, bouncing off the sofa. "I had a good long think about it when we were sorting the washing out, and I reckon it'll be great to have a sister. I can't wait to tell all my friends at school. My teachers too, especially Mr Wilkins, he's my favourite. Do you think I should tell Grace, mummy?"

Sarah spent the next half hour nervously attempting to make Emma-Lou promise to keep the skeleton firmly in the closet. "Just for the time being," she said. "Just until we get to know her a bit more. Please, Emma-Lou, you do promise, don't you?"

Emma-Lou looked at her mother. "Oh, but it's such a huge big gigantic secret to keep, mummy," she said, putting her fist in her mouth. "Almost as big as when you run over next door's cat."

"Please?"

"Well, I'll try."

"It'll be for the best, sweetheart, you'll see."

"Do you think she'll like me, mummy? I hope she's nice and kind. Rosie's older sister makes her eat frogs."

"I'm sure she'll melt your heart," Sarah said, kissing the top of her daughter's head.

The following morning, over breakfast, Sarah made Emma-Lou reiterate her promise to keep their visitor's existence secret.

"Are you okay, mummy?" Emma-Lou asked through a mouthful of muesli. "You look very tired."

"I'm fine, darling," Sarah replied. The truth being she hadn't slept at all.

As promised, the doorbell chimed at six o'clock sharp. Toby was first to the door, his tail doing an impersonation of a helicopter rotor-blade. Sarah and I were close behind.

Emma-Lou remained in the living room, where she sat in her best dress, picked out herself.

Sarah stood inside the front door for a few seconds, checking her appearance in the hallway mirror. Despite her best attempts with some artfully applied make-up, she couldn't hide the worried sag her face had suddenly adopted. She took a deep breath, smoothed her knee-length skirt, and opened the door.

"Well, hello again, mum," the skeleton said.

Toby yelped and slobbered like a lunatic as he circled the young girl's legs.

"Toby, leave the poor girl alone," Sarah said, sounding like she'd borrowed my throat-mouse. Toby ignored the instruction and continued bouncing around like a Rodeo bull.

"So, can I come in?" the stranger asked, ruffling Toby's head.

Sarah stepped aside and allowed her first born child over the threshold of her cosy existence. "Shall I take your coat?" she offered.

The prodigal daughter removed her coat, revealing clothing that no sane mother would allow their fifteen year old daughter to go out in. A very tight, low cut t-shirt struggled to contain a very full set of teenage breasts, and a short leather mini-skirt left little to the imagination. There was no evidence of a bra, and black knee-high stilletoed boots completed the ensemble. I'm not sure whose mouth opened widest, mine or Sarah's.

Sarah managed to keep herself upright with the help of the hallway telephone-table, and I immediately concerned myself with any possible public display of affection.

The youngster caught sight of herself in the hallway mirror and tossed her head like she was in a hairspray advert. "I assume you've told Emma-Lou who I am?" she said.

Sarah managed to nod.

"Good, then let's get this party started."

As soon as her big sister entered the room, Emma-Lou leaped off the sofa and flung herself into her arms. "Well hello to you too," the stranger said, spinning Emma-Lou around. "My, we are going to have such fun. I'm going to teach you some really cool stuff. That's what big sisters are for you know?"

"So you're not going to make me eat frogs?" Emma-Lou asked.

The elder girl put Emma-Lou down and frowned. "Why, certainly not," she said. "I'm going to teach you how to dress nice, like me. I'm going to tell you what make-up to wear, and what music to listen to. My favourite is Eminem." She leaned into Emma-Lou and lowered her voice. "And I'll teach you all about boys."

I couldn't help but praise Eminem for his obvious ability to appeal to women of all ages. (He was number 10 on Elaine's list).

Sarah had made her way shakily into the living room and was hanging on to the back of an armchair.

The new family member turned to her. "Any chance of a drink, mum?" she said.

Sarah was doing an exceptionally good impression of a stroke victim. "Of course," she replied, through one side of her mouth. "What would you like? I've got some hot chocolate. Free-trade in case you're worried about that type of thing."

The girl frowned and shrugged her shoulders. She didn't seem like the type who would worry about where, or how, Sarah obtained her goods. "I'd prefer something stronger."

Sarah tightened her grip on the back of the armchair. "I don't keep alcohol in the house," she said. "Anyway, aren't you too young to be drinking?"

The girl laughed. "Thanks for the concern. I suppose hot chocolate will have to do then." She turned to Emma-Lou and winked.

Emma-Lou and her sister settled themselves down on the two-seater sofa, whilst Sarah used various items of furniture to help make her way to the kitchen. I stood in my corner, the one Toby had backed me into, and found my eyes alternately drawn between our visitor's chest and legs.

Mother was going berserk.

"Mark, what on Earth do you think you're doing? What have I told you about ogling? She's not even legal. You're one step away from finding yourself on a list, my boy. Wait until I tell Father. And what will poor Timothy's sister think when she finds out you've been eyeing up other girls?

Emma-Lou bounced on the sofa. "What's your name?" she asked her sister.

I noticed the stranger's face taking on the same wicked look Eric displayed whenever he was about to remind me of Elaine's activities. She turned her head towards the kitchen. "Emma-Lou wants to know my name, mum," she called. "What shall I tell her? Shall I give her the name my adopted parents gave me, or shall I give her the name you gave me?"

There was the sound of crockery falling to the floor, followed moments later by the sound of Sarah being sick in the sink.

"Are you okay, mummy?" Emma-Lou said, getting up to go and see what the commotion was about. Her sister grabbed her by the hand and sat her back down, shaking her head to indicate Sarah should be left alone.

A few moments later, Sarah appeared from the kitchen, looking distinctly ill. "Whichever you prefer," she said, setting down a tray carrying three mugs and some biscuits. Her hands were shaking so badly there was as much hot chocolate swilling around the tray as there was in the mugs.

"In that case," the stranger said, picking up two mugs and handing one of them to Emma-Lou, "we'll use the name *you* gave me when I popped out of your innards." She held her free hand out to Emma-Lou. "The name is Penny."

Emma-Lou giggled as she placed her chocolate on the coffee table and shook Penny's hand.

"Do you like it?" Penny asked.

"I think it's a lovely name," Emma-Lou said, still bouncing up and down. "Not as nice as mine, but still nice."

"Looks like our mother is good at picking names," Penny said. "Shame she's not so good at picking the dads, eh?"

Sarah sat in an armchair and held her mug of chocolate with two hands. She tried taking a sip, only to spatter the front of her blouse with stains. Her voice could just be heard above the ambient noise of the room as she asked, "So what name did your adopted parents give you?"

We all listened with interest as Penny told us her adopted parents had called her Jenny. Apparently, they'd a problem with the name Penny on the grounds their surname was Farthing. "It's a type of bike," Penny said, just in case we wondered.

Toby had stretched himself out at Penny's feet, and Emma-Lou gasped when her sister broke a house-rule by feeding him a biscuit from the tray.

"What?" Penny said, noticing Emma-Lou's horror.

"We're not supposed to feed Toby from our hands," Emma-Lou said. "Mummy says it's unhygienic. She only ever lets him eat from his bowl."

Penny fed Toby another biscuit, then settled back on the sofa. "I suppose you're wondering what's brought me to your door after all this time?" she said, looking at Sarah and smiling.

Sarah managed a nod and some form of grunt.

"Well, some of us girls were messing about on the computer," Penny continued. "You know, looking at family trees and stuff. To be honest, I hadn't really worried about my roots until then. But then I thought, why not? Go for it. Find out who decided to give you away I said to myself. Shit, it might even be fun."

Emma-Lou put her hand over her mouth at the breaking of another house-rule.

"What now?" Penny said.

Emma-Lou lowered her voice. "Mummy doesn't allow swear words. She says they show a lack of vocabulary."

"No shit," Penny said. "Well then I guess I'd best be careful, hadn't I, Ems? I can call you Ems, can't I? Emma-Lou is such a mouthful."

Emma-Lou leaned forward and looked across at her mother. "Can she, mummy?" she asked excitedly. "Please say yes. I think it's brilliant."

"Ah, now there's the first thing I'm going to teach you, Ems," Penny said, ignoring anything Sarah may have to think on the subject. "Whenever you want to say something is brilliant, say either brill, or better still, lush. It's way cooler."

"Excuse me," Sarah said, spilling more chocolate. She tried to place her mug back on the tray, but her hands were shaking so badly she gave up on the idea. She attempted to sound brave. "If anyone is going to teach my daughter how to speak, it will be me, if you don't mind."

Penny slowly turned and looked at Sarah. "And if *you* don't mind," she said, "I was having a conversation with my sister about some private shit." She theatrically put her hand to her mouth. "Oh sorry, did I just say shit again?" Penny didn't take her eyes off Sarah. She reached for another biscuit, which Toby gobbled out of her hand in one swoop. "Come on, Ems," Penny stood up and took the mug from Sarah's hands. "Let's go and make some more chocolate. You can show me where all the stuff is and shit."

I tried to follow them into the kitchen, but Toby growled as soon as

I moved and I decided to stay where I was.

Sarah had gone greyer than a heart-attack victim. She sat in silence as we listened to the low chatter of the two girls going about their chocolate-making business. Occasionally, the talk was interrupted by howls of laughter.

"Mummy, did you know Penny is in a home?" Emma-Lou announced, carrying a tray with more chocolate and biscuits back into the living room. The mug she placed in front of Sarah carried the slogan *World's Best Mum*.

Sarah grabbed the sides of her chair. "Home? What home? What are you talking about?" Her eyes started dancing.

Penny leaned against the archway leading from the living room into the kitchen and folded her arms. I couldn't help but notice that the action pushed her breasts almost completely out of the t-shirt. "Oh, don't worry, mum," she said. "It's just a home. No different to any of the others really."

Penny ignored the fact Sarah looked more dead than me, and took great pride in telling us she'd been in and out of institutions since the age of seven. Apparently, Mr and Mrs Farthing had lost the ability to look after their beloved Jenny after they'd both frazzled to death in a house-fire.

"The psychologists reckon I've blocked the fire from my memory or something," Penny said, moving from the archway and settling herself back on the sofa beside Emma-Lou. "They say I was found in the garden staring at the house as it burned. It's a complete mystery how I managed to get out." Penny fed Toby another biscuit. "I've had people poking around in me ever since." She turned to Emma-Lou and winked. "The guy who comes to me now is always looking down my top, the dirty bugger. He's quite good-looking though, which helps." Penny turned back to the almost comatose Sarah "I'd probably think about going with him if I didn't already have a boyfriend."

Sarah twitched, but seemed stuck, like the second-hand on a clock whose batteries have run out. It appeared none of her muscles were working. She looked like she'd been paralysed from the hair down. I don't think she was even blinking.

Penny turned back to Emma-Lou. "So, tell me all about school, Ems," she said. "Are there any boys you fancy?"

Emma-Lou giggled. "No," she said. "Mummy says I'm far too

young to be worrying about boys. But I'll tell you all about my teachers if you like?" Emma-Lou didn't wait for an answer before launching into a potted history of all the teachers she'd had since nursery.

"Can't say I ever got on too well with teachers," Penny said, when Emma-Lou had finished her list. "I've never really stayed in any one school long enough to worry about it that much. I did have a maths teacher once who made an impression on me. Giles his name was. Really good looking with a body to match, if you know what I mean?" She playfully nudged Emma-Lou in the ribs. "Yes, I got on very well with Giles. Very well indeed. I used to go round his house for extra tuition. My maths is still shit though."

Spittle ran from Sarah's mouth and dripped from her chin onto her chocolate-stained blouse. Her lips moved, trying to form words. We all had to concentrate hard to hear what she was saying. Through the jumble of almost silent words, we could just make out, "I'm sorry."

Penny placed her mug on the tray and stood up. "It's a bit late for apologies, mum," she said. "What's done is done." She turned to Emma-Lou. "Sorry, Ems, but I've got to go. I have to be back in the home by nine, and the bus takes a good two hours from here. Tell you what, why don't I come back tomorrow? Same time? Perhaps *mummy* will be in a more talkative mood, eh?"

Emma-Lou flung herself into her sister's arms. "That'll be lush," she said.

As Penny and Emma-Lou were saying their farewells at the door, I watched Sarah as she managed to make her way to the kitchen. Just before she started being sick in the sink again, she found the strength to throw the *Worlds Best Mum* mug onto the mock-Italian tiled floor, smashing it into a thousand pieces.

PENNY'S DROPPED

The following day, after Emma-Lou had been safely deposited at school, Sarah cancelled her clients and started her own family-tree research. She quickly discovered any authority dealing with child welfare are particularly reticent about giving out details. There were lots of apologies, but no information. No matter how hard she tried, she couldn't get to the bottom of where Penny had been for the last fifteen years, or of what had happened in that house-fire. After several hours of phone calls, intermittent crying, and internet surfing, Sarah popped out and did something which wasn't in her normal routine. She bought a bottle of wine.

By the time the doorbell announced Penny's arrival at six o'clock sharp, Sarah had already downed a large glass.

"Penny," Sarah said, "how lovely to see you again, come on in." The Dutch courage was accompanied by a slight slur. She took Penny's coat and waved her hand up and down Penny's spray-on leather trousers and figure-hugging top. "How nice to see you've dressed for the occasion."

Penny ignored the slight, and checked her face and hair in the hallway mirror before making her way into the living room. Emma-Lou greeted her sister with as much gusto as the day before.

"Wow! I'm sure you've grown since yesterday," Penny said, spinning Emma-Lou around again. "You'll be big enough to do all sorts of things soon. Like me."

As Penny sat down she spotted Sarah's empty wine glass on the coffee table. She picked it up and sniffed. "Mm, good stuff," she said, turning to Sarah, who'd slumped into her chair. "I thought you didn't keep alcohol in the house."

Sarah leaned forward and took the wine glass off Penny. "Now then young lady," she said, placing the glass back on the coffee table. "I need to know everything you've been up to for the last fifteen years." The word years came out as yearsh. "I need to know who your adopted parents were. Where you've been living. The address of this home you're in. Everything." Sarah waved her arms about like a demented windmill. "Because nobody will tell me a thing."

"Sounds like our mother has been checking up on me, Ems," Penny said, turning to Emma-Lou. She lowered her voice slightly. "Also looks like she's had a few." She made the motion of drinking with her hand.

Sarah smiled crookedly. "Of course I've been checking up on you, you silly girl," she said, the volume in her voice increasing a notch. "I'm your mother for goodness sake. I have a right to know where you've been. And I've had one. Not a few."

Penny laughed through the side of her mouth. "I think you'll find you gave up those rights the minute you handed me over," she said. "But don't worry. I might not be as bright as my little sister here," she hugged Emma-Lou to her, "but I've learned things I would never have learned if you hadn't seen fit to get rid of me."

Sarah visibly diminished. She took in a few large gulps of air, then closed her eyes. "I didn't want to get rid of you, Penny," she said. "You see, my mother…"

"Ah, good old granny," Penny said. "Shame she's kicked the bucket. I'd loved to have seen the look on her face when I rocked up. I bet she would have shit herself."

"You've got to believe me," Sarah said. I could tell from the way her bottom lip was moving that tears weren't far away. "I was desperate to keep you. It was my mother who forced me to put you up for adoption."

I recalled some of the things I'd been forced to do by Mother. Eat cabbage. Perform in the Sunday School nativity. Kiss relatives. Invite Timothy's spotty sister to the pictures. They'd all felt like the end of the world at the time, but now seemed insignificant compared to being forced to give up a child. The next time I spoke to Sarah's mother - there was a photograph of her on Sarah's dressing-table - I would get the new forthright Mark Ferris to give her a piece of his mind.

"Yeah, well it doesn't matter who forced who to do what," Penny said. "Because we're all one big happy family now, aren't we, Ems?" Penny snuggled Emma-Lou tighter, much to the delight of the younger girl.

Sarah struggled to get herself out of the chair. She wiped her face with the back of her hand, smudging her lightly applied lipstick. "I think I need a drink," she said, picking up the wine glass and making her way to the kitchen.

"I'll have whatever you're having," Penny called. She turned to Emma-Lou and winked. "And perhaps Ems would like one as well."

"Over my dead body," came the reply.

A few minutes later, Sarah returned with two large glasses of wine and a hot chocolate wobbling on a tray. From the way Sarah was teetering, it looked like she'd been helping herself from the bottle whilst waiting for the kettle to boil. She set the tray down and fell into her chair, spilling a small portion of wine over her blouse in the process. At this rate, I thought, she'd soon run out of clean tops. She took a large gulp of what was left in her glass, then found something mildly funny, then took another swig. "So, your life, Penny?" she said, sweeping her free hand in an arc. "Come. Tell all."

Penny took a small sip of her own wine. "I'd go easy on this stuff if I was you, mum," she said. "It can make you do some funny things. Especially if you're not used to it. Giles taught me that."

Sarah shrugged her shoulders and finished her glass with one more gulp. She allowed the empty glass to fall into her lap and rolled her tongue around her lips. She closed both eyes and only managed to reopen one of them.

Penny leaned forward and retrieved the glass from Sarah's lap, putting it on the coffee table. "Have you eaten today?" she said. "Because if you haven't, you can double the effects. Did you know that? And what about sleep? Lack of sleep can also have a drastic effect on alcohol consumption you know?" Penny turned to Emma-Lou. "So make sure the first time I ever take you out to get shit-faced, you have a good night's sleep and a nice big meal, okay?" The two sisters giggled at their scheming.

"The last time Sarah slept was the night before you arrived," I shouted from my corner. "And she hasn't eaten properly since that bowl of muesli yesterday morning."

Sarah attempted to say something, but her grasp on English had all but disappeared. After a few sentences of incomprehensible drivel, Sarah finally gave up her hold on alertness. She curled into a ball on the armchair and promptly fell asleep, twitching like a dreaming dog.

"Well now that's very rude, isn't it," Penny said to Emma-Lou. "Your mother hasn't set eyes on me for nearly sixteen years, and then when I make the effort to find her, she falls asleep."

"What's wrong with her?" Emma-Lou asked. "Shall we wake her up?" There was worried moisture in her eyes.

"No, let her sleep," Penny replied. "Your mum is fine. She's just had a couple of stressful days, that's all. I'm sure this has all been a bit of a shock to her. Anyway, this will give us chance to have some fun. I'm going to teach you some really cool shit. It's going to be lush."

Penny stood up, retrieved her coat from the hallway, and produced a half bottle of Vodka from a pocket. "Why don't you go and get us two fresh glasses?" she said, waving the bottle in the air. "And when you're at it, have a look to see if you've got any nice big bananas."

Sarah woke to the sound of someone retching. I glanced at the wall-clock: 7.15pm.

"Penny?" Sarah said. She winced and massaged her temples as she righted herself in the chair. "Is that you?" She tried standing up, but immediately fell back down.

If I thought she'd listen, I would have reminded Sarah that Penny had to be back at the home by 9pm. As it took her a couple of hours to get there, she'd left fifteen minutes ago. "It's not Penny," I said. "Try again."

"Penny?" Sarah repeated louder. She managed to get out of the chair and slowly made her way to the kitchen. She stopped dead when she reached the archway. "Emma-Lou!" Sarah ran to her daughter's side. "My God, whatever is the matter?"

Emma-Lou was incapable of replying.

Again, if only she'd listen, I could have told Sarah that Emma-Lou and her sister had had a jolly old time. I could have also mentioned that Emma-Lou had spent the last five minutes bodily disposing of the Vodka and blackcurrant Penny had plied her with.

After Emma-Lou had finished emptying the contents of her stomach, and Sarah had persuaded her to stop crying, Sarah carried Emma-Lou back to the sofa. The empty Vodka bottle and glasses were in full display on the coffee table, and from the general appearance and smell of her youngest I guess it didn't take long for Sarah to figure out what had happened.

"I'll bloody kill that girl when I get my hands on her," she said, covering the very delicate Emma-Lou with a blanket. Within minutes, Emma-Lou had slipped into a Vodka induced sleep.

Sarah sat in the armchair and curled herself up in a ball. She wrapped her arms around her knees and buried her head. "I really am the worst mother in the world," she whispered.

Then she cried.

Five minutes later, Sarah composed herself enough to go to the kitchen for some Kleenex to wipe her face. She returned to the chair and blew her nose noisily into the tissues, looking around the room as if she'd lost something. "Where's Toby?" she asked herself.

I could have told her, but knowing full well she'd take no notice, I decided to show her instead. I ran from the living room to the kitchen, then back to the living room. I ran halfway up the stairs and back down again. I did a quick twirl in the hallway, before running back into the living room and presenting myself in front of Sarah with a sort of star-jump.

Sarah still looked around the room, confused. "Toby?" she called. "Where are you, boy?"

"Don't you see," I said, hands on hips, trying to get my breath back. "I'm free!" I raised my arms in triumph as another song by *The Who* suddenly flitted across my memory. I had to stop myself from adding, *'and I'm waiting for you to follow me.'*

"Oops, nearly broke into song there, Sarah," I said. "Trust me, you wouldn't want that to happen. My singing is on an even keel with my dancing. Elaine used to say I sounded like a horse being castrated."

Sarah got up off the chair and started searching the house.

"It's no use, Sarah," I said, bouncing around behind her like Tigger. "Penny's taken him with her."

Understandably, Sarah needed to check I was telling the truth, and continued to search every room in the house. I followed her, whistling *Hound Dog*, until she finally slumped back in the armchair with the realisation Toby was nowhere to be found.

"Oh, and Sarah," I said, adopting a nonchalant manner that would have had Mother scowling at me. "Before I forget. You also missed the lesson with the condom and the banana."

The following morning, Sarah once again cancelled all her appointments. She also rang the school and told them Emma-Lou had picked up a stomach bug and wouldn't be in.

Emma-Lou surfaced around 11am. She looked like she'd been dragged through a wind tunnel. She sat silently at the kitchen table as

Sarah made her some organic wholemeal toast. When Sarah was confident Emma-Lou was looking a bit better, she sat opposite her and demanded to know exactly what had happened the night before. Sarah reminded her daughter that lying was a mortal sin and insisted Emma-Lou left nothing out.

Emma-Lou, who probably had no intention of lying anyway, didn't disappoint.

Sarah's kitchen became a distinctly uncomfortable place when Emma-Lou got to the part of the evening involving the banana.

Sarah's normal face disappeared in a host of ticks and twitches. "She… what?"

Emma-Lou looked at the floor. She sat on her hands and repeated how Penny had used the banana to demonstrate how to put a condom on a boy by using your mouth.

"It was a very impressive performance," I said, as Sarah slunk off her chair and landed on the floor.

Elaine had always been a firm believer in the condom. She insisted on putting them on me herself, stating, *'I don't trust you to do it properly, Mark. Anyway, by the time you've managed it, I'll have probably gone off the boil.'* Even despite Elaine's expertise in condom manipulation, I didn't think she'd ever once entertained the idea of putting it on with her mouth. I didn't even know the feat was possible. Not until Penny's little demonstration.

Emma-Lou jumped off her chair and started fanning Sarah with a tea-towel. "Penny said it was a life-skill that would make me very popular in a year or two," she said. "I wasn't very good at it though. I'd only get the top bit on and then it would fall off." Emma-Lou had obviously taken her mother's instructions about leaving nothing out to heart. "Penny was brill at it though," she added.

I nodded my head in agreement and put my hand up. "I can vouch for that," I said.

Emma-Lou helped her mother into the living room and settled her down on the sofa. "Penny said she'd come back to see us today," she said, stroking her mother's hand. "About six o'clock as usual. By the way, she took Toby with her. She said it didn't look like either of us were capable of looking after him. That was thoughtful of her, don't you think, mummy?"

"Listen, sweetheart," Sarah said. She looked at Emma-Lou as if she was about to ask for her soul. "I'm really not sure about Penny. I sort of get the feeling she's not a very nice girl." Sarah looked at the floor.

"I really don't think she should come round here any more."

"Oh, what!" I said, stamping my feet. "You can't be serious, Sarah. Can't you remember how boring it was around here until Penny came on the scene? Okay, so it's going to take me a thousand years to finish apologising to Mother for what was going through my head when Penny was playing with that banana. But still."

Emma-Lou stared open-mouthed at her mother for a few seconds, then marched off up the stairs to her bedroom. If the slam of the bedroom door was anything to go by, I think we could safely assume Emma-Lou was in a bit of a mood.

Sarah entered Emma-Lou's bedroom quietly. Emma-Lou was face down on the bed, her head in a pillow. "Go away!" she told her mother. Despite her voice being muffled, I could tell she was crying.

Sarah sat on the edge of the bed and placed a hand gently on her daughter's back. "She can't expect to just turn up on our doorstep after fifteen years and waltz into our home as if she owns the place, sweetheart. This is our house, she has to play by our rules. I'm not saying we can't see her again. I'm just saying I don't think she should come round here any more. Perhaps we can go and visit her at the home instead? That would be nice, wouldn't it?"

"Leave me alone!" Emma-Lou said. "This is MY bedroom and you're not allowed in here any more!"

"Okay," Sarah replied. "I accept you need some time to yourself. I'll be right downstairs if you need me, all right? It'll be for the best, Emma-Lou, you'll see."

Sarah made her way back downstairs. She went to the corner of the living room that housed the family computer and typed something into Google. "Now, where are you young lady?" she said. "And what the hell have you done with my dog?"

As promised, Penny returned at 6 o'clock sharp. Emma-Lou had kept herself in her bedroom since her little tantrum, and Sarah had spent another fruitless afternoon on the computer looking for needles in haystacks.

Sarah slipped the chain on the front door and only opened it enough to see out; just like she did when people called selling gas. I jumped up and down behind Sarah so I could see over her head. Penny and Toby emerged and disappeared from my view like they'd been caught in a flickering light-bulb.

"We've had a lovely time, haven't we, Toby?" I heard Penny say. I just caught sight of her ruffling Toby's head. I also momentarily caught sight of the tight white blouse with its top three buttons undone. I jumped as high as I could to try and see what Penny had on below the blouse, but I couldn't quite find the right angle. I eventually ran out of breath, and had to take a rest against the hallway wall. I really would have to think about getting fit, I thought.

I'd always had an uneasy relationship with exercise. I recalled one of my school reports, in which the PE teacher, presumably in an effort to find something positive to say, had written, *Mark is an enthusiastic spectator, and his kit is always clean, neat and tidy.*

Elaine loved sport. More particularly, she loved sportsmen, one of her favourite sayings being, *'Give me a man with the body of Nadal* (Number 8 on the shag-list) *and the face of Beckham* (Joint Number 11 with Cristiano Ronaldo) *and I'll give you one very satisfied woman.'*

"Don't ever take my dog without permission again," Sarah said through the gap in the door. "I've been worried stiff." Sarah poked an arm out and clicked her fingers. "Come on, Toby, here boy."

I looked at the opening afforded by the security chain and didn't need any knowledge of trigonometry - which was just as well - to know Toby would never fit through it without opening the door wider. I took a deep breath and started jumping again.

"Here boy," Sarah repeated.

Toby barked once, but remained sitting statue-like at Penny's side.

"Are you hiding someone in there?" Penny said, trying to peer around Sarah's head and laughing lightly. "Would you like us to come back in an hour or so? Give you time to get him dressed and on his way? I hope you're taking precautions, mum. Wouldn't want any little accidents now, would we? I can lend you some if you've run out. Oh, come to think of it, I left some in Emma-Lou's secret drawer. Of course, she says it's secret, but I told her you'd know exactly where it is. She didn't believe me by the way. She reckons you'd never do anything as low as snoop around in her private shit. I told her it's what all mums do."

Penny was right. Sarah knew exactly where Emma-Lou's secret drawer was. Its contents didn't normally add up to much. A few sloppy love poems she'd written about some boy a year above her in school. A ten pound note she'd found in the street. A picture of Mozart. Several more of some boy-band. And now, if Sarah cared to look, a few strawberry flavoured condoms.

"I don't need you to come back in an hour," Sarah said. She stood up straight and lifted her chin. "In fact, I don't think it's a good idea for you to come back at all. I'm really not comfortable with you coming here any more. Your behaviour is a bad influence on Emma-Lou, and, as her mother, I can't allow it. I have no problem with keeping in touch. Perhaps we could exchange e-mail addresses." She grabbed a pen and a piece of paper from the telephone table and scribbled quickly. She held the piece of paper out through the gap.

I jumped just in time to see Toby snatch the paper out of Sarah's hand and start ripping it to shreds. Sarah brought her hand back inside with a yelp of pain. She looked at it bewildered as a small trickle of blood run down her little finger.

"He bit me," Sarah said, mainly to herself. She quickly slammed the door shut and leaned her back against it, holding her finger in the air. It took a few moments for Sarah to slide down the door and start crying.

Penny opened the letterbox and spoke to the back of Sarah's head. "My, my, I have upset your cosy little applecart, haven't I?" she said. "If you think you can just ignore me, Sarah, you're very much mistaken. But then I guess you're used to making mistakes, aren't you? We all have to pay for our mistakes eventually, Sarah. That's the rules. And by God I'm going to make sure you pay for yours. I'll be back, Sarah. Don't know when, but I'll be back. You have no idea what I'm capable of. No idea at all." She allowed the letterbox to close noisily.

Emma-Lou, who I'd noticed had been sitting halfway up the stairs, walked into the hallway and sat down beside her mother. "We will see Penny and Toby again won't we, mummy?" she said, wrapping her arms around Sarah's neck.

I wandered into the living room, leaving Sarah and Emma-Lou crying together in the hallway. Despite being worried that, without Penny around, Sarah's life would slip back into tedium, I started to do my *Looks like Toby has gone for good* dance. It consisted of closing my eyes and whooping, whilst simultaneously displaying a cross between a native American rain-dance and someone on an epileptic pogo-stick. I'd worked up quite a sweat when I heard a gentle cough from the doorway. I recognised the tone and quickly stopped what I was doing. I opened my eyes slowly; one at a time.

"Very nice," Crimson said. "You'll have to teach me how to bust those moves someday."

"I... I... I thought a wasp had flown down my shirt," I said.

Crimson tapped her watch and caught hold of my hand. She was laughing too hard to say anything.

I could hardly see Mr T. over the stack of files in front of him. If it wasn't for the hat, I don't think I'd have known he was there. "How are things, Seven-Three-Five-Nine?" he asked, parting enough files so I could see him.

I opened my mouth to begin, but Mr T. held his hand up to stop me.

"Actually, as you can see, we are a bit busy, Seven-Three-Five-Nine," he said, accepting a file from one of the sidekicks. "So, no time for idle chit-chat I'm afraid. Now, the reason we needed to speak to you," he opened the file, "is to let you know we've conducted a thorough review of your case and..."

"My case?"

Mr T. closed the file and handed it back to the sidekick. "Yes, your case. There's no need to look so worried. It's all standard practice. Everyone has their case reviewed periodically, Seven-Three-Five-Nine. Think of it as a sort of job appraisal. If there's sufficient evidence to support sending you off to the Sanctum, then off you'll go. Personally, I hate review time. I mean, just look at all the work it creates." Mr T. scanned his hands over the files surrounding him. "Honestly, the sooner we get that Gates fellow here, the happier I'll be."

I closed my eyes and braced myself. If the job appraisals I'd gone through with the postal service were anything to go by, this wouldn't be good news. Don't get me wrong, the brass were always happy with the way I delivered my bag, but basically I ticked all the boxes that said, *This guy is going nowhere.* I opened my eyes to find Mr T. with his head stuck in another file.

"And?" I said.

Mr T. looked up and frowned. One of the sidekicks leaned over and whispered in his ear. "Oh, sorry, Seven-Three-Five-Nine," he said, slapping his forehead. "I forgot you were there for a minute. I think all this work is getting to me. I'm sure I'd forget my head if I didn't have this enormous hat to remind me where it was."

Oh Lord, I thought. Don't tell me Mr T's coming down with Alzheimer's as well.

"Anyway, you didn't make it," Mr T. said, looking over a note one of the sidekicks had just given him. He shook his head and let out a grunt. "Now, it looks like your messenger is… temporarily otherwise engaged, but not to worry, we'll send for you as soon as we're ready. In the meantime, I suggest you pass the time with your dear friend, Old Eric. No doubt he'll be absolutely delighted to see you again." Mr T. waved his hand in the general direction behind me. "Oh, and better luck next time, Seven-Three-Five-Nine."

I immediately found myself standing in front of a plain wooden door, and seemed to be holding a balloon on a short piece of string. The door was devoid of any words, but the balloon had *BETTER LUCK NEXT TIME* written on it in black marker pen. I turned back to Mr T. and the sidekicks, but they were far too busy to pay me any attention.

Through the door, a long table had been laid out. Displayed on the table were all the cards I'd received during my lifetime wishing me, *Better Luck Next Time*. There were the two off old driving instructors. Next to those was the one off Timothy's sister, hand delivered after she'd officially dumped me. There were several from various teachers, received after exam results, and several more from bosses, received after job appraisals. The penultimate card was the one off Elaine, received after the first time we'd made love, which, of course, she'd thought hilarious. That's Elaine's sense of humour for you. Finally, at the end of the table, just before I reached Old Eric's office door, there was the one from Mother I thought no one knew about; received the day after my marriage.

I settled myself on the edge of Eric's desk, balloon in hand. Unlike the balloon, the experience of being reminded of my many failures had left me somewhat deflated.

"Well, hello again," Eric said, frowning at the sight of the balloon. "What brings you to my humble domain?"

"Well, let's see," I said, tying the balloon around my wrist. "Oh, that's right, the committee wanted to make sure I hadn't forgotten what a useless failure as a human being I was… am… whatever."

"Ah, I see," Eric said. "Of course, it's review time again isn't it? I'm sort of guessing you still haven't made it in then, son."

"Bingo!"

Old Eric got up off his chair and made his way to me. "If it makes you feel any better, son," he said, putting his arm around me, "I've failed hundreds of reviews. It's no use beating yourself up about it. You've just got to accept it and move on. Look on the positive side. If you were in the Sanctum you wouldn't be here talking to me, would you?"

"I thought you said there was a positive side."

Old Eric made his way back to his chair, chuckling at what he perceived to be my attempt at a joke. "Anyway," he said, sitting down, "how's that assignee of yours? From what I remember she sounded a bit boring."

"Ah, but if you also remember, there was a skeleton in the cupboard."

Eric's smile brightened. "And has the skeleton turned up?"

I told Old Eric all about my time so far with Sarah. The story flowed out of me easily, and Eric listened without interruption, showing all the right emotions in the relevant places. I realised the new forthright Mark Ferris was getting reasonably adept at this story-telling lark. I could imagine him being the life and soul of those swanky parties Elaine never invited me to.

"Tarquin, you just simply have to listen to my husband tell you about the time he spent with a debt collector called - wait for it - Dai the Murderer." (Wait for Tarquin to stop gasping). *"Oh, and then, you'll utterly adore his telling of his time with an aromatherapist whose long-lost adopted daughter came and put a spanner in her cosy life."* (And here Elaine calls across the room to disturb my telling of these stories to an already captivated bunch of cocktail-dressed women who are hanging on my every word). *"Darling, darling, when you've finished with the secretarial department, you simply have to come and tell Tarquin all about the time you were dead."*

"I'll be there in the swish of a puppy-dog's tail, my sweet. I'm just telling these lovely ladies about the episode with the condom and the

banana."

"So, do you think Penny's gone for good?" Eric asked.

"Don't know," I said. "Like that Arnold what's-his-face from the movies, she's promised to be back. I just hope I've seen the last of that dog of prayer."

"Dog of prayer?"

"Yes. Whenever he appears, I pray."

Eric chuckled again. "See," he said. "What did I tell you? If you'd been sent to the Sanctum you wouldn't be here telling me all this stuff, would you?"

I stood up and leaned against the wall, the balloon bouncing after me. "So what would I be doing, Eric?" I asked. "You know, if I *was* in the Sanctum."

Eric leaned back in his chair and put his hands behind his head. "Ah, now there's the gazillion dollar question, son," he said. "You might as well ask me what the restaurants are like on Mars, because I've never been there either. You see, no one has ever come out of the Sanctum, so we can only take some educated guesses about what goes on beyond that door."

"But surely someone knows," I said. "What about the committee?"

"Don't think so. I've been here a long time, son. I reckon if they knew anything we'd have heard by now."

"But you once told me that to live the death I'd always dreamed of I had to get myself packed off to the Sanctum." I sat back on the desk. "How do you know that's the case when you don't even know what's behind the door yourself?"

Eric stood up and stretched himself. "Think about it logically, son," he said, over the clicking of bones. "Have you ever been anywhere, and I mean anywhere, that's made you think, *Wow! This is where I'm going to stay for the whole of eternity?*"

I opened my mouth with the intention of answering that I'd once had a very nice time in Scarborough, but Eric didn't give me the time.

"Of course you haven't," he said. "In life, it doesn't matter where people go or what they find when they get there. Eventually, they always end up back where they started. No place quite like home and all that malarkey. But, in death, nobody, and I mean absolutely nobody, has ever returned from the Sanctum. Not even a postcard, son. Not a bloody morsel of information about what's behind that sodding door. Goes to follow therefore that the place must be abso-bloodylutely fantastic." Eric sat back down.

"But that's just guesswork and conjecture, Eric," I said. "There could be all sorts of things behind that door."

"Could be," Eric replied. "And I suppose there's only way to find out. But it stands to reason it must be pretty amazing, doesn't it? Look, here's how I see it, son. We've established that nobody has ever come out of there, right? That's indisputable. Now, we all know that bad news travels faster than good, correct? So, no news at all must mean the place is beyond phenomenal. Let's face it, if the place was shite, like say, Swindon, we'd have heard about it, don't you think?"

"But you've got no proof, Eric. You're simply assuming."

"Look, you know like when you find something that's totally awesome and you want to keep it all to yourself? Well, that's what I think is happening here. I think that behind that door is the death you always dreamed of, son, and that's why we never hear about it. The selfish bastards in there want to keep it all to themselves. They think by being quiet we'll never get to know about it. That's my theory anyway."

I started playing with the print of the Last Supper. "You know what I've discovered since I've been dead?" I said.

"What's that, son?"

"Nothing! Absolutely nothing. I am the gatherer of all things nothing. Mr Nothing from Nothingshire, that's me. The committee tell me nothing, you tell me nothing…"

"I tell you things all the time," Eric protested.

"Huh!" I said, putting down the print. "The only thing you ever tell me is how many orgasms my wife is having…"

"Three yesterday," Eric said, holding up the required number of fingers.

"You see what I mean." I stood up and faced the door. The bottom lip was close to quivering. I was still facing the door when Crimson suddenly burst through it. She hung on to the handle, gasping for air.

"What have I told you about knocking?" Eric said. "Youth of today. Absolutely no manners."

Crimson apologised profusely, blaming lack of time for her indiscretion. She looked at her watch. "Oh shit," she said, walking to me and taking hold of my hand. "Come on."

She paused in the doorway and turned to Eric. "Mr Eric, the committee has said you may want to return to your assignee. Her and her lover are apparently searching desperately for the keys to the handcuffs she's stuck in."

Eric smiled and was gone. The balloon made a hissing noise and slowly deflated.

VISITING TIME

When I returned, Emma-Lou was lying on the sofa, still crying. Sarah was on the phone in the hallway. I listened to her half of the conversation.

"What do you mean you don't think this is a police matter?... I told you, my dog has been stolen... Yes, I know I said she was my daughter... Well, either Penny or Jenny... No, I don't know where she's living... Fifteen, nearly sixteen... It's complicated... Oh, forget it!"

For the next three days, Sarah alternated between peace talks with Emma-Lou, and searching the internet for clues.

"I will find you, even if it kills me," she whispered at the screen.

Late on the third night, with the house silent, Sarah was sitting in front of the computer drawing the normal blanks when she suddenly announced to herself how she remembered Penny saying something about the home she was in being two hours away by bus. Several hours later, after thoroughly researching bus routes around the area and cross referencing them with the types of establishments Penny may be holed up in, Sarah boiled down Penny's possible whereabouts to a local authority children's home forty miles away.

The following morning, before Emma-Lou got up, Sarah telephoned the home and used its website mantra that it liked to, *Work closely with visiting family and friends to enable and facilitate the rebuilding of broken relationships,* to get an appointment to speak with one of the home's managers. The appointment was for the following afternoon. Sarah decided not to mention anything to Emma-Lou.

I followed Sarah into the offices of the *Beachfield Secure Children's Unit*, a privately run, government sponsored establishment catering for children between the ages of 12 to 17 who'd been referred under section 25 of the Welfare placement act.

The name plaque on the desk suggested we were about to speak to a Mrs Julie Turner.

"Please, take a seat," Mrs Turner said, smiling warmly. She was one of those people who are difficult to age, and could have been anywhere between 25 and 45. On the desk in front of her was a bulging box-file, the contents of which were struggling to be contained within its grasp. Down the spine of the file, written in black marker pen, was the name, JENNY FARTHING.

After initial introductions and the offer of a cup of tea or coffee, Mrs Turner explained she was sure Sarah would understand any reluctance on her part to give out too much information.

Sarah agreed that Mrs Turner was in a difficult position, and fully accepted that Julie, *'she could call her Julie, couldn't she?'* had a duty to protect the welfare of her wards.

"I wouldn't expect it any other way," Sarah said in her best telephone voice. "But you see, Penny and I parted on not the best of terms. I'm desperate to put that right. If not for me, then for my proper daughter, who's not stopped crying since her sister stormed out on us. I suppose that's all I really want for now, Julie, is to know when visiting hours are. Actually, I was sort of hoping that I could have a few words with Penny today. Just to put a few issues to bed."

Mrs Turner sipped her tea and studied Sarah over the cup. "I'm afraid that's out of the question," she said, placing the cup back in its saucer.

Sarah drummed her fingers on the desk. "But surely I have rights."

Mrs Turner placed her hands on the desk and locked her fingers. "I think you'll find you lost those rights quite some time ago, Mrs Lloyd."

Sarah stopped drumming her fingers and narrowed her eyes. "Actually, it's *Miss* Lloyd."

Mrs Turner smiled. "Of course it is. I do apologise." She picked up the cup of tea and settled back in her executive leather armchair. "My hands are tied, *Miss* Lloyd. There really is nothing I can do. There's a million procedures you'd need to go through before I could even think about allowing you to speak with *Jenny*."

"But that's ridiculous," Sarah said. "You've had no problems with her speaking to me up until now. *She* came to find *me* for Christ's sake."

Mrs Turner stood up and made her way to the large picture window overlooking the well-manicured gardens. "Imagine if it were the case, Miss Lloyd, that you could put children up for adoption and then simply march in here years later demanding to see them. There'd be mayhem, don't you think? Rules are rules, Miss Lloyd, and I'm certainly not going to be the one who breaks them, especially not when we have a Government inspection due next week. Those people leave no stone unturned, Miss Lloyd. If I allowed you to speak to *Jenny* without all the relevant paperwork in place, they'd know as soon as they walked in and no mistake. They're like bloodhounds, Miss Lloyd. They've got noses that can sense misdemeanours from miles away. If they caught a whiff of wrongdoing, they'd skin me alive. They're like that, Miss Lloyd. Ruthless." The cup of tea Mrs Turner was holding could be heard rattling in its saucer. "Of course, if you've just so happened to bump into *Jenny* outside the confines of the home, then that's nothing to do with me, is it?"

"I will eventually go through the correct procedures," Sarah said. "Honestly, I will, but we're all adults here, right? Think about that poor eleven year old girl I've left at home sobbing her heart out. I mean, let's not forget, she's not only lost her sister, but the beloved family pet as well. Now, I'm damned sure you don't really want my dog cluttering up your lovely home. So what say I just spend ten minutes persuading *Penny* to give Toby back, eh? Just think, Julie, in ten minutes me and Toby could be out of your hair and on our way." Sarah tapped her nose. "And no one need be any the wiser. What do you say?"

Mrs Turner moved from the window and placed her cup back on the desk. "I'm positive I have absolutely no idea what you're talking about, Miss Lloyd," she said, sitting down. "What dog?"

Sarah laughed nervously. "You can't exactly miss him, Julie, he's like so big." Sarah indicated how big she thought Toby to be.

"I can assure you we do not have your dog here, Miss Lloyd," Mrs Turner said, shaking her head. "Or any other dog for that matter. Beachfield has a very strict no pets policy ever since our little darlings shattered the glass on the aquarium. Good Lord, can you imagine what the inspectors would say if they found a dog on the premises?"

"But he must be here."

"That's Impossible, Miss Lloyd." Mrs Turner's head shook a little faster.

"But he's got to be."

"Impossible." Mrs Turner's head started to blur.

"But he can't be anywhere else."

"Impossible." Mrs Turner's head was in danger of coming clean off its shoulders.

"But he's bound to be here."

"Impossible!" Mrs Turner slammed her fists down on the desk. "How could your stupid dog be here? We haven't even seen *Jenny* for the last five days!"

If the scene had been a stage-play, you could be forgiven for thinking the director had just told the cast to, *'Freeze.'*

Mrs Julie Turner eventually put her hand over her mouth, which did little to hide the look of horror on her face; the same look I'd once seen Elaine display after I'd tried to surprise her by dressing up as Superman.

Sarah gripped the desk for support. "What?" she said, her colour visibly disappearing. "What did you just say?"

"I think it's best you leave now," Mrs Turner said. She picked up a pen and pretended to write something. "You know the way out. Have a good day. Thank you for calling."

"You... you haven't seen her for five days? But that's impossible."

"Don't worry, Miss Lloyd. I'm sure she's fine. There's no need to get distressed. She'll turn up soon, just you wait and see."

"But what's she doing for money? For food? Oh, my God, you've lost her, haven't you? You've lost my daughter."

"We haven't lost her," Mrs Turner said, suddenly finding she was being forced to enjoy the company of one of those dreaded throat-mice. "We've just mislaid her, that's all. The relevant authorities have been informed. I'm sure they'll locate her very shortly. It's all standard practice. Now, if you don't mind, I do have a lot of work to get through."

"But how?" Sarah's fingers were going blue. "How the hell have you managed to lose her? Haven't you got systems?"

Mrs Turner's pretend writing got faster. "I hear what you're saying, Miss Lloyd, I really do, and I can understand how this must look. But we've got everything under control. I mean, we've always managed to find her in the past."

"This has happened before!"

"Please, there's no need to panic," Mrs Turner said, sounding like she was panicking enough for us all. "This isn't a prison, Miss Lloyd. Occasionally, *Jenny* has found ways of… shall we say, bypassing our routines."

"You mean she gets out?"

"Like I said, Miss Lloyd, we're not a prison. Our walls are to keep people out, not to keep people in."

"Oh my God!" Sarah said. "She's not coming back is she? Have you seen the way she dresses? She's probably been mistaken for a hooker. Oh my dear Lord, I can see it now. She's probably had her throat cut and been thrown in a skip. And Toby! Oh, my poor Toby. What'll happen to him?"

"Please try and stay calm, Miss Lloyd. I'm sure she's just playing one of her little hide-and-seek games. She'll be back with us in no time. Guaranteed."

"I think I'm going to be sick," Sarah said, putting her hand over her mouth.

Mrs Turner looked around frantically for something to offer. The best she could manage was to pass Sarah her wicker waste-paper basket, but the open-weaved sides of the bin were not designed to withstand projectile vomiting, and Sarah's lunch splattered through the slats. Mrs Turner's highly polished wooden floor had probably never seen such a mess.

The sight and smell of regurgitated food was obviously not something Mrs Turner was used to dealing with in the course of a normal working day, and she jumped from her chair with a scream. "I'll go and get you a glass of water and find one of the cleaners," she said, holding her nose and giving Sarah a wide berth.

By the time Mrs Julie Turner returned to her office, holding a glass of water and being followed by a foreign looking woman pushing a trolley full of cleaning materials, Sarah was passed out on the floor. Mrs Turner stopped dead as she spotted the open box-file, its contents rifled and strewn over her desk.

"Oh fuck," she whispered, dropping the glass.

A week after Sarah and I had left the office of Mrs Julie Turner, Sarah finally received the information from the prison location service she'd been waiting for. Jason Phillips, the biological father of Penny, slash Jenny, was coming towards the end of an eight year prison sentence for aggravated assault. The prison was seventy miles away.

Sarah completed all the paperwork and made the necessary arrangements for a visit. She still told Emma-Lou nothing.

Mother would have been horrified I was entering a prison. In her eyes it would make no difference that I was only walking through the prison gates because my assignee was visiting Penny's, slash Jenny's, biological father. Simply by association, I would be guilty of something.

"Mum, I'm just off to visit Jason Phillips in prison."

"Prison! What on Earth have you done now? Who's Jason Phillips?"

"He's Penny's, slash Jenny's, biological father."

"Who's Penny, slash Jenny?"

"She's the daughter Sarah gave up for adoption. She turned up on Sarah's doorstep a while back. But now she's disappeared. The children's home she was in have mislaid her."

"That's very careless of them, Mark. And what's all this about the lovely doctor Sarah giving children away? She seems far too nice for that."

"Anyway, Sarah and I managed to get a look at some confidential stuff that told us Penny, slash Jenny, has been regularly sneaking out of the home to visit Jason. Been going on for a while according to her records. According to the prison he's in, Jason is allowed two sixty minute visits every four weeks, so we're off to see if he's got any information about where Penny, slash Jenny, may be."

"What do you mean, managed to get a look? Mark, have you been snooping in other people's things again? Like that time I caught you going through my underwear drawer when you were twelve?"

"Mum, please. You said you'd never mention that again."

"Did I?"

"Yes. Oh, and one more thing."

"What's that?"

"We also found out Penny, slash Jenny, is pregnant. That's when Sarah fainted."

"Oh my God! What will I tell the Bridge club?"

"What? Mum, it's not mine for God's sake! She's only fifteen. What

do you take me for?"

"Well I never know what you're up to these days, Mark. You've become such a naughty boy since you died. Oh, this is all so very confusing. Perhaps doctor Sarah isn't the one for you after all. I do wish you'd stayed with Timothy's sister. She was so nice."

Passing through security became a bit tricky when the passive drug dog decided to go mental at me. Sarah was thoroughly patted down before we were led into a windowless, bare-bricked room, where several flimsy metal tables and chairs were arranged. Each of the six visitors, all women, were advised in turn which table to sit at. The prison obviously had no prior notification of *my* attendance and I had to remain standing.

Some minutes later, six prisoners, all men, were led into the room by several guards.

Jason was directed to sit opposite Sarah, who was staring at her shoes. Jason Phillips was about the same height as me, but much heavier. He obviously took full advantage of the prison gym. His head was shaved, presumably so everyone could see the jagged scar running from his temple to somewhere behind his ear, and I guess in his own menacing way he had a look that some women might find attractive. A bit like Jason Statham, I thought. (Number 9 on Elaine's list).

"You my new brief or something?" Jason said, making himself comfortable. "I didn't recognise the name when I filled out the visiting order. Almost didn't sign it." He ran his thumb over his lips. "Nobody said fuck all about any woman handling my release. What happened to Jerry? He get fired or something? Wouldn't surprise me. Little Jewish prick was useless." Jason lowered his head and tried to look at Sarah's face. "We'll get fuck all done if you can't even be bothered to look at me."

"I'm not your new brief," Sarah replied, without looking up.

"Then who the fuck are you? And to what do I owe the pleasure?"

Sarah slowly lifted her head.

I was just about to introduce myself to Jason, when I sensed someone standing behind me. I turned to find myself staring at a bright red tie with the word *Cymru* written on it just below the knot.

"So who's this then?" David said, pointing at Sarah. "And what does she want with my man?"

All the air in my lungs immediately went on vacation. My knees buckled, and David had to catch me in those enormous hands of his. When he'd been alive, I could only guess at the power contained in those hands. Now we were both dead, I could feel it for real. In between the moments of blackness swimming in front of me, I could just make out the two ragged gashes on David's wrists disappearing into the sleeves of his shirt.

"What the fuck's the matter with you?" David said, picking me up by my armpits so we could talk face to face. "You seen a ghost or something?" He laughed at what he believed to be a joke.

I tried replying, but nothing came out. David planted me back on my feet and let me go, presumably to see if I would stand up by myself. I wouldn't.

David gave me a dismissive grunt and left me sitting on the floor. He walked around behind Jason and stood there, arms folded, all kitted out in his visiting Mr Unlucky clothes, just the way I liked to remember him.

David wouldn't take his eyes off me, and I suddenly pitied all those poor unfortunates who'd seen David staring at them like this. I tried desperately to control my breathing and made several attempts to get my legs to understand their primary function. I also tried smiling, but thanks to various sections of my face actually being paralysed, I have no idea what facial expression finally materialised.

"You didn't answer my question," David said. "Who is she?"

I knew full well that David would shortly run out of words. Despite also knowing what happens when David runs out of words, I still couldn't force a reply. Fortunately for me, I wasn't the only person in the room with the knowledge to supply David with the answer he was looking for.

Jason had narrowed his eyes in concentration. He leaned forward until his nose was practically touching Sarah's, still rubbing his lips with his thumb. After several seconds of scrutiny, a slow smile started crossing his face.

"Well fuck me sideways with a wire brush," he said, clapping his hands loudly. "I remember you." He moved back from Sarah's face and started laughing loudly. "I never forget a face. And I certainly never forget a pussy." He stood up and called over to one of the guards. "Hey, Fat Mike. Lookee here." He pointed at Sarah. "Can't for the life of me remember her name. But I do remember dipping my dick inside it." Jason made thrusting movements and air-slapped what I assumed was an imaginary behind. The room fell silent as Jason continued to show everyone how he believed he'd dick-dipped Sarah. "Hey, Mike, can I take her to the special room? I'll let you watch. We all know how you like to watch."

Fat Mike showed no signs of moving. "Just sit back down, Jason, there's a good lad," he said. "And watch your language. There's ladies present."

Jason let out an orgasmic yell and rubbed his hands together. As he sat back down, the 20-plus stone prisoner sitting on the table next to us slowly turned in our direction.

"You're nothing but a prick, Phillips," the prisoner said. "And I'd appreciate a bit of peace and quiet so I can talk to my woman here." He pointed to a desperately thin, heavily face-pierced, nervous looking female sitting opposite him.

David marched over to the prisoner and looked down at the top of his tattooed head. "You say one more word and I'll rip your fucking head off and shit in your neck," he said. "You've got it coming, Slicer. Don't say I didn't warn you."

The prisoner thankfully ignored David's threat and went back to speaking to his woman.

David came back to our table with a satisfied grin on his face. The sort of grin I'd seen a thousand times. The one that said, *I've had a word. Everything's sorted.*

Sarah had gone back to staring at her shoes. We all had to strain to catch what she was saying. "There's something I need to ask you about," she said.

I looked at David and wondered who'd been the one to know him well enough to put him in his coffin wearing his favourite garb. Shaz maybe? Had she even attended the funeral? If so, then poor Jody would have been there as well.

"You fucking looking at me?" David said.

I broke my stare and shook my head vigorously. "No! God no. Sweet Jesus no. No, no, and seriously no. No with bells on."

"Then what's your problem?"

"You… you just remind me of someone, that's all."

"Don't tell me," David said. "Brad fucking Pitt. Get it all the time."

I nervously joined in his laughter, recalling that Brad Pitt was actually number 6 on Elaine's list.

"What do you mean have I had any visitors lately?" Jason said, in answer to Sarah's question. "Of course I've had visitors. I'm a very popular person. Pillar of the fucking community me." Jason looked over to Fat Mike. "Why, even the fucking Pope called in for a chat the other day, didn't he, Mike?"

Fat Mike half-smiled. "Whatever you say, Jason. Keep your voice down there's a good lad."

Jason leaned in towards Sarah. He put two fingers under her chin and lifted her head to meet his stare. "Last time I checked it had fuck-all to do with you what visitors I get," he said.

"I'm talking about one visitor in particular," Sarah said, closing her eyes. "I'm talking about Penny. Although she may have told you her name is Jenny."

Jason's fingers immediately let Sarah's head fall. I noticed Fat Mike taking a sideways step closer to our table and doing a bad job at hiding his interest in Sarah and Jason's conversation. Sarah lifted her head slightly.

"I assume you know who I'm talking about?" she said.

Jason studied Sarah hard. He rocked back on his chair and placed his feet up on the table. He started running his thumb over his lips again and used his free hand to start rubbing his crotch. "Every fucker in this room knows who you're talking about," he said, making sure his voice was loud enough for everybody in the room to hear. "But what's it got to do with you? You jealous or something? You want some of what she's been getting, eh? Hey, Mike, I reckon she's jealous. What do you think? Best start getting the special room ready. Looks like Jason has found himself another bitch on heat."

Before Fat Mike could offer a reply, Slicer gave out a groan and started heaving his weight out of his chair. He looked decidedly upset. Jason immediately pulled his feet off the table and picked up his own chair, holding it out like a lion-tamer.

"Sit down the pair of you!" Fat Mike said, jumping in between them. For a man who was a good thirty pounds overweight, he'd moved with surprising speed. "You've both only got a few months left. Let's not spoil it now, shall we?" He nodded to the other guards in turn to indicate he had the situation under control. Slicer growled and slowly returned to his chair. Jason waited until Slicer was comfortable, then set down his own chair. Presumably as a precautionary measure, Jason remained standing.

All attention in the room had been drawn to the two prisoners, so nobody, except me, noticed the ardent burning in Sarah's eyes.

Without warning she let out a long piercing scream and stood up, kicking her metal chair halfway across the room in the process. She caught hold of the table and flung it to one side, creating a clear space between herself and Jason.

"She's our fifteen-year old daughter, you sick, perverted bastard!" Sarah balled her hand into a fist, took one step closer to Jason, and took aim.

Mother had always instilled the doctrine that you should never, ever, under any circumstances whatsoever, absolutely no exceptions, hit a girl. Unfortunately for Sarah, Jason and Mother had never met, and the right hook Jason landed squarely on the side of Sarah's face robbed her of consciousness for a whole six minutes. It also kept wire in her jaw until the day she died.

Fat Mike moved like a gazelle - an overweight gazelle granted - but still like a gazelle. With the help of the other guards he wrestled Jason to the floor and applied handcuffs. In no time, and with no words, my last vision of Jason Phillips, the biological father of Penny, slash Jenny, was of him being dragged back through the door which he'd entered, restrained and silent.

As Sarah was being taken out of the room by medical staff, I noticed David wandering around like a lost child on a beach. I'd never seen him look so worried.

"He didn't know," he said to Slicer. "She never mentioned a word." He moved on to another prisoner and tried grabbing him by the shoulders. "She never said she was his daughter." He looked at each prisoner in turn. "Come on guys, we've all seen her. She's got to be older than fifteen, right? She's like what? Twenty, twenty-five?"

David sank down on Jason's vacated chair. "She never said she was only fifteen. She never said she was his daughter. He wouldn't have done it. Not if he'd known."

MELTING HEARTS

Two days into Sarah's hospital stay she got an unexpected visitor. She woke from a disturbed, pain-killer induced sleep, to find Fat Mike standing at the bottom of her hospital bed.

"Hi," he said, lifting a podgy hand. "Remember me?"

Robbed of any ability to speak by the metal contraption holding her lower jaw in place, Sarah nodded and drowsily lifted a hand in reply.

"I won't keep you long," Fat Mike said, grabbing hold of a chair and sitting at Sarah's bedside. "But I think there's some things you really should know. I hope you don't mind?"

According to Fat Mike, Sarah should know that Penny, slash Jenny, had never-ever told Jason she was his daughter. And under no circumstances had she ever once mentioned she was only fifteen. Hell, Fat Mike couldn't believe that himself.

Sarah pointed to a notepad and pen on her bedside cabinet. Fat Mike handed them to her. I looked over his shoulder as Sarah wrote.

So what did she tell him?

Fat Mike read the note and settled himself into the chair. He explained that Penny, slash Jenny, had written to the prison about three months ago stating she was doing some sort of university dissertation on the rehabilitation of violent prisoners. An appointment was set up with the Governor, who subsequently agreed that Penny, slash Jenny, could use Jason as her subject matter. Fat Mike had no idea how Penny, slash Jenny, had managed to persuade the Governor to let her regularly interview Jason in *The Special Room*. Hell, he wasn't even going to hazard a guess.

What's the special room?

Fat Mike looked at what Sarah had written. He got up off the chair and walked to the window, his back to us. "It's the room we keep for conjugal visits," he said. "There's not much in there. A bed. A sink. Conjugal visits aren't really allowed by law here, but the governor likes to be liberal about these sort of things. He's originally from Mississippi. They allow all sorts of things over there."

I don't think it had anything to do with the pain in her jaw, but Sarah winced and let out a groan. A solitary tear fell out of her right eye, rolled down her cheek, and disappeared through the cage around her mouth.

Fat Mike moved from the window and made his way back to the chair. "Are you absolutely sure she's his daughter?" he said. "And she's got to be older than fifteen, right?"

Yes, I'm sure she's his daughter, and yes, she's only fifteen. Why are you so concerned?

Fat Mike slowly shook his head. "You know you've signed his death warrant, don't you?" he said, reading the note. "You can get away with having killed your wife, your mother, even a bus stop full of blind grannies complete with their guide-dogs. But the minute you're tagged as a kiddy-fiddler." Fat Mike drew his index finger across his throat.

I'll repeat, why are you so concerned?

"Just call me an old softy," Fat Mike said, smiling, "but I've sort of come to like having him around. I wouldn't want to see any harm come to him just because of some old grudge. Because that's what this is, right? An old grudge?"

Old grudge! He's been taking advantage of his own mentally disturbed daughter you imbecile. He deserves everything he gets. I'm feeling tired now. Thanks for dropping by.

"Whoa, Sarah!" I said. "Who said anything about Penny being mentally disturbed? Okay, so she's bluffed her way into a prison and apparently started carnal relations with someone who she knew was her biological father, but come on, you're not qualified to make such sweeping statements. You're not a real doctor you know, despite what Mother thinks."

Fat Mike shifted in his chair. "Look, I can see you're upset with him. Hell, the whole prison could see that." Fat Mike attempted to laugh, but it came out more as a snort. I noticed sweat beads had started forming on his brow. "But I've sort of been wondering. Even if what you're saying is true, is there any chance you can help me out here? I mean, what's done is done, right? No point in making matters worse, don't you think? This whole thing is a mess, so why don't we, as responsible people, try and put it right?" Fat Mike stood up and wiped his brow with his sleeve. "Listen, I know you seem to have some issues with him, but I'm sure you wouldn't want to see Jason hurt. I mean really hurt. I mean hurt bad." Fat Mike made his way to the window. "So I was sort of hoping you could come and see him again. When you're better of course," he added quickly. "Then perhaps you could drop into the conversation that, oh, I don't know, something along the lines that you were really pissed off with him and you were sort of wrong about the whole fifteen year old daughter thing." Fat Mike remained looking out of the window. "Don't get me wrong, I think you should still press charges against him for punching you like he did. That alone will see him kissing goodbye to his release date and tag another year or two onto his sentence." Fat Mike turned from the window and made his way back to the chair. "But isn't that punishment enough?" Fat Mike cocked his head to one side and carried a look that suggested he was satisfied with his work so far. "Because she's not really his daughter, is she? And really? Fifteen? Come on. Perhaps when you come to tell him you got things a bit wrong, you could say it just loud enough for the other prisoners to hear. Especially Slicer. He was the guy on the next table. Remember him?"

Sarah had been furiously scribbling during Fat Mike's speech.

Sorry to have upset your cosy little arrangement. Jason was telling the truth when he said you liked to watch, wasn't he? I've already written a letter to your Governor, you fat, twisted sicko. By the way, Penny's pregnant. Jason will be the child's father and grandfather at the same time. How fucked up is that? Now go screw yourself!

Fat Mike put the note in his jacket pocket and left.

The day before we were released from hospital, Sarah and I received the news Fat Mike had anticipated. A silver-haired newsreader looked down at us from a small TV mounted on a swivel-arm above Sarah's bed.

'A thirty-two year old man was found hanged to death in his cell yesterday at East Moorlands Prison. Jason Phillips was coming to the end of an eight year sentence for aggravated burglary. A prison service spokesperson has announced an internal enquiry will be

conducted...'

Sarah slumped back in her pillows and closed her eyes, her chest rising and falling rapidly. If I could, I would have asked a nurse to fetch her a paper-bag. I immediately wondered how Penny, slash Jenny, would take the news. Not well was my guess.

It took several weeks for Jason's body to be released. The internal enquiry held by the prison service found insufficient evidence to support any theories of wrongdoing.

Without any reasons to think otherwise, the coroner recorded a verdict of suicide.

I was one of only four people at Jason's funeral, one of which was the vicar, who stood at the graveside struggling against a wind which threatened to blow him into the grave if he got too close. I started thinking the committee might need to revisit their fourteen day turn around period in cases such as Jason's. It had been close on two months since his death, and, given the right circumstances, there was every possibility he could easily have been witness to the paltry gathering who'd turned up for his final send-off. Fortunately, he didn't seem to be anywhere in sight.

The vicar, obviously in a hurry to get out of the wind, didn't hang about with too many platitudes, and was the first to march away from the graveside. Fat Mike, who we'd heard had since left the prison service and was now stacking shelves in Asda, disappeared a few moments later.

The wind started bringing with it the type of rain that pierces skin, and as Sarah and I made our way from the grave to her car, my twenty-three years experience of being eyed-up as doggy-dinner sent a message down my spine. We were being watched. I stopped and turned quickly, just in time to catch a glimpse of piercing green eyes disappearing behind an old Oak tree some distance away.

The real Mark Ferris would have undoubtedly followed Sarah back to the comfort of the car and a nice, warm ride home. However, the new forthright Mark Ferris decided to remain in a freezing wet graveyard, staring at an old Oak tree whilst his nice, warm, comfortable ride went home without him.

Two sextons filled in Jason's grave in double-quick time, then disappeared into the sanctity of a small shed at the edge of the graveyard. With the place as quiet as the dead, Penny and Toby emerged from behind the tree and slowly made their way to the side of Jason's grave.

I darted behind a headstone as soon as they appeared, yet could still see that gone were the porn-star looks of the days when Penny had first turned up at Sarah's house. She'd had her hair cut tight to her head; a sure sign of lesbianism according to Father. Her once brilliant blue eyes had dulled, and were ringed with dark circles. Her face, always so unblemished, was pock-marked with angry red spots, and her clothes were ill-equipped to deal with the weather. Sodden black leggings and trainers were accompanied with a plain white t-shirt, not long enough to cover the belly-button ring dangling from her swollen abdomen. A short denim jacket, too small to do up, was doing nothing to stop the rain from getting through to the t-shirt underneath. She looked like the sort of teenager Elaine reckoned the courts dealt with every day. From my distance, I couldn't tell whether the moisture on Penny's face was a result of tears, or simply the rain.

Toby didn't seem to be fairing much better either. His blackness had lost its sheen, and he was a lot thinner than he should have been. He'd somehow lost his collar, and moved with signs of a limp in a back leg. Despite being a creature spat out from the inner workings of the underworld, I couldn't help but feel slightly sorry for him. One thing he had retained however was his sense of me being about. Every time I stuck my head out from behind the headstone, he looked directly at me and barked.

Penny knelt down in the mud next to Jason's grave. She planted a small flower on the mound of earth, then lifted her head to the sky. "I'll make her pay, Jason, I promise," she said, shouting through the rain and wiping her face in the sleeve of her jacket. She placed both hands on her pregnancy and addressed her bump. "She robbed me of having proper parents. Now she's trying to do the same to you."

An hour later, Penny and Toby disappeared into the basement flat of a house which was well past its Victorian heyday. I had no doubt that at some time in the distant past, the house would have contained an English family of unquestionable pedigree complete with a retinue of servants and maids; but no longer. I sat on the steps leading up to the main door and asked the Jamaican gentleman sitting next to me what he intended to do with the piece of wood he was whittling with his switch-blade. I also asked him if he had any idea where we were.

"You see, I've sort of lost my bearings," I said. "I've been concentrating so much on staying out of Toby's sight, I haven't really taken much notice of where we've been walking."

Perhaps his English wasn't good, or perhaps he just wasn't in a talkative mood. Either way, the Jamaican ignored me, and we sat in silence watching all manner of creeds and colours making their way in and out of the house. Father would have used the comings and goings of the house as another justification for an attack on British immigration policy.

"I tell you, Mark, God is giving the world an enema, and all the shit is washing up on our shores. Sometimes, I think it would have been better to let the bloody Krauts win. At least the Germans wouldn't put up with this sort of nonsense."

Ironically, Father had no difficulty in dealing with the fact that the specialist who handled his Alzheimer's was a Mr Stanislovski; a gentleman who, no doubt, would have been in no position to practice medicine had the *bloody Krauts* actually won.

It was nearly dark before Penny and Toby emerged from their basement. I noticed Penny had attempted to hide the worst of her face by applying several layers of make-up, and was wearing an ill-fitting yellow summer-dress. Watching Penny struggle through the biting wind in a summer-dress reminded me that someone once said, *'There's no such thing as bad weather, just the wrong clothes.'* Wasn't it that swearing Scottish comedian who Father had to pretend he didn't like in front of Mother? At least the rain had stopped.

A brisk forty minute walk brought us to a darkened corner of an Asda car-park. Penny made her way to a black Volvo estate car with tinted windows, which was lurking just in front of some recycling bins. She walked around to the passenger door and put her hand on the handle before turning to Toby.

"Okay, Toby, you know the drill. You wait here and I'll call you if the dirty bastard gets too rough." Toby barked once and dutifully laid himself out on the floor. "Don't worry," Penny said, ruffling the dog's head. "The old git never takes too long." She rubbed her stomach. "And he can bloody well pay extra for this. When I've finished we'll get some supper, I promise." Penny opened the passenger door and the illumination afforded by the interior light gave me a brief glimpse of the portly, eager looking man sitting in the driver's seat. Penny got in and closed the door behind her. Everything plunged back into darkness.

It took a few seconds for me to fully understand the situation.

"Oh my God, Penny!" I said, making my way to the car. "Get out of there this instant." The new forthright Mark Ferris made his way closer to the car with the intention of opening the passenger door and dragging Penny out by any means possible, but Toby decided he liked the new forthright Mark Ferris about as much as he did the old one, and looked at me as if to say, *Take one more step. Go on, I dare you.*

During the ten minutes Penny was in the car, I wondered, from a safe distance, if I was ever going to find my way back to Sarah. As far as I was aware nobody knew where I was, including me. Was it normal for dead people to simply wander away from their assignees? Had the committee ever completely lost track of someone? Could I perhaps retire to the seaside without anyone noticing? I loved the seaside; Elaine hated it. She reckoned the combination of sand, sea, children, and old people, was a mix that should never be encouraged under any circumstances.

Almost as soon as Penny stepped foot out of the car, it sped off.

"Dirty bastard," Penny said, wiping her mouth with the back of her hand and spitting on the floor. She looked at Toby and waved a few twenty pound notes in the air. "Come on, Toby. Let's eat!"

Toby barked and got up off the floor, his tail bouncing.

Penny had only taken a few steps when she stopped and clutched her stomach, her mouth silently creating an *O*. I immediately recalled a documentary I'd once seen about some Danish soldiers on patrol in Afghanistan. The cameraman had bravely caught the instance a Taliban bullet had pierced the upper arm of one of the *Soldaats*, and the look of shock and horror on that soldier's face was the same look Penny was now displaying as she clawed at her stomach. I was pretty sure there were no Taliban snipers lurking around in Asda's car-park, and deduced that something else must be wrong. Toby sensed trouble too, and started circling Penny's feet, looking up at her, whimpering.

"Oh fuck, this hurts," Penny said, sinking to her knees. She managed to crawl over to one of the recycling bins and sat against it. She banged the back of her head against the bin in rhythm with her words. "Oh, fuck, fuck, fuck. It's not time yet, Toby. Something's wrong." Even in the darkness I could see the yellow of the dress showing signs of reddening around the groin area. Penny tentatively slid a hand under the dress and winced. She brought the hand in front of her face; it was completely sodden with blood.

"Oh my God, I need help, Toby," Penny said, lying on her side. Toby sniffed the bloodied hand several times, then licked it clean. Penny closed her eyes and bit her bottom lip until it bled, her face as full of pain as that poor Danish soldier's.

I ran across the car-park to the entrance of the store, and, after getting my breath back, screamed in the ears of the bored looking woman manning the customer service desk. I begged her to call an ambulance, but she was more interested in the customer who was requesting a bunch of flowers to be gift-wrapped. I continued screaming until I could scream no more. I remembered that within seconds of being shot, that Danish soldier was being attended by an army medic, who immediately arranged for a helicopter to whisk the poor guy off to the nearest field hospital. Unfortunately, Penny was not a Danish soldier, and I was only a postman, not an army medic or helicopter pilot. By the time I started running back across the vast expanse of car-park to Penny, the rain had started again.

I'd never been good with blood and gore; even old black and white Hammer horror movies were enough to send me scuttling behind the sofa. Elaine loved horror movies, and enjoyed a good carve up, counting *Texas Chainsaw Massacre* as one of her all time favourites. She may have been better equipped therefore to deal with the sight presenting itself when I got back to the recycling bins.

Whatever had been growing inside Penny's stomach was now lying in a bloody puddle between her legs. If it was a baby, it wasn't like any baby I'd ever seen. I couldn't make out if it was actually moving, or if it was just the weight of the rain pushing the viscous blob around. Penny's eyes were shut, and her stomach was violently contracting as if there may still be more to come. Her bottom lip was dangling at a strange angle where she'd almost chewed it off, and the original colour of the summer-dress was unrecognisable for the amount of blood it had accepted into its fabric. Something flitted across my mind about cotton holding four times its own weight in liquid.

Toby licked Penny's face in an effort to revive her from her loose grasp on consciousness, then turned his attention to the bloody mass on the floor between her legs. He sniffed at it several times before dragging it away behind the bins, leaving a smear of red on the floor behind him as he went. At the sound of Toby devouring his promised supper, I made a mental note to ask the committee if it was normal for a dead postman to spend so long being sick.

Crimson found me four hours later. I was leaning against one of the recycling bins, occasionally still retching. Penny and Toby were long gone.

"Oh, thank Christ," Crimson announced, resting her hands on her knees and gasping for air. "I've been looking for you for hours. The committee are going mental."

"Why?"

Crimson looked around to make sure no one was listening. "You're not supposed to wander away from your assignee like this," she said. "Nobody had any idea where you were." She lowered her voice. "And what's this I hear about you visiting brothels?"

"What? Crimson, what are you talking about?"

"Just something I heard, Mark, that's all." Crimson looked at her watch. "Come on, time to get you back to your assignee. Where you belong!"

"We can't go," I said, as Crimson took my hand. "You see there was this girl and… and she must need medical attention. We need to find her and get her to a hospital. I mean, look at all this blood." I swiped my arm in the general area around me, but the rain had washed most of the evidence of Penny's labours away.

Crimson gripped my hand tighter. "Sorry, Mark," she said. "I can see you've been having a bad day, but honestly, we really do have to go."

For the next two months, Penny and Toby disappeared from the radar. Sarah constantly bombarded Mrs Turner with telephone calls, but the home had not seen or heard anything. The relevant authorities only had limited resources to try and find someone who, in their opinion, obviously didn't want to be found, but insisted they were doing all they could. All hospitals in the area were on alert for anyone fitting Penny's description, as were all dog pounds for anything resembling Toby's. Sarah took to pinning photos of Toby on lampposts; checking in the odd skip for Penny as she went.

I was ignored, naturally, when I tried to tell people that the last time I'd seen Penny she certainly hadn't looked like the blonde bombshell the police photo-fit had drawn up. I also tried telling anyone with any interest in the matter that if they checked the basements of all the squalid houses within a forty minute walk of a certain Asda's car-park, they may be on to a winner. Especially if they could find one with a Jamaican gentleman whittling wood on the front steps. As expected, I was also totally cold-shouldered when I mentioned Penny wasn't pregnant any more.

Sarah was also struggling to appease Emma-Lou's anguish. She constantly had to find ways of reassuring her that Penny and Toby were safe and sound, repeating that she was sure Penny would be in touch as soon as she got over her *issues.* Sarah conveniently left out telling Emma-Lou anything about Mrs Turner, Jason Phillips, Fat Mike, the funeral, the baby; basically all the things that might have suggested Penny was anything but safe and sound.

In an effort to relieve what was evidently an increasingly troubled mind, Sarah had slowly built up to doubling the dose of painkillers prescribed to ease the constant ache in her shattered jaw. Before bed she now regularly downed a large glass of wine, and, with the aid of a few over-the-counter sleeping tablets, Sarah subsequently found no problem in sleeping soundly through the dark hours of the night.

She therefore failed to hear the return of the skeleton.

My ears picked up the faint noises of movement from downstairs. I looked at the bedside clock: 3 am.

I called upon the new forthright Mark Ferris to help me make my way out of Sarah's bedroom to investigate. I noticed even he couldn't stop my hands from shaking as we crept down the stairs and into the living room. Another faint sound from the kitchen had us both diving for cover behind the sofa, him trying to persuade me it was probably only next door's cat.

"How can it be next door's cat?" I whispered. "Sarah ran it over, remember?"

The new forthright Mark Ferris had nothing else to offer, leaving me with no option. If I was to find out who, or what, was in Sarah's house, I would have to go and look for myself. I eventually crawled from behind the sofa, hiding behind as much furniture as I could on my way to the kitchen.

Penny's appearance was no better than it had been at Jason's graveside. If anything, it was marginally worse. The tight black t-shirt she wore showed evidence of painful looking rashes on her arms and neck. It also did nothing to hide her distended stomach. I was no medical expert, but my guess was she was carrying an infection of some sort.

"Oh, thank God," I said, making myself known. "Penny, you've had everyone worried sick. Emma-Lou is in bits. Mrs Turner is on the verge of losing her job. Sarah is going crazy mad mental." I made my way to her from the archway. "I've missed you as well," I whispered. "To be honest, things do get a bit boring around here without you. I don't like to speak out of turn, but your mother is a bit unexciting, isn't she? Did I ever tell you about my last assignee? No? Well why don't we settle down on the sofa and I'll tell you all about him. I'm very good at telling stories these days."

Penny ignored the opportunity to be regaled by my story-telling abilities, and remained standing at the kitchen sink, where she'd started peeling some organic potatoes.

In the excitement of Penny's return, I hadn't immediately noticed Toby sitting like an Egyptian statue in the corner of the kitchen. For once, he remained silent at my presence. He looked in desperate need of feeding.

"Ah, I see," I said, keeping one eye on Toby. "Of course, you're both hungry. Tell you what, you should have broken into mine and Elaine's house. You wouldn't have had to go to the trouble of preparing food there. Elaine says any food that takes longer than four minutes in a microwave is a complete waste of time. Our freezer is a homage to the ready meal, I can tell you. You could have been in, fed, and out, in no more than ten minutes max."

I sat on one of the kitchen chairs and replayed Elaine's lack of cooking skills in my mind. When I'd been alive, her refusal to cook had been somewhat annoying. Now it felt endearing. "Isn't that funny?" I said. "How we always seem to think better of people when they're not actually around any more. Mother hardly said one good word about Father when he was alive, and yet you should have heard her at the funeral, Penny. You'd swear he'd been some sort of saint."

My daydreaming meant I paid only passing attention as Penny chipped the peeled potatoes and placed them in a much under-used chip pan, sizzling away courtesy of a complete bottle of extra-virgin cooking oil.

"Sarah doesn't do chips very often," I said. "If you do enough perhaps you can leave some for your sister as a treat."

When the pan was bubbling like a Jacuzzi, Penny placed a dry tea-towel over the top of it, then got herself on a chair and removed the batteries from the smoke-alarm. "Right, Toby, you go and make sure all the internal doors are open," she said in a whisper, placing the batteries in her pocket. "And be quiet about it, there's a good boy."

"Uh, Penny," I said, giving Toby a wide berth as he left the kitchen. "What the hell do you think you're doing?"

By the time Penny and Toby left through the back door, the fire was well under way.

For a while, I remained sitting in the kitchen, mesmerised by the flames. It was as if their deathly dance was sending me into some kind of trance. I recalled one or two of the boys in my class at school having a fascination with lit matches, and could sort of see the attraction. I never played with matches myself of course. Mother would have had a heart attack if I had.

"Mark! What on Earth do you think you're doing?"

"It's only a match, mum."

"A match with fire on the end of it, Mark. Fire! If you ask me, fire should be banned."

"Mum, stop talking rubbish. Fire is arguably one of the most important discoveries man has ever made."

"Try telling that to that poor Mr and Mrs Farthing... Or Joan of Arc."

Eventually, I snapped out of my stupor and realised exactly what Penny had done.

"Jesus Christ!" I said, springing off the chair and running upstairs. I tried shaking Sarah awake, but my hands cut through her shoulders like they were made of air. I ran into Emma-Lou's bedroom and tried the same exercise. Same result.

"Emma-Lou, wake up!" I screamed. Emma-Lou had always been a good sleeper and remained ignorant of my presence.

I ran back downstairs to check on the fire's progress in the vain hope it had miraculously extinguished itself. The kitchen was fully ablaze, and flames had started licking their way into the living room. Thick acrid smoke began meandering towards the stairs like a creeping snake. I blew on the smoke with all my strength to try and divert its inexorable journey upwards. After what seemed no more than a few minutes the flames had spread to the hallway, cutting off both front and back doors. Even if Sarah woke now, escape would be almost impossible. I ran back upstairs and into Sarah's room. She hadn't moved. I ran into Emma-Lou's room. She hadn't moved either. My legs were weak from all the running around, and I was forced to crawl back along the landing to Sarah's room. I sat amidst the swirling smoke on Sarah's bedroom floor and cried as hard as I had ever cried, the heat drying each tear the second it appeared. I wasn't sure if it was the smoke or the mouse that stopped any noise coming from my mouth.

The sound of a downstairs window exploding from the heat finally opened Sarah's eyes. It took her several seconds to figure out she couldn't breathe, and with no clean air to fill her lungs, it took a mammoth effort for her to crawl across the landing into Emma-Lou's bedroom. She managed to lift the smoke-filled body of her youngest daughter from her bed and into her arms, but had only taken one step towards the door when part of the bedroom floor gave way. Both bodies disappeared into the flames below.

A tap on my shoulder turned my head.

"Come on," Crimson said, taking my hand gently. "The committee want to see you."

Over her shoulder, through Emma-Lou's bedroom window, I could just make out Penny and Toby standing in the garden staring at the house as it burned. Toby spotted me and barked.

ERIC'S BOY

I sat in the wooden chair, my head bowed. With no flames to dry my tears, they fell in a puddle at my feet.

"It'll take us a short while to arrange all the paperwork, Seven-Three-Five-Nine," Mr T. said. "But don't worry, we'll get you packed off to your new assignee as soon as we can." He pushed a dossier across the desk towards me. "It's all standard practice. We'll send for you when we're ready. In the meantime, I'm sure Old Eric will be beside himself to see you again. Off you go."

I lifted my head and went to wipe my tears, only to find the fire had burned away both sleeves of my postman's shirt. Further investigation showed I had also lost my shoes, socks, and the bottom half of my trouser legs. The smell of smoke was everywhere.

Mr T. pointed behind me. I immediately found myself standing in front of Old Eric's office door, my new dossier tucked safely under my arm.

"Bloody hell, son! What happened to you?" Old Eric immediately put away his crossword.

I sat on the edge of his desk and put the dossier down. "My assignee just died in a fire," I said. "Turned out Sarah was right. The skeleton she had in the cupboard was mentally disturbed after all. If you don't mind, Eric, I really don't feel like talking about it."

Eric tapped his fingers on the desk. "Okay," he said, "but like I've told you before, son. You really need to learn to get over these things as quickly as possible. Otherwise, it'll be you that's going mental."

"But I'm only a postman," I said, shaking my head. "I can cry for days watching soap characters die, Eric. How am I supposed to deal with this? These are real people feeling real pain. I can't just pretend they don't matter. Anyway, like I said, I don't want to talk about it."

Eric made his way to me and put his arm around my shoulders. "Okay, then I guess I'll have to do all the talking." His face brightened so much I had to close my eyes.

"Please don't," I said. "I really can't face hearing about Elaine right now."

"And what makes you think the only stories I have concern your widow?"

"Well don't they?" I opened my eyes slightly, and removed Eric's arm from around me.

"Of course not, son." Eric said, making his way back to his chair. He sat down and looked at the ceiling. "Oh, hang on, come to think of it, you're probably right."

I opened my eyes fully and picked up the print of the Last Supper. "You really have no soul, do you?" I said.

"Yeah, well, death does that to you, son," Eric said. He picked up his glasses and started chewing on one of the arms. "When you've been dead as long as I have you get to realise how temporary life really is. I've learned to accept my assignees aren't immortal, son, so I have no problem dealing with the inevitability of their death. Don't get me wrong, the first twenty or so hurt a bit, but…"

"Twenty!"

"Or so." Eric put down his glasses and crossed his arms. "Anyway, enough about dead people, let's get back to the living. Remember Charlotte?"

Eric must have had a dimmer switch secreted under his desk somewhere, because the brightness in the room suddenly reached Heavenly proportions.

"Charlotte?" I said, putting the print down. The only Charlotte I knew was my next door neighbour.

Eric winked. "Don't try and tell me you've forgotten Charlotte?" he said. "The object of your imagination when you used to see to yourself." He made the necessary motion with his hand in case I had any doubts about what he was referring to.

I opened my mouth, but only a few incoherent noises got past the mouse.

"Don't try and deny it, son. I was there, remember? I spotted you nipping off to the toilet when Elaine was sleeping. *'Oh, Charlotte, what are you doing to me? Oh, Charlotte, don't stop. Oh, Charlotte,*

Charlotte, Charlotte.' You weren't as quiet as you thought, son. Even Elaine heard you now and again, which always made us chuckle."

On an embarrassment scale, listening to Old Eric mock me about my masturbating practices was about as high as it could go. I could actually *see* the redness coming from my face; it was exuding more heat than the fire.

"Eric, you really are sick," I said. "Is nothing sacred to you?"

Eric shrugged his shoulders. "Not really, son. Do you want to hear about the lovely, delectable Charlotte or not?"

There followed several moments of awkward silence, during which I attempted to get an imprinted image of Charlotte sunbathing in her garden out of my head. Eric had been right of course, it was this image I used to help me along on the odd occasion I took sexual matters into my own hands and *Godlessly self-gratified.*

Mother was going nuclear.

"What sort of man have you become, Mark? You've just watched that nice doctor you were with die in a fire, you're sitting next to a picture of our Saviour's last meal, and all you can think about is some semi-clad harlot sunbathing in her garden."

"Sorry, mum. It's this death lark. It does strange things to you."

"You know, I'm seriously considering whether I should ever ask Timothy's sister over again. God only knows what you might do to the poor girl."

"Okay, what about Charlotte?" I eventually said, hurtling head-first into what I knew was likely to be a whole world of pain.

"Well," Eric said. "You really aren't going to believe this, son."

He was right. According to Eric, it appeared my wife had been hiding a long-held fantasy from me. Namely, she fancied introducing another woman into her sexual equation.

"Of course, as soon as she mentioned the possibility to that lawyer he got on the case without delay," Eric said, his eyes bulging. "He'd already built up a certain chemistry with Charlotte by flirting with her over the fence whenever she was out sunbathing. Didn't take long for his persuasive charms to get her interested."

"Eric, you've got to be joking," I said, my breathing struggling to remain under *need the bag* levels. "Twenty years I was with Elaine.

Surely she would have said something? Given some sort of clue? No, you're making things up. You must be. Anyway, what about Charlotte's husband?"

"Oh, he left her months ago," Eric said, opening a drawer. "You could tell she hadn't had any action for a while. The three of them writhed around for hours. Couldn't make out whose arms and legs belonged to who. Or who was making the most noise. She's coming round again on Sunday. I can't wait." Eric waved the bag at me.

I accepted the bag and moved to one of the side walls, sliding down it until I was sitting like a sleeping Mexican. "Eric, why do you have to do this to me?" I said, placing the bag over my mouth. I tried, unsuccessfully, to stop the torrent of tears waiting behind my eyes.

Eric got off his chair and sat on the edge of his desk. "Do what?" he said, leaning over me. "That's all I'm doing is keeping you informed. Admit it, you'd go mad with curiosity if I didn't."

"A simple *'she's doing fine'* would suffice, Eric." I tried to breathe without the aid of the bag but failed.

"Oh, don't be so boring," Eric said. "What fun would that be? Can't you just be happy Elaine is enjoying herself in your absence?"

I shook my head and talked through the bag. "No, I can't," I said, balling myself up as tight as I could. "I'd like nothing more than to curl up here and die. I wish I'd never been born. I feel like I never existed." I realised I sounded perhaps a tad over-dramatic.

Eric let out a deep breath and sat down beside me. "Of course you existed, son," he said, putting his arm around me. "We all existed. You just chose not to make much of a mark, that's all." Eric let out a single laugh. "Hey, that's funny isn't it? No mark for Mark."

"Hilarious," I said, the bag making the word sound like, *'hid eyes are us.'*

"Now there's no use beating yourself up about it, son," Eric said. "There's millions of people who've found themselves in front of the committee without ever having made an impression whilst alive. Think about it logically. If everybody was a somebody, who the hell would we ever look up to? Imagine a world where Elvis was just one *King* amongst many. There'd be mayhem, don't you agree? Yep, I'd say you're in pretty good company being a nobody, son."

Once again, Eric's attempt to cheer me up, if that's what it was, was not helping. It took a while for my breathing to sustain itself without the bag.

"So what about you, Eric?" I said, using the wings of his robe to wipe the tears from my face. "What mark did you leave on the planet? What wonderful legacy did you leave in your wake?"

Old Eric stood up and slowly stretched himself. "Haven't we already had this conversation, son?"

Here we go, I thought. Alzheimer's at play. "No, Eric, we haven't. We were about to, but then we got interrupted by Crimson."

"Crimson? Who's Crimson?"

I had to bite my lip and take a moment. "She's my messenger, Eric, remember?"

"Oh, that's right. She's the one you're…"

"Eric! Please can we stay on subject for a change?"

Eric sighed. "Okay, if we must," he said, putting his hands on his hips and bending back and forth. He stopped and frowned. "Sorry, what subject *was* that exactly?"

I closed my eyes and rubbed my temples. I took a few deep breaths and reminded myself that Alzheimer's was a cruel, cruel affliction. "You were about to tell me all about yourself, Eric," I said softly.

"Was I? I thought I was telling you about Elaine's threesome."

I put the bag to my mouth and shook my head.

Old Eric moved to the opposite wall and started doing press-ups against it. "Anyway, we don't need to delve into my life story, son," he said. "It's really not that interesting."

I'd always found being told I'm not going to be interested in something highly frustrating. Especially when you've not been told anything about the subject on which you're apparently not interested. I had no idea what Eric had done when he'd been alive, but telling me I wouldn't be interested made me more than interested to find out.

I took the bag from my face. "Please, Eric, I'd really like to know," I said

Eric made his way back to his chair. "Oh, all right. If you insist." He fussed with his robe, then put his glasses away and rested his hands on the desk, palms down. He puffed out his chest, giving the impression he was preparing to sit in the same position for quite some time. Buddha-like.

"Well don't stay down there," he said. "I can hardly see you."

I used the wall to help me up. I sat on the edge of Eric's desk and tentatively placed the paper bag in front of me. I gave Eric a look I hoped suggested I didn't want to hear anything that would require me having to use it again anytime in the near future.

"Believe it or not I used to be somebody in my day, son," Eric said, putting the bag away. "No, honestly, I did. You see, I used to be… how can I put this?" Eric closed one eye and looked at the ceiling, as if the right words were etched up there somewhere. "Called upon, I suppose you could say."

I frowned. "Called upon? What, like a plumber?"

Eric sighed deeply. "If you're not going to take this seriously, son, then I'm not going to bother," he said. "We'll just carry on with the story of Elaine's threesome."

"I'm sorry, Eric." I held up my hands in surrender. "Please, continue."

"Look, I know it's difficult to believe, son, but people really used to look to me for guidance. A sort of father figure I guess. Turned to me for all sorts of advice and help. In today's terms I suppose I'd be like one of those life-coaches. Or Google."

Experience told me people suffering with Alzheimer's occasionally talked gibberish, but Eric's illness had obviously become tinged with a hint of delusion. "Eric, what the hell are you talking about?" I said. "Google is a world-wide information super-highway. Simultaneously, it can be the most powerful source of knowledge known to man, or the biggest pile of gobbledegook you're ever likely to encounter."

Eric pondered for a moment, checking the ceiling for words again. "Yep, that pretty much sums up what I was all about," he said. "You see, I'd get asked all sorts of questions, son. Now, some I could answer, some I couldn't. Those I could answer I'd spout on about for ages, and those I couldn't… well actually I'd spout on about those for ages as well. It was one hell of a responsibility, son, I can tell you. People would hang on my every word. Can you imagine that?" Eric looked at me and smiled "What am I saying? Of course you can't."

"Eric, I have absolutely no idea what you're talking about," I said. "What sorts of questions? And how did people get to ask these so-called questions? Were you like a teacher or something?"

Eric clasped his hands together. "Telepathy!" he said.

"Telepathy?" I shook my head and rolled my eyes. "Eric, now I know you're talking rubbish. You do not have the power of telepathy."

Eric laughed and removed his crossword from the desk drawer, waving it at me. "Of course I don't," he said. "But five across just suddenly jumped into my head." He applied his glasses and looked at the crossword. "Communication of thoughts without using speech, writing, or any other normal methods. Nine letters." He took off his glasses and put the crossword away. "Now, what were we talking about?"

"Oh, for God's sake, Eric, we were talking about how you used to be some sort of omnipotent Guru delivering enlightenment to the masses. Although, we haven't quite yet established how this was managed." I noticed a sudden hint of sarcasm in my voice. Mother would be extremely displeased, as would Emma-Lou's geography teacher, Mr Wilkins. "Look, I'm sorry, Eric," I said, "but even with my limited knowledge of the ways of the world this all sounds a bit far fetched."

"Truth is often stranger than fiction, son," Eric replied. "But hey, if you want me to go back to that night Charlotte, Elaine, and…"

"No!" I stood up and waved my hands. "That's okay. Please, carry on." I sat back down.

Eric faintly nodded his head. "Very well. Like I was saying, I used to get all sorts of queries thrown my way. Some people would come and speak to me personally, others would send representatives." Eric lowered his voice. "And get this, son. Some would even say I'd spoken to them without ever having met me. How mental is that?"

"Okay, okay, hang on a minute," I said. "Let me try and get this straight. You were some kind of wise old sage?"

"If you like."

"And people would come to you from far and wide to ask you stuff?"

"Yep, something like that."

"And when did all this happen, Eric?" I asked. "What timeframe are we talking about here?"

Eric chose to ignore the hint of lightness my voice had found, and continued unabashed. "All well before your time, son." he said. "In fact, it was well before most people's idea of time."

"So before mobile phones and e-mails then?"

Eric drummed his fingers on the desk. "You might think this is all a joke, son. But it was no joke at the time, I can tell you. Everybody and his wife were after a piece of me. I had people coming to me with problems I didn't even know existed. Have you ever helped someone with a problem, son? Oh no, that's right, you were just a postman. Your primary function was to make sure people got their bills on time. You delivered evil. I delivered people from it."

I could tell Eric was upset.

"Eric, I'm really, really, sorry," I said. "But you must understand how this is all sounding to me? Look, were you like a doctor or something?"

"In a roundabout way," Eric said, still drumming his fingers. "People always said they felt better after talking to me, which correct me if I'm wrong, never happened in your lifetime."

Eric was right. I couldn't recall anyone ever saying they felt better for having had a conversation with me, but I was struggling to believe they'd feel any better after speaking to Old Eric either.

"So were you like a therapist?"

Eric's finger drumming got louder and more frantic. "No, I wasn't a bloody therapist!" he said. "For a start I never charged four hundred quid an hour for my services. My guidance was far more spiritual than finding out if you fancied having sex with your mother. It was more fluid. More intangible. More airy. More make of it what you want. More ethereal, so to speak."

The only other time I could remember someone using the word *ethereal* in a sentence, was when Father had told me about some music festival he'd attended on the Isle of Wight at the end of the sixties.

"Hundred and fifty thousand of us there were. Dylan was on great form. Hadn't performed in three years thanks to his motorbike crash. It was like the second coming, Mark. The bloody second coming I tell you. Ethereal even."

"Eric, did you perchance attend the Isle of Wight festival in sixty-nine?" I asked, still unable to remove the air of sarcasm from my voice.

"Sorry? What, where, when?"

"It's just you seem like the sort of person who would have fitted right in."

"Sort of person?"

"Well, can we safely assume the imbibing of illicit substances were involved in the dispensing of all this guidance of yours?"

Eric stood up and thumped the desk, making both myself and the print jump. "How dare you!" he said. "Never touched the stuff. Left all that bullshit to my son."

I had to grip the desk to stop myself from falling off. Perhaps it was because I couldn't envisage any woman finding an ancient, belligerent, soulless, oddly dressed, egotistical voyeur attractive enough to have children with, but I'd never have tagged Old Eric as being a father.

"Your son?" I said, squeezing the words past the mouse.

"Yes, my son." Eric sat back down. "There's no need to look so shocked. I was quite a looker in my day I'll have you know. Turned a few heads and no mistake. Plenty of notches on the Old Eric bedpost thank you very much."

"I'm sorry, Eric," I said. "It's just... I... well... I'm shocked, that's all. You, a dad?"

Eric must have touched the dimmer switch, because the room noticeably darkened. He started playing with the wings on his sleeve. "Yes, well, to tell you the truth I was a bit shocked myself at the time." Eric shifted uncomfortably in his chair. "I don't even think he was mine really. He was born when I was away on tour. Bloody well conceived when I was away on tour as well if you ask me."

I knew it. Eric *had* been in a band after all. "What instrument did you play?" I said. "I bet it was the drums. You look like a drummer. Did you have any hits? What was your name? I bet Father has heard of you. He knows all the bands from the sixties. Please don't tell me it was *The Doctors of Destruction*." I chuckled nervously at the possibility.

Eric shook his head slowly. "Sorry to disappoint you, son," he said. "But I'm about as musical as a fart."

"Oh, right. It's just when you said about a tour."

"Well, perhaps pilgrimage, or even crusade, would have been a better way to describe it. You see, through the grapevine, I'd heard people were grumbling about how difficult it was to find me. So I decided, what the hell? I'll go to them instead. Put myself out there so to speak. Should have seen some of their little faces when I started rocking up in various neighbourhoods. It was a sight to behold, son, I can tell you."

I had no idea what Eric was talking about, but decided it was comforting to have him rambling about something other than my wife's sexlife. I determined to try and keep it that way.

"So, what's the story about this son of yours?" I asked.

Eric ran his index finger over the top of the Last Supper. "The tour lasted a lot longer than I'd anticipated," he said. "Seemed people just couldn't get enough of me. I'd been away just over nine months when I started hearing rumours about the wife I'd left at home taking a fancy to the young carpenter we'd hired to put a new roof on the house. I decided to cancel the last few dates and go home to see what all the fuss was about. I was almost there when I got the news she'd popped a kid out. I'm sure I don't need to tell a bright spark like you that the maths didn't quite add up."

I thought about pointing out that my maths was appalling, but decided not to.

Eric let out a deep breath. "Let's just say that by the time I actually got home, the carpenter, the wife, and the boy-child she'd produced had all buggered off. I had to finish the bloody roof myself."

I was genuinely sympathetic, and under normal circumstances would have been happy to let the subject drop, but I didn't want to run the risk of Eric suddenly launching into tales of Elaine's activities. "So what happened next?" I said.

Eric stood up and stretched himself. "I used my connections to keep my eye on them as much as I could." He tapped the side of his nose as he sat back down. "There wasn't much happening back then that Old Eric didn't know about, son. I had people everywhere."

"And?"

The room's brightness seemed to dim further.

"That poor kid she brought into the world never stood a chance," Eric said. "In my opinion, all a kid needs to get on in life is strong parents, wouldn't you agree?" Thankfully, Eric didn't wait for an answer. "Truth is, the poor bastard didn't get one decent parent, let alone two. Firstly, that carpenter turned out to be at least half-gay, and then, work this out, the wife starts telling people she's a virgin!" Eric slapped his thigh and started laughing. "Have you ever heard of anything so absurd, son? Anything at all? It's no bloody wonder the kid went off the rails. Can you imagine being brought up by a half-gay carpenter for a father, and a mother who tries to persuade everyone she's unique in the art of insemination?"

I waited until Eric's forced laughter subsided. "If you don't mind me asking," I said, still eager to keep his mind away from any tales of Elaine's pleasure. "What happened to him?"

Eric rolled his head from side to side, letting out a sigh at the crick in his neck. "Well, at first, it looked like he was going to follow fashion and become a half-gay carpenter as well." Eric looked to the heavens and stretched out his arms. "But then his rationally-challenged mother lets him go on holiday with some dubious looking friends of his. And we all know what happens when youngsters get some sun, sea, sand, and shared saliva down their necks, don't we?"

I nodded sagely despite having had no personal experience of such holidays.

"Well guess what?" Eric continued. "Lo and behold! Miracle of miracles. He comes back with some right old slapper on his arm. Years older than him. More experienced in every department, if you know what I mean? I had my people do some digging and by Christ she didn't sound like good news. Apart from having been around the block a few times, she apparently also liked to dabble in certain mind-altering substances. Before you know it, she's persuaded the boy to give up his day-job and go on a bender to end all benders. Even took a few of his friends with him. We're not talking about a weekend in Prague, son. Oh, no. We're talking about three years on the piss."

"Three years!"

"Yep. Cut a long story short, the stupid, wine-soaked, drug-addled, prostitute-shagging hippy gets himself so far off the planet he starts rubbing people up the wrong way by believing he's some sort of *King*."

"Ah, now we all know there's only one *King*," I said, leaping off the desk and immediately adopting the pose.

"Do you have to, son?"

"Sorry, Eric. Go on." I sat back down.

"Well, as you can imagine, the authorities start taking an interest in the stupid bugger. Next thing I know he's been arrested."

"What for?"

"God knows. Being an arsehole probably. Although, if I remember rightly, there was some talk of him having vandalised a building or something. After the bloody lead to help pay for more drugs, no doubt. Anyway, just for a laugh, at the trial the judge asks him what he's actually meant to be the *King* of."

"What did he say?"

"Now there's the rub, son. The idiotic git was apparently so shit-faced on whatever that hooker was feeding him, he couldn't come up with an intelligent answer."

"So did he get sent to prison?"

"No. The judge must have got bored with the drunken buffoon's nonsense. He released him on the proviso he never set foot in his jurisdiction again. Told him to go home and get his shit together."

"And did he?"

"Did he hell! Him and his band of out-of-work, free-loading gypsies wandered into a notorious trouble-spot looking for kicks. My connections refused to follow him any further. Said it was too dangerous. Never saw or heard of him properly again."

"Oh my God, Eric. I'm so sorry."

"Ah, that's all right, son," Eric said, waving a dismissive hand. "It was all a long time ago. Like I said, I don't think he was mine anyway."

"So what do you think happened to him?"

"Lord only knows. There were reports he'd gotten himself beaten to death by a lynch-mob for stealing someone's donkey, but then I heard talk he'd been seen hanging about after that." Eric shrugged his shoulders. "All water under the bridge now."

"What about his mother and the half-gay carpenter?"

"Dropped off the face of the Earth. Wouldn't surprise me if the carpenter ran away with Mr Right. Also wouldn't surprise me if the wife ended up in a loony bin. Virgin my arse!... Anyway, enough of all this rubbish. Let's talk about something else."

Desperate to avoid Eric moving onto more disturbing matters, I quickly picked up my new dossier. "Shall we have a look at who my next assignee is?" I said, waving the dossier in the air.

The room brightened. "Ooh, yes please." Eric clapped his hands together like a child in a sweet shop.

I opened the dossier and removed the solitary note. Knowing there probably wouldn't be much information to keep a conversation going for long, I read as slowly as I could. "Roger Miller: Twenty-two years old: Unmarried: No kids: Lives and works with his father: Mother deceased: Practices Judo and likes to play cards." I gave the dossier a shake.

"Ah, I remember one of my sportsmen," Eric said, looking out through an imaginary window.

"I don't think cards can really be considered a sport, Eric," I said, checking the dossier in case I'd missed anything. I hadn't.

"Young football player he was," Eric continued, missing my attempt at a joke completely. "Tipped to go far, but got caught by his manager getting a quick blowjob in the dressing rooms. Now, don't get me wrong, I don't think the manager had anything against someone getting a quick blowjob, but he certainly didn't take lightly to the fact that the person whose mouth was clamped over his star player's manhood was none other than his own wife. Oh boy, oh boy, did he go mental or what? He picked up a boot and beat my assignee so badly the poor bugger was never the same again. By the time the surgeons had removed the studs from his noodle, my assignee had already been sold to a Finnish team in some unheard corner of the footballing world where he slowly festered to death. By the way, Finland is one fantastic place, son, I can tell you. Certainly made it onto my list of top ten places you should visit before you die. They're a crazy race of people, son, and no mistake. Not normal at all. Did you know they have an annual wife-carrying competition there? Now, if it was an annual wife-carrying-away competition, Elaine and that lawyer could enter, don't you think?"

I paced the room and waited for Eric's mirth to die down. "Well I hope my time with Roger Miller turns out to be normal," I said. "I reckon I've had enough excitement to last a lifetime... deathtime... whatever."

Eric stood up and moved to the door. He opened it and peered out, then closed it and made his way back to his seat. "Right," he said. "I reckon you've stalled long enough, son. Let's get back to Charlotte and the threesome."

"No, wait, let me just tell you something."

"What now?"

"Guess who I've seen?" I said, sitting back down.

Eric leaned back in his chair and closed his eyes. He put his fingers to his temples. "Was it Gandhi?" he said. "No, hang on, I'm getting the letter J. Was it John Lennon? JFK? Jim Morrison? Janice Joplin? Wait, wait, it's coming to me. Yes, yes, I see it now. It's, it's, ooh, wait, yes, it's," Eric opened his eyes. "How the bloody hell would I know? There's quite a lot of choice, son."

"It was David!" I announced.

Eric looked blank and shook his head slowly. "Sorry, but David is?"

Bloody Alzheimer's.

"For God's sake, Eric. David was my first assignee."

"Of course he was," Eric said, slapping his forehead. "The debt collector? Drowned or something didn't he?"

"He didn't drown, Eric. Granted he was in a bath, but he slit his wrists, remember? Anyway, I saw him when I went to visit Jason Phillips in prison. Now, Jason is, or at least was, the biological father of Sarah's skeleton in the cupboard, Jenny, slash Penny."

Eric held his hands up. "Okay, now you're really confusing me," he said. "Why don't we keep things simple and go back to the threesome? So, Charlotte comes over looking all sexy and..."

There was a knock on the door.

"Oh, you have got to be kidding," Eric said, thumping the desk. "I was just getting to the good bit."

As usual, Crimson was running with her breath in her fist, and was apparently about as late as late had ever been. Also, as should have been expected, my time with Roger Miller didn't turn out to be normal.

BAD HANDS

Roger's parents had been late in life having their only child. As a result, Roger was only seven years of age when his mother had passed away riddled with cancer at the age of forty-eight. Since then he'd been brought up by his father, Gary, now sixty-five and telling anyone who'd listen he was looking forward to his forthcoming retirement; to be celebrated with a well-earned round-the-world cruise.

Gary owned a reasonably successful property development company, and, after leaving school, Roger had gone straight to work in the offices of his father's business, where he now handled all the paperwork involved in the running of the firm. He was, of course, shortly expected to take full control upon his father's sail off into the sunset.

Roger had an unfortunate face; the type only mothers can look at for any length of time. His nose was too big, his eyes too close together, his lips too thin. He sported a mono-brow which grew to epic proportions despite constant pruning, and was tall and gangly with a wavy mop of black hair. Despite his man-equipment being in proportion with the rest of his appendages, in the six months since my arrival, there'd been no women willing to share his bed.

Roger and Gary lived together in a well proportioned detached house, which Gary had designed himself, and they sub-existed pleasantly enough. They talked sufficiently to get by, and rarely argued; a situation that would undoubtedly change if Gary ever found out Roger was systematically falsifying the company accounts in order to feed his two main hobbies: Poker and cocaine.

In the six months since Crimson had dumped me in the Miller household, I'd spent many an interesting hour watching Roger siphon off large portions of Gary's hard-earned income. At least my school's careers officer would be pleased I'd finally shown some interest in accountancy; albeit the creative type.

When I'd first arrived on the scene, Roger's poker had been limited to simple late-night TV games. A month later, he'd progressed to internet playing, and, two months after that, started getting himself involved in *proper* schools with serious players and serious money. The more recent cocaine habit helped Roger to survive on as little sleep as possible, which suited me fine as there didn't appear to be any photographs of Mrs Miller hanging around to keep me company. It also allowed him to stay awake during the marathon sessions of Texas no-limit he liked to attend. Both his gambling losses and his drug habit were, of course, funded unwittingly by Gary, and whilst I worried about the manner in which Roger found the cash to enjoy himself, I must admit I found the whole poker thing quite exciting.

Hey, Elaine, look what Roger has taught me to do. And here I would ruffle a pack of cards from one hand to the other like you see magicians do on TV. *Bet you'd be up for a game of strip poker now, eh?*

Once, and only once, had Elaine and I ever played strip poker. She'd come home from work slightly worse for wear after somebody's little retirement party at the office and suggested we give it a go. I eagerly fished out a pack of playing cards from a kitchen cupboard, thanking all the Gods I could think of for my luck. After all, it wasn't even a Thursday. Ten minutes later I was down to my socks, whereas Elaine hadn't removed a single stitch. She said something about not being in the mood any longer and suddenly decided she needed to go to Asda for some milk. As I gathered up my clothes from the living room floor, I tried telling her we had plenty of milk in the fridge. She didn't reply, but must have heard me, because when she came home a few hours later, all she had was a packet of biscuits.

Having never been a gambler, I had no knowledge of what separates a good poker player from a bad one. However, even I could work out that if you continuously lost, the possibility was you weren't that good. In the six months I'd been with Roger, I'd never yet seen him leave a game with more money than he'd entered.

Mother was going psychotic.

"What on Earth are you talking about, Mark?"

"Oh, mum, please keep up will you? Roger was holding a full house. He thought the other guy was bluffing, but it turned out he had a Royal flush. Long story short, Roger lost yet another three grand of his father's money."

"Does his poor father know?"

"Of course he doesn't, mum."

"Lord help me! Stealing from family, Mark. What sort of person have you turned into? Have you no shame? I thought it bad enough when you were bothering with that David the Murderer. You're going to end up back in prison, Mark, just like you did when you were knocking about with that doctor Sarah. I just know it. What will Timothy's sister think? Wouldn't surprise me if she never wants to see you again. You do know that gambling was invented by the Devil himself, don't you, Mark?"

I didn't have the heart to mention Father had secretly once told me he'd only managed to buy Mother's engagement ring thanks to backing the right horse.

As his dossier indicated, Roger practised Judo. Having never been sporty, I had no knowledge of what separates somebody who's good at Judo from somebody who isn't. However, even I could work out that if you continuously won, the possibility was you were pretty damned good. In the six months I'd been with him, Roger had won considerably more bouts than he'd lost.

Mother was perplexed.

"He does what?"

"He practices Judo, mum. It's unarmed combat which uses holds and leverages to unbalance your opponent. It trains the body and cultivates the mind through methods of attack and defence."

"Oh, Mark, you know I hate fighting. Remember that time I had to

come to the school because that girl picked on you?"

"Mum! You said you'd never mention that again."

"Did I?"

"Yes, you did. Anyway, it's not like real fighting, mum. It means gentle way in Japanese."

Roger was late, and it was obvious his Judo instructor, Paul Chang, was not happy.

"When one can use one's whole body at will, one can gain victory with one's body. Through further cultivation of the heart and mind, one can gain victory with one's mind. Having reached this point, how can one therefore be defeated by others?"

"Yeah, sorry I'm late coach. The traffic was mental." Roger quickly changed into his kit and joined the rest of the twenty or so people already involved in various grips and throws.

"Only when you have mastered all sixty-seven throws of Kodokan Judo, can you call yourself a master," Paul Chang shouted over the hubbub of grunts and groans as he slowly made his way around the melee. "And even then a true master will still better your mastery. A true master is master of all things. A true master is master of the wind, the fire, the soil. A true master is master of all masters. Remember this." Paul Chang reached the spot where Roger was having no difficulty in throwing the opponent he'd paired up with. "Please come with me for a moment, Roger," he said, taking Roger's elbow and leading him to a corner.

"What's wrong, coach?" Roger asked, wiping the sweat from his brow. "Look, I'm really sorry for being late. It won't happen again."

"I hope not," Paul Chang said. "Because it might spoil your chances of selection to the British squad for the European Championship in Helsinki next year."

It took a short while for Roger's face to finish its smile. "Are you shitting me?" he said. "You think I have a chance?"

"Of course you have a chance. Have you not noticed you are quite good, Roger? Your youth record speaks for itself, and your showing at the British Championship last month has stood you in good stead. I have spoken with some of my other colleagues within the performance cell programme, and as long as you remain medically fit and give us no other concerns to doubt you, I see no reason why you cannot be successful."

"Wow, boss, that's just fu…bloody wicked. I won't let you down, honest."

"Good. Now let us go to work on what I see as your only weak point, Roger. Your Yubisake Ate Waza."

"Fu…bloody hell, boss, speak English. My what?"

"Your Fingers Striking Technique, Roger," Paul Chang said, striking Roger with his fingers.

I'm not sure what might have constituted *other concerns* in the eyes of Paul Chang, but guessed that if he'd known Roger had been involved in a poker game for the last forty-eight hours, his keenness to include him in any squad would likely diminish. Especially when Roger had kept himself going by taking the occasional line.

"So, Helsinki," I said, following Roger back to his sparring partner. "You know, according to Old Eric, Finland is well worth a visit. Might even find myself entering the carry-a-wife-away competition, or whatever it's called. Best lay off the drugs though, Roger, eh? Maybe you should give up the poker for a while as well. We don't want anything messing up our chances, do we?"

Hey, Elaine, pretty soon I'm going to Finland and I'll be bothering with proper sportsmen. Might even get an autograph or two. What do you think of that? Bet that lawyer can't compete with that, can he? Do you know where my passport is?

Just as we left the training session, Roger got a text message inviting him to a game that night in a converted garage belonging to a bear of a man by the name of John Bolt, or *Johnny Two-Scars* for those brave enough to know him. In the underground world of unofficial poker, Johnny was a legend. He played hard, lost rarely, and was celebrated for the imaginative ways in which he never failed to collect his winnings. For a poker player, an invitation to one of Johnny's games was like receiving an edict from the Queen; it was something you simply daren't say no to. Roger's fingers worked like lightning as he eagerly accepted the invitation.

Daylight had started to filter through the gap underneath the garage door before Roger finally landed a hand. He was holding ace-king, and the flop had produced two aces, two queens, and a deuce. The only two players left in the pot were Roger and Johnny, and the sight of three aces had Roger's eyes rolling. He only had £500 left of the £5000 he'd entered the game with, and declared himself *'all-in.'*

I'd learned in the world of TV and internet poker that *all-in* is accepted for what it says. It means you have nothing left behind the money you're currently betting.

Unfortunately for Roger, Johnny's games were neither televised, nor to be found anywhere on the internet.

Johnny took a long draw on the cigar he was smoking and puffed the smoke towards Roger's face. "If you think I'm calling you've got another thing coming, boy," he said.

"So you're folding then?" Roger leaned in to gather the money in the pot. There was a collective intake of breath from the rest of the players. The sucking of air didn't go unnoticed by Roger, and he stopped short of collecting his anticipated winnings.

"What?"

Johnny blew another ring of smoke in Roger's direction. "Did I say anything about folding?" he said.

"But you either have to call or fold. You've got no other options."

"The question is, boy, what options do *you* have?"

"I don't understand."

Johnny got up from his seat and went to the makeshift bar in the corner of the garage. "Here's how I see it," he said, pouring himself a drink. "It's getting light outside, and I need my beauty sleep." Johnny made his way back to his chair and looked around the other players. "What do you say we call this the last hand of the night gentlemen?"

The other three players around the table all nodded their agreement. Johnny turned back to Roger. "Now, there's what? Two grand in the pot? Even if you win you'll still be three grand down, boy. I reckon if you're going to make any significant money out of tonight's efforts, it's got to be now."

"But I've got no money left," Roger said, holding out his hands as if to prove the point.

Johnny blew out more smoke and smiled for the first time since we'd arrived. The smile revealed a vast array of gold sitting in Johnny's mouth; it also stretched the two ugly, symmetrical scars on his cheeks into grotesque shapes. "Ah, but you do have that fuck-mobile you arrived in," he said. "What's that worth? Twenty grand? What is it again?"

Roger looked at the other players to make sure he had to answer. "It's a Mazda MX5," he said, when they all nodded. "But sorry, Johnny, I can't bet the car. You see, it's not really mine. It belongs to my father's company. Anyway, there's no way I'd bet that much."

Johnny turned to his fellow cohorts in turn. "Well that's fair enough, don't you think gentlemen?" They all made agreeable type noises. "I mean, it wouldn't be ethical to bet with money that doesn't rightfully belong to you, would it?" He turned back to Roger. "Come on then, let's turn the cards over and call it a night. I guess you'll just have to make do with being at least three grand down, boy. Call."

Johnny reached for his hand.

"Wait!" Roger said. I noticed beads of sweat forming on his brow, and his hands had started shaking badly. His right leg also began bouncing as if he had a troublesome baby on it. I couldn't tell if his actions were a result of the pressure he was being put under by Johnny, or simply a consequence of the cocaine he'd snorted the last time he'd visited the toilet.

"I need time to think," Roger said, re-checking his hand and calculating odds under his breath.

Eventually, he made a decision. The wrong decision.

Roger looked like he'd been electrocuted. He gripped the side of his chair, eyes bulging, his body stiff. He stared at the pair of queens Johnny had turned over. With the two queens in the flop, Johnny's four queens beat Roger's three aces any day of the week.

"But... but... this isn't fair," Roger said, looking around the other players for some sort of support. "I said I was all in. Didn't I say I was all in? The car isn't even mine."

"Oh well done, Roger," I said. "How are you supposed to drive to next week's training session now? Mr Chang won't tolerate you not turning up you know?" I could feel Finland slipping through my fingers.

Johnny puffed on his cigar and leaned into Roger until their faces were only inches apart. "Don't you ever say Johnny Two-Scars isn't fair, boy. I don't take kindly to it." Johnny leaned back and yawned theatrically. "Okay, gentlemen, time to go home."

"But I need the car!" Roger said, wiping his face vigorously. "How am I supposed to get home? What am I supposed to tell my father? Please, Johnny, it was just a joke, right? You're not really going to take the car off me, are you?"

The other players started packing things away and gathering their jackets.

"You can leave the keys on the bar on your way out," Johnny said, swilling the last of his drink around in his mouth. "As these gentlemen will testify, I'm not an unreasonable man, so here's the deal. I've got enough cars to last me a lifetime, boy, so I don't really need another one. Come up with twenty grand in the next two days, and I'll happily hand the keys back. If I don't hear from you by then, I guess I'll have to give the damned thing to the girlfriend. Only don't tell the wife."

I noticed the other players had strategically placed themselves around the garage to block any potential escape. Roger must have noticed it as well.

"Is there any chance I can get a lift home?" he asked, placing the keys for the Mazda on the bar.

With the help of several lines of cocaine, Roger spent forty-six of the next forty-eight hours doctoring enough pieces of paperwork to try and hide £20,000. The two hours he wasn't in the office were spent at various banks, cashing cheques onto which he'd forged his father's signature.

Johnny's house was set back further than the rest of the eight houses in the cul-de-sac. His doorbell played the theme-tune to *The Godfather*.

Johnny looked genuinely surprised. "Well, well, well," he said. "Look what the wind has blown to my door."

Roger hopped from foot to foot, and explained in short jerky sentences that he'd managed to find the £20,000 and could he please have his car back. He held out a black leather briefcase, purchased especially for the occasion.

Johnny ignored the briefcase and caught hold of Roger by the arm. "I don't do business on the doorstep, boy," he said, ushering Roger into the house. "Come on inside."

Roger was directed to sit on an opulent pink leather sofa in Johnny's living room. I noticed Roger's right knee was bouncing again.

"You'll have to excuse the colour schemes," Johnny said. "The wife likes pink."

"It's all there," Roger said, handing over the briefcase. "Just give me the keys and I'll be on my way."

Johnny accepted the briefcase and sat in a matching leather armchair opposite Roger. "All in good time, boy," he said. "I'm sure you won't mind if I count it first. It's all standard practice." He patted the briefcase. "Anyway, I'm sure you're going to want this back. It looks like good quality. Must have cost a pretty penny."

"That's okay," Roger said, wiping his face. "Really, you keep it. Call it a gift if you like?" He had started sweating quite badly.

"Oh now I couldn't do that, boy," Johnny said as he opened the briefcase. "I wouldn't be able to sleep at nights if I took something I hadn't had to work for. That's just the way I am." He started counting slowly. "No, you just sit tight, and as soon as I've finished you can have your nice shiny case back."

Roger rubbed his teeth. "You will give me my car back as well, won't you?"

Johnny stopped counting. "Something wrong, boy?" he said. "You seem… jumpy."

"I'm fine. Just need to get back to the office, that's all."

"Ah, I see," Johnny said, smiling. "Before daddy starts snooping around, eh?"

"No, nothing like that. I just have a lot of work to do."

"I bet you do, boy, I bet you do." Johnny closed the briefcase and placed it on the floor at the side of his chair. He stood up and made his way to a globe-style drinks' cabinet where he poured himself a measure of whisky.

"Want one, boy?" he asked.

Roger obviously decided some alcohol wouldn't go amiss and nodded his head.

"You know, you could always make this money work for you," Johnny said, handing Roger the drink and sitting back down. He nodded towards the briefcase.

Roger finished his drink with one gulp. "I'm not with you," he said, wincing at the whisky's after-burn.

"Well, I'm just thinking out loud here," Johnny said, picking up the briefcase and placing it on his lap. He used it as a makeshift table for his drink. "I've got another game set up for tonight. Same place, same rules, same players. So, instead of handing over this money, why don't you use it to join tonight's action? I'm sure with this sort of stack you'd have no problem in cleaning us all out. Think about it logically, boy. Tomorrow morning you could be driving into the offices of daddy's company in your fuck-mobile with enough cash in your pocket to take the books off the cooker and make all those funny looking entries seem almost right."

"I've no idea what you're talking about," Roger said, tipping his head back and sniffing away something running out of his nose.

Johnny placed his glass on the floor and opened the briefcase. "Suit yourself," he said. "I'll just finish counting before you go. Don't worry, it won't take long. Twenty grand can be counted in no time. Now, when you get up to sixty, seventy, eighty, even a hundred grand, that's the type of money that takes some adding up, boy, I can tell you. Help yourself to another drink."

Roger poured himself a large measure.

Johnny counted the money out loud. "I suppose that stuff you're shoving up your nose doesn't come cheap?" he said, getting to fifteen thousand. "Never bothered with the stuff myself, but from what I hear it can be an expensive pastime." Johnny looked up quickly. "I hope you don't owe any of those pushers money, boy. I hear they're nowhere near reasonable. Not like me."

Roger finished his drink and put the glass down on the table beside the globe. He made his way to Johnny and closed the lid of the briefcase just as Johnny got to eighteen thousand.

"You win," Roger said, taking the briefcase off Johnny's lap. "I'll see you tonight."

It was difficult to pinpoint exactly where things started to go wrong for Roger. Maybe it was the pot he lost when his ace-jack flush was beaten by an ace-queen flush. Or maybe it was when he folded a winning two-pair when his opponent bluffed him off the pot with a king-high. Wherever the trouble had started, made no difference to the fact it hadn't gone away. By the time the gap underneath the garage door announced the introduction of the sun, Roger was whisky-addled, full of cocaine, and down to £2000.

Roger fumbled with his cards, looking at them closely through one drunken eye. I looked over Roger's shoulder. He was holding the six and seven of spades. The flop had produced the five and six of hearts, the nine of clubs, and the ten and jack of diamonds.

Johnny threw twelve thousand pounds into the pot, which, when added to the previous bets and antes, made it a total of twenty thousand. The other three players folded in turn around to Roger.

"What do you want to do, boy," Johnny said, puffing out rings.

"Right, let's look at this logically," I said to Roger. "With what's on the table, there's no possibility of Johnny holding a flush. He'd have to be holding a seven-eight to make a straight, and you're already holding a seven, so that cuts down those odds. I reckon if he'd had a high pair in the hole, he'd have bet people off the pot before we even got to the turn, let alone the river. So, my guess is he's holding a jack. Top pair. Which of course beats your pair of sixes every day of the week and twice on Sundays. So, in answer to Johnny's question, Roger, what we want to do is fold faster than an Origami expert."

"I've only got two thou left," Roger said.

I leaned in to Rogers ear. "Doesn't matter how much you've got left," I said. "Johnny's holding a pair of jacks. Any fool can see that. Fold!"

Johnny puffed out more smoke. "If you really want to call, I suppose I could consider a short-term IOU," he said. "What did you say you had left? Two grand?"

Roger nodded.

Johnny reached into a jacket pocket and produced a pen and pad. "IOU ten grand," he said aloud as he wrote. He tore the sheet of paper off the pad and handed it with the pen to Roger. "There you go, boy. If you want to see what I've got just sign that and throw it in the pot with the two grand in front of you."

Roger signed his name.

"For God's sake, Roger, what on Earth are you doing?" I screamed. "There's no way you can win here. Can't you see that?" I was jumping up and down behind him, waving my arms around like a lunatic. "No, Roger, no, no, no. Fold for Pete's sake. Roger, think of Finland."

Roger threw the note into the pot along with his last £2000. "Call."

My poker skills had obviously become highly honed. Johnny had a pair of jacks. Perhaps I'd give up being a postman and become a professional poker player, I thought. Maybe the new forthright Mark Ferris could join me.

Roger let out a hearty laugh. "Gotcha!" he said, turning his cards over. "A straight."

Everybody in the room, except Roger, stared hard at the six-seven of spades on the table.

It was Johnny who broke the silence. "And how the fuck do you work that one out, laughing boy? Looks like the best you can manage is a pair of sixes to me. Does that look like a pair of sixes to you gentlemen?"

Everybody in the room, except Roger, muttered their agreement.

Roger looked at his cards, his laugh subsiding. He picked them up and turned them over. He looked around the foot of his chair. He got down on all fours and looked under the table. "Now hang on a minute," he said, climbing back into his chair. "These aren't my cards. I had a seven and eight of spades. I had a straight. Who the fuck changed my eight for a six?"

I assumed that in normal circumstances if anybody accused Johnny Two-Scars of somehow doctoring the cards they'd be lucky to leave the garage in one piece. But Johnny was laughing too much to do anything untoward.

I sat in a corner of the garage with my head in my hands and tried to close out the sounds of Johnny and the other players continuously mock Roger for his stupidity.

"Never in all my years," Johnny said, almost crying with laughter. "Thought his six… was an eight…"

Finland seemed to be a very faraway place.

By the time Roger and I had walked the 4 miles back home, the sun was reminding most people it was time to eat breakfast, which is exactly what we found Roger's father doing.

"By Christ, Roger, you look like shit," Gary said through a mouthful of cereal. "Where the hell have you been? You smell like a brewery. What's in the briefcase?"

"Please, dad," Roger said, kicking off his shoes. "What's with the third degree? I've just had the worse night of my life, so don't give me a hard time, okay?"

"Yeah, well sleep it off as quick as you can," Gary said, putting his bowl in the dishwasher. "I want you in the office by two at the latest."

"Not today, dad, please. Can't I take the day off? I've been working like a swamp-donkey for the last few days. Cut me some slack. I'm really not feeling too good. I just need to like totally crash for a day."

"Sorry, son, no can do. I've made an appointment for our accountants to come in this afternoon. Apparently the National Insurance boys are a bit twitchy about that Polish gang we employed to work on the new development. I just want to make sure everything's above board before we send the books in. And, as you're the one who looks after the books, I've already told them you'll be there to help. Have you got the Mazda back yet? I thought you said it only went in for a routine service."

What little colour there was left in Roger's face disappeared. He looked like he'd just been fished out of the Atlantic.

"Roger, the car?" Gary grabbed his jacket off the back of a kitchen chair.

"Sorry, what?"

"The car, Roger! Have you got the Mazda back yet?"

"Oh. Um. No, it's still in the garage."

"Problem?"

"Sorry?"

"For God's sake, Roger, is there a problem with the car?"

"No. I mean, yes. Something about the exhaust system. Dad, there may be something you need to know."

"It'll have to wait," Gary said, grabbing his keys off the hallway table. "I've got to make a few phone calls and clear my diary for this afternoon. I'll be back at one to pick you up. For Christ's sake use the time to get some sleep and tidy yourself up. It's like living with a bloody tramp. That's a really nice looking briefcase by the way."

The journey to the offices of Gary's company was the first opportunity I'd had to ride in Gary's Volvo estate. The tinted windows, so menacing from the outside, gave me the feeling of being able to spy on the world, and I made a mental note that if I ever passed my driving test and bought a car, I would invest in tinted windows.

We hadn't gone far, when Roger, who had taken his father's advice and attempted to tidy himself up, started heaving. "Dad, can we pull over? I think I'm going to be sick."

By the time we reached Gary's designated parking space and made our way into his office, two smartly dressed accountants were already there. Gary apologised for his and Roger's tardiness, explaining that his son had been taken ill along the way. He then instructed Roger to go and make the nice men a cup of tea before getting started.

Roger took the opportunity to slip out the back door and down the fire escape.

"For God's sake, Roger," I said, trotting after him, "don't run away.

You know it'll only make matters worse. At least make the tea first."

I continued remonstrating with Roger during most of the hour and a half it took us to walk back home. He took no notice and headed straight for the drinks' cabinet as soon as we got in.

Five hours later, Gary came home with a question for his son. Namely, what had Roger done with the £105,654.93 the two nice accountants were adamant was missing from the income stream of the company's accounts?

"I need another drink," Roger said, getting off the sofa and making his way to the cabinet.

Gary caught hold of his son by the arm as he past him. "Oh no you fucking don't," he said, snatching the empty glass from Roger's hand. "Everything in this house belongs to me, you little shit. In future, if you so much as even look at something that belongs to me, I'll poke your eyes out with rusty knitting needles. Now sit down!"

I thought it fair to assume Gary was not in a good mood.

Over the next hour Roger confessed everything. He included the loss of the Mazda, and the extra £10,000 he owed Johnny Two-Scars.

With each revelation Gary's face crumpled like an empty carrier bag caught in the wind. By the time Roger had finished, his father looked completely spent.

"I need to get out of this house before I hit you with something heavy," Gary said.

Roger chased after his departing father. "Dad! I need that ten thousand pounds in the next three days. Dad, please, I don't think Johnny Two-Scars is as reasonable as he makes out." We both watched as the Volvo disappeared, the smell of burning rubber lingering in the air. "Dad, I'm really, really sorry."

Gary didn't come home that night, or the night after. Roger was frantic. He'd tried calling his father on every number he could think of, but it appeared Gary didn't want to be found.

When Gary finally turned up at the house, Roger was a desperate mess. Gary didn't look much better himself.

"Oh thank God!" Roger said, as Gary walked in through the door.

He flung himself at his father, putting his arms around his waist and burying his head in Gary's chest. "Where have you been? I've been worried sick."

Gary peeled Roger's arms from around him and pushed him to one side. "Where do you think I've been, moron?" he said, making his way to the drinks' cabinet. "I've been at work trying to sort out the shit you dropped me in."

"But I've been trying to contact you," Roger said, close to tears. "The staff said they hadn't seen you. You've not been answering your mobile. I've been going out of my mind. All these different scenarios kept playing in my mind, and none of them were any good."

"The staff are under strict orders not to tell you anything," Gary said, before finishing his drink with one gulp. "I'm going to get some sleep. Make sure you don't make any noise."

Roger followed his father to the bottom of the stairs. "Uh, dad, I know this might not be a good time, but about this ten grand I owe Johnny…"

Gary spun quickly. "You are joking right?" he said. "I've just spent two days dealing with those smarmy accountants who tell me the Inland Revenue are asking for forty-two grand tax on undeclared earnings. Earnings that you, my wonderful son and heir, have either gambled or snorted away. Oh, that's right, Roger, I know all about the drugs. I mean, look at you. Your eyes are bigger than my dinner plate, and you're twitching like dying cattle. Doesn't take an Einstein to work it out, Roger. Now, add in the Mazda, the accountants' fees, and God knows what other sundry items might crop up, and by my reckoning you owe me nearly two hundred grand. So guess what, son? You can whistle Dixie. You're not getting another penny out of me, Roger. Not a brass fucking farthing. Understand?"

Fair to assume, Gary's mood hadn't got any better. I was mightily impressed with how quickly he'd done the maths though.

Roger couldn't contain the tears any longer. "I'll put it right, dad, honest I will. I'll spend every hour I breathe in the office making sure everything's in order." Roger rubbed his teeth, betraying the fact he'd recently taken a line. "I'll clean myself up, I swear. I'll pay back every penny. I'll even work for nothing until we're square. I'll do anything you want, dad, anything at all. I'll even sell my soul to the Devil if it'll help. But I just need this one last favour, dad." Roger tried laughing through his torment. "I mean, what's ten grand when I'm already in for two hundred?"

Gary joined in Roger's mock-merriment, then stopped quickly. "If your ugly, stupid, drug-ridden face crops up anywhere near my offices again, the staff have been instructed to shoot you on sight," he said. "You're not getting a nickel out of me, shit-head, let alone ten grand."

Roger sank to his knees and put his hands out in prayer. "Dad, please, what are you saying? You can't fire me. I'm your son."

"For God's sake get up, you look pathetic. You got yourself in this mess and you'll get no help from me in getting yourself out of it. What the hell did you think I was going to do? Welcome you back to work with open arms? You almost ruined everything I've ever worked for, Roger. I can kiss the cruise goodbye, and, thanks to you, I'll probably have to keep working until the day I die. You make me sick. I dread to think what your poor mother would make of it all."

Gary made his way to the hallway table and picked up the keys for the Volvo.

"Dad, I thought you said you needed some sleep," Roger said, shuffling after Gary on his knees. "I know I messed up big style, but please, I really need your help."

Gary reached the front door. "Just so you know," he said, without turning round. "I've had all the locks changed at the offices and altered all the alarm codes."

"Dad, please come back!" Roger screamed as Gary walked away. "If I don't come up with the money by the end of today, who knows what might happen. Dad!"

Roger was right. Johnny was not a reasonable man after all.

Maybe it was because I was on the other side of the doorstep, but the giant towering over Roger looked more menacing than David ever had. The guy had obviously just crawled down a beanstalk, and I knew from experience that he'd soon tire of Roger's pleas for more time.

After five minutes of listening to Rogers begging, I noticed the behemoth glance furtively from side to side.

"Roger, quick, close the door," I said. "He's checking to see if anyone's looking. Any minute now he's going to…"

The man-mountain picked Roger up by the collar and carried him into the house, kicking the door shut behind him. Roger flayed about as the beast carted him into the kitchen and unceremoniously dumped him onto a kitchen chair.

"Nice place you've got here," the visitor said, rubbing his hands together. His voice was thick, like he was chewing bricks.

Roger must have taken what his uninvited guest had said as an indication he was about to ransack the house. I guess Roger still had Gary's words about who owned everything in the house ringing in his ears, and, understandably, I assume he got worried that Gary would never believe it hadn't been Roger himself who'd sold off anything of value. Even given these facts, I couldn't help but think what Roger did next was somewhat foolish.

He got up off the chair and adopted one of those fighting positions you see in Kung-Fu movies; the crab or the monkey or something. He let out a sort of *'Heehah!'* and launched a textbook roundhouse kick which caught his adversary square on the jaw. The guy didn't flinch. The smile didn't even leave his face as he spat out a tooth and wiped the trickle of blood from his lip.

"Bloody hell, Roger," I said. "What did you do that for? Now you've got him really annoyed."

"Johnny said you were into all that martial arts crap," the brick-chewer said. "Never saw the attraction myself. Too many rules. All that self-discipline and self-control. Not for me. I like to lose it sometimes, you know what I mean?"

Roger tried to run, but the giant was deceptively nimble and caught him just as Roger got his hands on the handle of the front door.

"Please, just a bit more time," Roger said, being dragged back to the kitchen by the scruff of his neck. "I just need to work on my father a bit, that's all. One day. Two at most."

When back in the kitchen, the monster held Roger up against a wall with his left hand, and then delivered a punch to the solar plexus with his right that would have felled a charging rhino. Roger sank to the floor, letting out guttural noises that suggested his innards were trying to escape through his throat. He tried to snake away, but could only manage to spin like a dying fly.

Johnny's hit-man started whistling *Always look on the bright side of life* as he took a good look around the kitchen. His eyes finally settled on a heavy brass saucepan hanging from a hook above the range. He collected the saucepan and nodded his approval at its weight. He then waited patiently until Roger managed to get himself on all fours before swinging the saucepan with all his considerable strength into the side of Roger's head. The force of the blow flipped Roger onto his back. One look at his face confirmed he was out for well beyond the count.

The visitor continued whistling as he put the saucepan back on its hook and started rummaging through the house for anything of value. He took his time finding enough cash and items of jewellery to more than cover Roger's debt, then made his way back to the kitchen and knelt by the side of Roger's prostrate body. I'm sure the ringing sound of the saucepan as it had connected with Roger's head was still reverberating around the room.

"Now, what did the boss say?" the giant asked himself, closing his eyes and concentrating. "Big Nigel, he said to me, you make sure you leave a lasting reminder, you hear? I want the stupid, ugly fucker to carry a permanent reminder of the time he failed to pay Johnny Two Scars on time."

Big Nigel opened his eyes and picked up Roger's right hand in his massive paws.

"Now, if I work on two grand a finger," he looked to the ceiling and pondered for a moment. "Ten grand divided by two makes…" he muttered a few figures under his breath, "…five!" He looked back at Roger. "I think we'll break three on this one, and two on the other."

Despite my admiration of the monster's maths, I screamed and screamed on hearing Roger's bones snap. I only stopped screaming to be sick in the sink.

MIAMI VICE

Roger spent eight days in hospital before the doctors decided he was fit enough to be released into the wild again. When he came out he was a lot slower than when he'd gone in, both physically and mentally.

The following two months brought a series of painful physiotherapy sessions and follow-up medical assessments, during which one thing was established beyond all reasonable doubt. Roger's chances of ever practicing Judo again were somewhere between none and absolutely none.

Sorry, Elaine, but I won't be going to Finland after all, so I don't need my passport now. Thanks for looking anyway.

Roger's physiotherapist had done the best she could, but Roger's mangled fingers still took on the appearance of being permanently arthritic. She'd got them moving of sorts, but even simple things like picking up a pen or making a cup of tea weren't achieved without a high degree of concentration and a decent amount of pain. It became difficult enough for Roger to wipe himself after going to the toilet, let alone perfect his Yubisaki Ate Waza.

Just in case that wasn't enough to deal with, the blow to Roger's head had left him with a permanent dent in his cranium and a permanent ringing in his ears. It had also given him a gait which looked like he was shuffling along in a chain-gang and a slur in his speech which made him sound permanently drunk. The doctors were confident the ringing would eventually stop and the shuffle and speech would improve, but they couldn't give a timescale. They likened it to the recovery of a mild stroke victim.

All in all, I think it fair to say, Big Nigel had done what his boss had asked.

I suppose on the plus side, Roger hadn't looked for a game of poker or a line of cocaine since his release from hospital. On the down side, Roger hadn't looked for a game of poker or a line of cocaine since his release from hospital.

From the adrenalin filled days of poker, judo, drug use and embezzlement, Roger's days were now filled with the rather more mundane pastime of walking; something the doctors had embraced keenly, saying it would help with his overall state of wellbeing.

I'm not sure the doctors would have been quite so enthusiastic if they'd known Roger's daily outings regularly included a visit to the *Frog & Duck*, quite possibly the quietest pub in the universe.

Mother would have been disturbed to know I was spending my days in the pub.

"Mark, where on Earth have you been?"

"To the pub, mum. With my assignee, Roger."

"The one who used to go fighting, stole from his father, then got hit with a saucepan and had his fingers broken for not paying his debts?"

"That's the one."

"Oh, I don't like him, Mark. He seems a bit slow and dim-witted if you ask me. Is there something wrong with him, Mark? You know, up top?"

"I don't think his brain has stopped swaying from the clout Big Nigel gave him, mum. The doctors reckon he'll slowly get better. His fingers are damaged permanently though. Going to the pub is about the only thing he can do properly these days."

"Oh dear, what must his poor parents think?"

"His mother is dead, mum, and his father still doesn't really speak to him properly. Mind you, Gary has been very busy trying to get his company back in order."

"Well I hope you're not developing into an afternoon drinker, Mark. Maybe you should stop bothering with this Roger. I mean, only stupid people and alcoholics drink during the day."

"Mum, he has no more than three pints. And he takes forever to drink them. In some circles that might even be considered good for

you."

"Yes, alcoholic circles, Mark. Oh, what will Timothy's sister think when she finds out you're bothering with alcoholics? This is just like when you used to bring that Elaine woman over for dinner and she'd drink all your father's wine."

"That Elaine woman was my wife, mum."

Elaine prided herself on being a bit of a wine-buff. I tried telling her that simply drinking lots of it didn't make you any sort of expert, but she begged to differ, and would quite often drain a whole bottle of whatever was on offer before Mother had even served the soup.

Roger found having to use two hands to shakily hold a pint glass to his mouth far too embarrassing, and sat on a barstool slowly supping his drink through two brightly coloured straws. Believing him to be safe enough, I made my way over to the underused jukebox and attempted, yet again, to make its buttons depress. There was a whole page on the machine devoted to Elvis songs, and, despite my best efforts, it was so frustrating to have been coming in the pub every day for the best part of two months and not once having heard any of them. I eventually gave up trying to will *Suspicious Minds* to drop onto the turntable, and turned to make my way back to Roger. I had only taken one step when my eyes conveyed a strange message to the rest of my body.

Standing beside Roger, looking like someone from a 1920's gangster movie, was none other than Tony the Pony. On receiving the message from my eyes, my legs decided to stop working and I sank to the floor. Tony's pinstripe suit and snazzy hat had obviously attracted the attention of all the other punters in the pub as well, and they both left quickly. Presumably they were wary of people in suits.

"Hi there," Tony said to Roger, doffing his hat. "Lovely day isn't it?"

Roger concentrated on his drink and nodded.

Tony ordered himself a gin and tonic, being rudely reminded by the landlady that she wasn't an *'effing greengrocer'* when Tony requested a slice of lemon. He sat on the barstool next to Roger and sipped his warm gin. "I was just passing," he said. "Never been in here before. Does it get any busier?"

Roger shrugged his shoulders.

"Don't mean to be rude," Tony said, rummaging around in an empty ice-bucket, "but if you don't mind me asking, why the straws?"

Roger held his hands up in front of his face and stared at his oddly-angled digits. He then displayed them to Tony.

"Ooh, nasty," Tony said, giving up on his search for ice. "Arthritis?"

"Accident," Roger said, putting his hands back by his sides. "Should have been in Finland now. European Championship. Judo."

"Oh right. My commiserations. So, a recent accident then?"

"What are you? Police? Social security?" Roger used one of his unbroken fingers to draw a line across his lips.

Tony called the landlady over and asked if there was any possibility of her finding some ice, to which he was told the machine was broken. He waited for the landlady to move away before continuing the conversation. "No, nothing like that. I'm just trying to be polite, that's all. Call me an old softy, but you just looked like you needed a bit of cheering up."

"My lucky day," Roger said. "The cheering up fairy is here."

Tony laughed lightly. "Tell you what. Let me buy you a drink."

Over the next hour, Tony and Roger bonded over respective stories of being put in hospital by big, nasty men.

"The guy who done for me was called Dai the Murderer," Tony said with some pride. "He took me by surprise, otherwise I reckon I could have taken him easy."

"Three of them came knocking my door," Roger said. "Took two out, but the third crept up on me from behind. Did I tell you I used to do judo?" Roger got off his stool and tried to demonstrate to Tony the same pose he'd launched into in front of Big Nigel, but his legs were full of the alcohol Tony had steadily been supplying him with, and he stumbled sideways. Surprisingly, the more Roger drank, the better his speech became.

Tony caught Roger before he fell into a nearby table and carefully placed him back on his stool. "Listen, Roger," he said. "I can see life has been cruel to you recently, and if you don't mind me saying, you're looking a bit tired, mate. In my opinion what you really need - no, scrub that - what you really *deserve*, is a holiday." Tony closed one eye and started wagging a finger, as if some sudden great revelation had come to him. "Just give me a minute, Roger. Let me go and get something out of the car. Don't go anywhere. I'll be right back. I'm going to show you something that'll really blow your mind. It could be the answer to all your prayers, Roger."

Tony's passion and gusto as he worked his way through the magnificent colour brochure he'd produced was something to behold. Within twenty minutes of his visit to the car, he had me, Roger, and the landlady, drooling over a sumptuous looking beach-house in Miami.

"Ooh, good choice," Tony said. "Isn't she a beauty? Picture the scene, Roger. You've got your feet up. You're looking out on that beach. There's a constant stream of scantily clad women walking by. You've got nothing to worry about except where your next Pina Colada is coming from, or whether you should apply more lotion. Can you see yourself, Roger? Isn't it just paradise? You know, if I wasn't so busy I'd be out there myself. Now, here's the good news, Roger. I can do a cracking deal on that very house."

"Doesn't matter how good a deal it is," Roger said. "I can't afford it."

The landlady walked away to clean some glasses, muttering something about working too hard.

Tony leaned in to Roger's ear. "Didn't you say your father was worth a few bob?" he said, making sure the glossy paraphernalia about the beach-house remained clearly in Roger's view.

Roger supped his drink. "Did I?"

"I'm sure you mentioned it, Roger. Couldn't you ask him to help you out? Maybe lend you a few quid? I'm sure he could manage it."

Roger tried to close the brochure, but his fingers wouldn't quite manage it. "Forget it," he said. "We sort of fell out over money a while back. I won't get any cash out of him."

Tony looked around furtively. It was a theatrical exercise, we were still the only people in the pub. "Don't let what I'm about to tell you leave these four walls," he said, making sure the landlady was out of earshot. "But I don't necessarily need cash. Let's just say I'm open to… other arrangements."

Roger and I both frowned.

Tony continued looking around to make sure no one was listening, carrying on in no more than a whisper. "Listen, I don't always make these sorts of offers to people I've only just met, Roger. But I feel as though I can trust you. I can trust you, can't I?"

Roger nodded his head.

"Good. You see, let's just say, for argument's sake, that I may know certain people, who may know other certain people, who are able, just maybe, to convert things into ready, useable currency. Things, that may just so happen, accidentally of course, to fall into my hands."

"You're a fence?"

Tony put his finger to his lips. "Shhh," he said. "Not so loud. I like to think of myself more as a facilitator, Roger."

Roger took another sup of his drink. "Makes no difference what you call yourself," he said, keeping the straws between his lips. "I've got nothing to offer. I used to have a car once, sort of. But that's gone now."

"Okay," Tony said. "Let's put some cards on the table here." He continued checking for intrusions into the conversation. "There must be something you can lay your hands on, Roger? I mean, there's got to be plenty of value sitting inside that nice house you and your tight-fisted dad live in. We're only talking about what's owed to you, Roger. No more. Just a little break to get away from all this." Tony scanned his arms around the pub. "A reward for everything you've been through. We're not talking much. Let's just say, for argument's sake, five, maybe six grand. Seven tops."

"Joking, right?" Roger said, spitting out the straws. "Steal from my own house?"

"Bloody hell, keep your voice down," Tony said, picking up the brochure and placing it into a well-used briefcase. "It was only a suggestion. Forget I ever mentioned it. I've obviously thrown my dice to the wrong man. Sorry to have bothered you, Roger. I guess somebody less deserving will have to benefit from this ace of an opportunity. Personally, I don't see what the problem is. I mean, I bet the house is well insured. Hell, I bet your flush daddy would even add a few quid to the claim. As far as I see it, Roger, it's a win-win situation. But hey, if you want to spend the rest of your days moping around in places like this instead of mingling with the bronzed and beautiful people of Miami, then who am I to stop you? You know, if I was a gambling man, Roger, I'd have bet my bottom dollar you'd have been up for this. Ah well, never mind. It was nice to meet you."

Tony turned to leave.

In all the time I'd been with Roger, I'd never once known him to be overly interested in holidays, so I'm not sure what buttons Tony had pressed to make Roger say what he said next. Perhaps he'd simply preyed on Roger's sense of uselessness, or perhaps it was the liberal use of words like, *bet, cards on the table, flush, win-win, ace, gambling.*

"Big Nigel took most of anything that was valuable from my house," Roger said. He waited until Tony was almost out of the door, before adding, "But we could always look in somebody else's house."

Of course, it could also have been because Mother was right, and only stupid people drank in the afternoons.

Tony walked slowly back to Roger. "Let me buy you another drink," he said, clasping Roger around the shoulders.

FINGERS MILLER

Roger and Tony huddled together and spoke in low whispers.

I slumped over the bar and buried my head in my arms. "Roger, I really have a bad feeling about this," I said.

I was still muttering about how bad my feeling actually was when I felt hands squeezing me gently around the waist. Believing it to be Crimson, I lifted my head slowly. The grimy mirror behind the bar allowed me to catch sight of who was actually attached to the hands, and I immediately found myself falling to the floor, hitting my chin on the bar on the way down.

"Hello again," Mary said, staring down at me. "Remember me?" She cocked her head to one side. "What the hell happened to you?" She scanned her hand over me, laughing nervously.

Missing my shoes, socks, trouser legs, and the sleeves of my shirt, I guessed my appearance could be of limited concern. I called long and hard for the new forthright Mark Ferris to help me get some words past the mouse. All I eventually managed was, "Fire."

Mary shrugged. "So, you with this guy now?" she asked, nodding towards Roger. "He looks odd. He's what me and my friends would have called at least an eight-pinter." Mary giggled. "It means we'd have to drink at least eight pints before we sh…"

"I know what it means," I said, interrupting Mary's flow. "My wife explained it to me once."

Mary's sudden appearance had taken all the saliva from my mouth, and I attempted to find some moisture by licking my lips. Also, from my vantage point of lying face-up on the floor, my eyes had obeyed the very nature of man and had started tracing themselves up the expanse of leg on show beneath Mary's short denim skirt.

"Are you licking your lips and looking up my skirt?" Mary said, taking a slight step backwards. "Why, Mark, you dirty bugger."

Oh my God!

Mother!

"I really don't know how much more of this behaviour I can take, Mark. It's doing nothing for my nerves. I think it's time we signed you up for some help, don't you? Is there such a thing as dead perverts anonymous? Wasn't there a film about it once? With that Robbie Williams? I'll start looking in the telephone directory right away."

"It wasn't Robbie Williams, mum, (number 17 on the list) *it was Robin Williams,* (not on the list) *and the film was called Dead Poets Society."*

"Mary, I'm so, so, sorry," I said. I turned my head to one side and closed my eyes.

A few seconds later, I felt Mary's presence as she knelt beside me. She took hold of my hand. "It's okay," she said, stroking it gently. "It's perfectly understandable."

"You obviously haven't met Mother," I said under my breath.

Mary continued stroking my hand. "So how long has Tony been here?"

"A while. Long enough to get my assignee all worked up."

"Yeah, he does that. Has he shown him the brochure yet?"

I nodded my head.

"It's all a scam you know. None of those places really exist. Anyway, I'm sorry I wasn't here earlier. I've been in front of the committee. They took great pleasure in telling me they'd completed my review and that I still hadn't made it to the Sanctum."

"I know how you feel," I said, trying to ignore the fact I was in close physical proximity to a young woman who was now licking my fingers. "Did they give you a reason?" The mouse was having a field-day.

"No," Mary replied. She lay down beside me and rested her head on my chest. "Not really. They said my fainting didn't help."

I was struggling to keep from fainting myself, and could feel the unwelcome, yet unstoppable, stirrings of another public display of affection. "Your fainting?" I said. The mouse was as frantic as a hamster in a wheel.

Mary started stroking my stomach. "Yes, my fainting," she said. "You see, no matter how many times I see it, I just can't get over the size of Tony's... you know?"

For some reason, Mary had adopted a voice which I believed could only be found at the end of certain telephone numbers.

Once, and only once, had Elaine ever suggested we try phone-sex. It had been when she was away on one of her business trips, not long before I'd died. I must admit I'd thought I was doing quite well. Elaine seemed to be making all the appropriate noises. She'd even started screaming she was about to achieve something I couldn't normally get her to achieve when we were interrupted by what I believed to be a masculine cough in the background. I questioned her politely about it, but she angrily replied that I'd spoiled the moment and immediately hung up. We never spoke about the subject again.

"It's just every time he gets naked, I go all woozy," Mary continued. "I thought Star's was big enough, but that thing Tony's got is downright dangerous. It should come with a government health warning printed on it. There's enough room."

I covered my public display of affection with my hands and concentrated as hard as I could on the pub's smoke-stained ceiling. I remembered promising I'd call upon the new forthright Mark Ferris if I ever found myself in this situation again, and called and called until my mind was hoarse. But it seemed he'd heeded Mothers advice and didn't drink in the afternoons.

"Shouldn't we be checking on our assignees?" I said, sweat trickling backwards off my forehead and into my ears.

I sensed Mary's head rise slightly. "Ah, they look fine," she said. "Thick as thieves."

She replaced her head on my chest and slipped her hand underneath the remains of my shirt.

"Mary, I really don't think we should be doing this," I said. I tried to reduce the magnitude of my display by attempting to bring to mind all the ugly women I'd ever met. Oh God, I must have met ugly women. Where were they all?

"There's no need to be shy, Mark," Mary said. "There's no one around. Well, except for our assignees, and they can't see us can they, silly. I just need a cuddle, that's all. Hey, we could call this a proper date. What do you think?"

Mary raised a knee and rubbed it up and down my thigh, occasionally applying pressure to a certain area. She also started wriggling far too seductively to be appropriate, and moaned softly.

The display was teetering on the brink of explosion, and I recalled a self-help book that Elaine had once bought for me, which advised, *If one has a tendency to fulfil one's sexual pleasure well in advance of one's partner, try doing the nine times table.* I decided now was as good a time as any to put my difficulty with maths to one side and apply the exercise.

I only got as far as five nines.

Mary stopped wriggling and stroking and rubbing, and lifted her head off my chest. Even through closed eyes, I knew the smile she was offering me was one of pity and disappointment. I'd felt the same smile from Elaine many times.

I apologised over and over to Mother.

"You didn't even buy the poor girl dinner, Mark. I'm disgusted with you."

I rolled over onto my side and curled into a ball, vowing to remain exactly where I was for the rest of my life… death… whatever. Under no circumstances could I ever face the outside world again.

I sensed Mary's breath close to my ear. "Glad I could be of service," she whispered. "But I'd open your eyes if I was you. You have a visitor."

I opened a quarter of one eye and looked up. Crimson was standing over me, her mouth open wide. I immediately re-closed my eye.

Crimson bent down and caught hold of my wrist, grasping it between her thumb and forefinger as if picking up something disgusting. "Come on, the committee want to see you," she said.

Mr T. was engrossed in paperwork, and only looked up when one of the sidekicks nudged him and pointed in my direction.

"Ah, Seven-Three-Five-Nine," he said, "what a pleasant surprise." He looked to his sidekicks and lowered his voice. "Sorry, but you'll have to remind me. Why have we brought Seven-Three-Five-Nine here?"

One of the sidekicks whispered in Mr T's ear.

"Oh, that's right," Mr T. said, slapping his forehead. "I'm afraid we have some bad news, Seven-Three-Five-Nine."

Given the circumstances, I couldn't for the life or death of me think what news could possibly be considered bad.

"Elvis has finally left the building," Mr T. announced. "He passed away peacefully at his Peruvian mountain-top home yesterday morning. His nearest and dearest were with him. We just thought you'd like to know."

The news should have been devastating, but I guess I'd already mourned enough when alive. Instead of grief, a new emotion surfaced. "Will I be able to meet him?" I asked, unable to hide the excitement from my voice.

"Good Lord, no!" Mr T. said, looking at his sidekicks, who both shook their heads in disbelief at my request. "When you've lived a life as pious as his, Seven-Three-Five-Nine, it's straight off to the Sanctum as soon as you get here and no mistake. No autographs, no meet and greet, no questions, just straight in. It'll be the same for that Webb chap when his time comes, which, despite rumours he's going to live forever, shouldn't be too far away now. Anyway, enough of this idle chit-chat. As you can see, we do have quite a lot of work to get through. It's not every day we get to prepare for a *King's* arrival."

One of the sidekicks passed Mr T. a note.

He read it and sighed with annoyance. "Looks like your messenger is... temporarily otherwise engaged, Seven-Three-Five-Nine," he said. "No matter. Here's what I suggest."

Mr T's suggestion wasn't quite what I'd expected. Apparently, Old Eric had gone to Paris for a romantic weekend with Elaine and that lawyer.

"You can wait in there," Mr T. said, pointing behind me. "It's all standard practice. We'll send for you when we're ready. Off you go."

The door had the word *BALLET* written on it.

Elaine professed to love ballet; I hated it. I couldn't get to grips with spending a week's salary on tickets to see a bunch of people interpreting dance in a manner which I had no chance of understanding. After all, I was only a postman.

I stared at the door and recalled Elaine once dragging me along to see a version of Delibes' *Coppelia,* which she'd informed me, *'Despite being a comedy, was a portrait of man's conflict between idealism and realism, art and life.'* To which I'd almost replied, *'Despite being a comedy, I feel like I want to kill myself.'*

I should have known. Through the door wasn't just *like* the same version of *Coppelia* I'd seen all those years ago, it *was* the same version. Except I was the only patron.

Three hours later, with the same willingness to end it all, Crimson appeared. She held me gingerly by the wrist and kept me at arms length, as if I was something that needed to be cleaned. "Come on, it's time to go," she said, looking at her watch. "In fact, I should have been here in the interval."

When I got back to Roger, he was back at home studying the back of a beer-mat Tony had scribbled on. I looked over his shoulder to discover Tony had written down an address. It was an address in an area of some salubriousness that Roger and I often walked by during our daily rambles.

"How hard can it be?" Roger mumbled to himself. "I'll be in and out like an eel."

"Eels don't go into other people's houses uninvited, Roger!" I screamed. "They stay in water, where they know they belong. If they venture outside of it, they die. Honestly, Roger, as far as I'm aware, eels do not make good housebreakers. For God's sake what are you thinking? Even I can tell you're not cut out for this sort of thing. And I'm only a postman."

Over the next two days Roger *practiced* around the house, trying to pick up pieces of jewellery and other small items of value. The results were disastrous.

Gary started going mental at all the *stuff* he kept finding over the floor when he got home from work.

"What the hell are you doing, Roger?" he said, tripping over a trinket box. "Why can't you just leave things where they are? Brain still not working straight, is it?"

Roger had rehearsed his reply. "If I'm going to function properly in the civilised world, then I need to be blind to my disability," he said, getting up off the sofa and standing like a soldier to attention.

Gary moved towards Roger until their noses were almost touching. "But that's the whole point, dickhead," he said. "It's because of your disability that you *can't* function properly in the real world any more.

Get used to it."

"I used to do judo you know!" Roger caught hold of his father's lapels the best his fingers would allow. "Should have been in Finland. European Championship."

Gary laughed and slapped Roger's hands away. "Yeah. Well the only chance you've got of going to Finland now is if they have an annual competition in *dropping shit*."

Gary disappeared into the kitchen, still laughing.

"I wouldn't put it past them," I shouted after him. "They're quite a strange bunch apparently."

Three days after their meeting in the pub, Roger telephoned Tony in some despair. He put him on speakerphone as he paced around the living room.

"I can't do it, Tony," Roger said. "I can't pick anything up! The only thing I'll succeed in doing is making the place look untidy."

"Just calm down, Roger," Tony's voice filled the room. "There's more than one way to skin a cat."

"What do you mean?"

"Perhaps we'll have to do this in stages, Roger."

"Huh?"

"You're still serious about wanting to go to that paradise I showed you, yes? Because if you've changed your mind then we can always…"

"No! I'm still serious."

"Okay. Good. Now, I assume you're okay with picking up cash, yes?"

Roger stopped pacing and sat on the sofa. "As long as it's notes. Why?"

"Well, let's just say, for argument's sake, that I may know certain people, who may know some other certain people, who may have come across an address that may have some cash lying around in it. Not the sort of sums we were hoping for, but it'll be a start, Roger. It'll be a good couple of hundred guaranteed, maybe even a grand or two."

"But that's not enough."

"It'll be enough for me to hold as a deposit, Roger. A commitment if you like. Let's just say, for argument's sake, that I'll put it in a special high-interest account I have."

"But it'll still take ages to be enough."

"Listen, I can't think of anyone who deserves a break more than you, Roger. So I'll tell you what I'll do. You bring me whatever you can, and I'll match it. No, hang on! Keep this between us, Roger, but you bring me whatever you can, and what the hell? I'll double it!"

"You'd do that? Why?"

"I agree it's not standard practice, Roger, and please don't tell anyone else. If people knew I was dealing out these kind of cards they'd be banging my door down. Now quick, go and get a pen and take this address down, before I change my mind."

"Okay, but you'll have to speak slow, because I don't write very fast."

I looked over Roger's shoulder as he clumsily wrote down the address. It was an address I knew well. It was an address that once housed a rusty Metro in the front garden and a new swing in the back yard.

"Oh, Jesus Christ, Roger," I said. "What are you doing? That's David's old house."

Roger duly altered the route of our daily walks.

For the next four days we stopped for an hour or so every time we got to David's old abode and observed it from what Roger deemed to be a safe distance. When our daily *stake-out* was complete, Roger would make his way to the nearest pub.

Instead of the Frog & Duck, our afternoons were now spent in the Buckets.

"Roger, please listen to me," I said, as we settled at the bar. "You really don't know what type of neighbourhood you're dealing with here."

I looked across at the table from where David used to conduct his business. There were two men sitting at it, looking so uninterested in Roger it was obvious they were interested.

"Have you not learned anything in the last four days? Just have a quick look around. This isn't the Frog and Duck, Roger. Look at all these eyes on you. Trust me, I spent the first eight months of my death living around here, and even if you so much as sneeze, the whole neighbourhood will know about it before you get to *Shoo*. Roger, I'm telling you, the minute you set foot inside that house, they'll be on to you. And one other thing to take into consideration, Roger. People around here don't always rely on the law to look after their justice either."

Roger ignored me and supped his drink through his straws.

"I mean, I don't mean to be rude, Roger, but you're not exactly inconspicuous are you? You walk like your feet are tied together, your hands don't precisely look like they should, and you're drinking through two multicoloured straws for Christ's sake. Did you not hear those people talking about you as we walked by Sundip's mini-mart yesterday?"

Roger continued to ignore me.

"Come on, let's just go home." I tried tugging on Roger's sleeve. "We'll phone Tony and tell him the deal is off. He'll understand. I think Tony must have got the address wrong in any case. I mean, why would there be any money in *that* house?"

In the time we'd spent outside the house, we'd not once seen the person, or persons, who currently lived inside it. We had, however, witnessed a whole host of visitors come and go, and, even though Roger's brain wasn't firing on all cylinders, he hadn't missed the fact that all the callers were men, most of whom looked far more relaxed and satisfied coming out compared to when they went in.

"Just a whore on her own," Roger mumbled, one of the straws stuck to his bottom lip. "How easy can it be? I'll be in and out like an eel."

"Now let's not go there again, Roger," I said. "I told you all about the criminal qualities of eels, didn't I? Tony's just a conman. Surely you can see that?"

Roger obviously couldn't see that, and started playing with the front of his jumper.

"Oh, for God's sake, Roger, stop fiddling with it," I said, nervously keeping an eye on the two men at David's old table. "I told you stuffing a tyre-lever down the front of your jumper was a stupid idea. It sticks out like a sore thumb, excuse the reference."

Just before teatime we left the Buckets and made our way towards David's old house. Obviously feeling peckish, Roger decided to call into Sundip's mini-mart for some light refreshments along the way.

"What the hell are you doing?" I whispered as the door-chime tinkled. "This place is like air-traffic control around here. Oh, God, Roger, why did you have to dress all in black? It's not even dark."

Roger seemed unaware of the odd looks he was getting as he completed his purchase of a sausage roll, packet of crisps, and a bottle of diet Coke. He even acknowledged a woman in her slippers with a cheery "Evening" as he left.

We watched David's old house from across the road. Roger leaned against a garden wall and fumbled for an eternity to open the sausage roll wrapper.

"That's right, Roger," I said. "What can be more normal than being all dressed in black in broad daylight, a tyre-lever down your jumper, leaning against a garden wall, and eating a sausage roll? Have you not noticed the guy looking at us out of his caravan window? Or the curtains twitching over there? What about that woman in her slippers who strapped a mobile to her ear as soon as you were out of earshot? Or those two men who walked by when you were struggling to open your crisps? Didn't see them, did you? Well they were the same two men who were sitting at David's office in the Buckets! Roger, this is madness. Please, let's just go home and wait until your brain stops swilling around."

It took Roger around twenty minutes to finish his snack, most of which had been spent fighting with the various packaging. In that time we'd not seen anyone go in or out of the house.

"Maybe even prostitutes take a day off," Roger said through a mouthful of crisps. "After all, it is a Sunday."

Roger pushed himself from the wall and started shuffling across the road. We had to stop halfway across to allow a hooded youth on a bicycle to pass.

"Evening," Roger said, nodding his head once. The reply was a solitary finger.

As we closed in on the house, I noticed the overgrown garden still showed a bare patch where David used to park the Metro, and latterly, Tony's BMW. Roger shuffled up to the door, and, given his fingers couldn't form a proper fist any more, he knocked on it as best he could.

"Bloody hell, Roger," I said. "What are you doing now? Do you think whoever lives here is just going to invite you in and show you round? Roger, I really don't think this is a good…"

I lost all capability of speaking, thinking, or standing, when in answer to Roger's knocking, the door was opened by a once beautiful young girl who used to have pools of blue for eyes, a blemish-free round face, and full curly blonde hair reaching halfway down her back. She was still tall, but no longer that thin, and was sporting a baby-doll nightgown.

"Well, don't just stand there," Penny said. "We wouldn't want the neighbours to start talking now, would we?" Penny turned and walked back into the body of the house.

"Easier than I thought," Roger mumbled to himself as he followed Penny.

I only just managed to crawl through the door before Roger closed it behind him.

"Roger," I whispered, still on my hands and knees. "I know this girl. I reckon the best thing we can do is turn around and get the hell out of here as quickly as possible."

Roger ignored me and followed Penny into the unlit living room.

"Okay, big boy, let's get the finances out of the way first," Penny said, standing far enough away to be no more than a shadow in the gloom. Despite still being light outside, the heavy drawn curtains made David's old living room distinctly sunless. "It's fifty quid for my hand, hundred for my mouth, or two hundred for the full works. I'll dress up for free, but if you want me to do something really kinky it'll cost you extra."

Roger started fumbling down the front of his jumper. "Sounds a bit expensive," he said.

"It'll be the best money you've ever spent," Penny replied. "So what's it to be, lover-boy?"

The tyre-lever fell out of the bottom of Roger's jumper, landing with a loud clank on the floor. Roger bent down, and, by using two hands, eventually managed to pick it up.

"What I'd really like you to do," he said, waving the implement triumphantly in the air, "is give me all the money you've got." Roger was attempting to sound as if threatening prostitutes was something he did on a regular basis, but he'd attracted his own member of the mouse family, who was quite happily destroying any attempt at menace.

Penny took a step out of the shadows and laughed. "Now why would I do that?" she said.

Roger continued waving the lever. "Because if you don't I'll crack your skull open with this. I used to do judo you know. Should have been in Finland. European Championship."

I groaned and got up onto my knees. "Please, Roger," I said, trying to tug on his trouser leg. "Let's just turn around and go when we still can." I could feel the bottom lip quivering. "Nothing good is going to happen here. You really don't know who you're dealing with."

"Listen, I'll give you one chance and one chance only," Penny said. "Leave here in the next thirty seconds and we'll put the experience down to… well, experience, I suppose."

"Please do as she says, Roger," I said, trying to get to my feet but failing. "You don't know what this girl is capable of."

"I'm not going anywhere until I've got what I deserve," Roger replied. "I know there's money here. Just tell me where it is and you needn't get hurt."

He clumsily swung the lever over the top of Penny's head.

"That was a warning shot," he said. "The next one will be straight into the side of that pretty face. Can't imagine you doing much business with a mashed up face," Roger waited a few seconds before adding the word, "bitch."

"Oh, I'm so scared," Penny said, covering her face with her hands. "Please don't hurt me. I suppose I'll just have to give you all the money I've got and hope you go away. Follow me. I keep it all in a biscuit tin in the kitchen."

"Roger! Do you hear that?" I screamed. "That's the sound of sarcasm. Just like when Brian Fletcher asked Mr Wilkins if all the starving people lived in Hungary. Don't you dare go in there."

"I said this would be easy, didn't I?" Roger whispered, following Penny into the kitchen. "In and out like an eel."

"How many times have I got to tell you?" I shouted after him. "Eels are no good in criminal situations."

As my eyes adjusted to the darkness of the room, I sensed I wasn't alone. "Crimson, are you here somewhere?" I said. "Stop messing about and come out."

"She doesn't keep any money in there," a voice said. "She keeps it all in a drawer by the side of her bed." The voice had come from the direction of the large armchair in the corner. The voice was distinctly Welsh. I could just make out a bright red tie with the word *Cymru* written on it just below the knot.

I fell face first to the floor and attempted to find enough air to inflate my lungs.

"Why, I remember you," David said, lifting me up by my elbows. He turned me round to face him. "You're the little twat who came to the prison that day." He threw me into the armchair he'd vacated, then stood over me clicking his knuckles. "Do you know what Slicer and his goons did to my man?" He didn't wait for a reply. "First, they beat him half to death with shoes. Then, they held him down whilst Slicer carved the word *perv* onto his dick with a piece of broken glass. Finally, they strung him up with a belt. Belts are not made for hangings, did you know that? Took ages for him to strangle to death."

I curled into as tight a ball as I could manage. Tears had started to soak what was left of my shirt. "Please don't hurt me," I pleaded. "I'm only a postman. I went to the funeral."

David let out a long menacing laugh and circled the armchair. "I suppose there's little point in snapping you in two," he said. "After all, you're already dead. However, I am getting this strange feeling that causing you some grievous bodily harm would somehow make me feel a whole lot better. Call it an urge if you like. Odd that, don't you think?"

David's urgings were thankfully disturbed by the sound of something metallic landing on the floor in the kitchen, followed by a scream.

David stopped circling and sat on the sofa opposite me. "This used to be my house, did you know that?" he said, smiling. "A man's house is his castle, so they say, and this used to be mine." He waved his arms around the room, but in a way that indicated he was referring to a much wider realm. "Ruled the roost around here I did. King of my own domain. Nobody messed with Dai the Murderer. Nobody. Oh, yes, that's right, my quivering friend, that was my name. Dai the Murderer. Used to make people quake in their shoes whenever good old Dai the Murderer came a knocking. But, hey! Guess what?"

"What?" I said, the word coming out as nothing more than a noise.

David leaned forward and paused for effect. "I know this is going to be difficult to believe," he said, "but I'm not the most aggressive thing in this house any more. In fact, I'm decidedly docile compared to what's in there." David nodded towards the kitchen. "The poor bastard hasn't been fed for a day or two either. Why the committee think Penny needs me to look after her when she's got that beast following her about I'll never know." David patted me on the knee. "If I was you, I'd go check on your assignee."

It took me a while to compose myself and get out of the armchair. I kept one eye on the giggling David as I crawled slowly to the kitchen door.

Roger was pinned with his back to the fridge, his mouth open in a silent scream. He was on tiptoes and holding onto Toby's ears as best he could, frantically trying to shake the dog's grip on his testicles. The tyre-lever was lying harmlessly on the floor some distance away.

"Not too tight, Toby," Penny said, picking up the lever. "Not yet."

She opened a drawer and put the tyre-lever away, then made her way to Roger and fished some money out of his trouser pocket. She took a step back and counted out the notes.

"Thirty quid! What sort of a girl do you take me for, Roger Miller?" she said. "Oh, that's right, I know your name, Roger. In fact, I know everything there is to know about you." Penny put the money down her cleavage and put her mouth to Roger's ear. "Did you honestly think you could spend four days outside my house unnoticed?"

"See I told you!" I said. "But would you listen? No!"

The sound of my voice made Toby turn his head, which in turn twisted Roger's testicles. "Oh God! Please. No more!" he pleaded, his eyes bulging with pain and panic.

"You know, getting a blowjob from a dog is speciality stuff, Roger," Penny said. "Should be costing you a lot more than thirty quid."

She started making her way out of the kitchen.

"Please. Come back." Roger tried to prise Toby's jaws apart, but his fingers carried little strength. "Please, get this thing off me. I promise I'll go. You'll never see me again. I'll move to Finland." A trickle of blood could be seen running out of the bottom of Roger's trousers. "Oh, God, please!"

Penny stopped in the doorway, her back to Roger. "Sorry, Roger, but when Toby is in this sort of mood he's very difficult to control. Anyway, I've got to go and change now. You see, I've got to go out. Got to go to Asda. I've got a date with a regular. Dirty bastard will only ever do it in his car. It's a big black thing, Roger. The car I mean, not the punter. Volvo, I think, with tinted windows. Still, he pays well."

She turned and blew Roger a kiss. "You couldn't do me a favour when I'm upstairs changing could you, Roger? Feed Toby for me, there's a love."

Penny made her way out of the kitchen and disappeared upstairs. I crawled out of the kitchen and back across the living room floor as quickly as I could. I searched for somewhere to hide, eventually settling for underneath the armchair. I stuck my fingers in my ears and hummed loudly, but my actions did little to drown out Roger's screaming.

"Ooh, now that does sound painful," David said, getting off the sofa and following Penny. "Very painful indeed."

I was still under the armchair two hours later when Crimson's face appeared before me. "There you are," she said, reaching under and grabbing me by the foot. "I've been all over the house looking for you. I haven't got time for games of hide and seek, Mark. The committee are going mental." She checked her watch. "This house looks familiar. Have I been here before?"

I nodded, but could find no words.

"Thought so," Crimson said. "By the way, did you know there's a dead body in the kitchen?"

CHOICES, CHOICES

"Well, hello again, Seven-Three-Five-Nine," Mr T. said, without looking up from a file he was holding. "Why it only seems like a few days since you were here last."

"It was a week ago," I said. "Why are you doing this to me? I'm only a postman." I curled up into my defensive position.

"Oh, now there's no need to be so melodramatic, Seven-Three-Five-Nine. Nothing lasts forever. Well, except death of course. Oh, and apparently that musical *Phantom of the Opera.*" Mr T. looked into the void above him. "We had the chap who wrote that here the other day. Had some strange idea about actually being the Lord."

Mr T. shook the idea from his head.

"Anyway, Seven-Three-Five-Nine, we're still preparing for Mr Presley's arrival, so we haven't got time to chatter about your whys and wherefores. I'm sure you understand. Now, it will take us a while to complete all the paperwork, but we'll send for you when we're ready. Here's your new assignee. I hope you like television." He pushed a dossier towards me. "It's all standard practice. In the meantime, I'm sure your good friend Old Eric will be more than happy to see you again. Off you go."

I looked behind me and couldn't work out whether I was relieved or not to discover Old Eric's office door waiting for me.

"Eric, I don't know how much more of this I can take," I said, settling on the edge of his desk.

Eric put his crossword away and removed his glasses. "What's happened?"

I left nothing out. Well, except for everything with Mary.

Somehow, I didn't think Old Eric would treat that bit with the compassion it needed.

"A lovely tale," Eric said. "Now, if you've finished, can I tell you all about my weekend in Paris?" Eric looked like a child desperate to show his mothe the painting he'd done at school.

I stood up and paced the room. "For God's sake, Eric, I'm in trauma here. Can't you give it a rest?"

Old Eric retrieved the crossword and reapplied his glasses. "Okay, so you pick a subject," he said. "I'm getting a bit fed up of always being the one who provides the entertainment around here anyway."

Mother was in my ear.

"I always thought I'd brought you up to respect your elders, Mark. I know you're an alcoholic pervert these days, but that shouldn't stop you from being polite. Let the poor man talk about whatever he wants to. I'm sure he's earned the right. By the way, I've made an appointment for you to see Dr Connolly about this whole pervert thing. Remember Dr Connolly? He was the one who gave you those pills to clean up that little problem you picked up on your honeymoon."

"Mum! You said you'd never mention that again."

"Did I?"

"Yes. Anyway, Elaine said she must have caught it off a toilet seat."

"Didn't she go to Ibiza with her friends just before you got married?"

"So? What's that got to do with it?"

I sat back on the desk and played with the Last Supper. "Well, you never actually got round to telling me how you died, Eric," I said, hoping to keep his mind away from Paris. "You just bit my head off about having something called *end syndrome*, remember?"

"It's not that important, son."

"Important or not, I'd really like to know."

Old Eric sighed and put his crossword away. "Well, if you insist," he said, removing his glasses and placing them on the desk. "But honestly, the weekend in Paris is far more riveting. Are you sure you wouldn't rather hear about that?"

"Positive thanks."

"Okay, where to start?" Eric looked at the ceiling. "I suppose you could say I simply allowed myself to drift off." He stood up and paced back and forth behind the desk. "Disappeared into the sunset never to be seen again. Took my nose off the grindstone and gave myself a permanent holiday. Decided to drop out of the rat-race." Eric sat back down. "There, satisfied? Can I tell you about Paris now?"

"Eric, you're not making much sense," I said, putting down the print. "I mean *what* actually killed you? What does it say on your death certificate?"

Old Eric giggled to himself. "No such thing as a death certificate in my day, son."

Eric obviously wasn't going to make this easy. I'd once dabbled in trying to trace my family tree (Mother had forced me to stop when she found out) and knew that death certificates had been in existence for 175 years or so. "Okay," I said, playing along with his game. "But if there had been, what might it have said?"

"God knows," Eric said, still giggling. "Probably some fancy bloody name. I mean, they find names for everything these days don't they?"

"Not quite with you, Eric. What do you mean?"

"Well in my day, son, if you were a bit thick, then you were a bit thick. If you were an evil shitty kid, then you were an evil shitty kid. If you were mental, then you were mental. If you were a miserable bugger, then you were a miserable bugger. It was a simple system, son, and everybody understood it. Nowadays, it seems no matter what's wrong with you, there's some medical name you can attach to yourself to excuse your actions. If you're a bit thick, there's always Dysthickia, or whatever the hell it's called. If you're an evil shitty kid, there's Evil Shitty Kid Syndrome. If you're mental, there's that Schizophrenia lark. And, if you're a miserable bugger, there's always good old Depression to fall back on. Whatever happened to failure, son? That's what I'd like to know. Why do people today insist that their egos can only cope with differing levels of success?"

Old Eric stood up and made his way to me.

"That's why I like you so much, son," he said, putting his arm around my shoulders. "You're a throwback to the good old days. You understand failure."

"I wish you could have met Father," I said, taking Eric's arm from around me. "I think you'd have got on really well."

Old Eric made his way back around the desk and sat down. "So, anyway, the action started as soon as Elaine and that lawyer got to the airport," he said. "They checked in and immediately made their way to the nearest toilet…"

"Eric!"

"What?"

"We weren't talking about Paris."

"Weren't we?"

"No."

Mother was screaming at me to keep calm; to remember Eric's Alzheimer's. I took a deep breath. "We were talking about how you died," I said.

Eric picked up his glasses and pondered for a moment. "Surrendered," he said with some triumph.

"Pardon?"

Eric retrieved his crossword from the drawer. "Nine down," he said. "Stopped resisting. Eleven letters."

I stood up and pretended to bang my head against the wall. "Eric, why can't you ever give me a straight answer? That's all I asked is how you died. Surely nothing could be simpler?"

"Oh, I'll have to disagree with you there, son," Eric said. "If you look hard enough you'll find the path to death littered with an uncountable number of choices. It's almost impossible to put your finger on which one actually brings you in front of the committee, wouldn't you agree?"

Eric sucked his brilliant white teeth.

"Let's try this," he said. "Imagine you've got a thousand beautiful women lined up in front of you all desperate to be your wife, but you've been told you can marry only one."

"Eric, for me, the scenario is highly unlikely."

"So, anyway, you make your choice, and for a while you're in Heaven. But did you make the right choice? After all, the mother-in-law has turned out to be a bit of an ogre, and, no matter how green people keep telling you your grass is, you start thinking about all those lovely women you passed over. Doubts start creeping over you like climbing Ivy. It begins to drive you mental. You had all those choices. You could have picked any one of them. Your mind starts to fry in a bubbling cauldron of uncertainty. Did you make the wrong choice? Your desperation eventually drives you to drink. Your therapist suggests you start taking antidepressants to get you through the day. Your beautiful bride starts to abhor you and runs off with your best friend. You lose your job. You often find yourself waking up on park benches. Or in skips. One day, unable to process the amount of abuse it's being given, your liver explodes into a thousand pieces. You die. Now, what's the cause of death here, son?"

Eric cocked his head to one side awaiting a reply.

"Eric, I have no idea what you're…"

"Go on. Give it a stab. What's the cause of death?"

"I don't know… Sclerosis of the liver?"

"Ah, now that's undoubtedly the fancy name they'd put on the death certificate," Eric said. "But what's the *real* cause? Which choice finally did you in? The choice of woman? The one to start drinking? Your choice of best friend? Sleeping in skips? Should you have made any choice at all when confronted with all those women? Why didn't you just walk away? Would you still be alive if you had?"

"Eric, I really have no idea what you're on about," I said. "In fact, I think I can actually feel a headache coming on." Were dead postmen even supposed to get headaches? "That's all I wanted was a straight forward answer. Like, I got run over by a bus, I fell off the edge of a cliff, I had a heart attack."

"Okay, okay," Eric said, putting the crossword away. "If it's one definitive answer you're after, here it is. In the final analysis of things, son, the only true cause of death has got to be life itself. I mean, look at it logically. It's impossible to achieve the one without the other, right? I suppose the trick is to make sure you get them in the right order. And don't listen to these people who tell you that life's too short, son. When all said and done, it's the longest thing you'll ever do. Well, except death I suppose."

"I give up. Eric, what are you on about?"

"To summarise, the cause of all death, mine and yours included, has to be because we lived." Eric's brightness increased by a few thousand lumens. He looked like he'd just discovered something important, like the cure for cancer, or a new planet.

"No, really, I give up," I said, sitting back on the edge of Eric's desk.

"Good. *Now* can I tell you about Paris?"

"No!"

Old Eric leaned back in his chair and whistled quietly to himself, occasionally glancing at me and offering a smile. I couldn't quite make out what he was whistling, but thought it may well have been the French national anthem.

"Eric, I do not want to hear anything about Paris, okay?"

"If you say so," Eric said. "But sooner or later, we're going to have to talk about something."

I stood up, walked to the door and back again. "Okay, if you're not going to tell me how you died, tell me what happened *after* you died," I said. "Tell me about your first meeting with the committee. Tell me anything except what happened in Paris."

Old Eric closed his eyes and shook his head slowly. "Oh my, the first meeting. Were the committee pissed off or what? You should have heard them, son. Dragged me over the coals until I felt like I'd been run over by a steamroller."

"What happened?"

Eric opened his eyes and put his hands behind his head. "Well, like I told you before, son," he said. "I had a lot of people hanging on my advice. Even the negative publicity surrounding the antics of my supposed offspring hadn't dampened people's enthusiasm for my wisdom. And the fact my missus had run away with that half-gay carpenter somehow only served to increase my popularity. So, I guess I left a lot of people up shit-creek when I disappeared. The committee went mental."

"What did they say?"

"They said the crap had really hit the fan since I'd left the stage. Told me I was like a drug. People had to have their fix, they said, and without me around to give it to them, things had apparently started to go a bit haywire. They said I'd abandoned my followers with no explanation; that I'd left my people all alone in the wilderness with no hope or salvation. There were hunger strikes and protests, so they reckoned, even the odd tribal war. According to the committee, there was so much wailing and moaning going on it could be heard from where they were. Told me I could forget any ideas about ever getting into the Sanctum, and that I was nothing but a selfish, worthless piece of doggy-doo, who'd never be forgiven as long as I lived… died… whatever."

"What happened next?"

"Well, I told them I wasn't looking for forgiveness anyway. Told them I firmly believed in the eye for an eye thing and had no time for turning the other cheek. By my reckoning, that just meant you'd end up with two sore cheeks. So I told them straight. Whatever you want to do to me, I said, do it. And let's not have any more idle chit-chat."

"So what did they do?"

"Made my death hell, son, that's what they did."

"How?"

"Oh, this and that. We needn't go into details. After all, isn't it within the detail where you supposedly find the Devil? Suffice to say that over time they've mellowed bit by bit. Did I ever tell you I'm the only dead person to have an office?"

"I think you mentioned it."

"I even get some credit now and then for the work I did when I was alive. It's not a lot, but it helps to stave off thoughts that my work was a complete waste of time. Still don't think I'll ever get to the Sanctum though. I left far too much of a mess behind for that to happen."

"I don't mean to be rude, Eric," I said. "but if you were as important as you say you were, how come nobody's ever heard of you? I mean, wouldn't there be books written about you? Films even?"

Eric's smile reached biblical proportions. "Yeah, you'd think so wouldn't you?"

There was a knock on the door.

Thank God, I thought, as Crimson entered the room. I've managed to keep him talking long enough to avoid Paris.

"Damn!" Eric said. "We never got round to finding out who's in your dossier."

BILLY'S BELTERS

Billy White had his own prime time television show. If you were lucky to be stupid enough to get your little mishap aired on *Billy's Belters*, you received the princely sum of £200.

The end of each show had Billy announce, *'Don't forget guys, nobody in tonight's show got seriously hurt, because if they did, it just wouldn't be...'* Billy would then take a deep breath and the studio audience would join in with the final word of the evening, drawn out for as long as possible, *'fuuuuuuuuuuuuun.'*

And oh, how everyone would laugh.

Billy's charismatic TV persona, coupled with his over-abundant sex-appeal, had made him one of the nation's favourite celebrities. He'd appeared in cameo roles on numerous soaps and had advertised everything from aardvarks to zygotes. He'd hosted a range of game shows down the years and was a regular and popular guest on chat-shows. Forty-five, but only admitting to thirty-nine, he'd risen from humble Northern routes, leaving school with no qualifications to speak of. His first paid job had been working as a runner for a local TV channel, and his first break came when the producer's wife suggested Billy host the channel's new late-night game-show; a cheaply produced affair wherein contestants competed to test which of them had the greatest pain threshold. The show itself was an unmitigated disaster, but Billy's looks and ease in front of the camera hadn't gone unnoticed. Soon, Billy started to climb the rungs of the TV-land ladder, and had women of all ages wishing he was theirs.

Including Mother.

"He seems like a very nice man, Mark. I'd love to invite him

around for tea one day. Best not ask Timothy's sister around at the same time though, had I? One snap of his fingers and she'd be gone."

As well as Mother's admiration, Elaine also took pleasure in often reminding me Billy White was number 3 on her shag-list, stating, *'the only way I'd ever turn him down, Mark, was if numbers one* (Richard Gere) *or two* (Orlando Bloom) *asked first.'*

At least whilst I'd been alive I could always pretend to ignore Elaine as she drooled over Billy showing her footage of some grown man driving his bicycle through a shop window or the like. Even when Sarah and Emma-Lou snuggled up together and guffawed their way through watching kids falling out of trees into paddling pools, or animals riding skateboards, or women getting their fingers stuck in the claws of crabs, I could still retreat to my corner and disregard their merriment.

Now I had no choice.

It had been three months since Crimson had dumped me in the middle of the studio in which Billy's Belters was televised, and I still couldn't get the appeal of the show; or of Billy.

Father had always conjectured that Billy was, *'A bit of a knob,'* and it appeared he'd been right. Off-screen Billy was nowhere near the jocular, agreeable character as on-screen Billy. Whether Billy had always been how Father suggested was, of course, unknown to me, but for the last three months he'd certainly lived up to Father's description. It had been three months in which I'd had to witness Billy treat most people he knew as inferior to himself. This included his long time manager and agent, Harry.

Billy and Harry had been together ever since Billy had first come to the attention of the populace, and, despite their notorious spats, I'd come to learn that Billy's career would have been nowhere near as successful without Harry's expertise and input; something I believed Billy fully understood, but decided not to acknowledge. In the early days, after Harry had eventually negotiated Billy's move away from that dreadful first game-show, one tabloid had even suggested their relationship might be more than purely professional, but had been forced to issue a very public apology when Harry arranged for a porn actress to testify that Billy certainly wasn't gay. I recalled Elaine, presumably along with most of the female population, breathing a sigh of relief at the time. *'Oh thank God for that. I thought for a moment I was in for another George Michael episode. Broke my heart when I had to take him off my list.'* Poor old George had been number 7 until he came out. He'd since been replaced by Jake Gyllenhaal.

The cameras had stopped rolling and the studio was winding down. As soon as the last of the audience had left, Billy marched onto set, obviously in one of his moods - or a *Billy's Belt* as I'd often heard some of the workforce call them.

"Where's that useless twat of a make-up girl?" he screamed to all within earshot. "This fucking eyeliner is running like diarrhoea. I'll put her arse in a vice if she's made me look like a cunt on national TV. Harry, where the fuck are you?"

Harry appeared from the wings, where he'd been talking to one of the cameramen. He looked as colourful as ever in a gold-coloured sports jacket and lime-green skinny jeans.

"Billy, please don't get yourself worked up," he said. "It's no good for your blood pressure, not to say anything about your complexion." Harry adjusted the lapels of Billy's handmade Italian jacket. "I'm sure it's just the heat from the lights." He licked his thumb and run it under Billy's eyes. "Look, there's hardly anything there." He showed Billy the evidence. "I'm sure no one noticed."

Billy stared hard at his small, bespectacled manager-come-agent. "I noticed!" he said. "So get her fired, Harry. I'll not have my reputation spoiled by some kid straight out of face-painting school who has no fucking idea how hard I've worked to get where I am today."

"She's twenty-six, Billy," Harry said, taking a monogrammed handkerchief from his top pocket and wiping Billy's face. "She's worked with the best of the best for Christ's sake. She's in very high demand. I had to negotiate my arse off to get her. We were really lucky she chose us."

"Wrong, Harry!" Billy shouted. He snatched the handkerchief from Harry's hand and started making his way back towards his changing room. "She was lucky we chose her. Anyway, she's obviously a lesbian, and, as you are fully aware, I can't stand working with lesbians or gays."

"She's not a lesbian, Billy," Harry said, trying to keep up with his employer. "She's married to an extremely sexy Spanish football player, and, if I remember rightly, she also used to date Russell Brand. I can only assume you're basing your prejudices on the fact she turned you down for dinner?" (Russell Brand had been a constant on Elaine's list and had been number 19 the last time I'd looked.)

"Just do your job and get her fired you miniscule gay dwarf," Billy replied. "And make sure I'm not disturbed for a while. I need some peace and quiet. I've been working like a third-world-well all day. I need some Billy-time."

Billy slammed his dressing room door behind him, leaving Harry outside.

The smell of freshly cut flowers overpowered the sumptuous dressing room. Billy was very specific about his flowers and had been known to throw the most amazing tantrums if they weren't right. He slumped into one of three velvet covered armchairs and removed a state-of-the-art mobile phone from his jacket pocket; the one he only ever used for personal calls.

"Hi, it's Billy White," he said into the phone. "Yeah, yeah, I'm fine. Still overworked and underpaid. How about you? You still getting criminals off?" Billy laughed at whatever the recipient of the phone call replied. "Listen, I'm thinking of staying in town tonight, so how do you fancy hooking up? Perhaps we could meet at that swanky club of yours?" Billy reached over and picked out a yellow carnation from a spray and sniffed it appreciatively. "Great, say around eight?"

Billy put the mobile away and poked his head out of the dressing room door. "Harry!" he screamed. "Get your skinny gay arse in here now."

Harry was never too far away, and no more than thirty seconds had passed before there was a tap on the door. "You rang, master," Harry said, poking his head into the dressing room.

"Don't try and be clever, Harry," Billy said. "It doesn't suit you. And where the fuck have you been? I called you ages ago. Have you been shagging that cameraman again?"

"Ooh, you bitch," Harry said, entering the room. "Anyway, he's not my type."

Billy poured himself a whisky from a well stocked drinks' trolley. "Don't tell me. Too short?" He sat back down in one of the armchairs.

"No. Straight," Harry replied, puckering his lips in disappointment. Harry went to the trolley and poured himself a pineapple juice. "Now, to what do I owe the pleasure of your summons?"

"Have you fired Picasso's daughter?"

"No need. She overheard. She quit."

"Good." Billy drained his drink and got up to pour himself another one. "I'm staying in town tonight. Meeting up with an old friend. I want you to phone Ruby and tell her I won't be home. Tell her there was trouble with the shoot or something and I'm stuck on set."

"Why can't you phone her yourself?"

Billy swilled his drink around before devouring it in one go. "Because I don't keep a dog just to do all the barking myself you stupid bent midget. Why the hell do you think you take that huge amount of my earnings, Harry? To sit on your arse all day? Anyway, she'll believe you."

"And who is this old friend?" Harry said, making for the door. "Female, I suppose?"

Billy sat down at his preparation area and checked his hair in the wall-length mirror. "No, *he's* not female," he said. "Now fuck off and phone Ruby for me. After all, if it wasn't for you I'd never have married her in the first place. Why the hell do I need a wife when I can have any woman I want? Oh, and by the way, that pineapple juice is coming out of your wages."

Harry turned in the door and blew Billy a kiss. He managed to close it just in time to stop the hairbrush Billy had thrown from connecting with his head.

As was Billy's norm he was fashionably late, and turned up outside the swanky club he'd referred to in his telephone conversation at ten minutes past eight. His old friend was waiting. As soon as I stepped out of the taxi, I felt like I'd triggered off a landmine.

I'd met Billy's friend once before. Five months before I'd died.

We were in a hotel at some party Elaine's law firm was throwing; someone's retirement do I think. Elaine was circulating the room, looking sexy in a tight white blouse and split to the thigh pencil skirt. I was just pleased to have been invited, and was towing along behind under strict instructions to remain as quiet as a librarian, and under no circumstances to break out into any Elvis stories.

After half-an-hour of mingling, during which Elaine managed to sink two large glasses of wine, she spotted a man over the crowd and let out a little girly moan. I noticed the man in question had an uncanny resemblance to number 1 on Elaine's shag-list and she waved her fingers at him before making a beeline in his direction. I followed in her wake, and, after Elaine had tried unsuccessfully to hide her disappointment that I had actually followed her, she introduced the man to me simply as her *colleague*.

Half an hour later, after Elaine had devoured another two glasses of wine, and I was listening to someone boast to his assembled crowd about the time he'd prosecuted some famous politician, I lost sight of her. I searched the room, but couldn't find my wife anywhere. I thought about asking her *colleague* if he knew where she might have got to, but I couldn't find him anywhere either.

Ten minutes later Elaine suddenly appeared at my side, looking slightly dishevelled. I pointed out that the buttons on her blouse didn't seem to be done up right, and on asking where she'd been, she replied she'd been to the toilet, reminding me angrily that she didn't need my permission to take a piss. I also asked what had happened to her *colleague,* as he seemed to have disappeared.

Elaine made some vague reference about him having *'come and gone'* and we never spoke about him again.

The sight of Billy's friend had rendered my body numb from the waist down. I was forced to follow the pair of them past the liveried doorman and into the club by using my elbows to pull myself along like a snake. By the time Billy and his friend got themselves settled into two leather armchairs around a highly polished table, the exertions of my snake impression caught up with me, and I fell face-first into the luxurious pile of the club's carpet. I fought hard against the darkness creeping around me, eventually managing to roll over onto my back. My efforts were done just in time to witness the ordering of two bottles of wine that would have devoured a few weeks' worth of salary for a postman.

I decided the minute I could find enough air to speak properly, I'd use the new forthright Mark Ferris to tell Billy's friend exactly what I thought of him.

"You just wait until I can stand up," I said, rolling around like an upturned turtle. "Then you'll be sorry. I might not have done anything about you when I was alive, but I'm dead now, so… so… so…" I couldn't finish the sentence. Tears rolled out of my eyes and started filling my ears. I called hard for the new forthright Mark Ferris, but he obviously hadn't been allowed into the club; perhaps he'd forgotten to wear a tie or something.

I cried hard as Billy and his wife-stealing friend exuded spare pheromones for fun, engaging each other in relaxed conversation.

"Damned, you're looking good," Billy said to his friend. "What's your secret?"

The reply came back in a voice that could smelt gold. "Doesn't come easy, Billy. My personal trainer is a real taskmaster. Ten miles on the machine. Fifty lengths in the pool. An hour on the weights."

"What, every day?" Billy said.

A waiter arrived and presented the wine as gently as if it were a new born babe.

"Yeah. It's hard work, but worth it," Billy's friend said, excusing the waiter with a flick of his hand.

"How do you find the time?"

"Life isn't all about work, Billy. You should always find time for yourself. When I'm not busy in court or at the gym I like to fit in a game of squash here and there, or even the odd round of golf. I'm off a handicap of eight these days."

"Bloody hell," Billy said, swilling his wine around in a crystal-cut glass. "You must be knackered all the time."

The lawyer laughed. "Far from it, Billy. I find the physical exercise actually gives me more stamina, especially in the bedroom department, if you know what I mean?"

I recalled Father once telling me, *'Everyone has faults, son. It's just they're easier to find in some than others.'*

I forced myself to look up from the floor and study the lawyer. "Hah!" I said, weakly lifting my hand and pointing a finger in the general direction of some grey strands of hair on the side of his head. "You're going grey."

Then I remembered Elaine found men with grey hair distinguished and sexy. There were certainly enough of them on her shag-list.

I continued studying the lawyer with all my might, but could find nothing wrong with the man. His greying hair was immaculate. His made to measure clothes were immaculate. His tanned face was immaculate. Even his fingernails were immaculate. He smelled of success and oozed confidence like it was freely available from supermarkets. I guessed if medical science ever wished to create the perfect man, they wouldn't go far wrong using Billy's friend as a template.

How could I, Mark Ferris, a dead postman, ever hope to compete? The scent of my wife was all over him.

"Talking of which," Billy said, leaning forward in his chair as if involved in some conspiracy. "You still with that sexy thing you started seeing after your daughter passed away?"

"Yep, still with her," the lawyer confirmed. "Been nearly three years now. Be going in for my long-service award soon." He giggled at his quip as he reached into his jacket and produced an ornately wrapped cigar. "Had this given to me yesterday by a grateful secretary," he said. "Didn't have the heart to tell her I don't smoke. Would you like it?"

Billy took the cigar and immediately started unwrapping it. "Wow, thanks," he said. "None of my bloody employees ever give me presents." Billy sniffed the cigar and let out a satisfied moan. "Listen, I'm sorry I wasn't around. You know? When all that crap happened with your daughter."

"That's all right."

"No, it's not. What are friends supposed to be for? You were there to help me out when I got into that spot of bother, and I should have been there for you when you needed a shoulder to cry on."

"Ah, but don't forget, Billy, you paid for my help. Anyway, you're a very busy man these days, Billy. I bet it can't be easy keeping all those adoring females away."

"Almost impossible," Billy said, laughing.

"Can't believe you got married," the lawyer said, sipping his wine. "Okay, so if you're going to get married then what better than a lingerie model? But still, you, married? Doesn't seem right. Came as a bit of a shock when I read about it in the press."

Harry had introduced Billy and Ruby to each other at the launch of a new lads' magazine that was using Ruby as one of their models. Ruby's career up to that point had been sporadic and un-noteworthy, but their brief courtship and subsequent marriage had been covered in a blaze of publicity and had helped propel Ruby to the forefront of most magazines' wish-lists. The wedding itself, completely arranged by Harry, had been limited to fifty guests, all of whom were handpicked. Small, but lavish, and held in a castle in Scotland, it had cost a leading magazine a small-fortune to get exclusive rights for photographs, and had been hailed as one of the most glamorous weddings of the year.

However, in the three months I'd been witness to the union, I'd come to the conclusion Ruby had no love for her husband.

But she did love his money.

Money equalled power. And power opened doors. Therefore, to the outside world at least, Ruby gave off the air of being one of the most loved-up women on the planet, and females in general struggled to hide their jealousy.

Wasn't she just the luckiest woman alive?

"Yeah, sorry we couldn't get you an invite," Billy said, still admiring his cigar. "But the guests were all arranged by Harry. In fact, the whole thing was arranged by Harry. Reckoned it would be good for my image. Said it would get certain rumour-mongers off my back."

"Rumour-mongers?"

"Believe it or not, my friend, there are still a few people out there who question my sexuality. I mean, I ask you, how many women have I got to be seen with for them to understand I'm not gay for God's sake?"

"So the whole marriage thing was just for the cameras?"

Billy nodded his head as he took a swig of wine. "Ruby's quite happy with the arrangement," he said, putting down his glass. "After all, it hasn't done her career any harm. And, I don't know, she's sort of handy to have around, you know what I mean? Don't get me wrong, I couldn't give a flying fuck what she gets up to, but she's probably the closest thing I've ever gotten to having someone who'll listen if I need to let off some steam."

"So do you and Ruby. You know? Get it on."

Billy laughed. "Once."

"Once!"

"On the night of the wedding. Just to make it legal and all that."

"But she's bloody gorgeous. How do you keep your hands off her?"

"Plenty of fish in the sea, my friend. If women insist on throwing themselves at my feet, it would be rude for me not to pick one or two of them up along the way, don't you think?" Billy leaned forward and looked around to make sure there was no one within earshot. "You know that stunning seventeen year old who just won that reality pop show thing?" He formed a circle with his thumb and forefinger and pushed the cigar in and out of it.

"You didn't?"

Billy leaned back in his chair and smiled. "Oh yes I did."

"But she built her whole story on being such a sweet little thing who'd never been touched." The lawyer's face suddenly collapsed. "My God, Billy. You did treat her okay, didn't you?"

"Like an angel."

"Hang on. That's not why you've suddenly called me up is it? You haven't been stupid again?"

"Of course not." Billy rolled the cigar around his lips.

"Because if you have there'd be no hiding place this time, Billy. You're a household name these days. Not like back then."

"Stop panicking," Billy said. "I was the perfect gentleman. Don't get me wrong, she reckoned it was her first time and all that bollocks. Struggled a bit at first I must admit, but when she got going she was like a feral bloody cat. If anyone's going to make a fuss, it should be me. I had cuts and bruises all over me by the time we'd finished. She just couldn't get enough."

The night in question had happened a month after I'd arrived.

They met at some TV-land party and the girl was as lovely, sweet, and demure in real life as she'd been on the TV. She was surrounded by a posse of male admirers, but fell for Billy's charms and flirted with him outrageously.

Towards the end of the evening, Billy invited the girl back to his hotel room. She agreed on the basis it would be for a quick nightcap and nothing more. Once in the hotel room, Billy lost all his charm and swooped on the girl like an owl on a vole.

When she finally gave up all hope of fending Billy away, the girl begged him to be gentle. Billy ignored the request, and the girl cried in pain all the way through the *act* itself. When he was spent, Billy practically threw the girl out, not even allowing her to use the shower. He reminded her who he was and told her if she ever breathed a word about what had happened, he'd personally see to it that her career went down the drain quicker than rainwater.

Harry later arranged for the bed sheets to be clandestinely cleaned of the girl's virgin blood.

"Well as long as you're keeping things legal," the lawyer said.

"Because, thankfully for me, nobody is above the law, Billy, not even God himself."

"You think so?" Billy said. "Watch this."

He popped the cigar into his mouth and called the waiter to the table.

"I need a cigar cutter and a light," he said, pointing at the cigar dangling from his lips.

Without a hint of emotion, the waiter replied, "Sorry, sir, but this is strictly a no smoking establishment. There is a shelter out back if sir is desperate."

"Do you know who I am?" Billy asked, narrowing his eyes.

"I do believe you're Billy White," the waiter said. "The wife and I never miss your programme, sir. Even the dog finds it funny."

"And you're telling me you can't even bend the rules for someone who makes your fucking dog laugh?"

"I'm afraid not, sir."

"Perhaps I should follow you home and introduce myself to your wife, you overgrown penguin. I bet I make her nice and moist, eh? I bet you get extra action on the nights she's been watching me, don't you?"

The waiter turned to the lawyer. "I must insist you control your guest, sir, otherwise we shall have to respectfully request you both leave the premises."

"Yes, yes, of course," the lawyer said, exchanging a polite nod with the waiter.

"Hey, come back here," Billy said, as the waiter walked away. "Nobody walks away from Billy White."

The lawyer leaned forward and caught hold of Billy's arm. "Billy, give it a rest will you?" he said. "It took me two years to get accepted in here."

Billy leaned back in his chair and closed his eyes. "Ah, I'm sorry," he said, taking the cigar out of his mouth and throwing it on the table. "I'm working too hard. What I need is a good woman." He opened his eyes and smiled. "Tell you what. Why don't we get ourselves a couple of high-class hookers? The Singleton is just down the road. I've got a suite on retainer."

"Wow, that must cost a pretty penny."

"Yeah, it's a fair sum, but Harry manages to get it palmed off as tax deductible, and at least they give a hefty discount for signing up long-term. The main beauty though is its staff are nice and discreet. What do you say?"

The lawyer shifted in his seat. "I don't think so, Billy. Really? Hookers?"

Billy downed his glass of wine, refilling it immediately. "Look, I've been working like a dog," he said. "You might be full of energy thanks to your personal bloody trainer, but I'm absolutely fucked. I just feel like having a woman who'll ride me rotten and ask no questions. Anyway, hookers are safer. Never know what you might catch from some floozy you pick up in a bar. Plus, hookers don't mind if you get a bit kinky."

"It just seems like false economy, Billy. Don't know about you, but I've always managed to get as many kicks as I need for free. Surely hookers are for the poor unfortunates who are too ugly to get action anywhere else, aren't they? I mean, look at us. If we want women we only have to snap our fingers, right?"

Billy finished his glass and poured out the remains of his bottle. "Ah, I suppose you're right," he said. "Why should we have to pay when there's hundreds of women who'd sell their children to sleep with us? Come on, drink up, let's get out of here and find some action." He drained his glass.

"Whoa!" the lawyer said, waving his bottle of wine in the air. "I've still got half a bottle here. It's too bloody expensive to leave. Anyway, what's the rush?" He topped up his own glass and poured out a measure for Billy. "Here's to beautiful women and all who sail in them." He lifted his glass, indicating for Billy to do the same.

Over the clink of their glasses the strains of the theme tune to *Mission Impossible* emanated from somewhere within the lawyer's jacket. "Excuse me, Billy," he said, retrieving a mobile from his pocket. He looked at the incoming caller's number and stood up. "Sorry, but I have to take this." He walked a few paces away, but not far enough for Billy and I not to hear his half of the conversation.

"Hi, babe, what's up?... No, I'm just out with an old friend… Actually, you'll never believe who it is… What do you mean I need to get home right away?... You're joking?... What, the whole thing?... What about the glasses?... The boots?... Gloves and hat?... Okay, don't move. I'm on my way."

He put the phone away and made his way back to the table.

"Uh, Billy," he said, without sitting back down. "Something's cropped up. I'm really sorry but I'll have to take a rain check on our little woman-hunt."

His phone chirped again. He turned it sideways to look at it. "By Christ," he said, quickly putting the phone away. "She really is wearing the whole thing."

"But what about the wine?" Billy protested, as the lawyer accepted his coat off the waiter. "You just said it was too expensive to leave."

"You have it," the lawyer replied, signing his name on a credit chit the waiter had brought. "My treat." He quickly made his way out of the room.

"Hey, come back here," Billy shouted. "Nobody walks away from Billy White."

I rolled off my back and eventually managed to pull myself up into the seat vacated by Billy's old friend. I dried my face and watched in silence as Billy finished off the wine.

"Hey, penguin boy," Billy shouted over to the waiter. "Fetch me my coat. I'm leaving. Don't forget to tell your wife who you've been serving tonight. Bet there'll be a blowjob in it for you at the very least."

After leaving the club, Billy had continued drinking steadily at The Singleton and was extremely uneasy on his feet when he went to answer the knock on his hotel room door. He looked at his watch. "Bang on time," he said. "I like it when they're punctual."

In the three months I'd been with Billy we'd only stayed at his room in The Singleton twice before. Both times I'd had to turn my head away from the violent pornography Billy liked to watch on his laptop, but this was the first time he'd arranged company. It dawned on me that despite his sex appeal, and for all his fame and fortune, I'd only known Billy to have sex with two women. One was a street prostitute he'd picked up after a furious row with Harry, and the other was the young singer he'd boasted about earlier. On both occasions he'd not exactly been gentle.

Billy opened the door and ushered in his company. She was dressed in a tight lace-up leather mini-dress accompanied by thigh-high leather boots, a-la Julia Roberts in that film with number 1 on Elaine's shag-list. Underneath her garish make-up, I could still tell Billy's companion once had beautiful pools of blue for eyes, a blemish-free round face, and full curly blonde hair reaching halfway down her back.

Penny strutted into the room confidently, quickly followed by David. I immediately lost the ability to remain standing.

"What the fuck are you doing here?" David asked, picking me up and placing me in the bedside chair. He started cracking his knuckles. "You know, I get this strange feeling I knew you when I was alive," he said. "Just can't place the face. Perhaps I should rearrange it a bit and see if anything comes to mind."

I curled up on the chair and was only vaguely aware of Penny negotiating prices with Billy. "Can't we just talk instead?" I said, the words struggling to bypass the mouse.

David laughed. "I've never been one for talking," he said. "Anyway, what the hell would *we* talk about?"

"Penny?" I suggested.

Thankfully, David stopped cracking his knuckles; it always amazed me how even the half a finger still cracked. "What about her?" he said.

"Well, how's she been?" I asked, trying to inflect as much pleasantness into my voice as I could. "You know? Since her dog ate my last assignee. I would have thought having a mangled dead body in the kitchen took some explaining."

David moved towards me. Oh, God! I must have said the wrong thing. Bloody foot and mouth. I put my hands over my face and felt the bottom lip giving way.

David sniggered as he picked me up under the armpits and sat me on the floor, taking the chair for himself. "Now don't you go worrying your pretty little head about Penny," he said. "She can look after herself. She called in a few favours and got any trace of her existence out of that house before the night was out. Let's face it, it's not like her name was on the rent-book."

I took my hands away from my face. "But what about Roger's body?"

"Poof!" David made a motion with his hands of something magically disappearing. "Vanished into thin air. Well, into a nice deep grave in the New Forrest actually, but we'll keep that to ourselves, eh?" David tapped his nose.

"Oh my God, poor Roger. Poor Gary. What about the police? I mean, I assume Gary reported him missing?"

"Ah, they wouldn't have got any answers," David said, looking over to the raising voices from Penny and Billy. "They probably didn't ask too many question anyway." David's face started to look worried as he concentrated on the obvious decline in any pleasantries between our assignees. "Let's face it, your assignee was a bit of a dickhead. My guess is his case-file is already rotting away in some dusty storeroom.

I'm sure the police have better things to do than go looking for an ugly stupid wanker like…"

David's assessment of Roger was interrupted by the crunching noise of Billy's fist connecting with the side of Penny's face.

David leaped from the chair and flew across the room.

I attempted to stand up, but only managed to get myself to my knees. I watched, helpless, as David tried in vain to exact pain and suffering on Billy.

"I'm going to fucking kill you," David screamed, raining blows on Billy that would, under normal circumstances, have given medical staff a whole lot of work. "I'm going to rip that fucking smug head clean off your shoulders and feed it to the birds, you shit-hole."

I sat back on my heels and buried my head in my hands. "Jesus Christ, Billy," I whispered. "What the hell are you doing?"

I peeked through my fingers as David continued to try and stop Billy from doing what he was doing.

The blow Billy had delivered to Penny's head had landed her face-up on the bed. I could tell she wasn't quite unconscious because I could hear her mumbling incoherently and her right arm was rising and falling spasmodically.

Billy was shaking his hand vigorously. "You little bitch," he said. "I think I've broken a knuckle. I'm going to have to make you pay for that."

Billy proceeded to extract a handkerchief from his jacket pocket and stuffed it into Penny's mouth. He then straddled Penny and used his belt to tie her hands behind her back. Slowly, he began to strip off her clothes.

When she was naked, except for the boots, Billy undressed himself.

David made his way back to the chair. He'd all but spent every ounce of energy he possessed attempting to carry out his various threats against Billy. "You best do something quick," he said, pointing at me. "If he lays another finger on her, I'm blaming you."

I responded in the only way I knew how. I curled myself into a ball and burst into tears. How long I remained like that before David picked me up and planted me on my feet, I'm not sure. I may have even passed out for a few minutes.

"I don't care how hard you think things are," David said, catching me under the chin and turning my head towards the bed. "Because they can always get harder. Look!"

Penny, who still hadn't regained full control of her senses, had her ankles bound together with some sort of cord. She used what little strength she had to resist in vain as Billy tied a leather strap around her waist. Closer inspection, forced upon me by David thrusting my head into the action, showed that attached to the leather strap, was a gleaming silver vibrator.

Not that I was any kind of expert, but it crossed my mind it looked like the same model I'd once found in Elaine's secret drawer.

With the device in place - protruding upwards from just below Penny's bellybutton - Billy stepped back and admired his handiwork.

"Now for the real entertainment," he said, wearing a grin that would have competed with Old Eric's for wideness. He retired to the bathroom, reappearing almost immediately with a jar of lubricant. After applying a liberal dose to the toy, he placed the jar on the bedside cabinet. He then climbed onto the bed, straddled Penny, and slowly lowered himself down.

I desperately wanted to crawl into a corner and hide away, but David was holding my head in his huge vicelike hands, insisting I witness the unfolding events.

Billy closed his eyes and worked himself up and down on the vibrator.

"Everybody I ever meet eventually fucks me up the arse," he said. "Harry, Ruby, the producers, everybody." He started moving faster, and with every other word he'd taken to slapping Penny hard across the face. "They're all parasites living off the Billy White bandwagon, so why should you be any different? Just like the rest of them, you might as well fuck me up the arse, you parasitic whore."

Despite her body being out of commission, Penny's eyes were alive and burning with hatred. "Billy! This really isn't a good idea," I said, "You really don't know who you're dealing with."

David turned my face to him. "The very first opportunity I get," he said. "I'm going to pull his eyes out with a spoon."

After what was probably no more than a few minutes, but seemed like an eternity, Billy let out a scream and allowed himself to explode over Penny's stomach and breasts.

David and I could do nothing but watch as Billy slowly dismounted. He made his way gingerly to the bathroom, leaving Penny still bound and gagged on the bed. Seconds later the sound of the shower filled the room, and David finally released my head from his grip.

"David, I'm really, really sorry," I said, as he sat back in the chair.

"He's been under a lot of stress lately. You know, with work and everything."

"One day I'm going to catch up with that motherfucker," David said. "And when I do, I'm going to chop his dick off with the bluntest, rustiest thing I can find... Hell, I might even just pull it off."

No more was said as we listened to the sounds of Billy whistling the theme tune to his own show as he showered. When he finally returned to the room, wrapped in a towel and cleaning his ear with a cotton bud, he took one look at Penny and sucked air through his teeth. "Whoa!" he said, giggling lightly. "Did I do all that?"

Penny's eyes, partially closed by swelling, were puffy and beginning to show signs of bruising. There were deep cuts on her cheeks and lips where Billy's wedding ring had connected, and her nose looked undoubtedly broken.

"Okay, well we can't leave you there forever," Billy said, throwing the cotton bud into a bin.

He sat on the bed beside Penny's head.

"I'm going to have my handkerchief back now," he said, pointing at Penny's mouth. "You even think about making a noise, and I'll ram that dildo so far down your throat it'll come out the other end. Understand?"

Penny made no sign of pain or emotion as Billy ripped the handkerchief out of her mouth.

"Good girl," Billy said, scrunching up the handkerchief and throwing it in the bin. "Now, let's put this away as well, shall we?" He removed the vibrator from around Penny's waist and replaced the toy in the bedside cabinet drawer.

He stood up and paced the room, tapping his forehead with a finger. "Now, I do hope you're going to keep all this quiet," he said. "But then I don't suppose you've got much choice, have you? I mean, who's going to listen to a cheap whore like you, eh?"

Billy sat back on the bed and started to untie the cord from around Penny's ankles. "After all, I suppose this is all in a day's work for you. Occupational hazard." He rolled Penny over onto her back and started untying the belt from around her hands. He'd only partially done so when he caught hold of Penny's hair and roughly lifted her face off the bed. He put his mouth to her ear and whispered, "Because you breathe one word of what's happened here, and I'll crucify you." He released Penny's head, untied her hands, and stood up. "Now get the fuck out of my room."

Penny rolled off the bed and started gathering up her clothes.

Billy poured himself a drink and watched her dress. "I mean it," he said. "One word and you're dead. I won't just tie you to that bed, I'll fucking nail you down. Got it?"

"Can I use your bathroom?" Penny asked, her swollen face and broken nose making it sound like she was talking underwater. "I need to do something with my face. I'm sure you don't want me walking around the hotel with it looking like this. Oh, and by the way, this is going to cost you extra."

Billy followed Penny towards the bathroom and postured himself in the doorway. "Well see, that's where we may have a problem," he said. "By my reckoning, I did all the work here. I mean, all you did was lie down, right? Hell, if anything, you should be paying me. Now get yourself cleaned up, and fuck off!"

Billy turned, poured himself another drink, switched on the TV, and lay on the bed.

Penny emerged from the bathroom a few minutes later. She left without saying another word.

David stopped in the doorway and turned to me. "You know?" he said, "I have a funny feeling your twisted mother-fucker of an assignee hasn't seen the last of us yet. In fact, if I was a betting man, I'd put money on Penny getting to him before I can."

The following morning, Billy rang his agent. He put Harry on speaker-phone and padded around the large hotel room, completely naked, drink in hand.

"I need a holiday, Harry," Billy said without preamble. "You're working me too hard. I don't know what sort of work ethic you guys live by in Lilliput, but I'm out on my arse here. Get someone to cover the show for a few weeks. Then get me on an island with sexy cocktails and even sexier cocktail waitresses. Now!"

There was a long pause, then a sigh. "Billy, it's six-thirty in the morning. For God's sake go back to bed."

"I've been to bed you stupid pink imp. Now go and book me a holiday."

"Look, I'll call the producers and get you the day off, okay? I'll tell them you've got man-flu or something. Now go back to bed." The phone went dead.

An hour later there was a faint knock on Billy's hotel room door.

"Now who the fuck is that?" Billy grumbled, turning down the TV and wrapping himself in a complimentary bathrobe. "I thought I told those pricks on reception I didn't want to be disturbed."

He opened the door to find a young boy standing there. The boy was dressed in the hotel's uniform, and the badge pinned to his waistcoat told us his name was *Ivan*. Ivan was looking down at his shoes.

"What do you want?" Billy said. "What part of *'I don't want to be disturbed,'* did those stupid dickheads on reception not understand?"

Billy picked the *Do Not Disturb* sign off the door handle and waved it underneath Ivan's downcast eyes. "And doesn't this count for anything?" he said. "Do you not understand plain English? Fucking muppet."

"I am very sorry, Mr White," Ivan said. He had an accent that sounded Eastern European. He held out a small envelope with Billy's full name scrawled across the front of it - *William Graham Charles White*. "But person who gave envelope said very urgent you would like to have it."

Billy snatched the envelope and was about to shut the door when the boy coughed.

"What?" Billy said.

The boy coughed again.

"I think he wants a tip," I said.

"If I was you I'd get something for that cough," Billy said, slamming the door.

The envelope contained a single piece of paper. It simply read, *Haven't worked out how much yet - be in touch soon.* It was signed - *Parasitic whore.*

"The fucking arse-shagging bitch," Billy screamed, ripping the note into several pieces. "Who does she think she is? Nobody fucks with Billy White. Nobody! I'll have her fucking head on a spike!"

"Wow, he doesn't seem in a good mood," Crimson said, materialising in the doorway leading to the bathroom. She checked her watch. "Damn, I wish I had time to stay until he got out of that bathrobe." Crimson's body shook as if it had received a small electric current.

"Honestly, Crimson, you wouldn't want to go anywhere near this one with a bargepole," I replied. "He's nothing short of a rapist."

"Actually, I've always had a bit of a rape fantasy," Crimson said.

"Anyway, come on, we haven't got time for this." She shook the fantasy from her head and caught hold of my wrist. "The committee want to see you."

Once, and only once, had Elaine and I attempted to act out a rape scene; her idea of course. It had started well enough, with me dragging her up the stairs by her hair as she pleaded theatrically for mercy. But then things went horribly wrong when I attempted to rip her blouse off and succeeded in falling backwards, knocking myself unconscious against the corner of a bedside cabinet in the process.

When I came round, Elaine had gone.

She'd left a note though - *Gone shopping to Asda. Don't wait up.*

RABBITS & RAINBOWS

"We thought you'd be interested in the result of your recent review, Seven-Three-Five-Nine," Mr T. said, his head stuck in a file. He didn't wait for a reply. "We've taken everything into account, but unfortunately you still haven't made it into the Sanctum. So back to business as normal I'm afraid. Better luck next time, eh?"

"Business as normal?" I said, pulling my feet up onto the wooden chair and wrapping my arms around my knees. "I wouldn't say my business was normal, would you?"

"Depends where you want to draw the parameters, Seven-Three-Five-Nine," Mr T. said, reading over a note handed to him by one of the sidekicks. "Who are we to judge what constitutes normality? In my experience even those who are deemed to be the most normal of people will have some trait hidden away; some perversion that's kept from the outside world. Even Michael Jackson and Hitler were considered normal once upon a time and look what happened there. Anyway, we haven't got time for idle chit-chat, Seven-Three-Five-Nine. We've got far too much work for that. Now, it appears your messenger is... temporarily otherwise engaged, so we'll send for you when were ready. It's all standard practice. In the meantime, here's what I suggest."

Mr T. pointed behind me. I turned to find a door with the word *COUNTRYSIDE* written on it.

"You'll find Old Eric's office out there somewhere," he said. "Off you go."

Through the door wasn't just somewhere that looked *like* an expanse of good old English countryside, it *was* an expanse of good old English countryside. Elaine professed to love the country; I hated it. Why anybody would want to live forty miles away from their nearest loaf of bread was beyond me. Then there's the cows, the horses, the sheep, the constant smell of methane, farmers, the unrelenting belief that a day begins at half-five in the morning and finishes at eight at night, cake baking competitions, and finally - wasps.

Lots and lots of wasps.

Father had once told me Germany had used the wasp as the template for the Doodlebug. They'd apparently studied the panic created when the mere sound of a wasp was close by and calibrated the sound of the Doodlebug's engine to be as similar as possible.

After dogs, wasps were my next least favourite creature. I had no idea what the size ratio of the average wasp compared to the average postman might be, but what I did know was if I ever came up against something that was somewhere in the region of a gazillion times bigger than me, then I wouldn't make any attempt to annoy it, let alone cause it any physical pain.

Most wild animals are perfectly happy to leave you alone unless you accidentally step on them or try to steal their children, but the psyche of a wasp is programmed for attack, no matter what the odds may be. The wasp will stalk you for hours, following you wherever you try and hide. It'll bide its time, happily waiting for that opportune moment when you're carrying a cup of tea or the like, before disappearing up your sleeve or down your shirt to cause its pain and mayhem.

Experts have studied brain patterns between someone in the throes of an epileptic fit and someone fending off a wasp attack, and found the differences to be miniscule. There's even been recorded instances of people throwing themselves under trains in order to get away from a carefully co-ordinated pincer wasp attack.

By my reckoning, when considering wasps - just like Doodlebugs or paedophiles - there's no such thing as a nice one.

I wandered up vale and down dale for an hour before finally spotting Old Eric's office door at the far end of a field. Lo and behold! Dangling from a tree branch, not three feet in front of the door, was a nice big wasps' nest, around which hundreds of the creatures were buzzing.

I crept through the grass to within about twenty feet of the nest. I knew the creatures had seen me, but they were playing that trick of pretending to be busy; undoubtedly whispering to one another about what tactics to employ in order to cause me as much pain as possible.

"Okay, Buzz, do you see what I see?"
"I see him, Sting."
"Right, here's what we're going to do. We'll just keep pottering around the nest like we're busy and can't be bothered with him. Then, when he least expects it, we'll get Stripy and Frank to go for his head. When he's busy swatting them away, I'll fly up his sleeve, and you go up his trouser leg."
"Sting, do we really have to take Frank? Remember what happened last time?"
"Okay, good point. We'll ask Drone instead."
"Uh, Sting?"
"What?"
"Don't mean to put a spanner in the works here, but that human appears to be deficient in the sleeve and trouser leg department."
"Good Lord, so he does. Okay. Gather round boys. Plan Bee."

I tried to think of various means of getting around the nest, but eventually plumped for the only strategy my mind could come up with. I closed my eyes, took a deep breath, crossed myself, and bolted for Eric's door as fast as I could. As I normally did when in the company of wasps, I made sure I had my head down, screamed like a Banshee, and waved my arms around like someone who's drowning.

I burst in through Eric's door without knocking and slammed it shut behind me. I quickly checked myself over by patting myself down like my clothes were on fire. Despite still having a buzzing in my ears, it looked like my tactics had worked as I could find no evidence of any of the devil-creatures having followed me in. I did notice however that my bare feet were covered in something unpleasant and smelly.

"Didn't your mother ever teach you to knock?" Eric said.

I lifted my head to apologise and explain the situation, but the scene in front of me, together with the smell from my feet, took all the air from my lungs.

Eric was sitting in his chair and readjusting his robe, his face a mixture of anger and embarrassment. Standing by his side was a woman. She was bent over smoothing down her skirt, and, when she'd finished tidying herself up, she quickly brushed by me and disappeared out the door. Despite the fact she'd kept her head down, I had the distinct feeling I knew who she was.

"Hang on," I said, pointing at the door and trying to make my head comprehend what my eyes had just witnessed. "That looked like Grace. I used to work with her."

"I'm afraid I didn't quite catch her name," Eric said, continuing to adjust himself. "She's new. Committee put her on the messenger rota. She just popped in to get some advice."

"Is that so? What sort of advice, Eric?"

"Just general, son, just general."

Eric retrieved his crossword from the desk and started sniffing the air. "In God's name what is that smell?"

I sat on the edge of Eric's desk and looked down at my feet. "Sorry," I said. "I seem to have stepped in something."

"Here," Eric said, producing a box of tissues from one of the desk drawers.

"So, poor old Grace is dead then?" I said, wiping my feet with the tissues. "Old age I expect."

"Apparently not," Eric replied. He stood up and opened the office door, indicating for me to throw the dirty tissues outside. A quick peek as I did so told me the wasps and the countryside had disappeared into the void. "As far as I can gather," Eric continued, making his way back to his chair, "she took an overdose of sleeping pills by mistake. Says she tried to explain to the committee she was struggling to sleep because of the Godless immorality of today's youth or something and got the dose wrong. If you ask me, I can think of a thousand things more worthy to lose sleep over than Godless social decline, but everyone to their own, eh? Anyway, if you hadn't barged in when you did, I reckon her misplaced moral barrier would have been well and truly down by now."

I was almost sick. "Please, Eric," I said, finishing off between my toes and throwing the last of the tissues out the door. "I really don't need to know."

"Good, because I wasn't going to tell you anyway. Now, what brings you ignorantly crashing into my office with your shitty feet and all?"

I closed the door and sat back on the desk. "The committee wanted to tell me they'd conducted another review and I still hadn't made it to the Sanctum."

"Ah, yes, review time again." Eric looked at the ceiling. "Mr T. doesn't even send for me any more. Just sends one of the messengers along with the good news that I haven't made it. That's why what's-her-face was here."

"Her name is Grace, Eric."

"Whatever," Eric said, putting his crossword away. "Boy, have I got a story to tell you, son. It's all about what Elaine was wearing when that lawyer got home yesterday…"

"No!" I put my hand up in front of Eric's face. "Not interested, Eric. Think of something else to talk about."

"Like what?"

"Anything! Anything at all." I trawled through my mind. "What about continuing our conversation about what's behind the Sanctum door?"

"What conversation?"

There it was. Alzheimer's again. "Well, you once told me you have no idea what's in the Sanctum, right?"

"Did I?"

"Yes."

"And you want to talk about that instead of…"

"Yes."

"Well, okay. If you insist. But honestly, you wouldn't believe what Elaine…"

"Eric!"

"Okay, okay," Eric held his hands up. "I get it… Actually, I don't get it. You *really* want to talk about what's behind the Sanctum door?"

"Yes please."

Eric sighed. "Well, like I'm sure I've already said, son, there'll only ever be one way to find out." He stood up and stretched himself. "But like I think I also told you, I reckon it's the death you always dreamed of." He sat back down.

"But I didn't think death would bring me anything," I said, playing with the print. "Well, except the norm I suppose. You know? Nothing. Darkness. Oblivion."

"There you go then," Eric said, opening his arms in triumph. "If that's what you truly believed death was all about, son, then the word on the street is that's what you'll get if you ever go through that Sanctum door."

"But that's impossible," I said, putting the print back down. "Think about it logically, Eric. What about people who believe in God? What about those who believe they're going to get virgins and stuff? Are you telling me no matter what you believe in it's going to be found beyond the Sanctum door?"

"Difficult to comprehend I know, but that's the buzz, son."

"Okay, okay, hang on. What if, for example, I believed that in death my God was a giraffe called Jerry? Are you trying to tell me the minute I walk through that Sanctum door, Jerry will be sitting there waiting for me?"

"You'd probably be the only person he'd seen in a while, son, but yes, in theory, Jerry would be sitting there smiling his big giraffy smile and…"

"Eric, this is ridiculous," I interrupted. "If what you're saying is true, then every God exists. Even if he's a giraffe called Jerry."

"I know, mental or what?" Eric made his way from his chair and sat beside me. "You see, son, as far as I can gather the Sanctum's premise is simple." Eric put his arm across my shoulders. "In fact, nothing could be simpler. Believe in what the bloody hell you like and the Sanctum will provide it. Like I mentioned, son, nobody has ever come out. So it obviously caters for everyone. Absolutely everyone. It's the only logical answer."

"But, Eric, I can't get my head around this," I said, extricating myself from his embrace and pacing the room. "If this is true it's like the biggest news, well, like ever! And you're talking as if it's nothing more important than what colour socks to wear."

Eric stood up and made his way back to his chair. "If you like we could always talk about something else," he said. "That story about what Elaine was wearing is still on the back burner."

I had to turn my back on Eric to avoid the brightness from his eyes. "No thanks."

"Sure? It really is a hell of a story."

I sat back on the edge of the desk. "Eric, can you please forget what Elaine was wearing for a minute and imagine if we could get the message across?"

Eric's smile and far-off look told me he hadn't forgotten for a moment what Elaine had been wearing. "What message, son?" he said, the room taking on the brightness of freshly polished silver.

I clicked my fingers in front of Eric's luminescent face. "The message about the Sanctum," I said. "Imagine all the problems that would disappear overnight if only people knew no matter what they believed in, it actually existed."

Eric shook his head slowly. "And how do you suggest this message is conveyed, son?" he said, the brightness dimming slightly. "Do the committee suddenly appear on the six o'clock news and announce there's a place waiting for people after they've died where all their desires are fulfilled?"

"Could they do that?"

Eric laughed loudly. "Of course they bloody couldn't. Can you imagine Mr T. rocking up in that ridiculous hat and announcing to the world there was a place called the Sanctum waiting for them after death? Furthermore, as long as they got in, it contained whatever they wanted it to contain. There'd be mayhem, don't you think? They'd lock him up and throw away the key. Just take a peek through history, son, and have a look at what's happened to anyone who's tried to say they know exactly what the afterlife is all about. Trust me, it's always the messenger who gets shot. No, some things are best left secret, son, and the existence of the Sanctum is one of them."

"But surely something so big can't be kept secret forever? Can it?"

"Had you ever heard of it before you got here, son?"

"Not exactly, no. A version of it perhaps. But I was always taught if there was a God, then He was the one true God, and if we didn't believe in Him we'd be destined for a death of eternal misery. The minister of our church certainly never mentioned anything about a giraffe called Jerry."

"Bit restrictive, don't you think?"

"Maybe. I suppose I just went with the flow and never really thought about it that much. Anyway, how long has the Sanctum been here, Eric? Ten years? Ten million years? Since the dawn of time?"

"Nobody really knows, son. The only thing we can ascertain is it must have been created by somebody who was good with wood. Have you seen the workmanship on that door? It's a shame some of it's covered with that painting."

I recalled the painting I'd seen when Mr T. had first shown me the door.

"And what's that all about?" I said. "Why the rabbits and rainbows?"

"My, my, you've really found your tongue today haven't you, son? It's like talking to Mr Question from the Planet Question. Are you sure you wouldn't rather I tell you about Elaine's outfit? It's far more interesting than this rubbish."

"Positive, thanks."

"Well, if you insist, but don't blame me if you get bored."

"I won't."

Eric closed one eye and frowned in concentration. "Sorry, where were we?" he said.

"The painting, Eric," I said, keeping my irritation at bay by reminding myself of Eric's battle against Alzheimer's.

"Ah, of course, the painting," Eric said, nodding his head. "Yes, the painting. Indeed, the painting… What about it?"

I took a few seconds to compose myself. "Well, for a start," I said. "Do we have any idea who painted it?"

"Not really," Eric replied, shrugging his shoulders. "What we do know is that whenever a bunch of school kids arrive at once; a coach disaster, some lunatic running amok with a shotgun, a mountain subsiding, a stray American missile, etcetera, etcetera, the committee always give them paints and stuff to keep them entertained whilst they're waiting to be processed. They don't allow them to write anything of course, just paint."

"That's nice," I said. "They made *me* wait in my dentist's waiting room."

"Well, to be honest, I don't know if it's *that* nice. Not when you look at it logically. I mean, I can't imagine painting a picture to be high on the list of some poor traumatised kid whose only crime was to be in the wrong place at the wrong time, can you? Anyway, even if one of the poor buggers did feel like creating a masterpiece, they'd have to be bloody quick about it. The committee don't hang about when it comes to processing kids. There's some age-old rule they follow about suffering children being brought to the front of the queue or something. It's always been the case, son, that anyone under the age of sixteen gets automatic entry to the Sanctum. Only fair, I suppose. I mean, when you think about it logically, it's only us adults who mess things up."

"It's a bit odd though isn't it?" I said. "The painting."

"Odd?"

"Well, the rainbows are black. What child would paint black rainbows?"

Eric drummed his fingers on the desk. I could see he was getting bored. "I may have been the font of all knowledge when I was alive and kicking, son, but I've been dead a long time now and the old synaptic gaps don't open up like they used to. How the hell would I know what goes on inside the head of a child? Especially one who's been blown up, squashed, shot, burned, drowned, starved, or split in half. Now, are we finished with the bloody rabbits and rainbows? Can we please move on to something else?"

"As long as it's not Elaine," I said.

Eric buried his head in his hands and pretended to cry. "But it's just too good a story to keep to myself," he mumbled. "You should have seen her, son."

I recalled the look of desire on that lawyer's face when he'd gazed at whatever was on his phone and was desperate to keep Old Eric away from any description of what might have caused him to seem so excited. "So what did you believe in, Eric?" I asked. "What did you think death would bring?"

Eric lifted his head up slowly. "Ah, it's so bloody long ago I can't remember," he said. "So I guess that if by some miracle I ever do find myself going through that infernal door, it'll be a nice surprise to be reminded. Now, really, son, enough of this nonsense, let's get back to real-life."

"Okay, but please, nothing about Elaine, okay? I'm really not in the mood."

Eric sighed theatrically. "If you insist," he said. "Look, if you're so keen on not allowing me talk about my assignee, at least tell me all about yours."

"Right, so let me get this straight," Eric said. "Billy White, the nation's darling and object of most women's desire, including Elaine's, is nothing more than a dirty depraved dickhead who's hiding his latent homosexuality behind a sham marriage."

"One way of looking at it I suppose."

"Just goes to show you can't judge a book by its cover, son, eh?"

"Unless it's by Jeffrey Archer."

"Pardon?"

"Oh, nothing. Just something Father used to say."

"I remember one of my assignees who had a bit of a sick problem in the bedroom department," Eric said, the room brightening. "Radio announcer he was. Quite famous in his day. Had the perfect face for radio; ugly as sin. Voice like velvet though. Women fell in love with that voice, I can tell you. Just as well they couldn't see him."

"Don't tell me… he killed his brother?"

"Nope."

"Got caught having sex with the station controller's daughter?"
"Nope."
"Their son?"
"Nope."
"Wife? Aunty? Cousin?"
"Nope."
"I give up."

"Well, ugliness must have run in the family, because his poor sister was inflicted with it too. I guess the only action they could get was with each other."

"Urgh, Eric, that's disgusting."

"Used to do it almost every day in his booth after he'd read the evening news. I suppose they weren't doing any real harm, but one evening the daft ugly bugger forgot to switch himself off air. Now, that was one busy day, son, I can tell you."

There was a knock on the door.

"Bugger! I was just getting to the good bit," Eric said. "Come in."

EASTERN PROMISE

Crimson got me back to Billy's house just as he was arriving home. I watched from a bayed front window as he parked his Bentley convertible on the gravelled driveway and quickly made his way through the rain to the house.

"Ruby!" he called, as soon as he entered the mock-Georgian spread he called home. "Ruby, where are you?" He deposited his coat on the coat-stand in the hallway and checked the downstairs rooms in turn for his wife. He eventually found her in the kitchen, seemingly enjoying a cup of coffee with her tennis coach, Oleksiy.

"Hi, darling," Ruby said, getting off a breakfast stool and giving Billy a peck on the cheek. "The rain has spoiled my tennis lesson, so me and Olly are taking a break."

"Has the rain made you deaf as well?" Billy asked. "Didn't you hear me calling?"

Ruby sat back on the stool and crossed her long, fake-tanned legs. "Sorry, darling," she said. "But you know how much noise that kettle makes when it boils."

After Elaine and Crimson, Ruby probably had the finest legs I'd ever seen, and I was dumfounded that Billy didn't seem to appreciate what was right in front of his nose. If I'd been Billy I'd have been sending Olly on his way and ripping Ruby's tennis outfit off her right here in the kitchen. Well, as long as the new forthright Mark Ferris wasn't busy elsewhere of course. My close observance of Ruby helped me notice she looked a little flushed; like she'd been exercising. Olly looked like he'd also been working out as there were sweat beads on his forehead and his shirt was sticking to him like a second skin.

At six-three or thereabouts, Oleksiy looked like a bronzed Adonis. With the body of Hugh Jackman (number 4 on the list) and the face of

Enrique Iglesias (number 15) he exuded sporting prowess. How good Oleksiy actually was at tennis however was something of a mystery. In the three months I'd been with Billy, I'd never once actually seen him and Ruby play. In fact, the more I thought of it, I couldn't remember him having ever turned up with a racket.

With my suspicions aroused, I meandered over to the kettle and clandestinely checked its temperature; stone cold. I stood on tiptoes and peeked into the two coffee cups on the breakfast bar. As suspected, both were completely devoid of any signs of coffee. Using my new-found powers as a super-sleuth, I quickly came to the ever-developing conclusion that Olly was tutoring Ruby in a completely different sport altogether; a conclusion confirmed when further investigation spotted a pair of frilly sports-knickers poking out from behind the toaster.

"Well when you've finished I need to talk to you," Billy said. "I'll be in the drawing room."

"What do you want to talk about, darling?" Ruby stood up and peered out through the French doors, giving the impression she was checking to see if it was still raining.

Billy looked Olly up and down. "It's private," he said.

"Perhaps I go," Oleksiy said, wiping some of the sweat from his brow. "The rain not stopping, Mrs White. Perhaps I give discount because we not finish."

"No, no," Ruby protested. "Look there. I think I see some blue sky, and I really need to practice my forehand technique, Olly."

"Like I said, I'll be in the drawing room having a stiff one," Billy said, turning and making his way out of the kitchen. "Looks like you've already had one," he added, just loud enough for us all to hear.

Half an hour later, Ruby entered the drawing room. She found Billy folded into his favourite chair; the type that engulfs its leather around you. She had changed out of her tennis whites and donned jeans and a t-shirt.

"So what's so bloody important?" she said, pouring herself a large gin and tonic from a drinks' cabinet.

Billy obviously decided to get straight to the point. "I spent last night with a hooker," he said, disentangling himself from his chair and pouring himself another glass of whisky from the cabinet; the third glass since he'd got home.

Ruby leaned against the mantle over the large unlit fireplace. "Male or female?" she asked, without a hint of surprise.

"Jesus Christ, Ruby," Billy said. "How many times have we got to go through this? I am not gay."

Ruby placed her drink on the mantle. "Of course you're not, darling," she said. "I just wish you'd prove it to me every now and again." She blew Billy a kiss; Marilyn Monroe style. "We could do it right now if you want to."

"Would have thought you'd have been too worn out after your *tennis lesson*," Billy said. "I can smell the foreign twat from here."

Ruby laughed and picked up her drink. "Well, what is a girl supposed to do?" she said. "Anyway, I trust this hooker of yours was old enough?"

Billy settled back into the folds of leather. "Of course she was bloody old enough. What do you take me for?"

It took me a while to do the maths. Penny had been fifteen, nearly sixteen, when she'd come knocking on Sarah's door. Five months later she'd burned the house down, frazzling Sarah and Emma-Lou in the process. Then I'd spent nine months with Roger. Add in the three months I'd been with Billy, and Penny would be… about seventeen and a half. Almost old enough to vote, I thought.

"Well at least that's a start," Ruby said. She made her way over to Billy and started massaging his shoulders. "Now, we all know you're a sick perverted bastard, Billy. So come on, why are you telling me all this? What have you gone and done to the poor girl? She is still breathing I hope." Ruby giggled lightly to show she was joking.

Billy closed his eyes and rolled his head, moaning softly as Ruby's hands moved to his neck. "Of course she's still breathing."

"So what then?"

Billy rolled his drink around in its glass, staring at it intently as if it was some wonderful work of art. "I made her wear a strap-on."

Ruby stopped massaging and looked to the heavens. "God give me strength," she said. "And he says he's not gay… What next?"

"Pardon?"

"Come on, Billy, I'm not stupid. If that was all, you wouldn't be sitting here drinking whisky like it's gone out of fashion, and these lovely broad shoulders of yours wouldn't feel like they're made of lead. So, what next?"

Billy bolted his drink. "Well, I may have got a little rough," he said. "But I'd had a real bad day, Rube," he added quickly. "First the make-up girl made me look like Coco the fucking Clown, then I called up an old friend to help blow off some steam and he left me high and dry. I mean, what was I supposed to do?"

"How rough?" Ruby said, making her way back to the mantle.

"Just a few bumps and bruises. Nothing much."

"How rough, Billy?"

"Okay, cuts on her face, a broken nose maybe. I don't know."

"Jesus, you're nothing but a prick, Billy. Why the hell don't you just find yourself a man and get all this bullshit out of your system?" Ruby finished her drink. "I hope you paid her well."

Billy seemed to disappear further into the chair. "Well now there's the thing," he said.

Ruby's eyes narrowed. "What, Billy? What's the thing?"

"The little whore demanded extra for her troubles. Can you believe it? I'm Billy White for fuck's sake. She should have paid me. Hell, I reckon she enjoyed it more than me anyway."

Ruby calmly placed her empty glass on the mantle and walked over to Billy. She stood over him for a few seconds before slapping him hard across the face.

"Bloody hell!" Billy said, rubbing his cheek. "What was that for?"

"Jesus Christ, Billy!" Ruby said. "What do you think is wrong with the following three things? One, you get some hooker to shag you up the arse. Two, you smack her about. Three, you refuse to pay her. What the fuck were you thinking?"

"I'm sorry, okay," Billy said, still rubbing his reddening cheek. "Like I said, I was having a bad day." He produced a handkerchief from his jacket pocket and mopped up the whisky that Ruby's blow had forced him to spill on his shirt.

"Where did you find her?" Ruby demanded, making her way back to the mantle.

"What?"

"This hooker. Where did you find her?"

"Does it matter?"

"Yes it fucking matters. Where did you find her? Which agency? Because we'd best make some donation to their favourite charity or something. Ananomously of course. We'll get Harry on the case straight away. So, where did you find her, Billy?"

Billy got out if his chair and poured himself another whisky. "I found her number in a phone-box," he said, just loud enough to be heard. "I called her up on my way to The Singleton."

Ruby threw her hands in the air and started laughing. "Oh, well done, Billy," she said. "Ten out of ten. I can see the newspaper headlines already. The great Billy White, who could have his pick of any woman in the country, gets his kicks from being sodomised by cheap hookers he finds in phone-boxes. Who do you think you are? Hugh bloody Grant. You stupid, stupid, man!"

Despite Hugh Grant's misdemeanours, he'd still managed to work his way onto Elaine's list. (Number 13).

Ruby went to leave, but stopped in the doorway. "Hang on, there's something else isn't there?" she said, making her way slowly back into the room. She mixed herself another gin and tonic. "I mean, even if this whore does go to the press, we get Harry to sweep it all away like usual. Who would people believe anyway? It would be the word of a bargain basement call-girl against the blue-eyed boy who can do no wrong. So, I have to ask myself, why are you so worried, Billy? What is it you're *not* telling me here?"

Billy returned to his chair and swallowed a large portion of his whisky, his hand visibly shaking. "She sent me a note," he said. "It's just a feeling, Rube, but I don't think this one is going away without a fight."

A disquiet fell over the room.

"How much are we talking about?" Ruby eventually asked.

"I don't know," Billy replied, with one of those horrible throat-mice playing around in his mouth. "She says she hasn't worked it out yet."

Ruby finished her drink with one gulp. "I suggest you get Harry over here as soon as possible," she said. "Get him to really start earning his money." She rolled the empty glass around in her hand a few times before throwing it into the fireplace and leaving the room.

"Do you think she knows who you are?" Harry asked, stomping

around the drawing room. "Because if she does, God only knows how much this is going to cost."

Billy was slumped in his chair. I'd lost count of the number of times he'd refilled his glass since Ruby had stormed out of the room. "Of course she knows who I am," he said, his words badly slurred. "Everybody knows who I am, you stupid gay twat. I'm Billy White. No, wait, I sit corrected. I'm *The* Billy White, and no two-bit, arse-fucking whore is going to get a penny out of me. Hell, she should be paying me for the privilege."

Harry groaned. "And I suppose you told her that?"

Billy closed his eyes and nodded his head. "Maybe."

Harry groaned louder and poured himself another pineapple juice. "If this gets out, Billy, we're finished. Do you understand? Finished."

The ensuing silence was broken by the chirping of Billy's mobile; the one he only ever kept for personal use. He drunkenly struggled to fish the phone out of his trouser pocket and flipped open the lid. "Hello," he said, more as a question than a greeting. It was the only word he spoke before closing the phone and allowing it to fall into the folds of the chair.

Harry put his hands to his lips in prayer. "Oh my God, that was her, wasn't it?"

Billy nodded his head slowly.

"Okay, how much does she want?" Harry closed his eyes and grimaced. "Did she threaten to go to the press?"

"She didn't say."

Harry opened his eyes. "What do you mean she didn't say? Billy, please try and make sense. If she didn't say what she wanted, what the hell did she say?"

"She said she'd be here in five minutes."

I looked at the ornate clock hanging above the fireplace: 3.55pm.

"Oh Jesus Christ almighty," Harry said, putting his hands on his head and turning his back on Billy. "That means she knows where you live. Bloody hell, Billy, how much information did you give her? She knows where you live. She knows your personal number…"

"I didn't tell her anything, Harry. Do you think I'm stupid?"

"I'd rather not answer that right now," Harry replied, pacing the room. "Okay, okay, I need time to work things out, so here's what we'll do. When she gets here *I'll* answer the door. Hopefully she won't have a clue who I am, so I'll tell her she's got the wrong address and send her on her way. I doubt if it will keep her away for long, but with any luck it'll just give us enough time to come up with some kind of strategy. Where's Ruby? I need her to stay out of sight. If your whore knows who you are, she's bound to know who Ruby is as well."

Harry left the drawing room muttering expletives under his breath.

"Hello," Harry said, after opening the door. "Can I help you?" He put on as cheerful a voice as he could muster.

It was the first time in my death that I'd seen Penny in what could be described as normal clothing; standard fitting jeans and a plain white blouse.

Standing beside her, arms folded across his chest, was David.

"Hi, you must be Harry," Penny said. She removed the large frog-eyed sunglasses from her face and held out her hand.

At the sight of Penny's face, both Harry and I held on to the door frame. Harry tried to speak.

"Oh, did he not mention this?" Penny said, circling a finger around her face. "Well, when you've got time you can quite clearly see how it all happens on this, Harry."

Penny rummaged in her handbag and retrieved a CD.

"You can keep that one," she said, handing the CD to Harry. "I think I've burned enough copies for everyone. Ooh, I thought I'd bring these along as well." Penny handed Harry a bundle of photographs, held together by an elastic band. "A good friend of mine took them minutes after I'd left the room. Apparently, one press of a button and they could be all over the internet in no time, Harry. They're very good quality. Ivan reckons he'd like to open his own photographic studio one day. When he's saved up enough money of course. Which shouldn't be too long, Harry. You see, there's a lot of well-known people with suites at The Singleton. And, just between you and me, Harry," Penny tapped her nose and winced with the pain, "Ivan tells me it only takes him five minutes to set up all the equipment. Tells me he likes to hide the cameras in air-conditioning vents and the microphones in lampshades. Or is it the other way round? Well, no matter, he's got money coming in from everywhere, Harry. How clever is that? And he's only the same age as me! Anyway, shall I come in?"

Penny walked past Harry's rigid, silent frame and stopped in the hallway. "Wow, look at all these doors. Which way, Harry?"

"Said you hadn't seen the last of us, didn't I?" David said, pushing me out of the way.

Harry eventually found the strength to close the door and lead us all into the drawing room. Billy was curled up in his chair, slowly but surely losing his battle against alcohol-induced sleep. He only had one eye open and was making strange mumbling noises. Harry ushered Penny into one of the other chairs in the room.

"You'll have to forgive my client," he said. "He's not feeling too well." From the way Harry's face had gone a strange yellow-green colour, I guessed he wasn't feeling the best either.

"That's okay," Penny replied. "I much prefer to speak to the organ grinder than the monkey anyway."

Harry made his way to the drinks' cabinet. "Can I get you a drink? Miss…"

After a moments thought, Penny replied, "Harding."

"So, can I get you a drink, Miss Harding? You are old enough to drink I assume?"

"Not legally, no. But I'll have a Vodka and orange if you've got one. The bigger the better."

Harry looked to the ceiling and started chewing his bottom lip. "One Vodka and orange coming up," he said. He mixed the drink, added some ice, and handed it to Penny. "So, Miss Harding, I'm sure you're a very busy person, as indeed am I. So what exactly can I do for you?"

Penny retrieved a chunk of ice from her drink and ran it over her swollen lips. "You know, you really should send him to see someone special, Harry." She nodded in the direction of where Billy was now fast asleep. "He's obviously got issues. I've still got the numbers of some people who've rummaged around inside me if you'd like them."

"Thanks for the offer," Harry said. "But if need be, I think we can find our own people." Harry closed his eyes and pinched the bridge of his nose.

"Suit yourself," Penny said. She drank her Vodka in one go. "Anyway, in answer to your question, Harry. I reckon four hundred thousand will help make my memory somewhat foggy. It might even help me forget everything about last night completely."

Harry opened his eyes. We all looked from one to the other. Even David looked shocked.

Harry eventually gave out a laugh-come-cough. "Surely you don't mean pounds sterling?" he said.

Penny stood up and made her way to the door. "What other kind is there, Harry?" she said. "I'll be back tomorrow." She nodded towards the clock above the fire. "Shall we say the same time? Make it cash, Harry, and not too big in denominations. People ask awkward questions if you start waving large notes in the air. I'll see myself out. Thanks for the drink."

David sidled up to me as he left. "See you tomorrow," he said.

After Penny had gone, Harry and I left Billy sleeping in his chair and went to find Ruby. She was reading a magazine in the kitchen; her semi-clad form plastered over the cover.

"Can I assume from the fact you look like you've been eaten by a fox and shat over a cliff, Harry, that the meeting with the whore didn't go particularly well?" she said, flicking over a page.

"Afraid not," Harry replied. "I think we have a real problem on our hands this time."

"What's she after?"

"Four hundred grand."

Ruby stopped flicking pages and lifted her head. "If it had been me I'd have rounded it up to a cool half-mill?"

"It's a lot of money, Ruby." Harry started making himself a coffee; black with four sugars.

"Of course it's a lot of money. My darling husband made her shag him up the arse, beat the living daylights out of her, then threw her out on her ear. That's not the sort of thing a woman will forget for twenty bloody quid, Harry."

"I know, I know. But four hundred grand?"

"And what's she got by way of evidence?"

"Quite a lot by the seems of things," Harry replied. "Just so happens a friend of hers is a fucking expert in covert surveillance. She's given me a CD which I assume won't make easy watching. There's photographs as well. From the one or two I've seen, they don't look pretty, Rube."

Ruby went back to reading her magazine. "You do know even if we pay her she'll be back for more, don't you?" she said. "People like her have no idea how to handle those sums of money, Harry. She'll probably blow the lot in a week; two at most. She'll be back with her cap in her stinking whore-hands in no time. Mark my words, Harry, she'll be fleecing us dry for the rest of our lives."

Harry sipped his coffee before adding another sugar. "Then I guess we'll just have to make sure we get hold of everything she's got," he said. "Discs, photographs, everything. I'll get some sort of paperwork drawn up. Make her sign to say she's got to hand everything over before we pay her."

Ruby laughed loudly. "Don't be so bloody stupid, Harry," she said. "The stupid bitch probably can't even write. What good is some piece of paper? She can hand over discs and photographs until we're all blue in the face. She's bound to hang on to something. I mean, wouldn't you?"

Harry hopped up onto one of the breakfast stools. "So what would you suggest?" he asked.

Ruby buried her head in the magazine, flicking over pages at a rate that suggested there was no way she was reading them. "There's only one thing for it, Harry. We've got to get rid of her."

"Yes I know we've got to get rid of her, Rube, but how? If paying her off isn't the answer, then what is?"

Ruby looked up from her magazine and stopped flicking. She held Harry's stare for quite some time.

Harry's coffee cup fell to the floor.

"Oh, come on, Harry," Ruby said, making her way to a cupboard. "Don't tell me you haven't thought of it?" She produced some cleaning materials and started mopping up Harry's coffee. "I mean, what harm would we be doing? That's all we're talking about is some halfwit whore. Let's face it, I doubt if she's a valuable member of the local society, Harry. Highly unlikely to be on the church roof committee now, is she? People like her are nothing but a drain on the resources of normal people, Harry, and I'll be damned if I'm going to allow the bitch to be a drain on mine!"

Harry's eyes had widened to epic proportions and his mouth opened and closed as if he were catching small insects. "Jesus Christ, Ruby, will you just listen to yourself? We can't just wipe her away like dust. She's a crying, talking, sleeping, walking, living human being."

Some song by Cliff Richard automatically sprung to mind. Sir Cliff had been number 18 on Elaine's list for quite some time, but had gotten himself replaced with Robert Pattinson just before I'd died. According to Elaine, she didn't think Sir Cliff would be any good in the sack anyway. No track record to speak of, so she said. Too chaste. She also added that Mr Pattinson could be interchanged with someone called Taylor Lautner depending on what camp she was in that day. I had no idea what she was talking about, until Grace told me one was a vampire and the other a werewolf. Apparently, Grace's church group were running a campaign denouncing the works of the author and she'd therefore been forced to read the books and watch the films just to see what all the fuss was about.

"Yes, a human being that's probably being housed, fed, and clothed by the likes of us, Harry," Ruby said. "I for one have no intention of making her life any easier at my expense. If she will go putting her number in phone-boxes, then what does she expect?"

"I doubt if she expected to end up looking like this," Harry said. He retrieved one of the photographs from his jacket pocket and placed it on the breakfast counter.

Ruby refused to look at the photo and started putting the cleaning materials away. "She'll undoubtedly have a drug problem," she said. "Probably registered with one of those council-run clinics that are paid for by the taxes of honest hard-working people like us. I tell you, Harry, society will give us a bloody medal if we make her go away." She began making Harry a new cup of coffee.

"Ruby, will you please stop talking like this?" Harry said, accepting the cup. "What about her friends and family? You can't just make people disappear. Somebody somewhere will miss her."

Ruby let out a derogatory snort. "What friends and family do street-whores have, Harry? She probably ran away from home when she was like twelve or something. Trust me, no one will bat an eyelid."

Harry looked on the verge of collapse. If I'd had a paper bag to offer him I would have done so.

"Did she come on her own today?" Ruby asked, turning the photograph Harry had left on the counter face-down.

Harry nodded his head.

"Actually," I chipped in. "That's not strictly true. She had David with her."

"Okay, and where has she asked for the money to be delivered?" Ruby reached over and took Harry's coffee off him before he spilled any more.

"She's coming here tomorrow," Harry said, his voice distant.

"Perfect!" Ruby announced. "Don't you see? She hasn't even considered the fact we may have something else up our sleeves. She's just a stupid little whore, Harry. A boil on the backside of humanity. Come on, Harry, it's the only sensible option. You know it, I know it, and as soon as Billy's sober enough, he'll know it as well. The only person who doesn't know it is her."

"I'm going home," Harry said, sliding off the stool. "I'll be back in the morning. Hopefully you'll have seen some sense by then."

"Right, I've been thinking," Harry said, as soon as he, Ruby, and Billy were settled in the drawing room. I looked at the clock: 12 noon. "I've spent the morning talking to the banks and our accountants, and with a little bit of ducking and diving we can come up with the cash without too many questions being asked. It'll be tight and we'll have to make a few trips into the city to sign some stuff, but if we get a wiggle on I reckon we can do it. I've already phoned the studio and told them your man-flu hasn't got any better, Billy. They say it's not a problem. As long as you're back within the week they've got enough pre-recorded stuff to last. Now, I've also drawn up a statement for our little problem to sign." Harry started unzipping a leather folder he'd brought with him. "It's effectively like a gagging order. With any luck she'll use the money to bugger off somewhere and we'll never hear from her again. What do you think?" He held out the paperwork.

Billy and Ruby remained silent and were both smiling at Harry.

"What?" Harry said. "What's so funny?"

"You," Billy replied, taking a large swig of whisky. "Do you honestly think I have any intention of paying this… this… thing?"

Harry put the paperwork back in the folder. "For God's sake, Billy, what choice do we have? I watched the little home-movie she gave me. It's a bit grainy, and the sound dips in and out, but there's enough on there to worry about, and no mistake. I also had the pleasure of looking through the photographs she gave me. She's got us by the proverbials, Billy. We're in no position to negotiate." He placed the folder on the small coffee table in front of him. He looked from Billy to Ruby and back again. They were both still smiling. "Oh, no. Oh, no, Billy. Please don't tell me you buy into Ruby's theory that the only way out of this is to actually dispose of the poor girl."

Billy poured himself a new drink and made one for Harry. "And why not?" he said, handing Harry the glass. "As Ruby has succinctly pointed out, we'd never stop paying the bitch. She's nothing but a piece of shit on our shoes, Harry. She needs to be scraped off and thrown away."

"But, Billy, this is ridiculous. Have you two completely lost your senses? You're a television celebrity, Billy, not Tony bloody Soprano. We're talking four hundred grand here. We can cover that easy. It's like buying another Bentley or two. It's nothing."

Billy's lips curled, showing his expensively whitened teeth. "Harry!" he said, snorting like a bull. "I'd cheerfully bury the bitch for four cents, let alone four hundred thousand quid. If she thinks she can piss all over Billy White, she's got another thing coming. When I tossed her out of that hotel room she should have slunk back to whatever hovel she crawled out of, licked her wounds, and put it all down to experience. How dare she come to MY house and try to fuck me over. Anyway, Ruby's come up with a plan. Tell him, Rube."

According to Ruby, the plan was simple enough. Harry would lead Penny into the drawing room the same as yesterday, where Billy would be waiting - sober. They'd make sure she was nice and comfortable in the chair facing away from the door by engaging her in polite conversation. Then, Ruby would sneak into the room and hit Penny over the head with the fourteen inch length of scaffolding pipe the builders had left behind when they'd had the new windows fitted last month. If the blow didn't kill her outright it would surely render her senseless enough for Billy and Harry to carry the girl to the master bathroom, where they'd drown her for good measure. Apparently, the patch of ground underneath the large Oak tree at the back of the house would be a perfect resting place for the body. Might even be good for the Rhubarb, so Ruby thought. What could possibly go wrong?

It dawned on me their plan was to be carried out by Mrs White with the lead piping in the drawing room. I loved Cluedo; Elaine hated it. Although, she had once put Professor Plum on her list just for fun (Number 14). He'd since been replaced by Ashton Kutcher.

"You're both as bloody mental as each other," Harry said, re-zipping the folder and tucking it under his arm. "I don't want anything to do with this. I'm off."

Billy stood up and closed the drawing room door. "You're not going anywhere, Harry," he said, standing in front of it. "Ruby said you wouldn't be up for it. But you see, it would be far too dangerous for us to just let you go now. What if you and I fell out and parted company some time in the future? I'm sorry, Harry, but there's no way Ruby and I can run the risk of you knowing about this without you being involved. Call it insurance, if you like. Oh, you might say you'll keep quiet, Harry. But I know what you gay people are like for gossiping. Just look at that bloody hairdresser at the studio. Always droning on about who's doing what to who. It's in your genes, Harry. You people just can't stop blabbering. No, I'm afraid Ruby and I have decided you're going to get your hands dirty on this one, Harry. You've got no option. Now, why don't you sit down and have another pineapple juice, and we'll go over the plan again."

Harry opened the door as planned and greeted Penny with a lopsided smile. "Come in, Miss Harding," he said. "So nice to see you again. Billy is in the drawing room. Please, follow me."

"Here we are again," David said, barging his way past me.

"If you don't mind I'd just like to use your bathroom," Penny said, entering the house. "It's been a long journey, and that cup of coffee I had a while back is dying to get out."

Fortunately for Harry the house had several bathrooms, and he was therefore able to direct Penny away from the one Ruby was in, steadily filling up the bath with water.

"I'll only be a jiffy," Penny said.

David made to follow her.

"David, stop," I said, catching him by the arm. "They're planning on killing her. There's no money. They're going to kill her and then bury her in the garden."

David snatched his arm away from me and gave me a look suggesting if I ever touched him again he'd consider ripping my hands off. "Don't you think she's thought of the possibility?" he said.

Five minutes later, Penny entered the drawing room. Harry indicated for her to sit in the chair facing away from the door. Penny made herself comfortable.

"Would you like a drink, Miss Harding?" Harry asked, moving to the drinks' cabinet. "Vodka and orange isn't it?"

Penny kept her eyes firmly fixed on Billy. Billy stared back and made a motion with his hands suggesting he'd like to wrap them around Penny's throat and throttle her right there and then.

"No thanks," Penny said. "I'll just take the money and be out of here."

"The money will be here shortly, Miss Harding," Harry said, he turned and handed Penny the drink anyway. "I'm sure you understand that four hundred thousand pounds - sterling - was not an easy sum of money to find at such short notice. It's being sent over by courier as we speak."

"Five minutes," Penny said, still not taking her gaze from Billy. "If the money's not here by then, I have an appointment with a national newspaper to keep."

I shuffled over and stood at David's side. "David, we have to do something," I whispered. "Any minute now..."

Harry and Billy both unsuccessfully tried to hide the fact they had momentarily glanced at the doorway. Penny's eyes remained on Billy, but David and I followed their furtive glances. Ruby was inching her way into the room, scaffolding pipe in hand.

"I'd stop right now if I was you, Ruby," Penny said, still glaring at Billy.

For a brief moment the scene stood still. Then, Ruby let out a scream and launched into the room. However, instead of making her way to where Penny was sitting and clouting her over the back of the head as planned, she appeared to be propelled into the room by some unseen force from behind. She fell face first to the floor, losing her grip on the pipe, which rolled noisily across the wooden flooring to within a few inches of Penny's feet.

David put his arm around my shoulders and squeezed until I thought I'd snap. "See, told you she'd thought of the possibility, didn't I?" he said, nodding towards the door. Replacing the space that Ruby's form had been filling was Oleksiy. In his right hand he held a short rope, on the end of which was a snarling, slobbering Toby.

Ruby got herself into a sitting position and turned to investigate the cause of her airborne entrance. She cocked her head to one side as if the vista might somehow be different if she did so. "Olly?" She looked to Harry and Billy with a questioning look in her eyes, as if wondering why they hadn't let her in on this part of the plan. Both were incapable of offering any explanation and stared, open mouthed, at Oleksiy and Toby.

Penny picked up the piece of pipe, got out of her chair, and made her way to the doorway. "Bang on time, darling," she said, giving Oleksiy a peck on the cheek and running her free hand over his torso.

"You?" Ruby said, pointing at Penny. "And him?" She pointed at

Oleksiy. She then started to laugh. A laugh which got louder and progressively more manic.

"That's right," Penny said, burying her head in Oleksiy's chest. "Oleksiy and I are going to be married. How forgetful of you not to tell Ruby about our plans, Oleksiy."

Billy extricated himself from his chair and stood up. "You filthy bitch-whore," he said, puffing out his chest. He took a step closer to the doorway, but must have thought better of going any further when he noticed how much Oleksiy was struggling to keep Toby on his tether.

Penny meandered back into the room, swinging the scaffolding pipe by her side. She walked around Billy, then Harry, and finally Ruby, as if participating in some weird contemporary dance. "Now then, on the understanding I'm not going to get my money, we'll just have to think of something else, won't we?" She turned to Harry. "You see, I'm not really interested in destroying your client, Harry. All I wanted was enough money for Oleksiy and I to go to his home in Ukraine and settle down. You really wouldn't believe how far four hundred thousand pounds - sterling - will go out there, Harry. So, if only you could have managed to persuade your fucked-up client to come up with the money, it would have been the last you'd have seen of me. Still, never mind, here's what I suggest." She made her way back to the doorway and snuggled back into Oleksiy's chest. "You three amigos can stay here, all nice and comfortable, whilst Oleksiy and I have a good look about. I think I'll leave Toby tied to the door handle here, just in case you think about leaving." Penny patted the dog on the head.

Billy took a step forward. Toby went mental and Oleksiy struggled to keep the dog on its leash.

"I really wouldn't come any closer," Penny said. "Toby is exceptionally hungry."

Billy stood his ground. "The first chance I get, I'm going to tear you into tiny little pieces," he said.

"Over my dead body," David said, clenching his fists.

I didn't have the heart to point out the irony in his threat.

"Whatever," Penny said. "Right, shall we start upstairs, Oleksiy? Most ladies like to keep their valuables tucked away in bedrooms. I tell you, by the time you and I have finished turning this place over, it would have been cheaper for them to stump up the cash." Oleksiy nodded and started to tie Toby to the door handle.

There was a low growl in the room. I immediately looked at Toby, but it wasn't coming from him. Further investigation indicated the noise seemed to be coming from Ruby. The growl suddenly turned into a yell; something how I imagined a marauding Viking might sound. Ruby leaped to her feet. "You worthless, crack-whore bitch!" she screamed, taking a few purposeful strides towards the door. "Keep your filthy fucking hands off my stuff."

Toby went nuts. Oleksiy had only managed to loosely attach the beast to the handle, and he could hold him no longer. Toby felled the oncoming Ruby with one pounce. Once on top of her, a single flick of his head opened Ruby's neck like it was made of nothing more than paper.

"Get him off her!" Billy shouted, running at Penny. "I'm going to tear you apart, you worthless piece of shit."

It was Oleksiy's turn to move. He tackled Billy around the waist, hoisting him in the air before dumping him on the floor. Oleksiy had all the advantages you could think of in a wrestling match-up with Billy. Size, weight, age, muscularity, you name it. But Billy had adrenalin and fear on his side; a potent mix that had him slowly get the better of his adversary. Billy pinned Oleksiy to the floor and raised a clenched hand in the air. "I'm going to ram my fist so far down your throat I'll be able to pull your liver out, you foreign fuckwit." Billy was halfway through delivering his promise when Penny decided to intervene. She took a few steps closer to the action and swung the scaffolding pipe she was still holding into Billy's head with all her strength. The noise was very similar to when Big Nigel had clobbered Roger with that saucepan. Billy immediately fell off Oleksiy and collapsed into a crumpled heap.

The whole episode was too much for Harry who fainted on the spot.

Penny turned and finally instructed Toby to leave Ruby alone, but it was obvious it was too late. Ruby was twitching her final throes. Her eyes had bulged to twice their normal size, and the blood emanating from her throat, which had initially been showering the room, had now slowed to a gentle foamy bubble.

"Excuse me," I said to the room, stepping over Ruby's dying body. I quickly made my way into the kitchen, where I was duly sick in the sink.

Over the sounds of my continuous retching, I could hear Penny and Oleksiy frantically ransacking the house for anything of merit.

After several long minutes David emerged behind me, his shadow plunging the sink into darkness. He started patting my back. I'd never been *patted* so hard. "Now that was a busy day, wasn't it? " he said.

"Whoa! Look what I find?" I heard Oleksiy call from somewhere in the hallway. "Keys for Bentley."

Five minutes later, Penny, Oleksiy, David, and Toby all left the house with as many valuables as Billy's Bentley could handle. I stood in the front doorway and watched them disappear down the gravel driveway. David waved at me from the back seat, a huge grin across his face. I half-heartedly waved back, then sat down on the doorway step and allowed the tears to flow.

I was still crying some time later when the unsteady figure of Harry made his way out of the house. Slumped across his shoulders was the even more unsteady figure of Billy. Harry struggled to get Billy into the back of his bilious pink car - the one with flowers all over it - before driving away. I didn't have the energy, or the inclination, to go with them.

And I was still crying when I felt a hand lightly touch me on the shoulder. "Do you know there's a dead body in there?" Crimson said. Out of the corner of my eye, I noticed her taking a glance at her watch.

"I suppose the committee want to see me?" I said, my voice muffled by tears.

"Not exactly," Crimson replied. "Anyway, you're okay, we've got a few minutes yet." She sat down beside me and cradled my head to her chest.

I knew she was lying.

CONFESSION TIME

After I'd spent a further ten minutes or so crying into Crimson's *Doctors of Destruction* t-shirt, she finally admitted she was running a bit late and we should really be going.

"Just another five minutes?" I said, sounding like a child.

Crimson gave an affirmative sigh. "Okay," she said. "But if I get into trouble it's all your fault. Deal?"

"Deal," I mumbled.

Despite my distress, I couldn't help but notice that the wetness being produced on Crimson's t-shirt as a result of my tears was helping to endorse certain attributes of her form. In turn, those certain endorsed attributes were helping the image of Ruby being torn apart to somewhat diminish.

There was even one part of me that was ignoring the trauma completely.

After the allotted time, during which Crimson kept stealing glances at her watch, she playfully punched me on the shoulder. "Right, come on," she said. "We haven't got time to sit here all day. I should have got you back to your assignee like ages ago."

"But I thought the committee wanted to see me," I said, confused.

"No, they were your words, Mark. The committee caught wind you and your assignee had become separated. They sent me to get you back together again."

"But I was with him up until like seconds before you got here," I protested. "How did they know so quickly?"

"I have no idea," Crimson said. "But what I do know is the committee will kill me if I don't report back soon."

I didn't really want the embarrassment of Crimson possibly noticing a certain public display of affection if I stood up, so stalled for more time. "Please, just another minute," I said. "Tell you what, why don't you tell me what *did* actually kill you? I'd love to know."

"Mark, we really haven't got time."

"Please. Pretty please. Pretty please with all the bells and whistles attached. I mean, if you're already late what's an extra minute or two? I really don't feel like seeing my assignee just yet. He's a bit of a jerk to be honest." I made my best begging face and mouthed another *please*.

"Oh, okay, but this will have to be quick, Mark."

Surprisingly, Crimson rested her head on my shoulder, which did nothing to alleviate certain stirrings. "I had a heart complaint," she said. "One of those things that go undetected until it's too late. One day, I was rushing down the corridor at university, late for my next lecture as usual, and it just exploded. Dead before I hit the ground apparently."

"My God, that's terrible," I said. "You poor thing." I snuggled Crimson closer to me and found myself lightly kissing the top of her head. I'm not sure, but I think I even started smelling her hair.

"Well, when I say it was undetected, that's not entirely true," Crimson said. She didn't seem to object to my extra attention, and even laid her palm on my chest. "What I mean is, it was undetected by everyone except me. I knew there was something wrong, but chose to ignore it, or at least not tell anyone about it. The committee gave me a right roasting. I remember Mr T's words as if it were yesterday. *'In our eyes your failure to seek out any help for your condition constitutes a voluntary act towards your own downfall, young girl.'* I've been told they give the same lecture to euthanasia victims."

"But that's ridiculous," I said. "How could you have known your condition was so serious?"

I was aware Crimson had started crying, and I gently lifted her head by placing my fingers under her chin. I used my thumb to stroke away her tears. What the hell was I doing? The new forthright Mark Ferris must have decided to join us and take complete control of the situation.

Mother was flipping her lid.

"Mark, put that young girl down. Now! You're old enough to be her father. Oh, I thought Dr Connolly would have cured you of all this pervert stuff by now. For pity's sake, why couldn't you have just stayed

with Timothy's sister?"

In counteracting the argument, I could hear Father chipping in.

"Remember son, the best time to get any action from a woman is when they're in an emotional mess. The best sex I ever had with your mother was the night of the funeral of your grandmother."

I have no idea if it was the new forthright Mark Ferris who made the move, or whether it was Crimson herself. What I do know is within seconds of wiping away her tears, Crimson and I were kissing each other gently on the lips.

"Oh, my dear God! I'm so sorry," I said, pulling my head away. "I… I don't know what came over me. It's… it's this new forthright thing that gets inside me now and again. Crimson, please, please, forgive me."

I was pushing my elbow down on my display so hard it was hurting.

Crimson looked at her watch. "I'm so late you wouldn't believe," she said. "But this time it really is your fault." Crimson smiled and took me by the hand. "Come on, let's get you back to your jerk."

I was surprised to find myself immediately back in Billy's kitchen. Furthermore, I was still attached to Crimson's hand. "Uh, Crimson," I said, "what are we doing here? This is Billy's kitchen. Why have we only gone from the front step to the kitchen? Billy definitely isn't going to be here. I saw him go."

"I know," Crimson said, her voice full of concern. "But I can't bloody find him. You made me spend too long on the step with all your crying and kissing and stuff and I've lost the trail. Oh, God, how am I going to explain this away?" Crimson looked to me for help. I could offer none. "Listen," she continued, "the only thing I can do now is leave you here and go back to the committee for an update on his whereabouts." Crimson looked at the ceiling. "They are going to be so mad at me."

"Tell them it was all my fault," I said. "Tell them I held you against your will."

Crimson looked me up and down. "Somehow I don't think they'll believe that," she said. "Don't worry, I'll think of something. I'll tell them you were hiding and I couldn't find you in time… again. Don't move. I'll be back as soon as I can."

And then she disappeared.

It was five days before I saw her again.

Ruby's body was found later that evening by the Somalian housekeeper; who'd presumably fled Somalia to avoid scenes of brutality. I watched as she ran around the house screaming before she finally found the strength to use the house phone in the kitchen to call the police. Fifteen minutes later the first squad car arrived. Fifteen minutes after that the house was teeming with police from all sections of the force. Even an interpreter had been drafted in to help with the poor housekeeper's statement.

Within two hours of the housekeeper's call, the house was sealed off.

Ruby was declared dead at the scene. Her body was duly photographed, bagged, and removed. The forensic pathologist advised the lead detective, DCI Staines, that in his opinion the time of death could be determined as within the last 4 hours, and that ultimately the cause of death was laceration of the jugular vein. He'd let him know more as soon as a post-mortem had been carried out.

Shortly after Ruby's body had been removed, DCI Staines received the news that Billy White had been located at the studio where he worked and had been duly informed that a body, believed to be that of his wife, had been found at his home.

Detective Staines gave the order for Billy to be taken to the nearest police station and kept until he himself could get there to speak to him. "At the moment," he informed anyone with an interest, "the official line is Billy White is simply helping us with our enquiries. Nothing more."

I jumped in the back of detective Staines' unmarked car and accompanied him on the drive to the police station. I had to duck my head to avoid being spotted by the ever growing horde of reporters that had started congregating at the bottom of Billy's drive. There was no way I could risk Mother finding out I was being ferried to a police station courtesy of one of her majesty's law and order officers. She'd have been hysterical.

"I told you you'd come to no good, didn't I, Mark? Ever since you stopped seeing Timothy's sister you've become a different person. Molesting young girls, bothering with murderers, thieves, vagabonds and perverts. Whatever next! I just don't recognise you any more, Mark."

A further gathering of journalists and photographers were waiting for us on the steps of the police station. "How the hell do these hounds get their information so quickly?" detective Staines mumbled as he got out of the car. "We could do with a few of them on the force."

"Okay, break it up please," I said, as we fought our way through the scrum. "Nothing to see here. No comment... No comment... No comment."

Detective Staines sat himself down in front of Billy and introduced himself. We were in a room not much bigger than Old Eric's office. A small metal table separated Billy from the detective. Detective Staines removed his jacket and threw it over the back of his chair.

"I know this isn't easy, Billy," he said. "But I need to ask you a few questions, okay? Now, the first thing I need to point out is that you're not under arrest. However, if you'd feel more comfortable having your legal representative here, then that's fine."

Billy shook his head.

"Good. Now is there anything I can get you before we start, Billy? Coffee? Tea?"

"No thanks."

"By the way, I know this isn't probably the right time to say this, but I love your programme, Billy. The wife and I never miss an episode."

Billy shifted in his seat. "When can I go home?"

Detective Staines ignored the question. "I bet there's a lot of hard work goes into making a programme like that, eh, Billy?"

"Could say that. When can I go home? I need to go home."

"So is that where you've been all day, Billy? Work?"

"Pardon?"

"I was just asking if that's where you've been all day. At work?"

"I guess so. Can I go home now?"

Detective Staines flipped open a notepad, into which he'd been making copious notes since his arrival at Billy's house, and began writing something. "And who could I speak to in order to confirm that, Billy?" he asked.

"Sorry?"

"I was just asking who may be able to confirm your whereabouts today, Billy?"

"Um… I suppose my agent," Billy replied. "He was with me all day."

Detective Staines flipped back a page. "That would be, Harry Bond, yes?"

Billy nodded his head. "Can I go home now?"

Detective Staines continued to ignore the question. "Now, I don't know how much my colleagues have told you, Billy, but it looks like the house has been burgled. There's been quite a spate of celebrity burglaries over the last few months, so I'm going to talk to other forces to see if they've got any leads, but at this moment in time we're working on the assumption that Ruby may have disturbed the perpetrators."

"Oh God. What did they do to her?"

"I know you don't want to think about it at the moment, Billy, and there's really no rush, but at some time in the near future I'm going to need a list of things that are missing, okay? Just so we can get a flavour of who we're dealing with. I would suggest you also inform your insurance company as soon as possible, Billy."

"I'll tell them as soon as I get home."

"Look, I'm really sorry, Billy, but it'll be a few days before we can allow you to go home. I promise we'll be as quick as we can, but the scenes of crimes officers have to be thorough, Billy. We have to satisfy ourselves that we haven't missed anything. I'm sure you understand."

Billy nodded his head.

"Talking of which, we will need to take your fingerprints. Just so we can eliminate them. Don't worry, it's all standard practice. And I could do with knowing who else has access to the house, Billy. Whose other fingerprints can we *expect* to find, apart from yours?"

Billy stumbled over his answer, but eventually confirmed that other than himself and Ruby, Harry visited the house regularly, as did the Somalian housekeeper and, of course, Ruby's tennis coach.

The detective's head lifted from his notepad. "Tennis coach?"

"Yes, Ruby's been taking lessons. He comes twice a week."

"What's his name, Billy?"

Billy shook his head. "Ruby only ever called him Olly. He was from Lithuania, or Latvia, maybe Estonia. I don't know, one of those places. Eastern European anyway. He was always drooling over my Bentley. Reckoned he'd never seen a yellow one before."

"Where's your car now, Billy? At the studio?"

"Um… no. Harry picked me up this morning. It should be parked on my drive. Why?"

Detective Staines scribbled furiously in his notepad. "Sorry, Billy, but I didn't see it there earlier, so it looks like that's the first thing I can put on my list of things that are missing. Do you know if this Olly might own a dog, Billy?"

"Sorry?"

Detective Staines put his notepad away. "Doesn't matter. Listen, I know you don't want to be answering stupid questions right now, so let's take a break. We'll get a cup of coffee, maybe a doughnut as well, and arrange for those prints to be done, is it?" Detective Staines stood up and collected his jacket.

"How did Ruby actually die?" Billy asked, as the detective led him out of the room. "I've not been told anything." A few tears could be seen rolling down Billy's cheeks.

"We're still waiting on the exact cause of death, Billy," detective Staines said, squeezing Billy's shoulder. "As soon as we find out I'll make sure you're the first to know, okay?"

"She was my rock," Billy said, allowing the tears to flow more freely. "What am I supposed to do without her?"

"We'll find out who did this, Billy," detective Staines said. "I promise."

"Thank you, detective."

"Just one last question for now, Billy. How did you get that nasty looking bump on your head?"

"Oh that," Billy replied, rubbing his temple at the point where the scaffolding pipe had connected. "Can you believe it? I walked into a lighting boom at work."

After he'd drunk his coffee, given his fingerprints, and confirmed that he would stay at his agent's house and not go anywhere until he was allowed back home, Billy was eventually escorted out of a back door of the station and ferried by an unmarked police car to Harry's address.

A scaled-down version of the media bandwagon we'd encountered outside the police station was also camped outside the gates of Harry's country pile. The police car had to stop outside the locked gates whilst Billy made a phone call.

"Open the fucking gates you dwarf!"

Harry looked twenty years older than when I'd last seen him just a few hours previously. "They know, Billy, I just know they know," he said, marching around his huge living room. "Do you think they know, Billy? I practically shit myself when they took me in for fingerprinting. The girl doing the prints had to keep asking me to calm down my hands were shaking so bad. If I get taken in for questioning I'll have a bloody heart attack, Billy, I know I will."

"Get me a drink," Billy said, sitting in one of several armchairs and reaching for the TV remote. "A big one."

He switched on the TV and tuned in to a 24 hour news channels. After a story about some famous footballer having an affair with his brother's wife, Ruby's death was the next big news. A slim, blonde-haired female newsreader announced that a body believed to be of the model Ruby White, the wife of TV celebrity Billy White, had been found dead at the White's residence earlier that day. The news footage cut to an aerial shot of the bagged Ruby being taken from the house on a trolley and into the back of a waiting ambulance.

The newsreader then confirmed a police spokesperson had said the death was being treated as suspicious, and that burglary was the possible motive.

If the hardly contained pleasure of the newsreader was anything to go by, I couldn't help but think women up and down the country were clocking that Billy White was now effectively single.

"We just need to stay calm," Billy said, taking his drink from Harry's trembling hands. "If we stick to the story we were at the studio all day, what can they do? We're each other's alibi, Harry, and don't you bloody forget it."

"But what if they start asking around the staff?" I could tell Harry was on the verge of crying. "It'll only take one of them to suggest they hadn't seen us and we're done for. Christ, I even rang in and told them you had man-flu. And what about the whore, Billy? What if she goes public?"

Billy closed his eyes and shook his head. "Think about it logically, you shrimp," he said. "There's no way the little bitch could risk it now. Even she wouldn't be stupid enough to draw that sort of attention to herself. After all, it was her bloody dog that killed Ruby. Look, I think I got that idiot Staines all worked up about Ruby's tennis coach. With any luck he'll be barking up that tree for the foreseeable future and won't even think about asking around the studio." He held out his empty glass to Harry.

"But what if he finds them, Billy? Oh, God, we're done for. I know it. I might as well kill myself now and get it over with."

"For Christ's sake, stop being so dramatic," Billy said. "I had Staines eating out of the palm of my hand by the time I'd finished with him. Anyway, with any luck the blackmailing whore and her greasy lover are halfway to wherever the hell they were going by now."

"Ukraine, wasn't it?" Harry said, handing Billy his drink. "Didn't she say four hundred grand would go a long way in Ukraine?"

"By Christ, so she did," Billy said. "Harry, you should have been a detective."

Later that night, the news coverage of Ruby's death included footage of a short press conference given by detective Staines.

"We can confirm that we are interested in speaking to a man who was employed at the White household as a tennis coach. We believe he is of Eastern European origin. Maybe Lithuanian, Latvian, or Estonian. It is possible he is in possession of a bright yellow Bentley motor car, registration number, Bravo, Whiskey, One, Five, - November, Oscar, Indigo. We would ask the public to be vigilant and to notify their nearest police station if they have any information. However, please do not approach this man, as he may be dangerous. Thank you."

I recalled the registration number. Billy had it spaced so it read, *BW 15 NO 1:* Billy White is number 1.

A crooked smile crossed Billy's mouth as he watched detective Staines' speech. "You know, Harry," he said. "I don't think Staines has got the brains he was born with. I think if there was any chance of him catching our little problem, he'd have had to have done so by now. I think the little bitch has actually got away. I have a funny feeling everything's going to be all right. Actually, if we play this correctly my little Oompa-Loompa, it'll do my career the world of good. Let's have a drink on it." He waved his glass in the air.

That night, as I watched Billy sleep, I reflected on the kiss with Crimson. What the hell had I been thinking? More to the point what the hell had *she* been thinking? Had I, Mark Ferris, really attracted the attention of a beautiful girl half my age? Or had Father been right, and I'd only got some action because she'd been in an emotional mess? Either way, how was I ever going to look Crimson in the eye again?

I paced around the sumptuous guest bedroom looking for answers when I suddenly caught sight of the new forthright Mark Ferris in a mirror. "Jesus Christ, are you smiling?" I asked him. "Do you think this is something to be proud of?"

"Actually, Mark," he replied. "I think it's bloody wonderful."

"God help me," I said, putting my head in my hands. "I'm going straight to Hell."

DCI Staines turned up at Harry's home first thing the following morning, disturbing Billy and Harry's breakfast of poached eggs. Accompanied by several burly policemen, detective Staines did away with platitudes and announced he was arresting them both on suspicion of conspiring to murder one Miss Penny Harding.

After the legalities were out of the way, Billy and Harry were handcuffed, then unceremoniously led away to separate police stations.

We were in a slightly larger room than the day before. This time, the table had three people around it. Billy sat on one side, whilst detective Staines and a colleague, who was introduced as detective Collins, sat on the other. On the table was a machine, which detective Collins advised would be used for the purpose of recording the forthcoming interview. After the machine had been told what date and time it was, who was in the room, and why, detective Staines removed Billy's handcuffs.

"Well, Billy," he said. "Looks like we've got ourselves in a bit of a pickle, doesn't it?"

Billy was unrecognisable as the debonair front man of *Billy's Belters.* Never a morning person anyway, his unexpected arrest had not given him time to groom himself as usual. DCI Staines had refused permission for either Billy or Harry to dress properly before bundling them out of Harry's house, which meant Billy's apparel consisted of no more than a vest, trousers, and socks and shoes; all of which were already a day old. His hair was lank, his breath smelled of eggs, and he was unshaven. Still, could always be worse, I thought. Poor old Harry had still been wearing his *Winnie The Pooh* pyjamas.

Detective Staines settled himself in his chair. "Right, Billy, would you like to tell me, in your own words, exactly what happened to Ruby?" he asked.

Billy remained silent for a few moments, looking around the room as if trying to find someone to reply for him. "I can only assume it's like you said. She disturbed some burglars."

Detective Staines let out a laugh. "Maybe," he said. "We'll see."

"Well I didn't kill her if that's what you're thinking." Billy tried to keep the statement light.

Detective Staines leaned back, rocking his chair on its back legs. "No, I don't believe you did, Billy," he said. "I believe your wife was killed by a rather vicious dog." He looked to detective Collins. "Name of Toby, wasn't it?"

"I believe so, sir," detective Collins replied.

I had to admit, I stood in some awe of detective Staines. How had he pieced together how Ruby had died on the evidence so far, and so quickly? And how did he know Toby's name? Was detective Staines a direct descendant of Holmes? Was detective Collins his modern-day Watson? Then I slapped my forehead for being stupid. It was obvious. Detective Staines had caught up with Penny and Oleksiy.

"There's no need to look so shocked, Billy," detective Staines continued. "We *are* detectives. Our job is to detect, right?" He looked to detective Collins who nodded his head in agreement. "So what else have we detected so far detective Collins?"

"Well, sir, I believe we've detected that Miss Harding was squeezing Mr White for four hundred thousand pounds - sterling - because he beat the living crap out of her whilst obtaining sexual favours."

"That's right," detective Staines said. "And we've also detected that when Miss Harding turned up at Billy's house yesterday, hoping to collect her booty, things started to go very, very, wrong."

"I believe you're correct, sir," detective Collins said "I also believe that we detected there was a plan afoot to murder Miss Harding. And that Mr White, Mrs White, and Mr Bond were all in on said plan. Our detection has further led us to believe that as soon as Miss Harding introduced her own accomplice to the scene, things started to go very, very, wrong."

"Why I do believe you could be right, detective Collins," detective Staines said. "I would suggest that further detection has led us to believe that Mrs White was attacked because Miss Harding and the tennis coach, who were, I understand, enjoying a romantic liaison, stated that they were about to start rummaging through Mrs White's *stuff*."

"I would concur with that detection, sir," detective Collins said. "And would add that when Mrs White moved with the probable intention of causing Miss Harding some hurt, Miss Harding's dog, Toby, took it upon himself to intervene."

"And that's when things started to go very, very, wrong," detective Staines said.

Billy sat rock-still.

"By the way, Billy," detective Staines continued, "the tennis coach is from Ukraine, and, to be honest, I don't think he's really a tennis coach."

"You don't say," I said.

Billy's face had started to collapse inwards, like it had a slow puncture. He looked like someone had put a funnel in his ear and sucked out every last ounce of colour from the neck up. Billy's collapsing face made his eyes look wider than the Mississippi.

"The Mississippi river can easily be up to eleven miles wide at Lake Winnibigoshish" - As taught to Emma-Lou by Mr Wilkins.

Okay, Billy's eyes maybe weren't quite *that* wide, but still very, very wide. He dropped his chin onto his chest. "It wasn't my idea," he said. "It was Ruby who came up with the plan."

"Oh, Billy," detective Staines said. "My wife is going to be so disappointed in you. She really thinks the sun shines out of that tight little backside of yours."

"If you've found them," Billy mumbled, obviously coming to the same conclusion as me, "does that mean I get my stuff back? What about the Bentley? Did they still have the Bentley? What else have you recovered?" He lifted his head. "I hope you're going to throw the book at the bitch. What have you actually charged her with? Prostitution? Extortion? Burglary? Owning a dangerous animal? What?"

Detective Staines leaned back and put his hands behind his head. His slow smile almost took on proportions that would have given Old Eric's a run for its money. "And what makes you think we've found them?" he said.

"Pardon?" Billy said.

"Yes, pardon?" I repeated.

"I said, what makes you think we've found them?"

"But you must have," Billy said.

"Yes, you must have," I repeated.

"Sorry to disappoint you, Billy," detective Staines said, "but the last sighting I have of them was boarding the Newhaven to Dieppe ferry. Probably halfway across Europe by now. We've got our friends at Interpol looking for them, but if they do actually make it to Ukraine we'll never get them out. No extradition rights you see."

"But I don't understand," Billy said.

"Neither do I," I added. Perhaps Staines and Collins were the new Holmes and Watson after all. At the very least, Cagney and Lacey.

"I thought you might not," detective Staines replied. "That's why I brought this along." He reached under the desk and produced a small shoe box. "I received this first thing this morning. Addressed to me personally. It really is one of the most interesting packages I think I've ever received, Billy."

Detective Staines emptied the contents of the box onto the table. Along with a pile of photographs and a handwritten letter, a CD landed on the table. It was clearly marked with black marker-pen: *Hotel.*

Detective Staines picked up the CD and waved it in the air. "Detetctive Collins and I spent a very interesting time watching this, Billy," he said. "The quality isn't always that good, but it's got everything on there. Very upsetting I must say. You really should see about attending anger management courses or something, Billy." He leaned into Billy and lowered his voice. "Or perhaps just find yourself a man."

"I am not gay!" Billy slapped his hands on the table, and looked at the CD as if it was the first thing he'd ever seen in his life.

"Now, this letter is quite illuminating as well," detective Staines said. "Would you like to read it, Billy?" He waved the letter in Billy's direction. Billy shook his head. "Please yourself. It goes into great detail. Even gives us the dog's name. Oh, by the way, she says she's sorry it was Ruby who had to pay the ultimate price for you being a... now how does she put it?" Detective Staines scanned the letter. "Ah, yes, here it is... *A sick, perverted mother-fucker who should have been drowned at birth...* Poetic, don't you think? Oh, and here, look, right here, Billy. There's a potted history of Oleksiy. The village he's from, how they met, how he and his young brother, Ivan, are experts in electronics amongst other things. Oh, and look at this, Billy. Right here on the back page. Oh, bless her. She's only gone and given us a list of everything they took from your house along with its expected value. So I guess I won't be needing you to supply me with that information after all, will I? It's quite a haul, Billy. Ruby did like her expensive jewellery, didn't she? And we would never recommend anyone leaving that amount of cash lying around, Billy. That's just asking for trouble. What, were you avoiding taxes or something? Oh, and look, there's even a PS saying they'd already got a hundred grand for the Bentley even before they boarded that ferry at Newhaven. Now that's industry for you, don't you think, Billy? Sheer bloody industry. My God, what is this girl capable of? I tell you, we could do with the likes of her on the force."

"I think I should call my lawyer." Billy said.

Four days later, despite the prosecution's pleas, a bored looking judge granted Billy and Harry conditional bail. They were both to hand in their passports, and both told to report to their nearest police station every day at 4pm. Furthermore, they were forbidden from communicating with each other, or any other person who may have a bearing on the case; excepting their own counsel. In order to try and avoid the media parked outside their respective houses, the judge ordered Harry to reside at the address of his sister, whilst Billy was to stay with his old friend and acting lawyer. The trial itself was set for a month's time.

"But your honour you don't understand!" I screamed at the judge. "You can't send him there. That's the same house my wife lives in. Your honour, it's the same house I lived in! Hell, it's the house I *died* in! Your honour, please don't make me go back there, I beg you." I dropped to my knees and actually begged. "Please! Have mercy on my soul."

I realised I was probably being a little melodramatic, but it made no difference. The judge completely ignored me and disappeared into his chambers, where apparently he was due his afternoon nap.

I slumped to the floor and listened as the courtroom emptied. I don't know what the collective noun for tears is, but I allowed a whole bunch of them to roll off my face as the idea of being sent to my old house took form. Did I really have to go? Perhaps if I crawled underneath the judge's desk and curled into a ball, just like this, no one would notice.

An hour later, Crimson's face appeared in my vision.

"There you are," she said, holding out her hand. "I wish you wouldn't keep hiding like this. I've been looking all over for you. Come on, I've got to take you to your assignee. The committee are going mental."

When I showed little enthusiasm for leaving my hiding place, Crimson leaned under the desk and started dragging me out by my foot.

"Where on Earth have you been?" I asked, straining against Crimson's tugging. "You said you'd be back as soon as possible. That was five days ago."

"Not now, Mark."

"Crimson, about that thing the other day," I said, struggling like a fish on a line.

"Mark, I really haven't got time right now." Crimson finally got the upper hand and got a grip of my wrist.

"But listen, I just wanted to say…"

I immediately found myself in a garden - my garden. Crimson rubbed her hands together and promptly disappeared.

"Oh my God," I whispered, staring up at the façade of a house - my house.

A movement from the upstairs window of the bedroom Elaine and I used to share caught my eye. I looked up slowly to see Old Eric waving at me furiously, his face beaming with the brightness of a thousand stars. He was jumping up and down like an excited puppy. From the look of him, it wouldn't have surprised me if he was actually wetting himself.

"Oh, Eric," I said under my breath. "I hope you've brought the paper bag with you."

I feebly waved back, took the deepest breath my lungs would allow, closed my eyes, crossed myself, and made my way slowly to the front door - my front door.

I stood looking at the door for several minutes before realising I didn't have keys any more and couldn't actually get in. "Oh, what a shame," I muttered. "I'll just have to go and wait somewhere else. Like Australia."

I turned with the intention of getting as far away as possible, only to find Billy and his lawyer marching up the garden path towards me. Billy, in particular, was showing signs of camaraderie that suggested he was quite pleased with how things had gone earlier. "You're the man," he said, grasping the lawyer's shoulders. "You are the absolute, fucking man. I never thought I'd get bail. You, my friend, are nothing short of being the man."

Their eagerness to get inside the house practically bowled me over. As they went by me, I caught the slight smell of alcohol. The lawyer fished some keys out of his pocket and opened the door. I noticed the key-ring he used was identical to the one I used to have. What were the chances of that? I thought.

Once in the hallway the lawyer shouted up the stairs - my stairs. "Elaine, sweetheart. Come and see who I've brought home." He then ushered Billy into the kitchen - my kitchen, where he flicked a switch on a space-age coffee machine before grabbing the remote control for a wall-mounted TV. Both items were new to me.

Moments later, Elaine - my Elaine, entered the kitchen wearing dark tracksuit bottoms and a white baggy t-shirt which professed *LIFE IS GOOD*.

Did I ever mention Elaine was a stunner?

I begged the new forthright Mark Ferris to stop me from passing out. It was no use. He must have still been hiding under the judge's desk.

FINAL CURTAIN

I opened my eyes to find Old Eric slapping me lightly across the face. I propped myself up on an elbow and took stock of my situation. I was on the floor in the kitchen, but, apart from Eric, the room appeared empty of people.

"How long have I been out?" I asked.

"About two hours," Eric replied, helping me to stand up.

"Two hours!"

"Yep. I've been popping in now and then just to make sure you weren't dying on me."

"Very funny. So where is everybody?"

"In the lounge," Eric said, nodding in the general direction. "Just finished off a Chinese takeaway. Elaine did consider cooking, but you know how Elaine hates to cook."

I knew only too well.

Just after we'd married, in an effort to impress, Elaine decided to invite her new boss over for dinner. For reasons best known to Elaine, she'd announced she would actually cook the food herself. After an afternoon of bangs, crashes, expletives, many burnt offerings, and with only half an hour to go before her VIP guest arrived, Elaine finally gave up and sent me on an errand to the nearest Marks & Spencer armed with a shopping list of shove-in-the-microwave foodstuffs.

Shopping for food was high up on my, *have no idea what I'm doing* list, and by the time I returned home, Elaine's guest was sitting in our lounge sipping an aperitif. I was instructed to go and entertain her whilst Elaine prepared the food. I duly breezed into the lounge as nonchalantly as I could and introduced myself to the frumpy looking woman sitting on my sofa. By using my God-given powers of observation, I immediately noticed the woman was heavily pregnant. Glad to have something to break the ice, I asked her when the expected joyous occasion would be.

Turned out she was just fat.

No amount of explaining how useless I was at meeting new people could retrieve the situation. Elaine changed jobs shortly afterwards.

"And guess what?" Eric enthused, clapping his hands together. "Charlotte is with them."

"Charlotte? What, as in next door Charlotte?" I felt a prickling climb up the back of my neck.

"The very one," Eric replied. He caught hold of my hand and started dragging me out of the kitchen towards the lounge - my lounge. I was reminded of all those times I'd been dragged anywhere I didn't want to go. The dentist, Ikea, the ballet, the school disco with Timothy's spotty sister, Marks & Spencer.

Like then, just as now, I felt powerless to resist.

My next door neighbour had lost none of the sex I used to find appealing when I was alive. She was wearing a little black number which left little of her form to the imagination. Her long brunette hair had been neatly and expertly fastened in a bob with just a few loose strands left untied to frame her small but perfectly made-up face. A pair of outrageously high black stiletto shoes had added several inches to her normal five-four, serving to accentuate the perfect curve of her legs. She was sitting on the sofa - my sofa, and, under normal circumstances, I would have been beside myself, even honoured, to have Charlotte in my house showing herself off like this.

However, these were not normal circumstances, and it would have taken a team of highly skilled medical staff to surgically separate Charlotte's face from my assignee's. They might as well have been sharing internal organs. She was wrapped around Billy tighter than cling-film on a hot dinner plate; her dress riding up slightly to reveal an enticing hint of stocking-top.

Sitting opposite them on a small two-seater - a new addition to the house - was the lawyer and Elaine - my Elaine. They were intently watching the exploits of their guests whilst occasionally turning to each other and touching each other inappropriately.

"I think I'm going to be sick," I said, managing to release my arm from Eric's grip. "I'll be outside."

I turned into the hallway and slid down the wall, bunching my knees into my chest. I cried hard, actually trying to force tears out in a futile effort to exhaust them quicker.

Mother was trying her best.

"Time heals everything, Mark. You just wait and see if it doesn't. Trust me, in the morning you'll wonder what all the fuss was about. I bet Timothy's sister would never have treated you like this. Shall I get Father to come and cheer you up?"

Five minutes later, Charlotte and Billy left the lounge and made their way upstairs, hand in hand.

No more than a minute after that, they were followed by Elaine and her lover. "Shall we join them?" the lawyer asked, hesitating at the bottom of the stairs.

Elaine nodded her head from side to side in contemplation. "No," she eventually decided on. "I've got a little surprise, and it's just for you."

Old Eric watched his assignee and the lawyer ascend the stairs before sitting down beside me. "I reckon if you want to fulfil a fantasy and really find out what Charlotte looks like naked, son, now's the opportunity." He put his arm across my shoulders.

"Twenty years, Eric," I said, through my tears. "Twenty years I spent with that woman. How can she forget twenty years just like that?" I clicked my fingers. "What did I ever do to make her treat me like this? Was I really that much of a disappointment?"

Eric looked up the stairs, then to me, then back up the stairs, then back to me again. "Listen," he said, with a resigned puff of his cheeks, "let's think about this logically, son. I know I once told you that you should have fought to keep Elaine, but I was probably only being polite. Let's face it, your death was probably the best thing that could have happened to her."

"Oh thanks a lot."

"No, what I mean is, when you were alive you were both miserable, right? Well at least now one of you is happy. Don't get me wrong, I know you loved her with all your heart and soul, and I also know her infidelity cut like a knife through butter, but if you love somebody that much, son, then surely your job is to make sure they're as happy as can be, yes? Even if it means letting them go."

My tears were still flowing. If I continued at this rate, I'd soon have a puddle around me that matched the Mississippi's deepest point.

"At Baton Rouge, Louisiana, The Mississippi river reaches a depth of one hundred and ninety eight feet." - As taught to Emma-Lou by Mr Wilkins.

Okay, maybe I wouldn't create something quite *that* deep, but still very, very deep.

"Trust me, in her eyes you're a hero, son." Old Eric continued, squeezing my shoulders as if in thanks for something. "If you'd never bothered to dive out of that attic, you'd both still be as gloomy as sin. But now... well you can hear that laughter for yourself, son. She's as happy as a kid with a new bike, and she's got your death to thank for it."

"Eric, is this the kind of wisdom people used to travel the length and breadth to seek you out for?" I reached over and used his robe to try and dry my face. "Because it sure as hell isn't doing me any favours."

The sound of another hefty laugh from my wife travelled down the stairs. The laugh tapered into a groan of deep satisfaction. Eric's face lit up like it had just been plugged in. He jumped to his feet with the agility of a cat. "Sorry, son, but I really do have to go," he said. "I actually know what her little surprise entails. I was with her when she bought it."

He took the stairs two at a time.

When the noises wafting down the stairs became too much to bear, and with my once-upon-a-time desire to see Charlotte naked completely destroyed, I made my way from the hallway into the kitchen. After deliberating on what to do next, I decided that curling up underneath the kitchen table was about as good an option as any.

At some point in the early hours, I briefly spotted Charlotte making her way gingerly to the front door. She was only partially dressed and was carrying her shoes in her hands. I couldn't be sure, but every step she took seemed to bring with it a gasp of pain.

The morning was still reasonably new when Elaine and the lawyer arrived in the kitchen together. They were hanging onto each other, giggling about nothing in particular. Elaine eventually extricated herself from her lover, grabbed a banana, and said something about being late for work.

"I think I'll ask Charlotte to come over again tonight," she said, striking a pose in the kitchen doorway. "The thought of having Billy White doing it in the next room sort of really got me going."

"I noticed," the lawyer said, blowing my wife a kiss.

Elaine caught the kiss and planted it on her lips. She then seductively peeled the banana and left.

I crawled out from my hiding place and used various items of furniture to help me get to my feet. I followed the lawyer around the kitchen as he made himself breakfast. He moved around with ease, as if he owned the place. Every time he walked by me, I used the new forthright Mark Ferris to stick out a leg. However, the lawyer was obviously well-balanced, and remained firmly on his feet. The new forthright Mark Ferris then decided to try kicking him, but with little result. Finally, in desperation, the new forthright Mark Ferris swung a few roundhouse punches, but successfully managed to avoid connecting with any of them. Ten minutes of using the new forthright Mark Ferris to exact any type of pain on the lawyer found me doubled over with exhaustion.

"I hate you," I said, hands on knees, gasping for breath. "You can only imagine how much." I crawled back under the table and curled myself up.

Billy finally put in an appearance some time around mid-morning. He was wearing a bathrobe with the lawyer's initials on the breast pocket, and his face bore the effects of the amount of wine he'd drunk the night before. "Is there any coffee in that thing?" he asked the lawyer, pointing at the robot coffee machine.

The lawyer pressed a button or two and within seconds produced a cup of steaming coffee. "So, I'm guessing from the noises I heard, someone had a good night," he said, passing the coffee over. "Charlotte still exhausted in bed?"

Billy took a sip of his coffee and winced at the warmth. "Gone when I woke up," he replied, shrugging his shoulders. "Shame really. I had something going on down below when I woke which could have done with seeing to."

"Save it," the lawyer said, smiling. "We're thinking of inviting her over again tonight."

"Great, can't wait. By the way thanks for all this." Billy saluted his lawyer with his coffee. "You really are the man."

"Who am I to argue?" the lawyer replied. "Now, as soon as you've finished that coffee, we've got the small business of your case to attend to."

Billy and the lawyer retired to the lounge and started talking legal jargon. I left them to it and made my way upstairs. I stood on the landing and stared at the hatch to the attic - my attic.

There it was. Just an ordinary hatch. I didn't know what I was expecting to see. A memorial of some kind? A plaque announcing, *Mark Ferris fell here*? Of course, there was nothing of the sort. I wandered around the rest of the house - my house, looking for signs of my existence. Nothing. Well, except for the photograph on the bedside cabinet, but even that was turned to the wall.

I made my way back to the lounge contemplating how forty years of life could disappear so quickly. Where was my stamp? My mark for Mark, as Eric had said? What had I left behind besides a horny wife? I'd sorted out all my personal finances before I'd died, making sure Elaine wouldn't have to worry about paperwork etcetera, and started to envy those who'd never bothered, or even those who'd left behind a mountain of debt. At least their loved ones still had something to remind them of their dearly departed, even if it was only bailiffs knocking down the door. What had I done to be remembered by? Nothing. I'd never written a well-loved song or delivered a groundbreaking novel. I'd never invented a lifesaving machine or won a medal at the Olympics. I'd neither gained nor lost a fortune. I'd never been the first man to do something, or the last. I started to wonder if I'd ever lived at all. I guessed I must have. Hadn't Old Eric said something about not being able to die unless you'd lived? But then, as he'd also suggested, perhaps I'd gotten them in the wrong order. My lifetime seemed like such a long time ago. And so pointless.

I remembered having read about something called *The Butterfly*

Effect where a very small change at one point in time - for example a butterfly flapping its wings - can result in huge differences at a much later point in time, and it dawned on me how drastically life can be altered by every little decision we make. What if Elaine hadn't been dumped by that rock-drummer? What if she'd never come running out of college that morning and literally bumped into the postman? What if I'd heeded Mother's advice and married Timothy's sister? What if I'd heeded Father's advice and never married at all? What if I'd had children? What if I'd never fallen out of the attic? What if David hadn't killed his unborn child? What if Sarah hadn't bowed to her mother's pressure and kept her baby? What if Roger had never set eyes on a pack of cards? What if Billy just admitted he was gay? What if I'd never kissed Crimson?

"If you'd never kissed Crimson," the new forthright Mark Ferris butted in, "then you'd be a bloody fool. Next time you find yourself with your lips clamped onto a young girl who's in an emotional mess, take the bull by the horns and drag her to the nearest bed. Idiot!"

"Oh go away," I told him. "You sound exactly like your father."

I re-entered the lounge - my lounge.

"So, here's how I see it," the lawyer was saying. "We're going to turn this thing on its head, Billy. Ultimately, we're going to make you out to be the victim." The lawyer started pacing the room. "You had a single moment of weakness, where, on the spur of the moment, you made the wrong decision to use the services of a prostitute. You were under a lot of stress, emotionally tired, and unstable. Unfortunately, due to these mitigating circumstances, your treatment of the prostitute turned out to be less than gentlemanly. For this you will humbly, and very, very publicly apologise."

"Still doesn't sound too good to me," Billy said. "At the very least, women are going to think I'm a monster."

"Listen, it's not difficult to discredit whores, Billy. Did you know that until recently crimes against prostitutes in America carried the acronym NHI."

"NHI? What the bloody hell is NHI?"

"No Human Involved." The lawyer sat back down. "That's how much the law thinks of them, Billy. Why do you think they're never used as witnesses? Anyway, let's not forget it was her who was blackmailing you. Even if they could, the prosecution would never risk sticking her on the witness stand."

"What do you mean even if they could?"

"She's long gone, Billy. Staines had confirmation that she crossed the Moldovan border a few days ago."

Billy allowed himself a small smile. "Well, good riddance to the thieving bitch," he said, "but I'm not actually at risk of going to prison because I got a bit rough with a whore, am I? I'm at risk of going down because I hatched a plan to kill her. I'm guessing there's a vast difference."

"But you didn't actually hatch the plan, Billy. We'll easily contend that Ruby was the instigator and main protagonist. I mean, even Harry will testify to that. Anyway, let's face it, Billy, the female element of any jury we put together probably already hate Ruby for marrying you in the first place. Even before we start they'll have her tagged a scheming bitch. I reckon if we play our cards right, Billy, and keep laying thick the mental stress you were under, we can persuade people Ruby was working you like a puppet and you had no idea what you were doing."

"Do you really think so?"

"Yes. Listen, I know it'll be expensive, but I've already employed the services of a team of top PR people. I tell you, Billy, by the time we've finished with this, we'll have the general public feeling so sorry for you, they'll demand you get a knighthood. Damn, I'm going to paint you so sweet, Billy, the prosecution will think they're trying jam."

"But I'm guessing people won't feel so sorry for me when they see that CD or those photographs. What are we going to do about them?"

"Haven't you ever heard of Photoshop, Billy? Anyone with half a brain can doctor a photograph. Don't forget, this Ivan geezer who took them has disappeared as well. We'll easily prove he would have known how to mock up a few photos. Anyway, you're in show-business, Billy, you of all people should know that with a bit of work you can make ugly people look fantastic. It therefore follows you can make fantastic people look ugly. As for the CD, I can't even see it being allowed as admissible evidence. It's what's known as a honey-trap, Billy, and judges tend to throw them out quicker than shit off a shovel. So, we'll accept you may have been a tiny bit rough with this girl, but we'll deny you caused the damage as it appears on those photographs. We'll simply say she exaggerated her injuries. It'll put reasonable doubt into people's minds, Billy, and that's all we need.

Reasonable doubt. Now, in the four days you've been in custody, those PR guys I mentioned have been working bloody miracles. Apparently, they couldn't find a lot of information about your whore's past, which means they've been able to be a bit creative. Especially as she's not around to deny it."

"You mean they've made it up?"

"Let's just stick to creative, Billy. Anyway, trust me, by now most people are thinking the whore deserved whatever she got. They've really gone to town on that Oleksiy and his brother Ivan as well, playing the illegal immigrant card. Okay, so there's no actual evidence to support either of them were here illegally, but no matter, it's reasonable doubt, Billy, reasonable doubt. Add in that all three of them were, quite possibly, almost definitely, maybe certainly, conceivably but unquestionably, alcoholics, drug-pushers, and sex-traffickers of underage girls from Belarus, and I think you get the picture. Then throw in the media coverage of poor Billy White's recent work-schedule, doctored slightly to prove you've actually managed to work more than twenty-four hours a day, and couple it with your absolute refusal to take holidays, hence putting any private life on hold in order to make yourself available to your adoring public, and we start to see what a crime it is that you're even on trial in the first place. Aaaand, just in case *that* wasn't enough," the lawyer took an intake of breath, "they've also constantly reminded the great British nation that you've just had your beloved wife chewed to death by a maniacal dog. A dog who just so happened to be owned by guess who? That's right, ladies and gentlemen, a dog who was owned, and trained, by our alcoholic, drug-pushing, sex-trafficking whore. Jesus, what more could we want? I tell you, Billy, as Paper Lace once said, you're going to be a fucking hero."

"Uh, actually, if you check your facts, you'll find they advised their Billy *not* to be a hero," I said. "In fact, their Billy died because he didn't listen."

"Now, where's that statement I've prepared?" the lawyer said, ignoring me.

Ladies and Gentlemen,
My client has asked me to read out the following statement.
Several nights ago, in a solitary moment of weakness, I, Billy White, the host of popular entertainment show Billy's Belters, entered

into carnal knowledge with a woman of ill-repute. I admit my actions during my time with her were less than gentlemanly, and, for this, I humbly apologise. I have never treated women with anything less than the respect with which they deserve, and can categorically state that I have never done this type of thing before, and have no desire to repeat it in future.

There is no defence for my actions, and I am prepared and willing to accept whatever punishment the authorities deem fit to thrust upon me. I am only an ordinary man. An ordinary man who feels the same pressures and suffers from the same weaknesses as any other man.

If my experience is to serve as any kind of lesson, I would urge people to do all they can to find a healthy balance between work and play, so as to avoid the type of stresses, both physical and mental, I put upon myself by my self-imposed work ethic.

Finally, I would like to take this opportunity to thank all the people who have offered me their support through this horrendous ordeal, and would now ask for some private time to grieve for the death of my beloved wife, Ruby.

Thank you.

"Do you think it'll work?" Billy asked.

The lawyer stood up and put his hand on Billy's shoulder. He smiled as he held the statement aloft. "Guarantee it," he said. "As soon as all this is over, Billy, we'll get Harry to set you up with some proper interviews. Not these wishy-washy gays who just take the piss all the time. I'm talking about real hard-hitting interviews where you tell the awe-struck nation how you travelled through the darkest tunnel and yet still managed to climb out into the light the other side. We'll put your story out to tender, Billy. Publishers will go mental. Hell, it wouldn't surprise me if they didn't make a film about you. Perhaps we'll even consider trying to crack America. I reckon they'd love you across the pond, Billy, bloody love you."

The lawyer looked at his watch.

"Right, let's get you down to the police station to check in," he said. "I've asked those PR guys to make sure there's plenty of media waiting for us to release this statement, so go and make yourself beautiful, Billy. It's show-time!"

The nearest police station was Mount Street. After going through the process of reporting in, the lawyer stood on the steps of the police station and read the prepared statement to the masses. Standing beside him, a silent and forlorn looking Billy managed a few tears.

"That was brilliant, Billy," the lawyer said, starting up his Mercedes. I could be wrong, but it didn't even look like he'd used a key. Was he so masculine that he could start vehicles just by looking at them? "The tears were an excellent touch. See, all those years in drama school have paid off after all."

"Uh, I never went to drama school," Billy replied. "Rarely went to any school if I'm honest."

"Well, the tears were an excellent touch anyway. Let's go home and celebrate. I think round one belongs to us."

The wheels started to come off Billy's wagon later that day; shortly after Elaine got home from work.

She found Billy and the lawyer in the kitchen, both partially full of wine.

"Can't I leave you boys alone for a minute," she said, playfully slapping her lover on the behind.

"I'm afraid we've started without you," the lawyer said, giving Elaine a welcome home kiss that wouldn't have been amiss in one of Father's secret stash of porn magazines. I say secret, but I don't think under the bed in the false bottom of a code-locked suitcase is really that secret, is it?

When Elaine had finally retrieved her tongue from down her lover's throat, she asked for half an hour to freshen up before suggesting she pop round to see Charlotte. As she left the kitchen there was a heavy knock on the front door - my front door.

"I'll get it," Elaine shouted.

There was the murmur of deep voices, the type you know are carrying bad news before you even know what they're saying. Moments later, detective Staines was ushered into the room by Elaine. He was followed by some of the same burly policemen who'd first accompanied him at Billy's arrest. The lawyer was the first to act.

"What's the meaning of this?" he said. "What do you want?"

Detective Staines ignored him and made straight for Billy. "Billy White," he said, "I'm arresting you on suspicion of sexually assaulting one Charlotte Cousins…"

That night, the news was full of Billy's re-arrest. Coverage included footage of Charlotte appearing on the steps of the same police station where only hours previously Billy's lawyer had delivered his *Sermon on the Mount*. (You've got to love the press and their way with words, haven't you?) She was wearing dark glasses, which, when compared to the bruising evident on the rest of her face, left to the imagination what horrors may lurk beneath their darkness. Standing beside her was detective Staines, who had his own prepared statement to read.

"Oh, Billy, Billy, Billy," the lawyer whispered at the TV. "What the fuck is wrong with you?"

Before the week was out, eighteen women of all creeds and colours, fifteen of them prostitutes, came wandering into the spotlight like hyenas drawn to a fallen deer. Every one of them had a similar story: Billy White, the host of TV's Billy's Belters, and one time darling of the nation, had been nothing less than a violent monster whilst gratifying his sexual desires.

If the reports were true, Billy's spree of sexual malice spanned back several years. With each revelation, Billy's pool of admirers shrank. Even the real diehard fans deserted Billy's ship when the nineteenth woman to come out of the woodwork turned out to be the sweet, demure, seventeen year old pop-star, who announced to the listening populace how Billy had savagely robbed her of her virginity.

First to sever all professional ties with Billy White were the PR team. They were quickly followed by the studio, who very publicly announced they were cancelling Billy's contract with immediate effect. They even went as far as to declare they'd already lined up Billy's replacement, and the show would henceforth be known as *Bruce's Belters.*

Finally, the lawyer resigned as Billy's counsel.

"I'm sorry, Billy," the lawyer said, sitting on one side of the small table in Billy's holding cell. "But this last week has been too much. I have a reputation to think of. If I continue to represent you, I'll never get a decent case again. People who defend sex-pests tend to get tarred with the same brush as their clients, Billy. I just can't run the risk. Anyway, to be honest, I don't think it matters who you get to represent you now. The only thing you can hope for is that the psychiatric reports declare you mental or something. Damage limitation, Billy, it's your only chance."

"But what about my bail hearing tomorrow?"

"It'll be my last act as your lawyer, Billy. I'll prepare a list for you of my possible replacements. They'll all be good people, Billy, I promise."

"But they won't be you, will they?" Billy stood up and poked his friend in the chest. "I should have known you'd fuck me up the arse." Billy turned his back on the lawyer. "You're just like the rest of them. Well let me tell you, friend, I don't need any fancy arsehole lawyer to fight my case. I'll represent myself. Should have done it from the very beginning." He turned back, finger at the ready for more poking. "Hey, where the fuck do you think you're going? I haven't finished with you yet. Nobody walks away from Billy White!"

Billy looked at his outstretched finger and frowned; as if he'd forgotten why it was there.

At the bail hearing, Billy's lawyer put up a very good argument for granting Billy conditional bail. He reminded the judge that Billy had recently lost his wife, quickly followed by his career. He was, of course, still technically innocent, and needed time to put a whole host of affairs in order before coming to trial; affairs he would have no chance of concluding if he remained in custody.

The judge, who was undoubtedly well informed about how overcrowded the prison system was already, agreed, accepting the lawyer's proposal that the system would therefore be better served if Billy went home and simply stayed home until his trial. He also accepted it would be impossible, given the media surrounding the case, for Billy to leave the house in order to check in at his nearest police station. The judge therefore decreed that a police officer visit Billy twice a day, just to make sure he hadn't gone anywhere.

Billy and the lawyer parted on the steps of the courtroom without a word.

They never saw each other again.

After the taxi had finally fought its way through the horde of journalists and photographers at the bottom of Billy's drive, it eventually deposited him outside his front door. Billy struggled to open the door, courtesy of the mound of post on the welcome doormat.

He picked up the pile with one of those groans that middle-age people have when bending, and made his way to the drawing room. He threw the post on a table and immediately poured himself a drink. He'd only taken a sip when he spotted the stubborn bloodstains on the wooden floor that the police clean-up team hadn't been able to remove. The drink fell from his hands.

Billy ran out of the drawing room, slamming the door behind him. He clung to the handle for a few seconds, looking at the door and shaking his head violently. He then made his way into the kitchen and fished out his mobile phone; the one he only ever used for personal calls. His hands were trembling so badly it took Billy a few attempts before he finally punched in the number he required. When it started ringing he put the phone on loudspeaker and placed it on the kitchen table. He then extracted a bottle of wine from the fridge.

Harry's voice suddenly filled the kitchen

"Is that you, Billy?" he said. "What the hell are you doing phoning me? You know we're not supposed to communicate with each other. This could jeopardise my defence, Billy. I shouldn't have answered."

"Harry, I'm at my wit's end here," Billy said, pouring the wine into one of those novelty glasses that hold a whole bottle. "I've got nobody else to turn to."

"Where are you, Billy? I thought you were still in custody."

"I'm at home," Billy replied, before taking in at least a quarter of the glass. "That fucking lawyer of mine worked miracles this morning and got me out."

"So why don't you talk to him?"

"I sacked him."

"You what?"

"At the end of the day, Harry, he wasn't the fucking man after all. Actually, he was nothing but a prick." Billy swigged his glass down to half-full, or was it half-empty? "Anyway, that's why I'm calling. I need you to find me a new lawyer, Harry. I want the best. I don't care what it costs. I want you to find me someone who'll drag these bloody women over the coals and send them back to their shit-holes. They're all whores, Harry. No humans involved. So just do your job and get them off my back you fucking gnome."

"Have you checked your mail, Billy?"

"What? No, of course I haven't checked my fucking mail. I've only just got here. Why?"

"You need to, Billy. You need to check your mail."

"Why? What's it got to do with you what fucking mail I get?"

"And you need to look for the letter with the blue calligraphy writing on the envelope."

"Harry, what the fuck are you talking about?"

"It's all in the letter, Billy. I'm sorry, okay, but under the circumstances I'm sure you'll understand I didn't have any…"

Billy threw the remains of the wine across the kitchen, the glass shattering against the wall. "No, it's you who has to understand!" he said, kicking over a breakfast stool. "I fucking own you. Without me you have nothing. Who the fuck would employ someone who wears green sports-jackets with yellow chinos and a spotted pink cravat? I've given you everything, you ungrateful fucking leprechaun. Well guess what? I don't fucking need you. I'm Billy White and I don't need anybody." Billy picked up the phone and threw it the same way the wine glass had gone; it too shattered into several pieces.

Billy started spinning on the spot and flailing his arms around. He looked like some medieval weapon. He began making strange noises, like a pig rummaging for truffles.

He ran into the drawing room and worked his way through the post, throwing envelopes into the air like they'd been caught in a malfunctioning shredder, until he came to the one addressed to him in blue calligraphy. He put the letter between his teeth and shook it like a dog as he ran back into the kitchen where he tore it open. I peaked over Billy's shoulder as he read the letter.

Mother was none too pleased.

"Mark! What have I told you about reading other people's stuff? You're so rude. This is just like the time you leaned over that poor man's shoulder on the train and read the letter he was holding, then blurted out to everyone his wife had left him for the gardener."

"Mum! Try and get your facts straight. It wasn't a train, it was a plane. It wasn't a letter he was holding, it was a book. Furthermore, the book was Lady Chatterly's lover. And I didn't blurt."

"Well, whatever, you're still rude, Mark. I hope you're not this rude with Timothy's sister."

The crux of the handwritten letter advised Billy that Harry had sought legal advice and he was perfectly within his rights to tender his resignation; effective immediately.

Billy let the letter fall from his hands and started laughing uncontrollably. He continued laughing as he made his way through the side door in the kitchen which led to the adjoining double garage.

"Where are you going, Billy?" I said, laughing along with him. "You haven't got a car any more, remember?"

As soon as Billy reached the middle of the empty garage, the fact must have dawned on him, because he laughed even harder.

We were both practically hysterical by the time Billy found a length of sturdy rope on one of the shelves and made his way back into the house. "Now what on Earth do you want that for?" I said, my laughing subsiding slightly.

Billy was still howling like a man possessed as he collected a small stepladder from the space underneath the stairs on his way back to the drawing room. Once in the drawing room, Billy climbed the stepladder and tied one end of the rope around an old beam which ran the length of the room.

"Billy, this isn't funny any more," I said. To prove the point I stopped laughing altogether.

Satisfied he'd tied a strong enough knot, Billy came down off the stepladder and poured himself a large tumbler of whisky. He sat in his favourite chair and raised the tumbler in the air. "Here's to me," he said. He downed the drink in one and threw the glass into the open fireplace before unfolding himself from his chair.

"Billy, please don't do this," I said, trying to hang on to the seat of his trousers as he re-climbed the stepladder. "Listen, I've read all about this on the internet." Billy ignored me and tied a noose around his neck. "You've got to work out load bearings and all sorts of stuff to make it quick. You could be dangling there for ages if it's not done correctly, Billy. Please, trust me, if you don't get it right it could be very slow, and very painful. Look, I think I can remember the websites. I'll give you the addresses if you like. Billy, please, just check them out. They'll tell you how to do it properly. Why don't we just have another drink and talk about it? Please! Billy!"

Billy continued to ignore me. I had to jump off the stepladder as he kicked it from under him.

When the realisation kicked in that he wasn't dying quickly, Billy desperately grabbed at the rope biting into his neck. His eyes bulged, cartoon-like, and his swelling tongue, slowly being depraved of oxygen, rolled out of his mouth, a strange blue-black in colour. When he couldn't release the tautness around his neck, he tried to relieve the pressure building in his head by grabbing the rope above it and lifting himself up, kicking his feet into the air like he was treading water. Except there was no water, and he only succeeded in bobbing himself up and down like an apple at Halloween. Urine and faeces starting running out of the bottom of his trousers, joining Ruby's bloodstains on the floor below him.

After five minutes his efforts became less frantic. After ten they became spasmodic. After fifteen they stopped altogether.

I slumped into Billy's chair and curled myself in a ball. In an effort to block out the sound of creaking as Billy turned slowly in half-circles, I cried hard.

END AWAY

Crimson appeared in the drawing room doorway six hours later. "Oh dear," she said, nodding towards the dangling Billy. "He doesn't look very well."

I jumped out of the chair, wiped my face with my hands, and smoothed my limited number of clothes. "Where have you been?" I said. "I've had to watch him turn like he's being slow spit-roasted for hours."

Crimson looked at her watch and sat herself down in the chair I had just vacated. "Well now here's the thing," she said, doing that crossing and uncrossing thing with her legs again. "Us messengers are all on a go-slow."

It took me a while to find some coherent words. "A go-slow?"

"Yep. We're protesting."

"Crimson, you're not making any sense. Go-slow? Protesting? Against what?"

"Well, you know that Gates fellow the committee have been waiting for?"

"The computer guy?"

"That's the one."

"What about him?"

"He finally arrived."

I lifted my eyes from Crimson's display of leg-crossing. "What? You mean he's dead?"

"Of course he's dead, stupid." Crimson stood up and gently caught hold of my fingers. "You don't get in front of the committee otherwise, do you?"

"No. Suppose not."

"Anyway, apparently he took one look at the system and went

totally mental. He's started reorganising the whole thing. Top to bottom. According to Mr T. we're currently going through a, *'Transitional period where things may have to get worse before they get better.'* It's chaos back at the ranch, Mark, total chaos."

"So what exactly are you protesting about?"

"Well, one of the other messengers reckoned she overheard this Gates chappy talking to Mr T. and, according to her, one of the first things he's planning on doing is to put measures in place so there'll be no need for any messengers at all."

"But that's ridiculous."

"I know! Anyway, we all got together and decided to show him just how valuable we are. We're all running three days behind."

"Three days!"

"Yep."

"But what does that mean?"

"It means we're running three days behind."

"I mean, for me. Now?"

"Sorry, Mark, but you're going to have to stay here for three days."

"But that's absurd," I said, nodding to where Billy was still swaying. "What am I supposed to do for three days?"

Crimson was still lightly holding my fingers. She checked the nails on her free hand and whistled tunelessly. "Entirely up to you," she said, glancing at me over the top of her eyes. She lifted up her arm and let out an exaggerated yawn. The motion lifted her t-shirt enough to bare her perfectly flat stomach.

I tried to let my attention settle on the dangling Billy in an effort to avoid any public display of affection from appearing unwontedly. "So if you're not here to take me back," I said. "Why are you here?"

"Just killing time," Crimson said, running a finger down my chest. "I've got a big meeting with the other messengers in half an hour and I was wondering what to do. Then I thought, I know, I'll go and see Mark." She ran her finger back up my chest and slowly turned my head towards her.

I searched and searched the drawing room in vain for the new forthright Mark Ferris. Once again, he must have been busy elsewhere, because as Crimson planted her lips on mine, I almost passed out.

After a long, lingering kiss, Crimson disengaged herself from me. She caught hold of my hand and led me slowly out of the drawing room towards the stairs. With every step I gently dug my heels in, like a dog on a lead being taken somewhere they don't want to go.

Eventually, we reached the guest bedroom door.

"Crimson, I'm not sure about this," I said, squeezing the words past the mouse. "I don't think you've really thought this through." My legs were becoming less and less supportive and my hands were shaking as if I'd been jack-hammering roads for the last thirty years.

Crimson turned to me and lightly kissed me on the forehead. "You're so sweet, Mark," she said. "But that thirty minutes is counting down. If I was you, I'd get a move on." She let go of my hand and entered the bedroom. She sat on the bed and patted the space beside her.

"This is a dream, right?" I said from the doorway. "Somehow I've managed to fall asleep in the chair downstairs." I held on to the frame of the door for dear life… death… whatever.

"Why do you keep putting yourself down, Mark?" Crimson said. She stood up, marched over to me, and dragged me into the room. "I mean, you're sort of passable in the looks department."

"Passable?"

"And you have a, oh, I don't know, a steady quality about you."

As Crimson led me to the bed, I took a deep breath, closed my eyes, crossed myself, and begged the new forthright Mark Ferris for help.

Mother was catatonic.

"I give up! I simply give up! You do know that the type of women who put themselves on plates are undoubtedly ridden with disease, Mark, don't you? If you go through with this, you're thingy will drop off. It's a known fact."

"Mum, that's rubbish."

"Oh, I wash my hands of you, Mark. What use will you be to Timothy's sister without a thingy?"

As Crimson lay me down on the bed, I opened my eyes slowly and caught a quick glance of the new forthright Mark Ferris in a mirror. "Oh thank God you've turned up," I whispered. "What the hell am I supposed to do?"

He winked at me. "Sod Mother," he said. "A man's got to do what a man's got to do."

"That's all well and good," I said. "But I'm not sure I can remember what a man's got to do."

The new forthright Mark Ferris licked his lips. "Don't worry, my friend, it's like driving a car."

"What!? You know full well I don't drive! Oh, sweet Jesus, Crimson, what are you doing?"

I sat in a post-coital haze; watching as Crimson dressed herself.

"So, are they my only qualities?" I asked, wearing a smile Old Eric would have been jealous of. "Steady and just about passable?"

"How many more do you want?" Crimson said. "It's two more than most men I know."

Crimson finished dressing, then tidied her hair at the mirror. She turned to me, looking at her watch. "Well, would you look at that," she said. "I've still got twenty minutes before my meeting. Ah well, at least I'll be early for a change."

And then she was gone.

An hour later, still basking in glory, I fished my boxers out from within the bedclothes. In his haste to disrobe, the new forthright Mark Ferris had torn what had been left of my shirt in half, rendering it completely useless. Also, no amount of searching could now turn up what the blazers he'd done with the remains of my trousers.

"Ah well, never mind," I said, stretching myself out like a starfish. "It'll just be easier to get naked next time."

The following morning, DCI Staines, accompanied by yet more large colleagues, broke down Billy's front door. Presumably, the police officer tasked with checking in on Billy's whereabouts had reported he couldn't get an answer.

No less than two hours later, the news was out.

Billy White, one time host of popular TV show Billy's Belters, and darling of the nation, had been found hanged to death at his home. The police confirmed there were no suspicious circumstances.

For the next few days I pottered around the house trying to fill the hours until Crimson's return. With an empty house full of the ghosts of Ruby and Billy, the nights became unbearable. The sounds were everywhere. Billy's strangled cries, the creaking rope, Toby's snarl, Ruby's gurgling neck.

I tried to overcome the night-noises by cowering in one of the bedroom wardrobes, but was forced to give up on the idea when an image of David dragging me out by my hair wouldn't disappear.

Early on the third morning after Crimson had left, I heard a noise in the hallway. "Is that you, Crimson?" I screamed, running out of one of the upstairs bathrooms, where I'd taken to hiding behind the shower curtain.

Standing in the hallway, shaking the rain off her umbrella, stood a thin, tall, powerful looking woman, who obviously was not Crimson. She removed her long raincoat, placing it on a hook. The badge on her navy blue jacket suggested she worked for *Hart & Hart, Estate Agents to the stars.*

I followed the woman at a distance as she pointed some form of laser device at walls and jotted things down on a clipboard. When it came to measuring up the drawing room, I politely refused to enter.

"I'll just wait for you out here in the hallway," I said. "But, please, you go on in." I stood to one side, allowing the woman to pass.

I'd been waiting five minutes when I heard the sound of someone breathing heavily behind me. I turned quickly, expecting to see Crimson with her hands on her knees, fighting for air as usual. Instead, I started at the sight of an old woman. Slightly stooped and smelling of mothballs, the woman reminded me of Giles' cartoon Grandma.

"I wish she wouldn't walk so bloody fast," the old woman said, leaning heavily on a walking stick. "Left me for dead when she got out of the car. Set off like a bloody racehorse she did. But then that's the modern way these days, isn't it? Rush, rush, rush. No time for anything. Now look at the state of me." The woman removed her steamed-up, horn-rimmed glasses, and rubbed them on the sleeve of her blouse. "I can hardly bloody breath. Oh, I do hope I've got my pump."

She rummaged through a large cloth bag slung over her shoulder. With each rummage, the bag gave off sounds of things clanking. After a few moments, the old woman gave up her search. "Now that's odd," she said. "I always make sure I've got my pump with me before I leave the house. Especially since that horrible Mr T. decided I couldn't use my frame any more. I tell you, if he's hidden my pump, I'll give him a bloody good clouting with this." She waved the walking stick dangerously close to my head.

"I'm Mark," I said, leaning back to avoid the arc of the stick and holding out my hand. "Very pleased to meet you."

Thankfully, the woman un-brandished the weapon. "Gertrude," she said, taking my hand with a surprisingly firm grip. "And that's my assignee, Saffy." She used her walking stick to point at her assignee, who'd just emerged from the drawing room. "Apparently, it's short for Sapphire. Stupid bloody name if you ask me. But then that's the modern way these days, isn't it? People do love to call their children ridiculous things, don't they? Do you know, I came across someone called *Moonbeam* the other day. Can you believe that? I ask you, how's the poor child supposed to get through school with a bloody name like Moonbeam? Tell me that."

Gertrude poked me in the chest with the walking stick as if it had been me that had been responsible for naming the child.

"I don't know, Gertrude," I said, trying to swat the tip of the walking stick away.

"Saffy's one of these estate agents," Gertrude continued. "Not the sort of job for a young woman if you ask me. But then that's the modern way these days, isn't it? Do you know, I came across a young woman who was joining the army the other day. The army! I ask you, what on Earth will a young woman do in the bloody army?"

Gertrude went to poke me again, presumably believing I was somehow to blame for the army's recruitment policy, but I managed to sidestep the lunge, and suggested we follow her assignee upstairs.

"This looks like a nice big house you've got here," Gertrude said, struggling, I believed somewhat theatrically, to get up the stairs. "Have you lived here long?"

"You do know this isn't actually *my* house, Gertrude, don't you?"

"Well I hope you're not here uninvited," Gertrude said, stopping and brandishing her stick at me again. "Because if you're here on the rob, I'll have to tackle you to the ground."

"Don't worry, Gertrude," I said, parrying the stick. "I'm supposed to be here."

On eventually reaching the top of the stairs, Gertrude moved into the first bedroom she came across and started making herself comfortable on the bed. "I think I'll just put my feet up when Saffy does whatever it is she does," she said. "Tell you what, a nice cup of tea wouldn't go amiss."

"Uh, Gertrude," I said, remaining in the doorway. "I think my tea making days are done."

"Oh, there's a shame," Gertrude said. She lay down and placed her walking stick across her chest. "I suppose a nice tongue sandwich is out of the question as well then?"

"Afraid so, Gertrude."

"Ah well, maybe I'll just have forty winks instead. Can you wake me up when Saffy's finished? Oh, and if I was you, dear, I'd put some clothes on. I know it's the modern way these days to walk about with practically nothing on, but you'll catch your death of cold wandering about in just your underwear like that."

Gertrude closed her eyes and within seconds was snoring heavily.

"I see you've met Gertrude," Crimson said, appearing at my shoulder and making me jump.

Ever since Crimson had left I'd been rehearsing what to say at this moment. The new forthright Mark Ferris and I had come up with a million fantastic conversation pieces all ready for Crimson's return, but all I managed now was to giggle like a naughty schoolgirl.

"The committee are completely baffled as to how she manages to do this," Crimson said, brushing past me and entering the bedroom. "It's against everything they've ever known. Gates insists on having a look at her himself. He wants to see if there's anything in her make-up that's different. Can you help me wake her please, Mark?"

"Oh, right, so you haven't come for me then?"

"Not yet. I've got to get Gertrude back first. Then I'll be back for you." Crimson checked her watch and gasped. "Come on, give me a hand," she said, shaking Gertrude's shoulders.

"Wait!" I said, pulling Crimson gently away from Gertrude. "Haven't you got ten minutes to spare? You know, the go slow and everything."

The new forthright Mark Ferris winked at Crimson to try and indicate what he had in mind. It was a reflex movement I wished he'd kept to himself. I'd never been good at winking. Elaine always said rather than looking insinuating and sexy, my wink made me look like I'd just had a stroke.

"No, I haven't," Crimson said, pulling away from me. "Thanks to that bloody Gates the committee can now track my every movement." Crimson produced a small fob from her pocket and waved it in the air. "Apparently pinpoints our position to within five feet. So come on, help me get Gertrude up and about."

After a few shouts and a few hardy shakes, Gertrude woke. "Oh, hello, dear," she said to Crimson. "What are you doing here?"

"The committee want to see you, Gertrude," Crimson spoke slightly louder than normal.

"Okay, okay, there's no need to shout, dear," Gertrude said, wiggling a finger in her ear. "I'm not bloody deaf. Have we got time for a nice cup of tea before we go? I'm sure that young man there wouldn't mind making us one."

"No, sorry, Gertrude," Crimson said. "We haven't got time. The committee want to see you straight away."

"Well I hope they're not going to talk rubbish," Gertrude said. "That Mr T. gets right up my nose."

After eventually getting herself off the bed, Gertrude poked Crimson in the chest with her stick as she made her way to the door. "And tell that young man to put some clothes on, dear," she said. "He'll catch his death like that."

Moments later, Crimson and Gertrude were gone.

Saffy left shortly after and I was alone again.

Crimson came for me early the next day.

"I thought you were coming straight back," I said, jumping off the bed. "I've been lying on this bed for the best part of twenty-four hours waiting for you. Where have you been?"

"Sorry, Mark," Crimson said, looking at her watch. "But as soon as I got Gertrude back, the committee called all the messengers together for a crisis meeting."

"Crisis meeting?"

"Yes, looks like they're getting rid of some of us. They say they'll work it on a last in, first out basis. Mr T. reckons that, *'The whole messenger service can now be run with far more efficiency, and therefore doesn't need to be so labour intensive.'* We all know they're not his words. He's just Gates' puppet these days."

I could feel the bottom lip starting. "So what about you?" I said. "There's plenty of people who've become messengers after you, right?"

"Not really," Crimson replied. "There's only about seventy-five of us altogether. New messengers are very few and far between. The most recent one has gone already. Grace, I think her name was."

"But what will that mean for us?" I said, begging the new forthright Mark Ferris to hold the tears at bay.

"Well, if I do get laid off, I suppose they'll allocate you one of the messengers who are left. Who knows? Maybe they'll train you how to get back and forth without a messenger. Like Old Eric."

"I don't mean like that, Crimson," I said. "I mean what will happen to *us*. As in you and me."

Crimson caught hold of my hand. She had the same puppy-dog-lost look that Timothy's sister had all those years ago. "There wasn't any you and me, Mark, was there?" she said. "Not really. I mean, come on, I don't think a minute or two fumbling around on a bed can be counted as a relationship, do you? I think we were both just feeling a bit lonely, yes? Look, I'm really sorry if I gave you the wrong impression, Mark… Oh, please don't cry."

As I turned away to hide my tears, the room filled with the sound of something bleeping like an alarm clock. Within seconds, Mr T's voice filled my ears. "Messenger Seventy-Two. Situation report please. You're behind schedule."

A quick glance around the room told me Mr T. definitely wasn't in it, so I turned back to Crimson. She was waving her fob-like devise in the air. She put the fob to her mouth and pressed a small button on the side. "Have just located Seven-Three-Five-Nine," she said. "He was hiding under the bed. ETA immediate. Repeat, ETA immediate."

The wooden chair had been replaced, and I found myself sitting on a very comfortable leather one instead.

"Well hello again, Seven-Three-Five-Nine," Mr T. said. "What do you think?" He scanned his hands in front of him, then swivelled in his own new chair, practically bouncing with excitement.

On the desk, placed neatly in front of each member of the committee, were 3 gleaming computer screens. There wasn't a scrap of paper or file in sight.

"We're sorry it took so long to bring you back after your assignee's death," Mr T. said, tentatively pressing a few buttons on his keyboard. He half closed his eyes with each touch, as if any one of them might set off a nuclear explosion. "You see, getting trained on how to use these things took a little longer than we thought. Still, we think we've ironed out most of the glitches. And at least we do have the luxury of having Mr Gates' office on twenty-four hour standby. Just in case we get stuck."

"Mr Gates' office? You've given him an office?"

"Of course," Mr T. replied, pressing a few more buttons. "We couldn't expect him to conduct his business without his own personal space now, could we?"

The noise of a printer started whirring from somewhere underneath the committee's desk.

"Ooh, I love it," Mr T said, clapping his hands together and glancing under the desk in awe. He reached down and produced an A4 piece of paper with some text typed onto it. He ceremoniously folded the paper in half and placed it into an envelope that had been handed to him by one of the sidekicks. With a final flourishing sweep of his hand, he presented it to me. "This is your new assignee, Seven-Three-Five-Nine."

I looked at the envelope. Through the window, where an address would normally be, were simply four bold numbers - **7359** - underneath which had been generated - **Assignment No. 5**.

As I stared at the envelope, Mr T. produced a fob similar to the one Crimson had been carrying. "Messenger Seventy-Two," he said into the contraption. "Seven-Three-Five-Nine is ready for despatch."

"Hang on!" I said. "Haven't you got paperwork to finish first? Aren't you going to make me go through some form of personal Hell to get to Old Eric's office? Won't he be delighted to see me again?"

Mr T. suddenly took great interest in whatever was on his computer screen. "I'm afraid we've had to redistribute our office space, Seven-Three-Five-Nine," he said.

"What? What do you mean? Oh, now wait a minute. You haven't kicked Old Eric out of his office have you?" Mr T. continued staring at his screen. The sidekicks also looked somewhat sheepish. "You have, haven't you? You've kicked him out to make way for this Gates chap."

"Not kicked him out exactly," Mr T. said. "Redistributed. Let's just say Old Eric is temporarily between offices. Now, if you don't mind, we do have a lot of work to get through. Off you go." He nodded to somewhere behind me. "It's all standard practice."

I swivelled in my chair to find Crimson standing there.

"Come on," she said, taking hold of my hand. "Let's get you gone."

THE DIVORCE

Crimson dumped me in a very large lounge. Then immediately disappeared without a word.

I could just make out the back of a woman's head. She was sitting on an enormous sofa, watching some daytime soap about Australians.

"So, who might you be?" I said, making my way round to sit beside her. I held my hand out in greeting. "I'm Mark. I'm your new watcher. I'll watch if you decide to slit your wrists open with a rusty scissors. Or burn to death in a house fire. Better still, I'll just sit here and watch whilst you get mauled to death by a monstrous dog. How about that? Although, if you decide to hang yourself, I beg of you to check it out on the internet first. It'll make it so much easier for us all."

The exploits of the Australians were obviously far too riveting for my new assignee to pay me any attention, and she ignored me completely. On reflection, it was probably just as well. If she had been taking any notice, I guess I may have come across as slightly disturbing.

The woman looked about my age, maybe a little younger, and seemed like she could have been beautiful if she'd wanted to be, but had decided against it.

"Okay, let's have a look what the committee have to say about you then, is it?" I said, opening the envelope Mr T. had given me.

It felt strange not to be sitting on the edge of Old Eric's desk reading the details to him. I could only imagine how upset he must have been at having his office taken away.

In *Times New Roman*, the A4 piece of paper informed me I was sitting next to thirty-nine year old Julia Barnes, who had apparently lived alone ever since her husband had left her a few years ago. The computer generated note also added, *Despite never being officially divorced, Julia reverted to her maiden name of Barnes as soon as her husband buggered off.* It also advised me Julia had, *Been a bit under the weather since the death of her daughter.*

"Oh, that's just great," I said, screwing up the note and stuffing it down the side of the sofa. "I suppose that explains why you're sitting here in your pyjamas at eleven o'clock in the morning with a glass of wine in your hand."

I settled on the sofa and joined in Julia's interest in the Australians.

As soon as the programme had finished, Julia made her way to an enormous designer kitchen and started making herself a sandwich.

"Let me help," I said, following her to the fridge. "I'm used to doing all the cooking. Elaine always said I made a mean egg sandwich."

It was one of those fridge-magnet photographs that rooted me to the spot, putting an immediate stop to any assistance I may have been giving. It was one of those souvenir types; taken coming down a log flume at some theme-park. Julia was at the front of the log, her mouth open in a silent scream. At the back of the log, his arms aloft in manly triumph, sat the lawyer. Sandwiched between them, looking as excited as a Russian border-guard, sat Mary.

I staggered backwards and fell against the large wooden table. "Oh my dear God," I said, sinking to the floor. Just before the darkness took me completely, it dawned on me this must be *the* kitchen table.

When I came to, the kitchen was empty. I couldn't trust my legs to carry me, so crawled my way back into the lounge. Julia was back on the sofa. On the coffee table in front of her were the remains of the half-eaten sandwich and evidence of yet more wine. I sat at her feet and unsuccessfully tried to stop myself from crying.

"I hope this being under the weather thing isn't because you blame yourself, Julia," I said, eventually hoisting myself onto the sofa. "Because everything is his fault. Absolutely everything."

I quickly scanned the room and found another photograph of the three of them taking pride of place on a wall. Professionally produced, it had obviously been taken some time ago. Mary was about ten, I guessed, and they all looked so happy and beautiful. I tried to put my arm around Julia, but she shifted slightly up the sofa and I missed.

"I've met your daughter, Julia, and she's a lovely girl," I said. "You should be proud of her. A bit forward for Mother's liking perhaps, but then that's the modern way these days, isn't it? Oh, now please don't look at me like that, Julia. I didn't take advantage. I mean, I'm old enough to be her father, although, as Old Eric would undoubtedly point out, I'm not. Anyway, I'm not the sort of guy to go around taking advantage of young girls, Julia, even if they are in an emotional mess."

Julia picked up the remote control and started channel-hopping.

"She didn't really want to kill herself, Julia," I continued. "If that stupid husband of yours had ever bothered to teach her to swim, she'd probably still be alive. See, like I said, all his fault. If he'd stopped nagging her about Sociology not being a proper degree, I'm sure she wouldn't have done what she did. Again, his fault. Perhaps if he'd given her a proper birthday present, like a car or a trip to New York, instead of taking her to that stupid theme-park, she'd still be with us. I mean, what father takes their twenty year old daughter to a theme-park? I don't know about you, Julia, but I'm seeing a pattern here. A pattern that tells me *everything* is his fault. Maybe if he'd stopped going on about her boyfriend... oh, hang on, that was you, wasn't it? Well I expect he put you up to it. See, everything is his fault, Julia. Absolutely everything."

Julia finally settled on a programme about some has-beens in a jungle, and we both curled ourselves into balls.

From the photographs around the house it was evident how Julia had deteriorated since Mary's death. Her once beautiful face was gaunt, diseased looking even. Her strawberry blonde hair, always long and free, was now almost entirely grey, and hung around her face as if a small child had glued the strands to her head. Julia's shapely body, shown off to best effect in a skimpy yellow bikini on a beach in San Tropez, now dropped from her neck like a pen-stroke, and her skin looked as withered and cracked as a decaying leaf. Her radiant smile, as witnessed in any photograph with her daughter, had disappeared behind lips that never saw the sun any more.

In the three weeks since I'd arrived in Julia's lounge she hadn't once left the house. Her only source of human interaction appeared to be the brief snippets of conversation with the delivery people who brought the small amounts of food she needed to survive.

On the days Julia decided to dress, she seemed content to wander about the house in jogging bottoms and scruffy sweat-tops; a far cry from the party dresses and evening wear that could be seen hanging in her wardrobe, or appearing in all their glory in some of those photographs. Julia never answered the house phone, allowing the answering machine to earn its keep, and I'd seen no evidence of a mobile. The state-of-the-art computer in the corner of the lounge served mainly to gather dust, only being used when Julia did her online shopping. Standing on the outside looking in, it appeared to me that Julia had deliberately disconnected herself from the outside world.

Obviously, the situation would not be deemed healthy by most, but it suited me fine. If staying indoors and following the plight of a bunch of Australians was how I was going to live out the rest of my death, then who was I to argue? I'd come to the conclusion I'd had enough excitement to last me a lifetime… deathtime… whatever, and apart from the face of that lawyer smiling his smugness at me every now and then, there was nothing here to upset me. No, I was quite happy to hide away with Julia somewhere in suburbia, thank you very much, and let the rest of the world do my worrying for me.

I should have known things wouldn't be quite so simple.

Julia and I were settling down to find out if it was indeed Bruce's body that had been washed up on the beach, when the house phone rang. As normal, Julia ignored it and let the machine pick up.

"You've reached the house of Julia Barnes. I'm not available to take your call right now, please leave a message after the tone."

"Julia, it's me. Listen, I'll come straight to the point. I want a divorce. I've worked a few things out. I've e-mailed you the details. Take a look and give me a ring or e-mail back, okay?"

Julia never took her eyes from the TV. To our relief, it turned out not to be Bruce's body after all. When the programme was over, Julia made her way to the machine and deleted the message. She then made her way to the kitchen for her midday sandwich and wine.

It was early evening, two days after the phone call, when the lawyer arrived at the house.

Julia and I were sitting in the kitchen enjoying a particularly fine bottle of chilled Chardonnay, and decided to ignore whoever was knocking at the door. Moments later, we looked at each other surprised and somewhat scared as we heard the front door opening. The fear dissipated, but the surprise stayed, when the silky smooth sound of the lawyer's voice called from the hallway, "Julia. Are you in?"

"I'll have that off you," Julia said, holding out her hand as soon as the lawyer entered the kitchen. He was decked out in a light brown suit of some quality and had freshened it up with a yellow shirt and matching tie. I could smell my wife on him.

"Have what off me, Julia?" He looked temporarily confused at Julia's attire; grey tracksuit bottoms, and a baggy white t-shirt sporting a large egg-mayonnaise stain.

"Your key," Julia said. "It's very kind of you to bring it over, but you could have posted it and saved the trouble. Goodnight."

The lawyer scratched his head and gave out a little grunt. "Julia, officially this is still *my* house," he said. "I'm perfectly entitled to have a key to my own house. If you'd answered the bloody door you wouldn't even know I'd still got it."

Julia remained sitting at the table with her hand outstretched. "You gave up your entitlement to anything when you left me for that whore," she said.

I jumped off my chair. "Ah, now hang on a minute, Julia," I said. "That's my wife we're talking about. Let's not lose sight of the fact that absolutely everything is his fault, remember?" I pointed at the lawyer. The new forthright Mark Ferris tried to jab him in the chest.

"If my memory serves me correctly," the lawyer said, ignoring the new forthright Mark Ferris. "I didn't leave. You threw me out."

Julia was still holding out her hand. "That's what you do with rubbish. You throw it out."

The lawyer sat on the chair I had just left. "Now, Julia," he said, scuttling the chair across the floor until they were face to face. He caught hold of Julia's outstretched hand in both of his. "I really was hoping we could be civil about this. I mean, come on, it's been what? Three years? I thought we'd be beyond the name calling stage by now." He released one of his hands and ran it through his perfect hair. "There's always two sides to every story, Julia. I don't see how you can put all the blame for what's happened on me."

Julia laughed and snatched her hand out of the lawyer's grasp. "Yes, silly me," she said. "How could I possibly have expected you to keep your dick in your wife?"

The lawyer shrugged and a slight smile appeared on his lips. Obviously, in his opinion, Julia had a point. Julia stood up and poured herself another glass of wine. She started circling the lawyer like a shark, staring down at the top of his head.

"Can I have one?" the lawyer asked, nodding towards the bottle.

Julia sat back down and took the bottle off the table, cradling it in her lap. "You're getting nothing from me," she said. She lifted her glass in the air. "Here's to a long and happy marriage."

The lawyer closed his eyes and shook his head slowly. "Julia, we can't keep on like this. I'm fed up of trying to make you see sense. Have you even looked at the e-mail I sent over?"

Julia took a large swig of her wine and gave a satisfied smack of her lips. "Nope. I have absolutely no interest in what you have to say or do," she said. "So, if you don't mind, piss off! You know where the door is. You can leave your key on the hallway table."

The lawyer stood up and made his way to the kitchen door. He turned in the doorway. "Julia, I have to say it, but since I last saw you, you look awful. It's obvious you've started drinking heavily again. Why don't you get out more? I mean, how many times have you left this house since I walked out?"

"You didn't walk out, arsehole. I threw you out."

"Ah, so we agree on something."

"Just go!" Julia drained her glass. "I don't know how many times I've got to tell you. Go back to your whore and leave me alone."

"And I don't know how many times I've got to tell you, Julia. Things can't stay like this. I'm not going to keep paying for you to live here. This is *my* house."

"Just fuck off!" Julia threw her empty wine glass in the general direction of the lawyer's head. It missed and shattered against the wall.

Three days after the lawyer's visit, Julia received a letter. I looked over her shoulder as she sat on the sofa and read it.

Mother was unhappy.

"Mark! Are you reading other people's stuff again? You can clearly see it's marked Private & Confidential. Is nothing sacred to you?"

The letter was from *Gunn & Gunn.*

"Bloody hell! That's the firm Elaine works for," I said, grasping the edge of the sofa.

The letter included all manner of legal jargon, but the gist was easy to understand. The lawyer was filing for divorce on the grounds of Julia's *Unreasonable behaviour.* He used the length of time they'd been apart as evidence there was no hope of reconciliation.

According to Gunn & Gunn, the lawyer had done all he could to save the marriage from meltdown, but Julia's unreasonableness following the death of their daughter had given him no option other than to leave the marital home. A list of her unreasonableness included: *Her drastic increase in alcohol consumption; Her refusal to participate in sexual activity; Her refusal to communicate;* and finally, *Her inability to cope on a normal level with the pressures of ordinary life.*

Julia made her way to the kitchen and refilled her glass of wine. "I'm going to take the bastard for everything he's got," she whispered.

"Oh, now I like the sound of that, Julia," I replied. "Good plan."

Later that day, after we'd watched Bruce tell his wife he was gay, Julia dusted off the computer and fired it up. After trawling the internet for a few hours, she finally settled on *Wyburn & Howells*, a firm of lawyers specialising in divorce proceedings, who, according to their blurb, prided themselves on being one of the few all-female firm of solicitors in the country.

Julia filled in the relevant e-mail document, giving a potted outline of why she wanted to use the firm's services, and, within an hour, received a reply stating Yvette Wyburn herself would be available to meet Julia next Tuesday at 11am. They'd noted Julia didn't drive, but not to worry. As part of their service, and despite the firm's offices being 50 miles away, Yvette Wyburn herself would be more than willing to come to Julia's home for the initial briefing.

Yvette Wyburn herself reminded me of a young Elaine. She wore a green knee length skirt over patterned tights which disappeared into a pair of black flat-soled boots. Above the waist, a white blouse peeked out from behind a green bolero-style jacket, and she'd completed the outfit with a green silk scarf. Her briefcase had her name embossed on it in gold-leaf, after which were added her letters of qualification. Her blonde hair was up in a bob, and her thin lips were decorated with bright red lipstick.

Like Elaine, Yvette Wyburn herself gave off the air of someone who knew they looked good, smelled good, felt good, and undoubtedly tasted good.

Yes, she could murder a cup of coffee - milk, no sugar - and yes, she'd love a piece of Marks & Spencer carrot cake.

After some small talk, conducted over the coffee and carrot cake, Yvette Wyburn herself got down to business.

"Now then, Julia, I want you to take your time and start at the very beginning. I need to know the complete picture." She took out an A4 pad from her briefcase and clicked the top of her Mont Blanc. "And please, don't leave anything out."

Julia had met the lawyer when they were both at university. He was studying law, she chemistry. She was still a virgin, he wasn't. Three months into the relationship, Julia found herself pregnant. Much against the wishes of Julia's parents, Julia and the trainee lawyer followed protocol and married. Seven months after the marriage, Julia gave birth to a healthy baby girl, who they called Mary; named after the lawyer's mother.

At first, the lawyer turned out to be an attentive enough husband and father, and, bearing in mind he was still a student, gave his new wife and daughter as much of his time and money as he could, even taking on several part-time jobs in order to supplement his grant. However, one thing the lawyer would apparently have none of, was the notion that Julia finish her own studies and become the forensic scientist she'd always dreamed of being. According to him, a mother's place, in particular Julia's place, was to stay at home with the child. Once more against the wishes of Julia's parents, she therefore gave up her studies to become a fulltime wife and mother.

Despite the offer from Julia's parents that they could live with them, home for Julia in those early days was a dingy one-bedroomed flat. Every morning she'd kiss her husband goodbye, babe in arms, and watch as he merrily left for university, leaving her to a day of drudgery. The lawyer wouldn't even talk about the offer from Julia's parents, suggesting they could manage perfectly well on their own.

After leaving university, the lawyer soon started to make the mark he'd always promised Julia he'd make. He began moving up the rungs of the legal-world ladder at an alarming rate, and, almost overnight, the dingy flat turned into a 3-bedroomed apartment. Julia liked the apartment itself, so she said, but couldn't understand why it had to be so far away from friends and family. According to the lawyer, the further away they were from outside influences, especially Julia's mother, the better.

However, what Julia didn't like, was the way her husband would howl with derision if she so much as mentioned finding herself a job or a hobby to get herself out of the apartment. He wouldn't even allow her to take driving lessons. The lawyer also insisted on taking control of everything financial, citing no wife of his was going to have to worry about anything other than being a good housewife. Julia also mentioned that on the rare occasions they went out together, the lawyer would dictate what she was to wear, even going to the trouble of sometimes buying the outfits himself; some of which were apparently only suitable if you were a certain type of woman. In short, the lawyer took control of all aspects of Julia's life.

By the time Mary started school, the 3-bedroomed apartment had been exchanged for the 4-bedroomed pile that Julia, Yvette Wyburn herself, and I, were currently conversing in. Despite looking like a happy family from the outside, with all the trimmings of English suburbia, Julia told Yvette Wyburn herself that she had felt like a Stepford wife, and, in order to stop herself going completely mental, Julia explained how she'd secretly joined the school's PTA.

The secret didn't stay secret for long, and the lawyer went crazy.

Apparently, he couldn't understand why Julia had tried to find stimulation outside the family home. Surely the lifestyle he was providing for his wife and daughter was enough? Julia was roughly reminded that food didn't cook itself, the house didn't clean itself, and he had no intention of sexually gratifying himself just because she'd been out with her PTA cronies and was too tired. According to Julia, he stopped just short of physical abuse.

Julia resigned from the PTA the following day.

Julia explained that from the day she'd married the lawyer to this, she'd rarely left the marital home unless it was in the company of her husband. She'd even had to argue hard to get permission to attend her mother's funeral. The lawyer himself was far too busy to go, and insisted on Julia catching the earliest train possible back home after the ceremony.

Julia also indicated that the lawyer had, without apology, missed Mary's first steps, her first tooth, her first words, and her first, second, third, fifth, seventh, tenth, thirteenth, sixteenth, seventeenth, and nineteenth birthdays. Apart from paying for it, Julia suggested her husband had had very little to do with Mary's upbringing.

"Okay, so let's just recap," Yvette Wyburn herself said, looking at her notes. "You were destined for a potentially successful career until he got you pregnant. Correct?"

"I suppose so, yes."

"Subsequently, he refused to allow you to complete your studies, and yet took no shame in making sure he finished his. Throughout your whole married life, you've been the one who's been the sole homemaker and child-carer, with little or no emotional help from your control-crazy husband. Shortly after the tragic death of your daughter, he started a relationship with another woman, eventually leaving the marital home to start a new life with her. Would you say that was an accurate précis of what you've just told me, Julia?"

Julia started crying gently and bowed her head. "Perhaps it was partly my fault," she said. "After Mary's death I admit I wasn't in the best of shapes. I started drinking quite heavily. I should have seen it coming."

"No! Don't even go there, Julia," Yvette Wyburn herself said, leaning over and cradling Julia's hands. "Don't you dare think this is anybody's fault but his."

"I told her that," I said. "Didn't I tell you that, Julia? See, I was right. Everything *is* his fault. Absolutely everything."

"He promised to look after you for better or for worse, Julia," Yvette Wyburn herself continued. "In my opinion, he's failed on both counts. Now, let's dry those tears and calm down over another piece of that delicious carrot cake."

Yvette Wyburn herself placed her crumb-strewn plate on the coffee table in front of her and licked her fingers clean. "Okay, I'm sorry to have to bring this up, Julia," she said, picking up her pen and pad. "But what about the sex thing?"

Julia took a deep breath. "Before Mary's death I suppose everything was okay, sort of. I didn't always want to get involved in the kinky stuff he'd suggest, but grinned and bore it all the same. Lie back and think of England and all that."

"And how many times a week would you say you and your husband enjoyed sexual activity?"

"Oh, I don't know. Once a day maybe."

If I'd had any carrot cake in my mouth, I would have spat it out. "What? Once a day! Nobody does it once a day."

"Okay, good," Yvette Wyburn herself said. "Above average, but not excessive."

"Not excessive!" I yelled. "What the hell are you talking about? She said once a day. Not once every other Thursday if you're lucky."

"And what about after Mary's death?" Yvette Wyburn herself asked.

Julia bowed her head again and struggled to keep herself in control. "He wanted to do it on the night of the funeral," she said. "He said I looked really sexy in black. We had a blazing row. We never touched each other again. At least not in that way."

"You know something?" Yvette Wyburn herself said, putting her pen and pad away in her briefcase. "I think I've heard enough. If you ask me, Julia, he's going to regret the day he ever decided to mention the word divorce."

Four months later, Julia and her husband found themselves in front of the Right Honourable Clive Cartwright, a district circuit judge appointed to hear the statements in the case of their divorce.

I looked around the assembled gathering and spotted Elaine sitting at the back of the court. I hadn't seen her since Billy and I had been staying at the house - my house. She'd changed somehow. At first I couldn't quite put my finger on what was so different, then realised she simply looked tired, or at least looked every minute of her age. I'd been dead 3 years, although it felt like 30, and like all dead people, would never effectively be any older than on the day I'd died. By this technicality, it dawned on me Elaine was now actually older than me. From what I could tell, it didn't look like she would age well.

Standing behind Elaine, waving furiously for me to join him, was Old Eric.

"You'll never believe what I've got to tell you," Eric said, catching hold of my elbow and indicating we should remove ourselves out of earshot. Once outside the door of the courtroom, Eric checked no one was listening. "She's seeing someone else," he whispered, still holding onto my elbow and looking up and down the corridor.

"What? Who? Eric, what are you talking about? Who's seeing someone else?"

"Keep your voice down," Eric said, moving us further away from the courtroom door. "Who do you think?" He didn't wait for an answer. "Elaine, of course. She's seeing someone else. Can you believe it?"

I couldn't. "Eric, is this your idea of a sick joke?" I said. "Because if it is, I'm not finding it very funny."

"Absolutely not," Eric said. "I'm deadly serious. About three weeks ago she was asked to prepare the defence for this geezer who'd been done for selling dodgy timeshares. He's as rough as sandpaper, but for some reason she sort of took a fancy to him. Hasn't been able to keep her hands off him since. Mind you, I'm not surprised, son. You ought to see the size of his todger."

I slid down the wall. "Jesus Christ on a stick," I said, refusing Eric's offer of the paper bag he'd retrieved from his pocket. Despite the mouse making things difficult, I did manage to push out, "Does the lawyer know?"

"What? Of course he doesn't know," Eric said, making his way to the courtroom door and peeking in. "I mean, look at him. He's still acting like the cat who's manufacturing, distributing, and retailing every ounce of cream in existence. Do you think he'd look so bloody pleased if he knew his lover was being serviced by a man who can put twenty pence worth of two pence pieces side by side on his love-pump?"

It took me a short while to do the maths. "No wonder she's looking tired," I said.

I knew it was wrong, but I couldn't help but feel slightly pleased; in fact, I think I was bordering on elated. The thought of the lawyer being cheated on filled my heart with all things fluttery and beautiful. I recalled all the times I'd wanted him to feel pain, both physical and emotional, and here was my chance. Now, how in God's name was I going to let him know?

As it turned out, I didn't need to say or do anything. Elaine did it all for me.

The Right Honourable Clive Cartwright gave the lawyer and Julia their divorce, but at some considerable financial cost to the lawyer. Yvette Wyburn herself turned out to be exceptional in court, and had judge Cartwright on her side from the opening salvo. She successfully painted Julia as having been systematically destroyed by her overbearing, bullying husband, who simply cast her aside for a new model as soon as things got a bit tough.

Every time the lawyer's lawyer (one of the Mr Gunns) tried to hone in on Julia's supposed catalogue of unreasonable behaviour, Yvette Wyburn herself skilfully managed to deflect the problem firmly back into the lawyer's lap.

By the time proceedings were finished, and we all started walking out of court, the lawyer had lost the house plus everything in it. He would also see a considerable amount of his future earnings being transferred to Julia's bank account, on top of which, he was given five days to prepare a one-off payment of huge proportions to cover Julia's missed opportunity of a successful career.

Despite his losses, the lawyer left the courtroom looking like he'd just been told all his dreams had come true. He ran towards Elaine at the back of the court and embraced her as if he'd just returned from sea. He then gathered her in his arms and marched her out of the building.

"You might be in for a treat tonight, Eric," I said, as we followed them out. "She always had a fantasy about being carried out like that after seeing that Officer and a Gentleman film."

"Oh, they've already done that one," Eric replied. "He even kept the hat on."

On the steps outside the courtroom, the lawyer planted Elaine firmly back on her feet, and waited until the rest of us caught up. Then, in full view of myself, Old Eric, Julia, and Yvette Wyburn herself, he sank to one knee. He looked up at Elaine with a huge smile and opened up a small velvet box. From where I was standing I couldn't exactly see what was in the box, but the shaft of brightness that emanated from it was surely a danger to low-flying aircraft.

In a voice loud enough to attract the attention of several passers-by, the lawyer asked, "Elaine Ferris, will you marry me?"

There were a few aahs and oohs as we all froze and trained our eyes on Elaine, waiting for her reply.

And then we waited some more.

And then a little bit more again.

"Hurry up, love," one of the passers-by shouted. "I've got a bus to catch."

"Well?" the lawyer said. I think I caught the hint of a throat-mouse. "You heard the man. He's got a bus to catch."

Elaine stared at the open box, her eyes moistening. Without saying a word, she turned and ran. She'd only gone a few paces when she stopped and removed her heels, which then enabled her to be gone much quicker.

Slowly the group on the steps dispersed.

First to go were the passers-by, who shuffled away muttering things between themselves. Next, Old Eric looked at me and shrugged, then disappeared in a blur of purple robe. Somehow, he'd left the essence of his smile behind. It suddenly dawned on me I hadn't asked him about his office. Finally, Yvette Wyburn herself linked her arm through Julia's, threw her head back, and marched them both off to a waiting car.

The lawyer snapped the box shut, placed it in his pocket, and got up off his knee. He looked around and smiled at the dissipating crowd. "She's just surprised, that's all," he said to no one in particular. He straightened his tie, coughed, and walked away briskly in the general direction Elaine had run.

Julia increased two things over the next few weeks. Firstly, her intake of wine. Secondly, her reticence to involve herself in the outside world.

It appeared to me that being unmarried didn't suit Julia particularly well.

"But you're better off without him, Julia," I said, as we settled down to see if Bruce could successfully defend himself against a trumped-up charge of child pornography. "Financially, spiritually, emotionally, and any other words ending in a-l-l-y you can think of. I mean, you can get on with the rest of your life now, can't you? Look at it as having your glass half full." I looked at the wine glass Julia was holding. Ironically, it was half empty. "Tell you what, tonight, why don't you get dressed up in one of those pretty dresses you've got hanging in your wardrobe, and go out?"

Julia sipped her wine and continued to stare at the TV.

Bruce was found guilty and sent to prison for 2 years. The gasps and shouts of astonishment from Julia and I almost drowned out the sound of knocking on Julia's front door.

"What have you ordered now?" I said. "What useless piece of rubbish has that smooth-talking shopping-channel host got you to buy this time?"

At the door was indeed a useless piece of rubbish. But not, as far as I was aware, one you could order off the TV.

Without any words passing between them, Julia allowed the lawyer into *her* house. They made their way into the kitchen, where Julia immediately replenished her wine glass.

"I just thought I'd bring this back," the lawyer said, holding out his door key.

He didn't look himself. Slightly unshaven, designer clothes marginally un-ironed, Italian shoes fractionally less polished, one or two hairs unplaced. He looked like someone who'd made an effort, but hadn't quite succeeded; someone who was on the way down rather than on the way up. There was also something else missing, something other than the grossly expensive watch and designer cufflinks. It took me a few seconds to work it out, then it came to me.

The smell of my wife was nowhere to be sensed.

"I was in the area," the lawyer continued. "Thought it would be a good opportunity to find out how you are."

Julia took a gulp of wine. "I couldn't be better," she said, sitting at the table.

The lawyer leaned against the fridge. "Glad to hear it." he said. "I've been a bit worried how all this might have been effecting you, Julia. I know how much you loved the whole being a good wife thing."

Through the kitchen window, I spotted the car the lawyer had arrived in. Despite my limited knowledge of cars, I knew enough to realise it wasn't the flashy Mercedes sports-car he normally paraded around in.

"Why worry about me now?" Julia asked. "You never bothered before?"

"Now that's not true, Julia," the lawyer replied. "I used to worry about you all the time." He pushed himself off the fridge and looked out of the window, his back to us. "I did love you, Julia, you do know that, don't you?" He waited for a reply but Julia offered none. "Actually, if truth be told, I think I still do."

"Well, what a lucky girl I am," Julia said, taking another swig of wine.

"Everything was fine between us until Mary died," the lawyer said, still staring out of the window. "Where did we go wrong, Julia? What the hell happened to us?"

Julia finished her wine and got up to pour herself another. "Well that's an easy one," she replied. "What happened was that you decided to have sex with another woman." Julia shook the bottle to get the last drops out into her glass. "How is the lovely Elaine?"

The lawyer turned from the window and looked down at his under-polished shoes. "We had rather a large argument after that day at court. I'm staying at The Singleton."

In true Mark Ferris fashion, I celebrated the lawyer's situation by dancing around the kitchen in my own unique style, letting out guttural noises only certain native tribes of Borneo would understand. As I spun around in jubilation, Julia and the lawyer's bodies came in and out of view like they were in one of those old *What the Butler Saw* machines.

Julia started to make her way back to her chair, but somewhere along the way her wine-laden legs failed to obey her commands. With a full glass in one hand, and an empty bottle in the other, she fell, arms outstretched, head first into the lawyer's chest.

"Whoa, tiger," the lawyer said, putting his arms around Julia's waist. "I think someone has had a bit too much. You should go easy on that stuff. I remember how it used to get you... well, you know?"

I stopped my epileptic dancing and hung on to the table whilst I got my breath back. Maybe it was because I was dizzy, but it looked like Julia's and the lawyer's heads were getting closer together? I closed my eyes and tried to shake the confusion from my head. When I opened them again, it was to find their heads actually conjoined.

I started jumping up and down and waved my arms around like someone practicing semaphore.

"No!" I screamed, the pitch coming out somewhere between the mating-call of a male sperm-whale and the hunting trumpet of a screech-owl. "No, no, and definitely no." I tried to pull their faces apart, but they'd obviously used an industrial strength glue to keep them together. "Julia, what the hell are you doing? Absolutely everything is his fault, remember? Don't even think about it. Let's go and see how Bruce is coping in prison. Julia! For Christ's sake, put him down. Julia!"

I fell to my knees, exhausted. Huge sobs started to engulf me.

"I give up," I said. I bowed from the waist and put my forehead on the floor. "I humbly grovel at your feet, oh lawyer Nemesis, God of love, God of making my life, and my death, a misery."

I lifted my head and allowed myself to cry uncontrollably.

The lawyer picked Julia up under her armpits. He was a good eight inches taller than her, and she dangled against him, arms still outstretched, holding the glass in one hand and the bottle in the other. With her feet off the floor, and their lips still welded together, it looked like the lawyer had picked up a human cross and stuck it to his face. He walked her the few paces to the kitchen table and laid her down, pushing his weight on top of her. He slid one hand down the front of her tracksuit bottoms and started undoing his trousers with the other. He finally released his suction on Julia's lips and stood up, looking down at her crucifix form.

"You always did love doing it on this table," he said, allowing his trousers to fall to his ankles.

Julia lifted herself into a sitting position, and, just as the lawyer reached out to push her back down, she swung the empty wine bottle with as much force as someone of her size and stature could summon, straight at the lawyer's head.

Surprisingly, the bottle didn't break, but the lawyer's skin did.

He looked at Julia with a look somewhere between confusion and pain as a trickle of blood run down his face from somewhere above his hairline. He opened his mouth to say something, but no words came. In slow motion, he staggered backwards as the message moved from his brain to his legs that he'd been dealt a considerable blow.

The trousers around his ankles aided his timber-like descent to the floor.

Julia jumped off the table and pulled her tracksuit bottoms back into position. She leaned over the lawyer's fallen form and stared into his fluttering eyes. "You stupid bastard!" she said. "*We've* never done it on this table."

Mother had always taught me that violence in women was ugly, but I couldn't help believe that what Julia had just done was a thing of sheer beauty. She stepped over the prostrate figure of her ex-husband, and, after collecting a new bottle of wine from the fridge, calmly made her way back to the living room and the anguish of Bruce's family and friends.

Almost as soon as we'd settled ourselves back down on the sofa, I became aware of a presence over my shoulder.

"So what's going on here?" Crimson asked.

"Well, see that guy there, the one with the ginger hair?" I replied. "That's Bruce's lover. Then the one sitting in the corner, crying, that's his mother. The really old biddy is the grandmother. She's only been given three months to live, but hasn't told the rest of the family because she didn't want to upset them during Bruce's trial. The young boy playing in the garden is Bruce's nephew, although, you've only got to look at his eyes to know he's Shayne's. Ah, the one that's just walked in is Uncle Digger. He's my favourite. He won a small fortune on the lottery a while back, but has lost most of it through his gambling addiction. His wife, Patsy, will go mental when she finds out…"

"Uh, actually, Mark, I meant what's with the semiconscious, semi-naked guy in the kitchen?"

"Oh, him," I said. "To be honest, it would be easier for me to explain about Bruce's problems than what's been happening there."

Crimson's fob beeped from somewhere within her jeans. "Oh for God's sake, I'm like five minutes behind," she said to no one in particular. "Come on, Mark, the committee want to see you."

TERMINAL

Mr T. and the sidekicks looked different somehow. Some things were still the same of course. Mr T's hat for one. But gone was the air of excitement Mr T. had displayed the last time I was here. Without their mounds of paperwork, Mr T. and the sidekicks looked - well lost, I guess.

Mr T. punched a few buttons before acknowledging my presence. "Ah, Seven-Three-Five-Nine," he said. "We thought you'd be interested to know we've been forced to adopt new guidelines."

"Sorry?"

"Yes, so are we, Seven-Three-Five-Nine. So are we. Anyway, Gates has decided our entry criteria for the Sanctum is ancient and outdated. According to his most recent report we have far too many dead people wandering about." Mr T. keyed something into his computer. "Ah yes, here it is. *'There are an unacceptable level of dead not fulfilling the true definition. Some of the dead I have interviewed are actually more alive, show more emotion, are less numb, feel more relevant to society, have a greater sense of importance, involve themselves in more activity, and are generally more excited than when they were alive.'"*

Mr T. cocked his head to one side and held out his hands as if apologising.

"So, as a result," he continued, "we've been ordered by the *new* audit department to streamline the amount of dead people we have outside the Sanctum with immediate effect." Mr T. pressed a few more buttons. "Bear with me, Seven-Three-Five-Nine," he said. "I'll find what I'm looking for in a mo. Ah, yes, here we are. Audit's direction following the forty-second edict of Gates. *'With immediate effect, our aim must be to achieve a more manageable level of dead outside the*

Sanctum.'"

He looked to his sidekicks in turn. "I suppose we should be thankful he's left us with anybody at all." They both nodded and muttered their agreement.

I remembered the first time I'd sat here. How my voice had been strangled by the mouse. How my hands had shaken. How cold and confused I'd been. It seemed nothing had changed. I knew my voice would be no more than a squeak if I tried to speak, and I had started shivering like a dog straight out of the sea. My head screamed for help from the new forthright Mark Ferris, but there was no sign of him. I started to wonder if he even existed at all.

Mr T. leaned back in his chair. "So, in order to comply with these wonderful new guidelines, Seven-Three-Five-Nine, we've had to open the door to the Sanctum to a whole host of people. People who up until now would have had no chance of getting in. Including, it would appear, people like you."

I curled myself into a ball, a lot easier to do in the new leather chair than the old wooden one, put my fingers in my ears, and hummed as loudly as I could.

Mr T. ignored my defence. "You see, Gates has insisted on a more liberal approach," he said, his voice loud and clear despite my actions. "Reckons we're on the dawn of a new era. An era, so it would seem, where you can get away with pretty much anything and still find yourself in the Sanctum." He removed his hands from behind his head and leaned forward to tap a few more buttons. "So, I suppose there's nothing left for me to say except congratulations, Seven-Three-Five-Nine. You're in." Mr T. pointed behind me. "Off you go. It's all standard practice."

I turned. The Sanctum door had materialised in all its glory. Why the hell were those rainbows black? I couldn't recall ever seeing anything so damned sinister.

I took my fingers out of my ears, and clung to my knees. The tears flowing off my cheeks splattered onto my bare chest with a thud. "Old Eric," I wailed. "I haven't said goodbye to Old Eric. Can I go and see him? Have you given him a new office yet? I'll do anything you want. I'll go to the dentist. I'll go through Ikea. I'll go down Excelsior Street. I'll fight wasps. I'll catch a bus. I'll go to the ballet. I'll go food shopping in Marks and Spencer. Eat cabbage. Take Timothy's sister to the pictures. Anything. Please, just let me see him one more time."

Mr T. buried his face behind his computer screen. From where I was sitting, it now looked like the screen was wearing his hat. "Sorry, no can do, Seven-Three-Five-Nine," he said. "Off you go."

"But I'll do anything. Name it."

Mr T's face popped back into view from behind his screen. Strangely, his hat seemed to stay where it was. "Makes no difference what you'd do, Seven-Three-Five-Nine," he said. "Gates reckoned we'd kept Old Eric from the Sanctum long enough. Gave us a bit of a roasting over it if truth be known. Apparently, we should have shown Old Eric the respect he deserved and sent him to the Sanctum the minute he'd got here."

My insides felt like I'd swallowed a grenade. "What are you trying to say?"

"Old Eric's already gone, Seven-Three-Five-Nine… Oh, now don't look so upset. Gates threw him a lovely little going away party. Thanked him personally, and over profusely if you ask me, for the work he did when he was alive, then presented him with a first edition of some ancient book he'd come across that he reckoned was written about Old Eric, and sent him on his way."

A sudden intense pain took a grip of my body. It wasn't a purely physical pain, more of an emptying; a hollowing out. Like a tree trunk being readied to be a canoe. I let out a noise which I didn't recognise and fell out of the chair, landing on my side.

Involuntarily, the cavernous pain rolled me around like a footballer looking for a penalty. How long the pain shook me for I'm not sure, but, like a man bleeding to death, I eventually ran out of energy. With a monumental effort I got myself to my hands and knees and looked up.

Mr T. and the sidekicks were leaning over the desk looking back.

"For God's sake, get up," Mr T. said. "We haven't got time for your hysterics, Seven-Three-Five-Nine. We're on a very tight time-schedule. Gates goes mental if we drop behind." The three of them sat back down in unison.

I crawled to the desk and used it to help me get to my knees. "But he can't be gone," I said, peering over the edge of the desk. "He always said you'd never forgive him."

"Yes, well, Gates is apparently all for forgiveness, Seven-Three-Five-Nine."

One of the sidekicks leaned over and whispered something in Mr T's ear.

"Do you think we should?" Mr T. said, studying me.

The sidekick shrugged and nodded at the same time.

"Oh, very well, but on your own head be it." Mr T. looked right and left before reaching under the desk and producing a small square piece of paper. He continued looking about him as he held it out for me, waving it in the air. "Come on, Seven-Three-Five-Nine. We haven't got all day."

With a hand that was shaking with a life of its own, I took the note.

When I first got here, the committee decided it wasn't enough that I didn't go to the Sanctum. They thought about it logically and came up with the idea of the crossword. Gave me some crap about having my own crossword to bear or something.

Anyway, final clue worked out yesterday morning, just before the committee sent for me.

42 across. Extreme and usually beyond cure or alteration. Eight letters.

TERMINAL.

Goodbye, son.

O.E.

PS. Guess what Elaine and that guy with the todger did last Monday in the George at Asda changing rooms? Bugger! The committee are going mental. Looks like I'm not going to get to the good bit.

I reread the note several times before the weight of my tears landing on it actually made it illegible. "How did he manage to write this?" I asked.

"He didn't," Mr T. said. "He dictated it to my colleague here." He pointed to the sidekick on his right. "Okay, come on, we can't have you grovelling around down there any longer." Mr T. pressed some buttons. "If Gates sees you with that piece of paper, he'll go mental. He can't stand anything written by hand. So, off you go, Seven-Three-Five-Nine."

I crawled quickly back to the leather chair and clung to its base. "No, please," I said. "Not yet. Crimson! I can't go without telling Crimson how grateful I am."

Despite not being able to see him, I sensed Mr T's eyes boring through the back of my head. "Grateful, Seven-Three-Five-Nine?

Grateful for what for goodness sake?"

I had no idea what trouble either of us would be in if I confessed to the few minutes of closeness Crimson and I had shared, but decided things couldn't really be any worse than they were. "Well, you see, we had a... a... thing." I let go of the chair and turned to face the committee. "And mother will never forgive me if I don't say thank you."

"What kind of a thing, Seven-Three-Five-Nine?"

"Please, I just need to tell her I'm truly, truly grateful for everything I've done to her... I mean everything she's done to me... I mean *for* me. Everything she's done *for* me."

Mr T. went back to his computer screen with that look I thought only Mother possessed; the one that said, *I don't care what I'm hearing, I know exactly what you've done.*

"Well, it doesn't really matter what you've got to be grateful for, Seven-Three-Five-Nine," Mr T said. "Frankly, I don't give a damn any more. Messenger Seventy-Two is unfortunately surplus to requirements. She's currently on her very last job. As soon as she gets back from Ukraine, she's following you through that door." Mr T. nodded behind me. "Undoubtedly she'll be late. I mean... temporarily otherwise engaged."

"Ukraine?" I mumbled.

"Yes, she's picking up Eight-Four-Two-Five, or as you know him, Dai the Murderer. He'll be off to the Sanctum later on today as well. Come to think of it, he's probably another one who'll kick up a fuss about going. He's loving Ukraine. Living like a king apparently." Mr T. pressed some buttons. "I'll put in a request for security, just in case." He looked to the sidekicks who nodded their agreement.

"So can I wait until Crimson and David get here?" I said. "Then we can all go through the door together. No fuss. I promise. I'll say thank you to Crimson, explain everything to David, and then be on my way like a good boy."

Mr T. sighed heavily and rubbed his temples. "Doesn't work like that, Seven-Three-Five-Nine," he said. "Gates has programmed the door to open in conjunction with the final keystroke of an individual's processing. He has some theory that if people get processed in batches, it wouldn't make them feel '*special.*' Now, please, off you go!"

"Mary!" I blubbered. "Oh my God, Mary, I've got to say goodbye to Mary. Please let me say goodbye to Mary."

"Why?" Mr T. said. "Don't tell me you had a thing with her as well?" He looked to his sidekicks and started laughing. They joined in momentarily, but slowly all three of them stopped when I offered no reply.

"Jesus Christ, Seven-Three-Five-Nine," Mr T. said, slamming his palms on the desk, making us all jump. "You can't go around having things with Marys." He again looked to his sidekicks. "You see, in my opinion, that's the sort of behaviour that should keep you out of the Sanctum for good." He looked back to me. "Defiling Marys indeed."

Despite my despair, I couldn't help but think Mary didn't need a lot of defiling. "No, no, I didn't," I protested. "Well, not really. Well, maybe, sort of, perhaps. Oh, I don't know. Anyway, it's not that. It's just I've got some information about her parents I think she should know."

"Yes, well, it doesn't matter what information you have, Seven-Three-Five-Nine," Mr T. said, obviously still annoyed. "She's already gone. God knows why, but Gates insisted we gave her a computer programme that teaches you how to swim before we sent her on her way."

The three of them shook their heads in puzzlement.

"But I can't go!" I wrapped myself tighter around the leather chair. "It's not my time. I'm not ready. What about Elaine? Oh dear God, Elaine! I never said goodbye to Elaine."

"Well you should have thought of that before you threw yourself out of that attic, Seven-Three-Five-Nine. After all, you only die once. Anything after that is just judgement. You never even left her a note. How do you think she felt finding you dangling on the end of that rope? You're selfish, Seven-Three-Five-Nine, totally selfish. Just had to end it all, didn't you? Weak, Seven-Three-Five-Nine. Nothing but a worthless, weak, selfish man. In my opinion your actions should be keeping you out of the Sanctum for a lot longer yet, possibly forever. But it's the law according to Gates these days, and as long as you never strangled a puppy, sexually abused a child, embarked on a spree of ethnic cleansing, invented a computer virus, or worked for the American Inland Revenue Service, you're safe. As long as you pass through Gates, you're in, Seven-Three-Five-Nine. Just like all the rest of your suicidal colleagues. Heaven forbid!"

I had no idea how I found myself standing at the threshold of the Sanctum door. I turned to look back at Mr T. and the sidekicks. They were pressing buttons.

Mr T. looked up and frowned. "You still here, Seven-Three-Five-

Nine?" he said. "Off you go. It's all standard practice."

THE SHAG LIST

1.....Richard Gere.
2.....Orlando Bloom.
3.....Billy White.
4.....Hugh Jackman.
5.....George Clooney.
6.....Brad Pitt.
7.....Jake Gyllenhaal.
8.....Rafael Nadal.
9.....Jason Statham.
10....Eminem.
11a...David Beckham.
11b...Cristiano Ronaldo.
13....Hugh Grant.
14....Ashton Kutcher.
15....Enrique Iglesias.
16....One Direction - Either individually or collectively.
17....Robbie Williams.
18....Robert Pattinson/Taylor Lautner.
19....Russell Brand.
20....Roger Daltry.

DISCUSS.